Napoleon Victorious

For Patty, the love of my life – my wife, dearest friend, conscience, counsellor, and the mother of three wonderful children!

Napoleon Victorious

AN ALTERNATE HISTORY OF THE BATTLE OF WATERLOO

Peter G. Tsouras

Greenhill Books

Napoleon Victorious: An Alternate History of the Battle of Waterloo

Greenhill Books

Greenhill Books, c/o Pen & Sword Books Ltd,
47 Church Street, Barnsley, S. Yorkshire, S70 2AS
For more information on our books, please visit
www.greenhillbooks.com, email contact@greenhillbooks.com
or write to us at the above address.

CIP data records for this title are available from the British Library

ISBN 978-1-78438-208-7

Typeset and designed by JCS Publishing Services Ltd
Typeset in 10.5pt Adobe Caslon Pro
Printed and bound in England by TJ International Ltd, Padstow, Cornwall

Prologue

I was barely 10 when I buried my father. Notre Dame glittered with uniforms of all the marshals of France, a battalion's worth of generals, and a regiment of colonels, not to mention the jewels and high fashion of their wives. The clergy added even more colour along with clouds of incense. The choir was perfect. The funeral itself had even been delayed long enough for the Pope to arrive to officiate. Nothing was spared. My regal mother's false tears were convincing to everyone but me.

Every eye seemed focused on the gilded bronze sarcophagus in front of the altar with the tricolour draped over it. On top of it rested his sword and simple black campaign hat. From corners of the coffin eagles flashed. All so regal, yet so cold. But my tears were warm and real. He called me his little eagle, and he loved me. I shall miss him till the day they lay me out in the same spot.

When the service was finished, his marshals flanked the coffin as official pallbearers while it was carried out by a dozen of the strongest members of the Old Guard. Mother and I followed, the mass of mourners rippling in bows as we passed. Outside, the Old Guard was massed. Our carriage rode past their ranks, and I could not miss the tears streaming down countless faces, as warm as mine.

Long after I was supposed to be asleep, I found my secret way, as 10-year-old boys are wont to do, to the garden and the moonlit bench in the arbour where Father and I would go to be alone. I could feel him still there, an invisible yet powerful presence. I remembered all the hours we spent there as he regaled me with stories of his wars, and – as I would realize later – much wisdom on the leading of men. The sergeant of the guard found me sound asleep. Through the haze of my sleep, I heard, 'Ah, Eaglet, what are you doing here?' as he gently scooped me up in his arms.

The next night I slipped out again and forced myself to stay awake until the sergeant made his rounds. This time he bowed as he said, 'Your Majesty should not be here alone. May I escort you back to your rooms?'

'My father said a little time alone was the most precious gift a monarch could have.'

'Ah, that sounds like the Emperor,' he replied.

He was an old soldier, grey in the service of my father, his moustache long and drooping, *de rigueur* for one of the Old Guard. Countless men had served my father, but how many had known him? 'Tell me,' I asked, 'where did you serve with my father?'

The sergeant laughed quietly and said, 'It would be a shorter list to say where I did not serve him, Majesty.'

'Were you at Mont St Jean?'

'Indeed, Your Majesty. I was with him when he broke the English.'

> Extract from the memoirs of Napoleon II,
> Emperor of the French

Contents

Illustrations

Maps

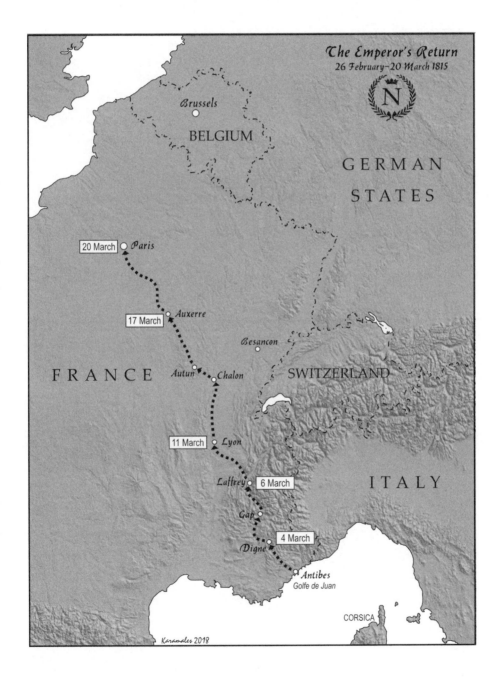

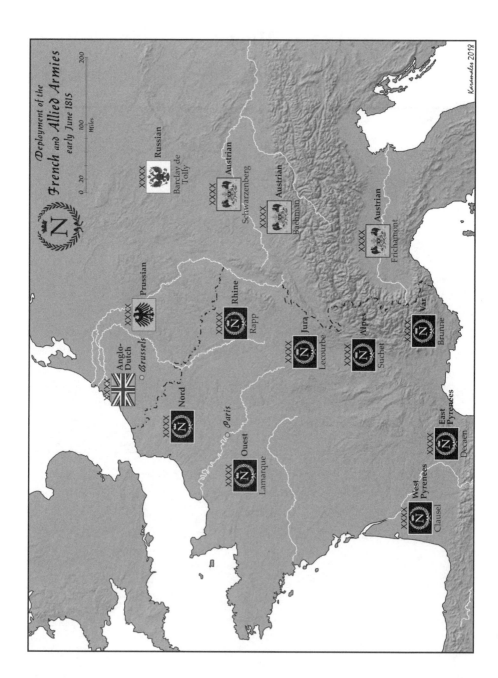

Deployment of the
French and Allied Armies
early June 1815

N

0 20   100   200
        Miles

Russian
Barclay de
Tolly

Austrian
Schwarzenberg

Austrian
Bachman

Austrian
Frichamont

Prussian

Rhine
Rapp

Anglo-
Dutch
Brussels

Jura
Lecourbe

Alpes
Suchet

Var
Brunne

Nord

Paris

Ouest
Lamarque

East
Pyrenees
Decaen

West
Pyrenees
Clausel

Kerimedes 2018

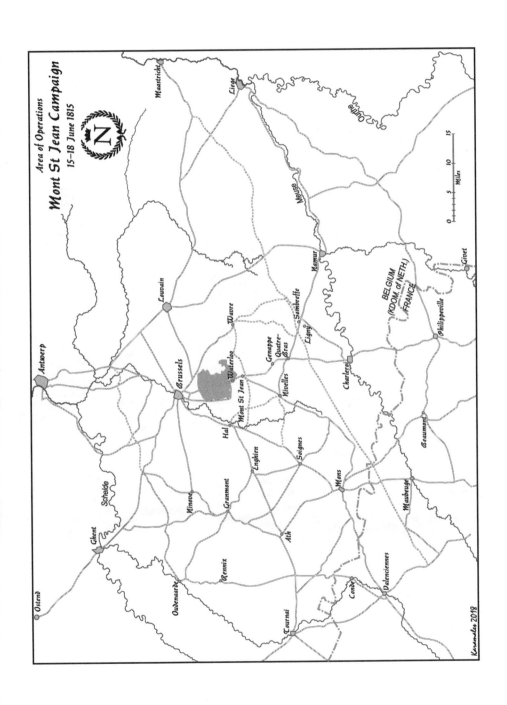

Area of Operations

Mont St Jean Campaign
15–18 June 1815

N

Ostend

Antwerp

Ghent

Scheldte

Louvain

Brussels

Waterloo

Mont St Jean

Hal

Soignes

Enghien

Grammont

Ninove

Oudenaarde

Renaix

Ath

Tournai

Condé

Valenciennes

Maubeuge

Mons

Beaumont

Charleroi

Nivelles

Genappe
Quatre-
Bras

Ligny

Sombreffe

Namur

Meuse

Liège

Maastricht

Ourthe

Wavre

BELGIUM
(KDOM. of NETH.)

FRANCE

Philippeville

Givet

0   5   10   15
Miles

Kessendee 2018

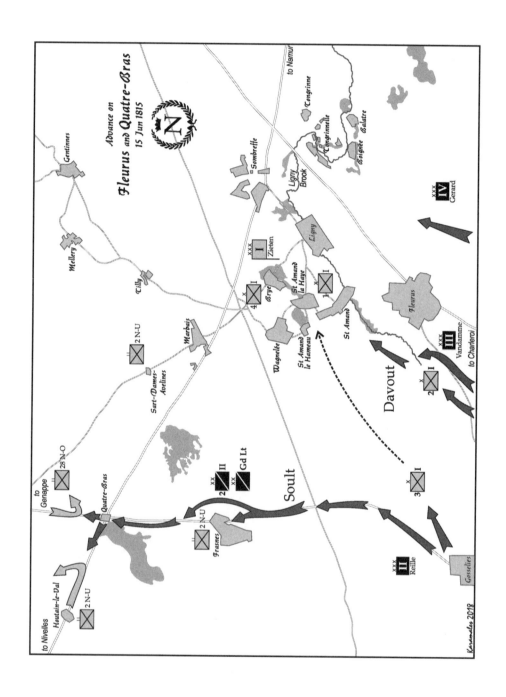

Advance on *Fleurus* and *Quatre-Bras*
15 Jun 1815

Krumades 2018

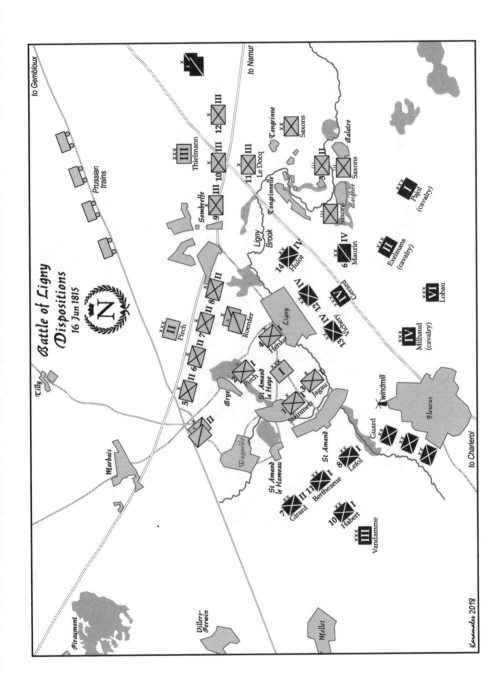

Battle of Ligny
Dispositions
16 Jun 1815

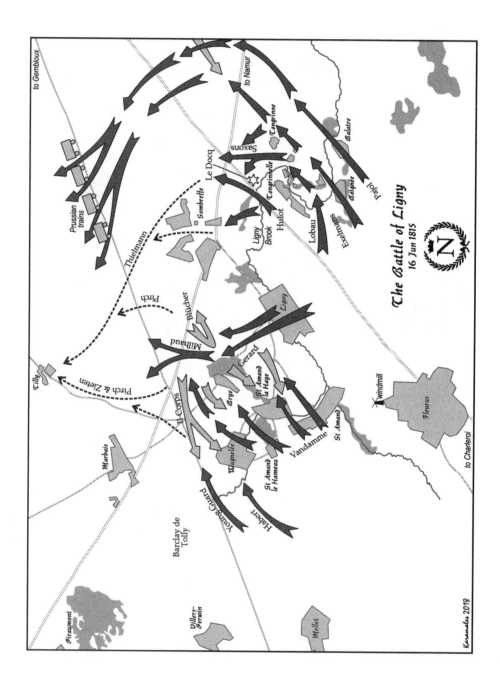

The Battle of Ligny
16 Jun 1815

to Gembloux

to Namur

Saxons

Le Docq

Tongrinelle

Tongrimme

Balatre

Boignée

Potel

Sombreffe

Hulot

Exelmans

Lobau

Ligny

Brook

Thielmann

Pirch

Blücher

Milhaud

Ligny

Pirch & Zieten

Gerard

Tilly

Brye

St Amand
la Haye

I Corps

St Amand

Marbais

Wagnelée

St Amand
le Hameau

Vandamme

St Amand

Young Guard

Habert

Barclay de
Tolly

windmill

Fleurus

to Charleroi

Villers-
Peroin

Pirraumont

Mellet

N

Karamellos 2018

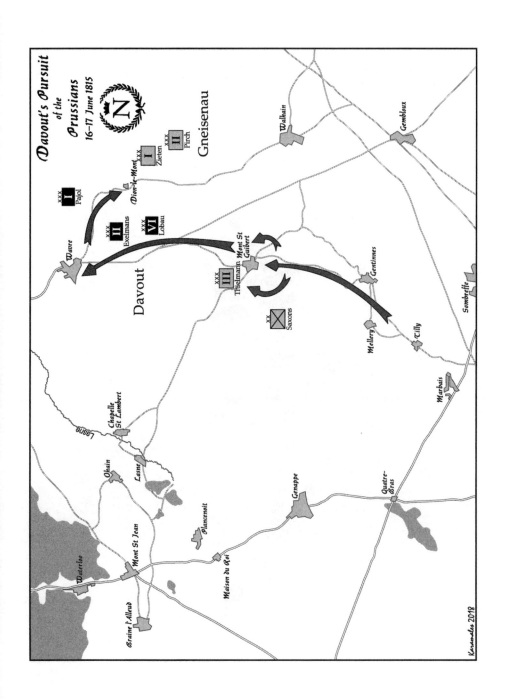

Davout's Pursuit
of the
Prussians
16–17 June 1815

N

Gneisenau

Walhain

Gembloux

I — Pajol
XXX

Dion-le-Mont

I — Zieten
XXX

II — Pirch
XXX

II — Exelmans
XXX

VI — Lobau
XXX

Wavre

Davout

III — Thielmann
XXX

Mont St Guibert

Gentinnes

Sombreffe

Saxons
XX

Mellery

Tilly

Marbais

Chapelle St Lambert

Lasne

Ohain

Lasne

Plancenoit

Genappe

Quatre-Bras

Mont St Jean

Maison du Roi

Waterloo

Braine l'Alleud

Kerameus 2018

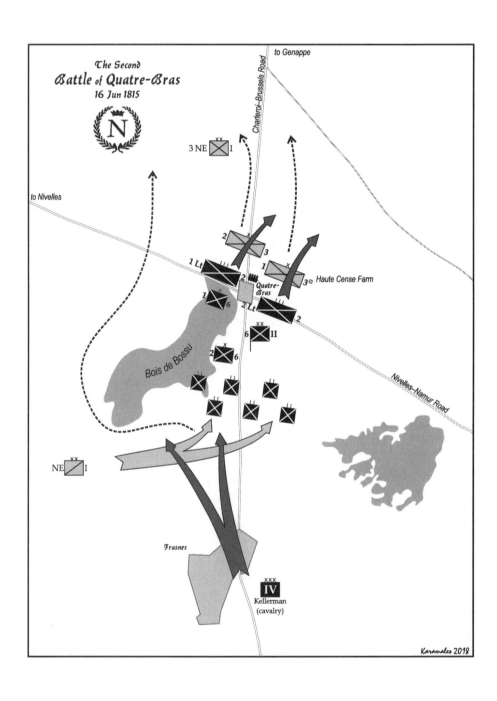

The Second
Battle of Quatre-Bras
16 Jun 1815

to Genappe

Charleroi–Brussels Road

3 NE [XX] I

to Nivelles

2 [X] 3

1 Lt [X] 2 1 [X] 3 — Haute Cense Farm

Quatre-Bras

1 [X] 6 2 Lt [X] 2

6 [XX] II

2 [X] 6

Bois de Bossu

Nivelles–Namur Road

NE [XX] I

Frasnes

[XXX] IV
Kellerman
(cavalry)

Karamales 2018

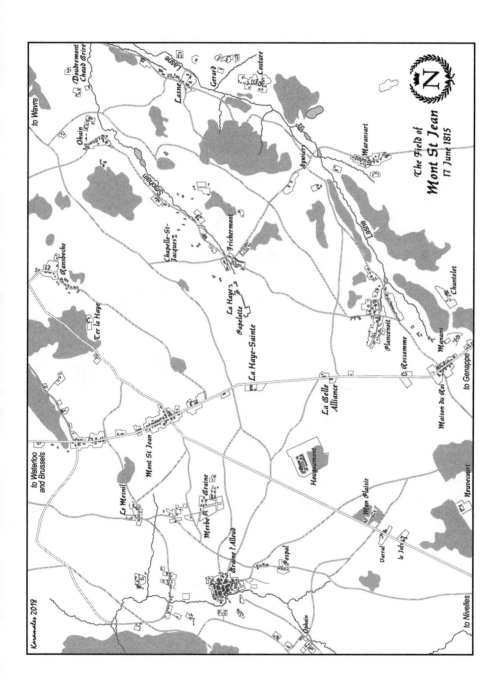

The Field of
Mont St Jean
17 June 1815

to Wavre

to Waterloo
and Brussels

to Nivelles

to Genappe

Kevander 2018

Lasne

Gerard

Couture

Maransart

Aywiers

Chapelle-St-Jacques

Frichermont

Lasne

Smohain

Ohain

Ransbeche

Ter la Haye

La Haye

Papelotte

La Haye-Sainte

Chantelet

Plancenoit

Rossomme

Manans

Maison du Roi

La Belle
Alliance

Hougoumont

Mon Plaisir

Neuvecourt

Mont St Jean

Le Mesnil

Merbe
Braine

Braine l'Alleud

Papol

Varval

le Jals

Ohain

Doubremont
Chaud Brite

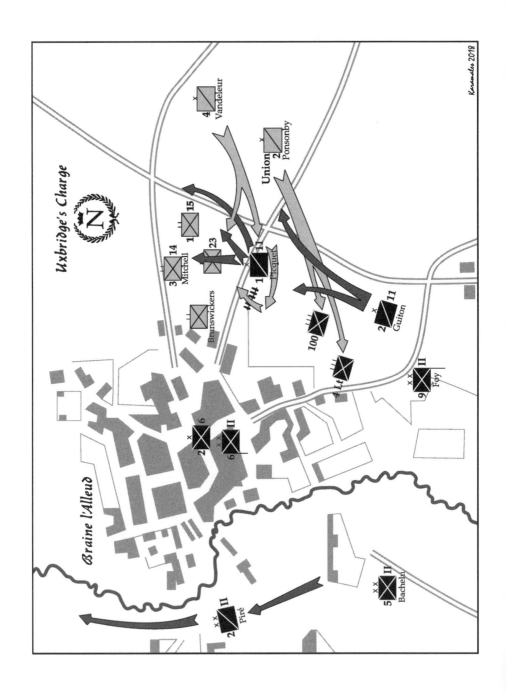

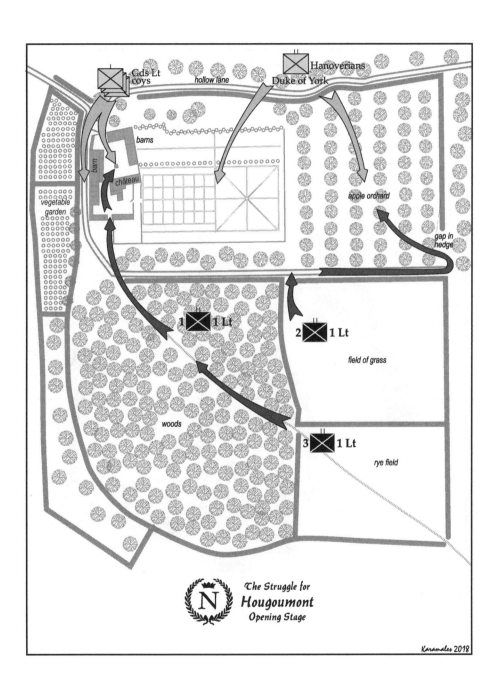

Gds Lt coys

hollow lane

Hanoverians
Duke of York

barns

barn

château

vegetable
garden

apple orchard

gap in
hedge

1 ⊠ 1 Lt

2 ⊠ 1 Lt

field of grass

woods

3 ⊠ 1 Lt

rye field

The Struggle for
Hougoumont
Opening Stage

Karamales 2018

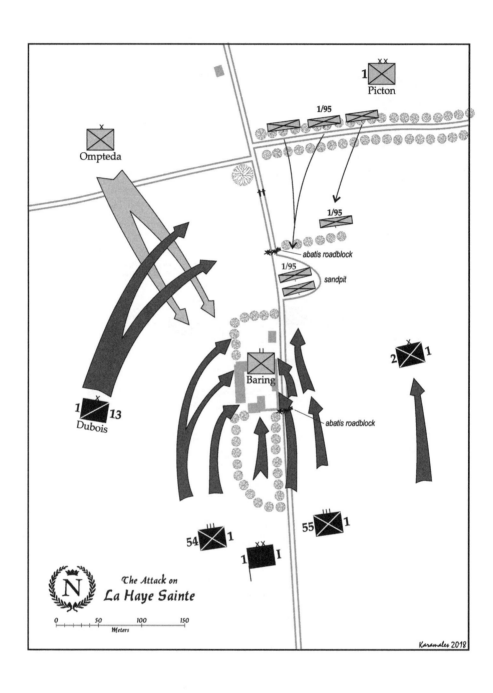

Picton

1/95

1/95

abatis roadblock

1/95

sandpit

Ompteda

2 × 1

Baring

1 × 13
Dubois

abatis roadblock

54 × 1

55 × 1

1 xx I

N

The Attack on
La Haye Sainte

0   50   100   150
Meters

Karamales 2018

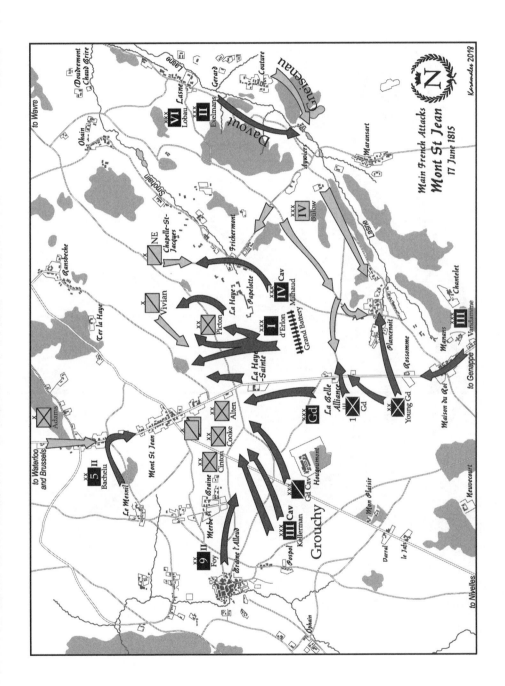

Main French Attacks
Mont St Jean
17 June 1815

Kosmodlos 2018

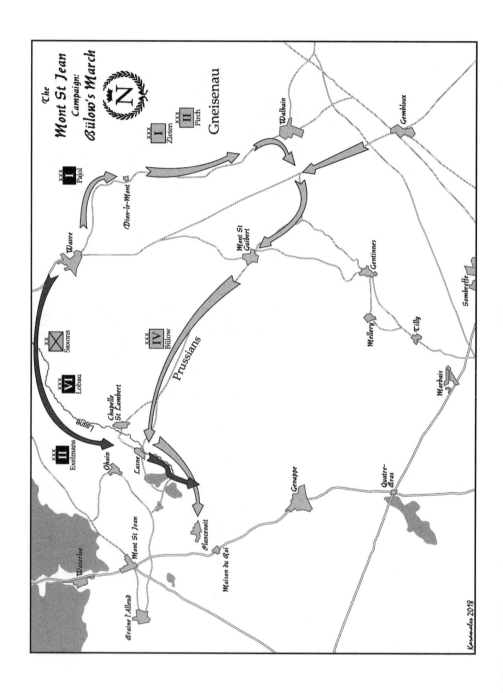

The
Mont St Jean
Campaign:
Bülow's March

Gneisenau

N

I
Zieten

II
Pirch

I
Pajol

Walhain

Gembloux

Dion-le-Mont

Wavre

Mont St
Guibert

Gentinnes

Saxons

IV
Bülow

Mellery

Tilly

Sombreffe

VI
Lobau

Prussians

Marbais

Chapelle
St Lambert

Lasne

III
Exelmans

Ohain

Lasne

Genappe

Quatre-
Bras

Waterloo

Mont St Jean

Plancenoit

Maison du Roi

Braine l'Alleud

Kristandlee 2018

Introduction

Grafenwöhr, the US Army Europe's tank gunnery range, was a strange place in which to become an admirer of Napoleon. There I was, a brand-new second lieutenant, in a very cold, snowy German February in 1971, down with pneumonia and ordered to quarters for three days. Quarters was a very general term for a long one-room cinder-block building with concrete floors, a barely working heater, and steel cots with no mattresses. I was curled up in my sleeping bag, gingerly trying not to impale myself on loose metal springs, when our company clerk brought in the mail. Lo and behold, there was a book – *The Campaigns of Napoleon* by David Chandler, all 1,093 pages of it, from the History Book Club. I devoured it in three days.

Years later I was finally to meet Chandler, that master of Napoleonic history and director of War Studies at Sandhurst. He had generously written a foreword to my first book, *Warriors' Words*, and invited me to Sandhurst after reading my account of how I had come across his book, where he devoted a day to showing me around. It would be difficult to find a kinder gentleman or a more eminent scholar. I encourage the reader to explore his numerous excellent books on the Napoleonic Wars. You will be richly rewarded.

That book sparked an admiration for the first soldier of Europe, whom Churchill would refer to as the 'Old Emperor' as he baulked at any comparison with Hitler. 'I certainly deprecate any comparison between Herr Hitler and Napoleon; I do not wish to insult the dead.'[1] Napoleon, like Alexander and Caesar, had the priceless ability to win men's hearts and propel them to incredible feats on the battlefield. He had the equally valuable ability to pick good men and reward them accordingly. Like Alexander he simply breathed the art of war and military glory. He dominated an era, and his reputation is still strong. Even Hitler, his sordid imitator, fell under its spell. It is no wonder that after the fall of France in 1940 Hitler gazed for two hours on Napoleon's sarcophagus in the Invalides. Thereafter, he ordered the body of the Emperor's son brought from Vienna and reinterred in the Invalides.

Napoleon's reputation ironically was transformed into myth by his defeat at Waterloo and his subsequent exile on St Helena. He presciently declared that by sending him to that bleak rock in the South Atlantic his vanquishers had fastened a crown of thorns on him. Even the British were to be ashamed of the insulting pettiness of the jailer they had assigned to him as governor of St Helena, thus spurring his transformation into a figure of heroic myth.

All of this hinged on his defeat at Waterloo. Had he been victorious the world would have become a far different place from what it is now, as imagined in Chapter 9. One predictable outcome would have been in the very name of the battle. The winner gets to name his victory. The French to this day disdain the name of Waterloo and refer to the battle as Mont St Jean. That likely would have been Napoleon's choice as well since the village of Waterloo was not part of the battlefield he had fought over. This book will therefore refer to the battle as Mont St Jean.

Napoleon Victorious is the fourth of my quartet of alternate histories on seminal battles that cover Gettysburg, Stalingrad, and D-Day. These three almost begged for Waterloo to be included among them. Not only is Waterloo a pivot of history as are the others, but like them its decision trembled on a knife edge. There was nothing inevitable about the outcome. If anything, the opening of the campaign that led to Waterloo was a tour de force by Napoleon in strategic conception and execution, causing Wellington to exclaim, 'Napoleon has humbugged me, by God!' In the battle itself, Napoleon tested Wellington as he had never been before. Repeatedly Napoleon was on the point of victory, yet it eluded him again and again. The Great Duke would later remark most rightly that Waterloo was 'the nearest run thing you ever saw in your life'.

How, then, did Napoleon fail? Since returning to power from Elba in February 1815 Napoleon had worked wonders in putting the French army back together after its reduction and shameful neglect by the Bourbons. The rank and file and junior officers were deeply and personally loyal to Napoleon, but many of the senior officers had compromised themselves by serving the Bourbons, which engendered intense distrust among their subordinates. Simply put, the soldierly did not trust many of their generals – hardly the way to create unity of purpose. The army Napoleon took to Waterloo may have been the most experienced he every commanded, but it was brittle.

Most of Napoleon's marshals were unavailable for one reason or another, but he misused the best of those that remained. As the army was moving to contact, he gave Marshal Michel Ney, a man now assumed to be suffering from post-traumatic stress, the major roles of holding off Wellington at Quatre Bras and managing the battle at Waterloo. Marshal Louis Davout, without doubt his most lethal marshal, he left in Paris as Minister of Defence. His next best, Marshal Jean-de-Dieu Soult, he made his chief of staff instead of giving him a combat command. The French general staff had been the creation of Marshal Louis Berthier and was the mother of subsequent military staffs the world over. Berthier retired to his estate in Bavaria and fell to his death from a window. Napoleon had first appointed Gen. François Bailly de Monthion, Berthier's highly capable deputy, as chief of staff. Reportedly, he did not warm to the man and replaced him with Soult, who did not understand the finely tuned instrument of the general staff. Events were to show that it did not perform well in inexperienced hands. Without it, the army did not work as smoothly or as quickly as it had in the past.

Neither did Napoleon take advantage of the considerable and often painful experience many of his commanders had in fighting Wellington and British troops. He asked their opinion but did not appear to incorporate their input into his decisions. This is all the more surprising since he had followed Wellington's campaigns with great interest and considered him to be the only general who approached his own abilities.

These problems taken together made it difficult for the French to apply breaking pressure on a number of the weaknesses in Wellington's own heterogenous army which spoke four languages – English, French, Dutch, and German. The British troops were in the minority, and by the end of the battle more of the Allied troops on the field were speaking German than English. Half of his troops were from the new Netherlands army, which included both Dutch and French speakers. Many of them had served in the French army and were of doubtful loyalty, especially the francophone Belgians. The Allied artillery was inferior in both numbers and ability to the French, and the cavalry was no match for the French in an open fight. Wellington famously distrusted the British cavalry, the domain of the aristocracy and relentlessly unprofessional. He also had to finesse the fact that the commander of one of his corps was the pretentious young heir to the Netherlands throne, William, Prince of Orange, foisted upon him by the necessity of alliance politics.

Yet, Napoleon's difficulties were not all pre-ordained. The essence of history is its contingent nature. It is a shifting kaleidoscope of human and natural interactions and chance, where opportunities quickly open and close. The opening of one such opportunity was in the American Civil War, on the second day of the Battle of Chickamauga in September 1863. A misunderstanding among Union generals resulted in a division pulling out of the line without a replacement available. Confederate Lt. Gen. James Longstreet's attack coincidently launched straight into the opening in the Union line, collapsing the entire flank and resulting in the flight of the Union army. Had there been more precise coordination among the Union generals, the Confederate attack would have run into formidable defence by experienced troops, and then it is highly likely that the battle would have resulted in a drawn affair or even a Union victory. In reality, Chickamauga was a terrible defeat for the Union, the first time that a major army in the Civil War had been routed. The difference between victory and defeat was a simple matter of careless coordination.

Make one change here, and its repercussions ricochet through all subsequent events. Replace a diffident officer with a dynamic one, and it becomes a completely different story. A chance encounter sets off a train of alternative decisions. The synergy of changes drives history in new and unexpected directions. Victories become defeats and defeats become victories. Few great battles offer more examples of the opening and closing kaleidoscope of opportunity and chance than Waterloo/Mont St Jean. For one man, it would mean a world of difference between being chained to that Promethean rock in the South Atlantic and being remembered as Napoleon Victorious.

Note. An alternate history, by its very nature, would have generated its own literature and works that in themselves give indications of how history took different courses. These sources will be reflected in the notes and are marked with an asterisk to preclude the reader from a fruitless search for new, interesting sources.

CHAPTER 1

'What a Canary!'

26 February–31 March 1815

'They have learned nothing and forgotten nothing.' Voltaire's comment on the Spanish Bourbons applied equally to their French relatives. The restoration of the Bourbon royal house to the French throne after Napoleon's defeat and abdication in 1814 had confirmed that intelligence was not a family trait. The grotesquely fat Louis XVIII himself did not inspire confidence either. The Duke of Wellington's comment was damning: 'A perfect walking sore, not a part of his body sound; even his head let out a sort of humour [odour].'[1] He was escorted by remnants of Napoleon's Old Guard, 'The wolf-bred offspring of the Revolution', in seething anger into a Paris still occupied by the Allied armies.[2] A witness wrote:

> I do not believe that human figures had ever expressed anything as menacing and as terrible. The grenadiers, covered in wounds, conquerors of Europe, who had seen so many thousands of bullets pass over their heads, who had smelt the fire and the powder. These same men, deprived of their chief, were forced to salute an old king, an invalid from age, not war, under the eyes of the armies of the Russians, Austrians and Prussians . . . Some, wrinkling the skin of their foreheads, worked their large bearskins down over their eyes as if not wishing to see, others turned down the corners of their mouths in scorn and rage, others again, below their moustaches, bared their teeth like tigers. When they presented arms, there was a crash of fury and the noise made one tremble.[3]

Things were to get worse quickly. Louis appointed his son, the Duke of Artois, a man of no military ability or experience but of great pretensions, as commander of the French army, aided by his two equally pretentious sons, the dukes of Angoulême and Berry. In every possible way, they insulted the French army in their attempt to purge it of memories of the Revolution and Empire. They had no idea of the bonds of brotherhood forged on countless battlefields. To them the French army was not a living institution with its own character and pride but a collection of peasants. A flood of incompetent émigré officers, many of whom had fought with France's enemies, flooded into the army. Such was their vast military experience that they suggested that, to prevent desertion, the trousers of the troops be collected in the evening and only returned in the morning. It 'was a strange new world where a man who possessed a title need not have earned it by charging through a crossfire of grapeshot or escalading heavily defended ramparts sword in hand'.[4]

The army was reduced in strength and 30,000 officers ordered back to their villages on half pay; for company-grade officers the sum was 'too much to starve to death on but not quite enough to keep them alive'. They were also forbidden to move, marry or find a new occupation. In return, the Bourbons were increasingly held in contempt, as bluntly expressed by the young Captain Duthilt.

> This family [the Bourbon family of King Louis] returned behind foreign bayonets, and its flag unknown and often fought against by us, replaced that under which we had subjugated by arms the kings of continental Europe; from one side, nobles, émigrés, men who in the past had served as an escort to this dynastic rogue . . . imbued with their old prejudices, desperate to reassume their privileges like feudal rights, hearts full of pride of bile and disposed to overturn the France of today in order to re-establish that which they did not want to forget.[5]

There was no better example of a half-pay officer than one Captain Jean-Roch Coignet. He had learned his soldiering in the old Royal Army and put that knowledge to better use fighting for the Republic.

Too afraid to disband the Old Guard, the Bourbons renamed them the Grenadiers of France in scattered garrisons with a loss of status and pay. They created in their place a royal guard of whom half were officers, who had to be of noble birth. To save money, crippled soldiers who had been cared for in the Invalides were sent back to their villages, as were the orphaned daughters of fallen soldiers, who had been maintained in boarding schools. Troops in their barracks were forbidden to discuss the events of the Revolution or the wars of the Empire. The huge numbers of returned prisoners of war, many of them sick, were simply abandoned. The public was outraged when the Bourbons purposely debased the Legion of Honour established by Napoleon in 1802 to reward the very best of valour and achievement. In less than a year they passed out more Legions of Honour than a Napoleon had in twelve years – for a price. Their only popular act was the abolition of the hated conscription.

Artois and his sons were despised, and seemingly took every opportunity to earn that sentiment. Berry had a rabid temper and openly struck officers. His brother and he openly paraded before the troops in the uniforms of Russian generals. Berry attempted to copy Napoleon's blunt familiarity with the troops, only to find that it fell flat. He told one soldier that now he was regularly paid, but under Napoleon his pay had always been in arrears. The man replied, 'What is it to you if we decided to offer him credit?' On another occasion one of the royals was going to review a large garrison mounted on one of Napoleon's white horses. No sooner had he put his foot in the stirrup than the horse began to sidle away, dragging him across the barracks square to the delight of Napoleon's veterans. All too often when troops were ordered to shout '*Vive le Roi!*', they instead thundered '*Vive l'Empereur!*' Bourbon paranoia soared. It was no wonder that the veterans kept a tricolour cockade safely hidden inside their shakos.

The large number of discharged or half-pay officers who gathered in Paris were contemptuous and rowdy and not above teaching a harsh lesson to any foolish young émigré officer who happened upon them. They openly referred to Louis as *le cochon* (the pig), 'and in playing cards they referred to the "pig" of hearts or spades instead of the king'. They sang the *Marseillaise* and would drink to *his* health, or ask in a low voice, 'Do you believe in Jesus Christ?' to which the answer was, 'Yes, and in his resurrection.'[6]

They would have given Napoleon's former marshals their opinion in blunt soldier language. After all, almost every one of those marshals had started out as an enlisted man to find a marshal's baton in his knapsack. All of his marshals, save Louis-Nicholas Davout, the Iron Marshal – and the only one whom Napoleon truly respected – had made their peace with the Bourbons, some more supinely than others. Davout was the only one of Napoleon's marshals whose martial ability bore comparison with the Emperor's. He was consistently successful whether as a subordinate or in independent command, the latter state in which most of the rest of the marshals failed. It was Davout who defeated with his one corps the major part of the Prussian army at Auerstedt in the 1806 campaign. After Napoleon's abdication in 1814, Davout marched his 26,000 men home from Hamburg, where they had stood siege, in such fine condition as to elicit the praise of British observers. He firmly refused to kiss the royal hand. He simply retired to his estate, defying his official disgrace and threat of prosecution. He was a Bonapartist to the core.

Marshal of France Louis-Alexandre Berthier, Prince of Neuchâtel and Wagram, had been referred to as the Emperor's wife, a backhanded compliment that showed how completely Napoleon and he formed the first great team of commander and chief of the general staff, the happy marriage described by Field Marshal Paul von Hindenburg of his relationship with Erich Ludendorf in a later war. Berthier held the singular position of Major General or Chief of the General Staff (*Etat Major Général*) in modern terms. The general staff was Berthier's domain, into which the Emperor never intervened. He never had to.

Berthier had begun his career as an officer in the Royal Army and fought in the American War of Independence with the French expeditionary force under Rochambeau. He supported the Revolution, but as chief of staff to the Versailles National Guard he protected the sisters of Louis XVI and helped them escape. He continued to distinguish himself in chief of staff assignments. A contemporary wrote of Berthier in 1796, when he became Napoleon's chief of staff in Italy, that he possessed:

> a remarkable grasp of everything to do with war. He had also, above all else, the gift of writing a complete order and transmitting it with the utmost speed and clarity . . . No one could have better suited General Bonaparte, who wanted a man capable of relieving him of all detailed work, to understand him instantly and to foresee what he would need.[7]

Years later Henry Houssaye would pen a summary of the work ethos of this unique man who made this system work:

> Indefatigable, conscientious, diligent, prompt in grasping the most complicated orders, executing them in every detail with admirable minuteness, clearness, and precision, very punctual in transmitting them at the appointed time, he had been a perfect instrument in Napoleon's hands. With him the Emperor's mind was at rest. The orders were always worded as to admit of no possibility of doubt or hesitation as to the manner of their execution. These orders always arrived safely, for Berthier would dispatch them, if need be, by eight different officers on eight different routes.[8]

Berthier had also created the general staff system later to be copied by the Prussians and eventually every other modern army. Under Berthier, the general staff became a hive of efficiency that gave the widest scope to Napoleon's genius. No one has described it better than the late, brilliant Col. John Elting.

> Berthier's operational instructions were simple and should be engraved inside every modern staff officer's skull. The chief of staff is the headquarters pivot. He must see everything that comes in and sign (or at least approve) everything that goes out. The assistant chiefs of staff must keep abreast of the general situation in addition to running their own sections. Speed and accuracy are the most important factors in staff work. The staff exists only for the good of the army and so has no regular office hours. It works as long as may be necessary, rests when it has nothing left to do, ready to move out, regardless of the hour or 'pain' involved. Up-to-the-minute intelligence on enemy forces and actions must always be available; therefore, reconnaissance must be continuous to the front and flanks, and results reported promptly. Finally, the commander-in-chief must always be told the truth, the whole truth, and nothing else – no matter how unpleasant the results may be.[9]

After Napoleon's abdication, Berthier threw in his lot with the Bourbons, more out of a sense of duty to France than any affection for a royal house that inspired none. Their favourable treatment of him may have had something to do with the aid he had given to the sisters of Louis XVI (brother to Louis XVIII). He had to watch in pained silence as the Bourbons disbanded his creation of the general staff. He was 61, had been wounded in 1814, had been at war for most of the years since he had served in America. By the time Napoleon abdicated, he was physically exhausted and morally drained.

Marshal Jean-de-Dieu Soult, Duke of Dalmatia, showed far more enthusiasm for the new regime. Soult was one of the first marshals made by Napoleon. The Emperor called him the *premier manoeuvrier* (first tactician) in Europe; he had a keen strategic sense and was one of the few to come close to reading Napoleon's mind. He was one of the even smaller number whose advice Napoleon took seriously. That had aroused the jealousy of Berthier, who could be depended on to make things difficult for Soult.

A sergeant in the old Royal Army, Soult rose in the wars of the Revolution to division command through a natural talent for leadership and a gift for aggressive and clever tactics. He was so highly recommended that Napoleon made him commander of the consular guard. Later, even more impressed, he put him in command of the French forces assembling for the invasion of England at Boulogne. Over two years of intensive training he essentially forged the Grande Armée – a term that came to denote the principal French field army commanded by Napoleon. At Austerlitz in 1805 his corps broke the enemy centre in the attack on the Pratzen Heights. He also fought well at Jena in 1806 and Eylau the next year.

Soult spent the next five years campaigning in Spain. A British officer would say of him, 'Every British officer who had the honour to serve against him had a great respect for him. If King Joseph had accepted his advice the fate of the War might have been different.' The British soldiers in their own way showed their respect when they referred to him as the 'Duke of Damnation' in salute. He went from victory to victory against Spanish forces and drove the British army under Gen. Sir John Moore out of Spain. In the Battle of Coruña, where Moore fell, Soult left a monument to his valour and ability. Despite the absence of unity of command among the French in Spain, over the next four years Soult's efforts were impressive – crushing Spanish and Portuguese armies, pacifying Andalusia, sending Wellington scurrying back into Portugal, and fighting a British–Portuguese army to standstill at Albuera although outnumbered three to two. While in Spain Soult earned the reputation of being 'a plunderer in the world class', making off with 1.5 million francs' worth of Spanish art.[10]

If Soult had a fault it was staying too far to the rear after committing his subordinates to battle. His flank attack at Albuera was brilliant, initially crushing the British line, but it petered our in the absence of the only man who could have pushed it forward. Wellington commented that Soult knew well how to bring his army to battle but was not quite sure what to do with it once it was engaged.

Napoleon recalled Soult to Germany in the spring of 1813, where he contributed much to the victories commanding the Guard at Lützen and Bautzen. With the collapse of the French position in Spain, Napoleon sent him back to defend the southern frontier, but Soult was unable to stop Wellington, who defeated him three times without being able to break his army, which Soult was always able to extricate skilfully.

Soult stood by Napoleon to the end in 1814 and only agreed to an armistice with Wellington when he received news of the Emperor's abdication. Although politically astute, he was not political; his loyalty had been to Napoleon and France. With Napoleon gone, France became his focus. An abrasive, cold man, he had few friends among the marshalate and no few enemies, which may explain why King Louis made him Minister of War. He was just the one to reduce the French army to the small force the Allies demanded, a task he accomplished with considerable ruthless efficiency. Nevertheless, he instituted necessary reforms and intensified training.

'The tallest, most loyal, most generally liked, and the only English speaker or writer [with an English mother] among the marshalate bore the names Marshal Édouard Adolphe Casimir Joseph Mortier. Genial, unflamboyant, and not self-seeking . . .', in 1804 he was one of the first men to receive his marshal's baton from Napoleon. Napoleon had been impressed with his considerable administrative skill as commander of the Paris garrison and his brilliant execution of the independent command to overrun and govern Hanover. For his performance at Friedland in 1808, Napoleon made Mortier Duke of Treviso. He was responsible for the French victory over the Spanish at Ocaña in 1809. His treatment of the British wounded left at Talavera earned him a letter of thanks from the future Duke of Wellington. In the invasion of Russia, he ably commanded the Young Guard, and in the 1813 campaign at the head of the rebuilt Young Guard he delivered the decisive attacks at Lützen and Bautzen. The next year in the defence of France he commanded the Old Guard in a brilliant series of actions. With the Bourbon restoration it was his sad duty to disband the Young Guard. Recognizing his ability, the King gave him command of the 16th Military Division at Lille.[11]

Louis made great efforts to cultivate and honour Marshal Michel Ney, whom Napoleon had once called 'the bravest of the brave'. Ney was the most popular of the marshals in France for his impetuosity, the *beau idéal* of the *furor franciscus*, and the King needed an intermediary who could tame this most Bonapartist element of the French nation. But Ney was not a temperate or thoughtful man, described as 'thoroughly insubordinate to any commander but the Emperor himself, besides being unreasonably touchy, quarrelsome, and uncooperative'. He was such an enemy of Soult that he had withheld the reinforcements that would have allowed

Soult to utterly destroy Moore's British army at Coruña.[12] Napoleon in his exile had not forgotten that Ney had taken the lead in demanding his abdication.

The Bourbons quickly soured with the general public as well; the economy was poor and unemployment high. Everyone who had acquired confiscated property from aristocracy or the Church because of the Revolution would see the Crown force its return. As the new year broke, people began to talk of violets, predicting that they would bloom again in spring, and the soldiers in their barracks spoke of the hoped-for return of Jean de l'Epée (John of the Sword), the army's affectionate nickname for Napoleon.[13]

Another irritant to the army was the presence of the Duke of Wellington, first as the commander of the Allied army of occupation and then as British ambassador. Count Maximilien Sebastien Foy was that rare French general who was on good personal terms with Wellington. He was one of the few generals who had fought in the Peninsula and still emerged with his reputation intact. He had been wounded by a shell splinter in the shoulder, left for dead, and captured in the last battle of Wellington's invasion of southern France early in 1814 at Orthez. To his surprise, he was visited by Wellington, who shook his hand, and, as Foy wrote in his diary, 'Nous avons parlé guerre' (We spoke of war). Foy was 'deeply moved' and retained his high regard for the man for the rest of his life.

Nevertheless, despite his high regard, he later refused the Duke's invitation to a ball at his official residence in Paris, writing on 26 October 1814:

We who were lately masters of Europe, to what servitude we are reduced? Lord Wellington is the Commander-in-Chief of the army of occupation in Belgium. Our telegraph is at his disposal two hours daily to send orders to his troops. He signs his letters from his headquarters in Paris; he has an air of saying to us: if you sit on the fence it will be me you will be up against. We see him coming away from the King en frac [morning coat] and in boots. The Princes go and dine with him after manoeuvres. O Napoléon, où est tou ['Oh, Napoleon, where are you?']14

26 February – Portoferraio, Elba

Napoleon stood on the quarterdeck of his 300-ton brig, L'Inconstant, in the dusk as his 607 grenadiers of the Old Guard boarded. They had all volunteered to come with him in his exile to this pleasant little island off Genoa. Now they looked up at him, waiting. They marvelled at the change in him since their arrival the previous May. The weight had dropped off him as he rode and walked the roads and trails of his operetta kingdom. Some of the older ones remarked how much he looked the man of Marengo and Austerlitz, his movements quick and supple. The flash of his eyes had new power. They did not know that in exile he had read the observation of

Socrates that a man should stay fit to be able to defend the state and, most tellingly, 'Besides, it is a disgrace to grow old through sheer carelessness before seeing what manner of man you may become by developing your bodily strength and beauty to their highest limit.' He had looked down at his paunch and was seized with the determination to rebuild the body that had given his genius wings.[15]

Now he told the men their destination was France. That was all he was able to say before they thundered back, 'Paris or Death!'

Timing is everything, and Napoleon had a special talent for recognizing it. All autumn and winter, visitors had been telling him that the Bourbons were alienating the French people and the army. He smiled when told that when the troops were ordered to shout, 'Vive le Roi!' they added under their breath, 'de Rome', meaning the King of Rome, the title Napoleon had given his son. 'So they still love me,' he said to this. The Allies at the Congress of Vienna appeared to be on the point of seriously falling out. Russia wanted all of Poland, and Prussia wanted all of Saxony. Austria and Britain were opposed, and Talleyrand, the French representative, had thrown his support to them, re-establishing France as a major player on the European stage. When their machinations came to light, an outraged Tsar Alexander I challenged the Austrian representative, Prince Metternich, to a duel and threatened to throw him out of a window. So, as February waned, Napoleon was ready to move. All it took was for his British minder to leave for Genoa to visit his mistress. Napoleon quickly had L'Inconstant painted in British colours, loaded his thousand followers on it and eight other small ships, and seized the main chance.

Fortune carried them unrecognized on a gentle breeze. L'Inconstant was actually hailed by a French warship. Napoleon had his guardsmen lie down, and he himself replied that they were a simple merchant ship. Despite the imperial tricolour flying from L'Inconstant's mast, the French captain readily accepted the explanation – so readily, in fact, that Napoleon made him an admiral a few months later.

He stepped ashore on 1 March at Antibes in Provence onto the very spot where he had landed on his return from Egypt so many years before. It was a good omen. From the wreck of his dreams of an oriental empire he had picked up the crown of France that he found in the gutter. He met no resistance now but quickly took the Alpine road to Paris; Provence and the lower Rhone Valley were royalist in sentiment. His goal was the arsenal at Grenoble. He walked much of the way with his Guard, eager to stay fit and exhilarated by his renewed sense of vitality and good health. No hand was raised against him, no bridge in his path was destroyed. He would tell his son, 'Some of the peasants took five-franc pieces stamped with my likeness out their pockets, cried, "It is he!"' Letters and proclamations were left in every town and village and rapidly flowed outwards. He astutely played on the all-too-real fears that the Bourbons would restore feudal rights, abolish equality of the classes and return the property of the nobility and Church that had been sold to countless peasants and shopkeepers.

5 March – The War Ministry, Paris

Soult was the only one to have kept his head when news of Napoleon's return arrived. Thirty thousand troops had already been ordered to concentrate in the area of Lyons. Talleyrand in Vienna had passed on an Austrian request for French troops to support the ouster of Napoleon's former Marshal Joachim Murat from his kingdom of Naples. The Duke of Artois, advised by Marshal MacDonald, would go to Lyons to command this formidable force. Berry was to proceed to Besançon to be advised by Ney to attack Napoleon's column. Angoulême, based in Nîmes, was to strike at Napoleon's rear.

6 March – The Tuileries, Paris

Ney had retired in a sulk to his estate outside Paris, stung by the insults to his wife about her lower-class origins and by other slights they had received from the Bourbons. Of late he had begun to remember all he owed to Napoleon. 'After all, this is the man who recognized whatever talents I have as a soldier . . . who promoted me to become a marshal of his, or rather France's, Empire. By comparison with him these Bourbons are pygmies! No wonder I nearly died for him so many times in battle.' Then a messenger from Soult arrived ordering him to Paris and then to a command in the south. He was stunned to be told upon his arrival that Napoleon was marching on Paris. His aide said, 'Everywhere, they say the people are flocking to him. It looks as if there will be terrible fighting.'

'No! At all costs it must be averted!'

His temper stirred to boiling point when he was told to report to Besançon, to an officer junior to him, Gen. Louis Bourmont, Comte de Ghaisnes, a favourite of Artois. He instantly understood that Bourmont was to spy on him. He demanded of Soult an immediate audience with the King. He found Louis resting on a chaise-longue, his feet in satin booties. The King was taken aback by Ney's agitation as he raged, 'France must not have another civil war. Bonaparte's enterprise is sheer madness. I am leaving at once for Besançon, and if need be I will bring him back to Paris in an iron cage!'

He stormed out. Looking bemused, Louis said, 'An iron cage? What a canary!'[16]

6 March – Laffrey, Hautes-Alpes

The events of this morning would go down in imperial mythology. Napoleon's scouts reported that ahead, between two wooded hills, a battalion of the 5th of the Line blocked the road. Bonapartist officers told Napoleon that their demi-bridge was sympathetic to him. Napoleon halted his column a short distance from them. He could see the ranks stirring as they recognized him in his grey coat. He ordered his Old Guard to ground their muskets. Alone, he moved towards the infantry that were waiting in profound silence. Their commander ordered his men to aim their weapons. He shouted, 'Fire!' Not a weapon discharged. Napoleon walked up to them, opened his coat, and said, 'If there is among you a soldier who wishes to kill his Emperor, here I am!'[17]

History held her breath for fleeting moment. Then, like the bursting of a dam, the troops shouted, *'Vive l'Empereur!'* and rushed to surround him.

The next day the 7th of the Line went over to Napoleon. He entered Grenoble in triumph. The rest of the 7th Division joined him and the people tore down the city gates to honour him. He would later say, 'On my march from Cannes to Grenoble I was an adventurer; in Grenoble I once again became a sovereign.'[18]

Every regiment in his path went over to him, and over the next two weeks he acquired an army. Former soldiers also rushed to swell the Emperor's growing army.

7 March – Café Milon, Auxerre

Half-pay Captain Coignet bore the Bourbon rule patiently and whiled away his time at the Café Milon nursing the cheap wine his meagre allowance bought. On this day one of the regulars came over to him and asked if he had heard any news.

'None at all,' he replied.

'You don't want to talk; you are afraid of compromising yourself.'

'I swear I know nothing,' a puzzled Coignet said.

'Well,' said another old gaffer, 'they say that a Capuchin has come over in disguise, and also another distinguished personage whom the prefect wanted to have arrested.'

'I don't understand you.'

'You are pretending to be ignorant.'

Another said, 'That is why he kept his horse; he is expecting the grey coat.'

Coignet was dumbstruck. Later he wrote, 'I withdrew, overwhelmed with joy, I can truly say, and I felt as if my Emperor was already back again.'[19]

8 March – Berlin

The 72-year-old Prussian Field Marshal Prince Gebhard Leberecht von Blücher slept unsoundly. He was in a constant roiling rage at the proceedings at the Congress of Vienna. He had submitted his resignation to the King and put his military career behind him. Called the 'Hussar General', he had been a relentless enemy of Napoleon and bore him a deep hatred for the humiliations he had forced upon Prussia in 1806. He had commanded the Prussian army in the 1813 campaign in Germany and in the invasion of France in 1814 and wanted to shoot Napoleon outright.

He was awoken that night by his chief of staff, Gen. August von Gneisenau, with the stupendous news that Napoleon had escaped Elba and was marching on Paris. Blücher was overjoyed.

He exclaimed, 'It is the greatest piece of good luck that could have happened to Prussia! Now the war will begin again. The armies will fight and make good all the faults committed in Vienna!' The King declined to accept his resignation and a week later made him commander of the Prussian army in Belgium.[20]

10 March – Lyons

Artois had been shocked at what he found in Lyons on his arrival on 8 March. There were only three regiments; Soult's 30,000 men had not arrived. That night Artois said to Marshal MacDonald, 'You take over command here. I give you the widest powers. Here we have neither ammunition, nor guns. The troops demonstrate and say they will oppose any resistance and the greater part of the populace has declared against us.' He was going to abandon the city, but MacDonald persuaded him to parade the troops the next day to appeal to their honour. That morning a delegation of junior officers informed MacDonald that the troops refused to parade for the princes but would do so out of respect for him.

It was a disaster. He formed the troops into a square and gave them a royalist speech, then shouted twice, *'Vive le Roi!'* He was met with dead silence. He called on Artois to do what he could, but the duke made things worse. Artois addressed a decorated veteran of the 14th Dragoons, encouraging him to shout for the King. The soldier just stood there open-mouthed as the duke and his entourage shouted, *'Vive le Roi!'* Outraged, Artois stormed off and promptly fled the city in his carriage. MacDonald was right behind him. It was just in time. Napoleon's hussars were already entering the city to the joy of the populace. That evening Napoleon accepted the keys to the city and slept in Artois' apartments.[21]

Almost everywhere the news of Napoleon's march on Paris was met with delight by the mass of the army – the enlisted men and junior officers particularly were for Napoleon. In many places divisional and regimental officers either futilely tried to keep the news of Napoleon's arrival from the men or stayed with them constantly – with equal futility – to try to maintain their allegiance to the throne. The loyalty of the soldiers was personal, and it was to Napoleon. The old soldiers had the memories of all the victories of the Grande Armée; younger ones remembered the defeats of 1813 and the invasion of the nation in 1814. The newly enlisted men and young officers wanted their share of glory. They all wanted revenge for the humiliations of France. The Cossacks and Prussians had not been kind, and the soldiery had long soured of the Bourbons.

Faced with their men declaring for Napoleon, those officers loyal to the King, especially the émigrés, discreetly departed, or followed the lead of the men. It would be hard to underestimate the enthusiasm of the troops. Lt. Chevalier of the Chasseurs à Cheval of the old Imperial Guard remembered hearing the news that Napoleon was marching on Paris, 'At this moment, there was joy, delirium throughout the regiment, everyone cried with pleasure. In a moment the silver *fleur de lys*, distributed by M. Le duc d'Angoulême, were broken and strewn on the ground.'[22]

11 March – The Tuileries, Paris

Soult had done everything possible to save the Bourbons, but it did no good. Napoleon's floodtide was rushing north as regiment after regiment went over to him. The King's ministers and court demanded a scapegoat, and their wrath fixed upon Soult. Everything he had done was interpreted through the lens of treason. The King did not believe it. Soult and he had genuinely worked well together, and Louis appreciated his worth. But the King was weak and sacrificed his faithful minister to the demands of his court. Soult quietly retired to his estate. The King had done Soult a backhanded favour.

12 March – Besançon

Captain Coignet travelled to Besançon on his way to report to his Emperor. Ney arrived with the 14th of the Line, as smart a line regiment as existed in the French army. Coignet heard to his horror that Ney had come to arrest Napoleon. He said to himself, 'It cannot be possible that a man whom I saw at Kowno take a musket, and with five men keep back the enemy – the marshal whom the Emperor called his lion – can lay hands on his sovereign.' The prefect of the city announced that by order of the government Napoleon was to be arrested. Coignet cursed when he heard cries of 'Down with Bonaparte' and 'Long live the King!' But the captain had little to worry about. It was all empty talk.[23]

Ney was told by his regimental commanders, '*Monsieur le Maréchal*, morale is bad, there are desertions. Napoleon's agents have brought two eagles.' Ney declared he would run through any man who tried to desert, but it was all bluster. His grievances towards the Bourbons festered. So, the timing of Napoleon's letter to him was perfect. He wanted to avoid bloodshed and knew that a conciliatory tone would tamp down Ney's impulsive nature:

My cousin, my major-general is sending you our order of march. I do not doubt that as soon as you have learned of my arrival at Lyons you will have had your troops re-display the tricolour flag. Obey Bertrand's orders and rejoin me at Châlons. I will receive you as I did on the eve of the battle of Moskowa.[24]

That was all Ney needed to make his decision. On the 15th he assembled his troops and announced, 'Officers, NCOs and soldiers, the Bourbon cause is lost. *Vive l'Empereur!'* The troops 'broke ranks delirious with enthusiasm'. They took out the tricolour cockades they had hidden in their shakos and haversacks and proudly affixed them to their shakos, their white Bourbon cockades littering the ground like snowflakes.

The next day a throng of soldiers and civilians left the town to meet Napoleon on the road. Napoleon recognized Coignet among the officers. 'So you are here, old grousser?'

'Yes, sire.'

'What rank did you hold on my staff?'

'Baggage master of the headquarters staff.'

Napoleon was eager to reward Coignet's evident loyalty as well as put the right men in the right positions. 'Very well; I appoint you quartermaster of my palace, and baggage master general of my headquarters.'

Then he asked, 'Are you mounted?'

'Yes, sire.'

'Then follow me, and join Monthion at Paris.'[25]

13 March – The Hofburg Palace, Vienna

The Congress of Vienna had been meeting in Vienna to settle the affairs of Europe since Napoleon had been safely caged on Elba. The Duke of Wellington had arrived in early February to replace Lord Castlereagh as British representative.

Wellington found the great continental powers, Austria, Russia, and Prussia, busy dividing up the spoils. The Allies created a Kingdom of the Netherlands by uniting Holland and the Catholic former Austrian Netherlands also known as Belgium. Austria, Russia, and Prussia dined on Poland once again. The Prussians devoured 60 per cent of Saxony, though they could not officially swallow it until the imprisoned Saxon king agreed. He resisted. At the same time the Allies kept his army under their control, sending 15,000 men to be divided between the Prussian army under Marshal Blücher deployed around Namur and a composite army of

Netherlands, British, and German troops from smaller states. Because Britain had been supporting Saxony, the Prussians redirected their anger to Wellington, who in his understated way outshone everyone else.

They were interrupted on 1 March by the shocking news that Napoleon had escaped. Further reports tracked his march on Paris. On the same day that Ney promised to bring Napoleon back to Louis in a cage, the Congress declared him an outlaw: 'Napoleon Bonaparte, by again appearing in France with a project of confusion and disorder, has placed himself beyond the protection of the law (*hors la loi*) and rendered himself subject to public vengeance (*vindicate publique*).'

15 March – Auxerre

Ney reported to Napoleon at Auxerre. He had a carefully prepared a manifesto on how Napoleon should govern France. The Emperor entered the room and said, 'Embrace me, Marshal!' Ney was overcome and gave the manifesto to him. He put it in his pocket, indicating he would give it careful consideration later. Ney attempted to justify his lead in forcing Napoleon to abdicate, but Napoleon was all conciliation and said, 'You need no justification. Your and my justification is the force of circumstances, which is stronger than men.' He then gave Ney command of a division and ordered him to meet him in Paris.

It was a cynical act. He needed to bind Ney to him to avoid civil war. When he read the manifesto, whatever goodwill he had for the marshal evaporated. The manifesto read, 'If you continue to govern tyrannically, I shall be your prisoner rather than your supporter.' It ended in a similarly impertinent tone: 'The Emperor must be occupied solely with the happiness of the French people, and with repairing the ills which his ambition inflicted on his country.' As soon as Napoleon finished reading it, he tore it up. 'This fine fellow is going mad.'[26]

16 March – Paris

The news flowed into Paris from all over France of the risings of people and army for Napoleon. People were thrilled by the line in one of Napoleon's proclamations that read: 'The eagle, with the national colours, will fly from steeple to steeple to the towers of Notre Dame.' Soon the French newspapers were printing variations of his progress:[27]

The Tiger has broken out of his den.

The Ogre has been three days at sea.

The wretch has landed at Fréjus.

The buzzard has reached Antibes.

The invader has arrived at Grenoble.

The General has entered Lyons. Napoleon slept at Fontainebleau last night.

The Emperor will proceed to the Tuileries today.

His Imperial Majesty will address his loyal subjects tomorrow.[28]

After hearing the news of Ney declaring for Napoleon, one wag left the following sign on public display in Paris: 'Napoleon to Louis XVIII. My good brother. It is unnecessary to send me any more soldiers. I have enough.'[29]

19 March – The Tuileries, Paris

As the last seconds ticked away to midnight, Louis abandoned Paris. The night before, he had said, 'I see it is all over. Let us not engage in useless resistance. I have decided to leave.' His last proclamation was being pasted up all over Paris stating that the King would not fight for the capital lest it bring on civil war. With him went marshals MacDonald and Berthier. Their destination was Lille initially, but the welcome there was less than warm. MacDonald left at this point, but Berthier accompanied the King to Ghent in Belgium. He considered himself still bound by his oath of loyalty. He found no comfort in Ghent. The court turned its hostility on him, and made it known that he could take his leave for his family in Bavaria. He left, a broken man, rejected for his loyalty to the King and alienated from the one man to whom he had truly been devoted.

20 March – The Tuileries, Paris

A travelling carriage drives rapidly through the gate. It is surrounded by a throng of horsemen of all arms and of all ranks, a confused mass waving their swords and roaring, *'Vive l'Empereur!'* The half-pay officers that fill the courtyard, the generals waiting on the porch steps draw their swords and rush forward. So dense is the crowd, so eager to see the rush that the horsemen are driven backwards and the postillions come to a halt, ten yards from the pavillon de Flore. The carriage door is flung open. NAPOLEON! The crowd seize him, drag him from his carriage, pass him from hand to hand into the entrance hall, where other officers tear him from them, hoist him shoulder high, and carry him to the staircase. Savage worshippers thee – struggling jealously to get near their idol – tigerlike in their caresses . . . The crowd pressing up and that pressing down the staircase would have crushed him had not Lavallette flung himself forward and turned his back on crowd, and clinging to the stair-rail, makes a buttress of his body, and thus he pushes his way backwards up the staircase, step by step, just a step above the emperor, murmuring ceaselessly, 'It's you, it's you.'

And he – he seems to see nothing, to hear nothing. He is borne forward. His arms are extended, his eyes closed, fixed smile upon his face. He seems like one walking in his sleep.[30]

Finally, his staff got him into his cabinet room and shut the doors. For him the time to celebrate was over. He went to work immediately, saying that France needed a government by the morning.

It was not long before Davout joined the crowd in Napoleon's apartments. He had come to seek a combat command. When at last all the others had been sent away, Napoleon asked the marshal to stay. Napoleon shocked Davout when he said that he had decided to appoint him as Minister of War. Davout protested vigorously that he would be of far more use as commander in the field. Besides, he had many enemies in the army and was known to be too severe and worked poorly with others. Napoleon laughed, 'You and Soult both.'

Then he grew serious.

Eh Bien! I will speak to you with an open heart and tell you all. I have let it be known and must continue to let it be known that I act in harmony with my father-in-law, the Emperor of Austria. It has been widely announced that the Empress is on her way bringing with her the King of Rome, that they will arrive any day now. The truth is that this is false, that I am alone, alone before Europe. This is my situation! Will you also abandon me?

Davout could no more resist the power of Napoleon's personality than Ney. He replied immediately, 'Sire, there is only one answer I can make, I accept the ministry.'[31]

That same day in Metz, the royal governor of the city, Marshal Nicolas-Charles Oudinot, declared the city in a state of siege. Oudinot had determined to maintain his oath to the King. The population and garrison were of a different mind and declared joyously for Napoleon. Known as the 'Father of Grenadiers' for his bravery, suffering thirty-six wounds on twenty-three occasions, Oudinot was not one to flinch from danger. Futility was something altogether different, and that described the King's cause. He and his family quietly slipped away to their estate at Bar-le-Duc.

21 March – The Tuileries, Paris

By the time Napoleon had gone to sleep at 3:00 in the morning, France had a new government. His appointments were of capable men who had been loyal to him through the events of 1814. The glaring exception was his choice for Minister of Police – Joseph Fouché. Fouché had begun his career as a bloodthirsty revolutionary who was one of those who voted for the execution of Louis XVI. He easily made the transition to the Empire and twice filled the position of Minister of Police, but in 1814 had conspired against Napoleon with the Allies. When the Bourbons would not employ him, he attempted unsuccessfully to plot against them with the Marquis de Lafayette and Louis Davout. Slippery as Napoleon knew him to be, his police talents for regime protection were simply too good to ignore.

Napoleon rose at 6:00. Five hours later the Tuileries courtyard echoed to rolling cheers and shouts of joy as the Emperor reviewed his regiments in a brilliant parade as 50,000 Parisians looked on, joining in the ovations. The noise only abated when he addressed 'the officers and non-commissioned officers gathered around him in a circle with a few of those beautiful, if vigorous phrases that belong to him alone, and that always made us forget our ills and defy all dangers'.[32] Master showman that he was, Napoleon knew that the enthusiasm of army and people had to be kindled and fed for the titanic struggle against great odds that he knew lay ahead.

He knew he could rely on the regimental officers, subalterns, and the enlisted ranks. It was those in command of regiments and divisions whose loyalty to the Bourbons was the price of their commands and were thereby suspect. At the review he stopped at each regiment and without hesitation replaced commanders whose loyalty was questionable.

One of the first men to rally to Napoleon was another former Minister of Police, Anne-Jean-Marie-René Savary. He was more than a capable policeman. He had been Napoleon's chief of *service d'espionage*, and a very good one too. He conferred privately with the Emperor that night: 'Your Majesty, there is an old friend that was one of the first to declare for you upon your return.' With a curious nod, Napoleon assented, and the doors opened. In walked a nondescript man. The Emperor looked at Savary, clearly not recognizing the newcomer. The man bowed, and as he did so made quick adjustments to his appearance. Napoleon burst out laughing. 'Schulmeister, this is the second time you have done this to me!'[33]

The Alsatian Karl Schulmeister had proved to be one of the greatest spies in history, at one time tricking Austrian General Mack to put his forces into the military trap at Ulm. Later he infiltrated the Austrian service to become its chief of intelligence. Missions took him all over Europe, even to England and Ireland. Napoleon recounted how Schulmeister had requested an audience in Strasbourg and asked for employment. Napoleon addressed him curtly. 'Where are your references?'

'Sire, I have no recommendations but my own.'

'You may go. We have no work for men without references.' Without another word, Napoleon rose and retired behind a screen, indicating that the interview was over.

But Schulmeister did not go. Instead, he made a few alterations to his dress and puckered up his face. In a moment the Emperor returned and, thinking that Schulmeister had gone and that here was a fresh recruit, demanded, 'Who are you?'

'I am Karl Schulmeister,' replied the candidate. 'You interviewed me a moment ago. Now that I have demonstrated my ability to change my personality completely, perhaps you could find me a job in your service.' Napoleon was thunderstruck and immediately employed him, a decision he was not to regret. Before long Schulmeister was the head of French espionage and its best spy. His most notorious effort was to kidnap the Duke d'Enghien. The duke had been organizing émigré resistance to Napoleon, who wanted an example made of him. After a quick court-martial he was shot. It was no wonder that Napoleon was to remark that the spy was worth a division, and Savary described him as all brains and no heart.[34]

'I have work for you, Schulmeister,' Napoleon said now. 'You must find out what they are saying about me in Vienna. Before you leave, see me again. I will have a special letter for you.'[35]

23 March – The Tuileries, Paris

Ney arrived in Paris with his division. Thinking he could see the Emperor, he was instead ordered by Davout to depart immediately on an inspection of the northern fortresses.

The Emperor had far greater regard for Soult. Unlike Davout he did not rush to seek a command from Napoleon. Twice Napoleon asked to meet with him, but Soult refused to come in from his estate. Napoleon was patient. When he wanted a man, he rarely failed to get him.[36]

One such rarity was Oudinot, whom Davout had urged to declare for Napoleon. He responded, 'I am faithful to my new master . . . I shall always remain the Grenadier Oudinot, a title I delight in.' He called in the officers of the garrison and asked them to shout for the King in front of the troops with him. There was dead silence until a junior officer informed him that the men would all cheer for the Emperor instead. Oudinot packed up and left for home.

At first Napoleon consigned him to his estates but later thought better of it and ordered him to Paris. He asked what the Bourbons had done for him that he, Napoleon, had not done better. Oudinot replied simply, 'Since I shan't serve under you, sire, I'll serve under no one.'[37] Napoleon accepted his sincerity and dismissed him with regret.

The task before the reinstated Emperor would have daunted anyone but a dynamo of energy like Napoleon. He had to rebuild the army that the Bourbons had allowed to shrink and rust to meet the inevitable Allied invasion. When he landed there had been eighteen marshals on the active list. Only nine of them eventually threw him their support: Davout, Soult, Brune, Mortier, Ney, Saint-Cyr, Masséna, Jourdan, Lefebvre, and Suchet. Of these, Saint-Cyr's support was only formal – he did not seek an appointment – and Lefebvre was sick. Masséna took a month to declare for Napoleon but was far too old for field service. The rest stayed neutral like Oudinot, or Napoleon rejected them as traitors in the 1814 campaign. Most of the rest of the officer corps considered their oath of loyalty to Louis to have been voided when he fled the country. Some declared for Napoleon with only a pretention of loyalty.

Napoleon understood that the Allies would surely reject his overtures of peace. He would need not only the army, but the people as well. He recognized that the French were in no mood for a return to his imperious rule. To win them over he proposed a bicameral legislature based on the British model, where both it and he would share power. He announced to the Council of Ministers that he was done with his past imperial ambitions and that 'henceforth the happiness and the consolidation of France shall be the object of all my thoughts'. He actually meant it.

After Davout had sent a crestfallen Ney on his tour of inspection, he was summoned to a private meeting with the Emperor, who made his plans plain: 'I will continue to send appeals for peace to the emperors in Vienna, but I expect nothing but war. Who knows?' He laughed. 'Perhaps the age of miracles has not passed.' Davout was not amused. Napoleon then got to the point. 'I expect their armies to converge on France. I cannot wait for them to do that; it would be just like last year's campaign. I must be able to fight and beat them one at a time. The closest enemy are the two armies between Brussels and Namur – the Anglo-Netherlands and the Prussians. I will beat them both, take Belgium, and drive that so-called new King of the Netherlands William out. He can flee back to his English pension.'[38]

He went on to describe how he would then turn east, cross the Rhine and strike the enemy armies one at a time before they could combine. 'A few more drubbings, and they will be only too glad to accept my offers of peace.'[39]

24 March – The Tuileries, Paris

Gen. Comte Pierre de Colbert-Chabanais took his time before throwing his lot in with Napoleon after his return. He was, however, a man whom the Emperor wanted to have with him. Colbert-Chabanais was both a brilliant and ferocious commander. For that reason, Napoleon had given him command of the 2nd Chevaux-Légers Lanciers, known as the Red Lancers. Originally part of the

Dutch Royal Guard incorporated into the Imperial Guard and issued a scarlet Polish-style uniform, they had earned a deadly reputation from the invasion of Russia to the campaign of 1814. Though some Dutchmen were still in the ranks, now it was a French regiment and just as deadly. After Napoleon's abdication, Colbert-Chabanais had declared for the Bourbons and been made commander of the lancers of the Royal Guard.

Napoleon gave him an icy reception when he presented himself to request a command: 'General Colbert, I've been waiting for you for three days.' Colbert was not intimidated and shot back, 'I have been waiting for you for a year.' Napoleon gave him back command of his lancers.[40]

26 March – The Tuileries, Paris

Napoleon did not have to test his patience in wooing Soult. The marshal's former aide, the Comte de Saint-Chamans and one of his division commanders from Spain, Gen. Bertrand Clausel, urged Soult to see the Emperor. Six days after Napoleon's arrival in Paris Soult presented himself at the palace. It was no doubt a tense meeting. Napoleon was fully aware of the harsh terms in which Soult had described him in Soult's last order of the day as Minister of War. Napoleon wanted him but was not yet sure of his loyalty. They discussed his returning to duty, but nothing was settled.

28 March – The Hofburg Palace, Vienna

The news of Napoleon's arrival in Paris had reached Vienna and shocked the delegates at the Hofburg. The initial reaction of many of the participants was that everything they had fought for was now in danger. Stronger voices soon prevailed. Wellington wrote, 'I am perfectly satisfied with the spirit which prevails here upon this occasion.' Emperors Alexander I and Francis refused even to respond to Napoleon's repeated offers of peace.

> In another show of solidarity, the allies publicly brushed aside Napoleon's declaration to the effect that nobody had the right to choose a ruler for France but the French people with a riposte that certain requirements of international law transcended the right to intervene in the internal affairs of another country in the name of the greater good of Europe.[41]

The sword was drawn and the scabbard thrown away. Each of the four powers pledged 150,000 men to the destruction of Napoleon. That number was beyond

Britain's ability: its contribution was the small force already in the region of Brussels and a £5 million subsidy for the others. The enormous subsidy was the linchpin of the new coalition. The finances of the Allies were exhausted. Without it they could not afford to buy a potato.

Wellington was offered a choice of remaining in Vienna as the British negotiator or taking command of the British-Netherlands forces. The young Tsar put his hand on Wellington's shoulder and said, 'It is for you to save the world again.' The Duke left for Brussels the next day.[42]

CHAPTER 2

Forging the Sword

1 April–29 May 1815

1 April – The War Ministry, Paris

Napoleon's support of a new constitutional order had been well received by the population in general, but the old royalist hotbeds in the Vendée and the Midi required more punitive action. The Vendée was a region south of the Loire in western France that had strongly resisted the forces of the new Republic and had been brutally suppressed. The Midi was that area of southern France bounded by the Pyrenees to the south, the Atlantic to the west and the Mediterranean to the east. The problem in the Midi was the most immediate. There the Duke of Angoulême was rallying support with a small army.

Napoleon had quickly dispatched Gen. Emmanuel de Grouchy to deal with that. Grouchy was an inspired choice. The scion of an old noble family, he had thrown his support in with the Revolution to become a skilled commander of cavalry who had all the ability of Murat but without the theatrics. He had commanded the Irish expedition of 1798, played an important part in the victories of Hohenlinden, Eylau, Friedland, and Borodino, and had led the Sacred Band in the retreat from Russia. His health broken, he had retired until the Allies invaded France in 1814, when he rushed back to the colours. Napoleon was deeply impressed with his brilliant performance at the Battle of Vauchamps and the capture of Troyes; he had been wounded three times. Napoleon had intended to make him a marshal, but the end rushed up too quickly. Grouchy had certainly earned it. Napoleon had not forgotten that he had stayed loyal right up to the abdication. Grouchy made his peace with the Bourbons but was relieved of his command of guard cavalry and fobbed off with a minor post of inspector of chasseurs and lancers.

4 April – The Tuileries, Paris

On 4 April Napoleon wrote to the Allies in Vienna that he was dedicated only to peace and the happiness of nations. His message fell on deaf ears.

4 April – Brussels

The first thing Wellington did after arriving in Brussels on the 4th was to inspect the terrain south of the Forest of Soignes to the crossroads of Quatre Bras. He found just what he was looking for near the village of Mont St Jean – a low ridge behind which an army could shelter to protect itself from the terrible fire of the French artillery. He had ridden over this ground the year before and marked it as exactly the sort of position he had used so successfully in the Peninsula.

Wellington arrived already worried about the Allied army he was to command. He was much displeased with the small staff and quickly dismissed the quartermaster general, Maj. Gen. Sir Hudson Lowe, who had the reputation of a small-minded jailer. Wellington needed the men he knew and trusted from the long campaign in the Peninsula. At first the only man of his old military family was his aide-de-camp and private secretary, the 25-year-old Lt. Col. John Fremantle of the Coldstream Guards, who had fought with his regiment as a junior officer. Wellington was a relative of his and transferred him to his staff, where his diligence and ability earned him the Duke's favour. He was given the high honour of carrying the dispatches of two victorious battles to London. Some of the Duke's anxiety was dispelled as more and more of his military family joined him.

A larger problem was the small contingent of British troops he found. There were only 8,000 British troops in the Netherlands. Too many of his best Peninsular army regiments were in America or mid-ocean. He needed tried and true men he had commanded and recommended contingents of the Portuguese army he had trained into crack troops, his 'fighting cocks', but nothing came of it. They had been disbanded, and the Portuguese leaders had seen enough of the British.

The British government had discharged so many troops after the peace of 1814 that there was only the thinnest reserve available for Wellington. The garrison of Ireland was stripped to send him 17,000 more men and even some regiments that had just put to sea were recalled. But there were not enough of the prized infantry which would be the rock upon which his army must rely. Except for the Guards, all these battalions were understrength. His request for more artillery was met with the explanation that there were enough guns and ammunition but not sufficient men and horses. The Regiment of Artillery had been reduced by 7,000 men. The only arm he had enough of were the cavalry, for which he had the least regard. He was appalled at his inexperienced staff, meant only for a small army of occupation. Eventually, he would gather thirty-three of his Peninsular veterans in a staff of thirty-six.

Eight battalions of the King's German Legion (KGL), as reliable as the British, were in the Netherlands awaiting discharge. In the end, of the British and KGL battalions Wellington would have, 75 per cent had fought with him in the Peninsula. The KGL was recruited mostly from the former soldiers of the Hanoverian army abolished by Napoleon when he had overrun Hanover. Refusing to accept French occupation, they had slipped into Britain determined to fight Napoleon and had been formed into the King's German Legion. Their professionalism and valour made them excellent soldiers whom Wellington valued highly.[1] The newly established Kingdom of Hanover was to provide seventeen infantry battalions, while the Germans from Nassau and Brunswick contributed another sixteen and a half battalions.[2] Wellington would have more German battalions than British in his command.[3]

As worried as he was about the number and quality of his British forces, Wellington's biggest problem was King William of the Netherlands, often referred to as 'Old Frog', who was to provide at least half his army. The King agreed with all of Wellington's suggestions but then found reasons to pick every one of them apart. Viewing William's forces, Wellington lamented that all of his officers had been in the French army and that his closest subordinates were all ex-French officials determined 'to get us out of Antwerp and Ostend'. The British had insisted that these two ports remain under their command, for upon their control and protection depended the lifeline and, if necessary, the escape route of the British should disaster befall them. Many of William's Belgian regiments had been in French uniform barely a year before. There remained a strong pro-French sentiment among the French-speaking Walloons in southern Belgium. The British had been badly disappointed that the promised Dutch rising against Napoleon in 1814 had never occurred. Their level of training was not high; most of the Belgian-Dutch troops were militia, though most of their officers and many of the men were veterans. The Catholic Belgians who had been promised independence upon the fall of Napoleon now found themselves forced into a union with Protestant Holland and reacted with sullen indifference. In the end, after all his intransigence, William was able to provide only seventeen Dutch and Belgian infantry battalions.

The Dutch King's son, William, the 24-year-old Prince of Orange, was another problem for Wellington. Exiled with his father in 1794 when the French overran Holland, he was educated as a soldier in Prussia and later attended Oxford University. At the age of 19 with the rank of lieutenant colonel he had joined Wellington in the Peninsula as an aide, where his courage and good humour made him popular. He stayed long enough to observe several of the Duke's campaigns, where he was referred to as 'Young Frog' for his broad, high, hairless forehead, wide mouth and prominent blue eyes which gave him a comical though engaging expression and 'Slender Billy' for his long neck. Back in England the next year he became the aide to the Prince Regent and was promoted to major general. In the chaos of 1813, William returned to the Netherlands as a lieutenant general. Due to royal favour he was rapidly promoted to full general in the British army by the end of 1814. When Wellington arrived, William was in command of the Allied, including British, forces in the Netherlands.[4] He had wanted to dispose his forces far forward ready to leap into France. The Duke had to restrain him and keep his forces concentrated further north to give him maximum flexibility.

While Wellington was personally fond of this engaging young man, he was aware that he had a dangerously inflated estimation of his own military virtues even though he had never commanded anything. He was possessed of 'the fatal self-sufficiency of military ignorance'. The Duke had said of him, 'The Prince is a brave young man, but that's all.'[5]

Wellington was far more fortunate in the selection of the man to command his II Corps – Lt. Gen. Rowland Lord Hill, a man of great ability who was also beloved for kindness as a 'zealous Christian' and called 'Daddy Hill' by his men. By 1811 he had risen to become Wellington's most trusted lieutenant in the Peninsula. When Wellington took command in Belgium, the government had the great good sense to send Hill to him.

> On 13 December 1813, during the Battle of the Nive, Hill performed what may have been his finest work in his defence of St-Pierre d'Irube. With his 14,000 men and 10 guns isolated on the east bank of the Nive by a broken bridge, Hill held off the attacks of Marshal Nicolas Soult's 30,000 soldiers and 22 guns. He fought the battle with great skill and 'was seen at every point of danger, and repeatedly led up rallied regiments in person to save what seemed like a lost battle . . . He was even heard to swear.[6]

Wellington had such trust in Hill that he was the only officer to whom he offered an explanation of his orders. He said of him, 'The best of Hill is that I always know where to find him.'[7]

Far less welcome to command his cavalry and act as his nominal second in command was Gen. Henry William Paget, second Earl of Uxbridge. Under Sir John Moore in the Coruña campaign he had won several spectacular victories that established his reputation. He promptly destroyed that reputation by abandoning his wife and children to elope with the wife of Wellington's brother. Ultimately, Paget was rehabilitated and became a favourite of the Prince Regent and the Duke of York, the commander of the British army, who foisted him on Wellington.

As much as he disliked Uxbridge, according to Sir Charles Oman, Wellington had never, until the Waterloo campaign, had an officer of such proven ability in chief command of his cavalry. In fact, Wellington did not regard the British cavalry highly, thinking them so unprofessional that they could not be easily controlled. He commented that he would trust one British cavalry regiment to beat one French regiment every time, but when the numbers increased, together with the necessity for control and discipline, he felt the French were superior.

Wellington was confident enough in the Hanoverian aristocrat Lt. Gen. Sir Charles Count Alten to entrust him with the command of his 3rd British Division, his largest, albeit made up largely of Germans. When Napoleon annexed Hanover in 1806, Alten had been one of the flood of 18,000 Hanoverians who fled to Britain to keep up the fight as the KGL. As was fashionable among young Hanoverian officers, he anglicized his name from Karl to Charles. He was already an experienced officer when he was assigned to Wellington, rising to command his famous light division.

The Duke also summoned the Welshman Lt. Gen. Sir Thomas Picton to command his 5th Division:

> Fame found Picton late in life, Sir Thomas having turned 50 by the time he became a celebrity as commander of Wellington's 3rd Division during the Peninsular War. Under Picton's tenure, this element of the Duke's army became known as the 'Fighting Division', and Sir Thomas gained a reputation as a fire-eating commander and disciplinarian. He also became legendary for vulgarity, Wellington pronouncing him a 'rough, foul-mouthed devil as ever lived'. But Picton got results.[8]

Unexpectedly Picton was reluctant to join Wellington in 1815. He had an overwhelming premonition of death, so powerful that, to the horror of his friends he jumped into an open grave to measure it for size. Yet he answered Wellington's summons.

Another one of Wellington's trusted Peninsular veteran commanders was Lt. Gen. Sir Henry Clinton, to whom the Duke entrusted the large 2nd British Division.

Lt. Gen. Sir Charles Coleville had commanded a brigade under Picton and had become one of Wellington's favourite brigadiers. Wellington insisted on his temporary promotion to lieutenant general when he arrived in Belgium and gave him command of his 4th British Division.

Wellington intended Lt. Gen. Sir Galbraith Lowry Cole, one of his ablest commanders, to command the 6th British Division, but Cole married on 15 June and departed on his honeymoon. The position was held open for him, but he never arrived. Another officer whom he wished he could have had with him was his brother-in-law, Maj. Gen. Sir Edward Packenham, who had taken command of British forces in North America and been killed at the Battle of New Orleans on 8 January. Wellington said of him, 'We have but one consolation, that he fell as he lived, in the honourable discharge of his duty and distinguished as a soldier and a man.'[9]

Thus, despite not getting all of his veteran regiments from the Peninsular War, Wellington was at least able to surround himself with men who had proven themselves on lengthy campaigns under the most difficult conditions and on many a hard-won field. The same could not be said of the three Netherlands generals who were to command the three Netherlands divisions, two of whom had spent their careers until 1814 in French service. These appointments were in the gift of the King of the Netherlands.

Lt. Gen. Henri-Georges Baron Perponcher-Sedlnitzky commanded the 2nd Netherlands Infantry Division. This Dutch soldier had been fighting the French since the First Coalition in 1792. When the Netherlands was overrun, he transferred to Austrian and then to British service, fighting in Egypt and briefly serving in the Peninsula without seeing action. He served in the disastrous Walcheren Campaign of 1809 but resigned in 1811 when Napoleon threatened to confiscate his hereditary estates. In 1813 he was instrumental in putting William I on the throne of the Netherlands. The King made him commander of the nascent new Dutch army, which he led in the 1814 campaign.

The career of Lt. Gen. David Hendrik, Baron Chassé, commanding the Netherlands 3rd Infantry Division, could not have been more different. Before the French Revolution, as a political exile, he entered the French army and then the armies of the Revolution. His career took off after the French overran his native Holland, first under the Batavian Republic and then in French service after the annexation of Holland. As a brigadier he became known as 'General Bayonet', which speaks for itself. He fought faithfully for Napoleon during the 1814 campaign, being made a baron of the Empire. Following the abdication, he entered the service of the new Kingdom of the Netherlands. Unlike his fellow Dutch generals, he was known, not unexpectedly, to be particularly anti-British.

Commanding the Netherlands Cavalry Division was Lt. Gen. J.A. Baron Collaert whose career, like that of Chassé, was tied to France. He served under the Batavian Republic, the Kingdom of Holland, and entered French service after Napoleon's annexation of Holland. In 1813–14 he served with distinction commanding cavalry brigades and participated in Napoleon's last victory at Saint-Dizier in 1814. He then joined the Netherlands army and was given command of the cavalry division and promoted to lieutenant general.

The Great Powers in Vienna and the British government expected Wellington to assume command of the Allied forces in the Netherlands. Nevertheless, for the rest of the month he had to fight a relentless battle with William I to make his command a reality. Wellington had taken the measure of William's forces. As a separate army, they were simply unreliable. The Duke wanted to mix the Dutch-Belgian forces with his British divisions as he had done in the Peninsula with his Portuguese brigades. The King would have none of it. Wellington resorted to threatening William that he would make known the reasons for the King's intransigence. That had the intended effect, and on 3 May William finally agreed to put his forces under Wellington's command with the rank of field marshal in the

Netherlands army and to integrate his divisions with the British. The price was the command of the Duke's largest corps for Slender Billy.

After his string of remarkable victories in the Peninsula and southern France, Britain and all of Allied Europe placed an almost mystical faith in Wellington. And well they might, for he had proven himself one of the great captains in history. An English visitor to Napoleon on Elba in October 1814 reported Napoleon's opinion of him. He said, 'There are but three generals in the world: myself, Lord Wellington and that drunkard Blücher.'[10] An Anglo-Irish aristocrat, born in 1769, the same year as Napoleon, Wellington had attended the French army school of equitation at Angers, where he learned excellent French and became a fine horseman. A military commission followed and eventually his family was able to purchase him the lieutenant colonelcy in the 33rd Foot in 1793. The next year his regiment joined the British expedition to the Netherlands which ended disastrously as half the army perished from exposure, sickness and starvation. He was to remark later of this experience, 'At least I learned what not to do, and that is always a valuable lesson.' Because of this experience he was to become one of the great logisticians in military history, his armies never going hungry or unsupplied.[11]

He had performed well in combat in the Netherlands and learned the value of steady infantry. Transferred to India in 1797, he achieved a remarkable series of victories with a combined force of Sepoy and British battalions that made his reputation as a successful general. Returning to Britain in 1805, he was promoted to lieutenant general and sent to Portugal, where he defeated the French invasion but was superseded by an incompetent who signed a shameful convention which allowed the French army to return. He was recalled but cleared, and the next year sent back to Portugal to command the British army there. Over the next five years he commanded Britain's only field army to one victory after another against a succession of Napoleon's marshals. He considered Soult to be the most formidable of all of them. After Napoleon's defeat in 1814 he was made Duke of Wellington as the nation's hero and made ambassador to France.

In the Peninsula he built upon his experience with mixed troops by training and incorporating Portuguese battalions into his brigades and brought them up to a high standard of performance. He became the master of the defence, allowing the standard French attacks in column to be shattered by the steady fire of his infantry in line which he had sheltered behind ridgelines until the moment of contact. He must have been amazed that the French did not modify their tactics in the face of repeated drubbings. His style of command was very much hands-on, drawing him like a magnet to each crisis point of a battle.

Aloof, aristocratic, and hard, Wellington did not engender the same sort of love from this troops that Napoleon did. His men trusted him to take care of them, though, and not to throw their lives away. His presence secured their confidence. Napoleon came to admire him from a distance as the only general who was his equal. Wellington respected Napoleon's military genius, saying that his presence on a battlefield was worth 40,000 men, but held him in contempt as a despot.

Lionized across Europe – where Beethoven wrote an orchestral piece, 'Wellington's Victory', to celebrate the Battle of Vitoria – Wellington felt that he had missed the ultimate test of generalship. He had not fought Napoleon. That omission was about to be remedied.

8 April – The Tuileries, Paris

Napoleon's chief concern was to prepare France for invasion by the overwhelming numbers the Allies were preparing. The Bourbons had hollowed out the French army and there were only 224,000 men on the rolls. Of that number, 32,800 had been sent home on leave without pay in order to free up funds for Louis' 10,000 'toy' soldiers in the Maison du Roi (royal household). Another 82,000 were listed as deserters – men who could not stomach serving the Bourbons. There were only 50,000 men fit for field service. Clothing and weapons were in poor condition; the French navy had simply been financially abandoned and the fortresses neglected. 'Every military commodity was in short supply – horses, harness, ammunition, clothing, weapons.' There were only 32,000 horses in the army, and 8,000 had to be loaned out to farmers to provide forage.

Now Napoleon turned his legendary powers of organization to the crisis. He ordered mobilization. Of the 114,000 men who had deserted or been sent home without pay, 82,446 had rejoined their regiments by June. Another 23,448 were at their depots in the process of being clothed and armed, with only 8,105 failing to respond to the recall. Seventy-five thousand veterans and another 15,000 volunteers rushed to the colours. French garrisons in Corsica and the Channel Islands were recalled and replaced with local volunteers. Those 10,000 men of the king's Maison du Roi who had not already deserted were dismissed unless they had had prior service with the Grande Armée; their weapons and horses were transferred to other units. Sixty thousand naval personnel were formed into Régiments de Marine to replace line regiments in coastal fortresses. He called up 200 National Guard battalions (over 91,000 men, and 25,000 veterans to train them) to take over the frontier forces to free up regular regiments for the field armies he was creating. The conscripts who had deserted in 1814 were pardoned and recalled to the colours, and many came. Within sixty days, the active army numbered 284,000, allowing Napoleon to field armies totalling 217,000 men and an auxiliary army of 220,000 men in the National Guard. The regimental depots were full of men in training and thousands of men were arriving at them every day.

The one measure the Emperor was hesitant to take was the reintroduction of the hated conscription for the class of 1815. Davout, however, argued that they had already been conscripted legally for the defence of France in 1814. Conscription would not be required; these men had deserted or had been released. They could simply be recalled to the colours. Napoleon agreed instantly. The measure was quickly enacted and met with no little enthusiasm from the men themselves. They were sent directly to line regiments where they were able to bring numerous understrength battalions up to strength, especially in regiments that would form the Army of the North (Armée du Nord). Thousands of the half-pay junior officers who had been ordered up by the Bourbons but balked, now joyfully complied for Napoleon. Many of them were sent to fill out the expanding battalions.[12]

With all of these measures Napoleon reasonably expected to have 800,000 men under arms by October.

It was not enough to raise an army. It had to be clothed, equipped, and fed. The Bourbons had essentially shut down France's arsenals and factories that fed the army. In a whirlwind of industrial mobilization, the arsenals were put back into operation to turn out new weapons and refurbish old ones. Foundries glowed night and day, pouring bronze into guns by the hundreds. Napoleon transformed the Bourbon high unemployment into full employment as he turned the nation into a workshop of war. Uniform factories reopened. There was not enough cloth available for all the needed uniforms, so large orders were placed to weave more cloth. Loaned-out horses were reclaimed, and 8,000 more were requisitioned. Cavalry regiments were allowed to make direct purchases. All this required money. A number of Dutch bankers, some say Dutch-English bankers, advanced large sums.[13]

Napoleon also attended to the spirit of the army. The new Bourbon regimental names were abolished and the old imperial numbers reintroduced. He issued new eagles to the regiments and he purged the Legion of Honour of the Bourbon disgraces. He resumed his method of reviewing regiments whereby any officer or soldier could step out from the ranks and address a grievance or petition to the Emperor. They were answered immediately unless further inquiry was required. It was also his style to address the officers and ask what soldiers were especially deserving of recognition, then there on the spot promote or decorate the soldier. He had a photographic memory, much like Alexander the Great, and knew thousands of men by sight. To call out an old soldier and recount his deeds in front of the regiment had a profound effect on everyone present, inspiring men to deeds that would merit the attention of the Emperor. The older soldiers commented how slimmed-down and energetic the Emperor was now – he was the man of Austerlitz again.[14]

The army that Napoleon was reconstituting was perhaps the finest he had ever had. Most of his men were veterans. Those newer junior officers and soldiers who had come to the colours since 1814 had been imbued with the ethos of the army and with an intense desire to achieve distinction. The loyalty of the army was to Napoleon personally. For them he represented everything they had achieved in his run of incredible victories, and when the victories turned to defeat, they clung to him too, for he was their hero. Even as the Allies had closed on him in 1814, he had led the men in a brilliant campaign against great odds until the numbers and treason told against them. The class of 1815, termed the Marie-Louises after the Empress, were trained on the march and in battle and performed beyond all expectations.

There was also another profound motivation – revenge. The thousands of returned prisoners from British prison hulks, and from Russian, Austrian, and Prussian confinement, who had been neglected by the Bourbons on their return wanted to get even. The men who had held out in garrisons in Germany and marched home in undefeated good order wanted to get even. The men who had fought to defend France in 1814 against the savage depredations of the Prussians and Cossacks wanted to get even. The army was united in the determination to punish their enemies should they again attack France.

The army that Napoleon was rebuilding was experienced, reasonably well-equipped, and with high morale. Yet it was brittle. So many men were new to their units that the bonding that normally takes long training had not completely set. Far more dangerous was the bitterness held by so many in the ranks for the generals that had betrayed Napoleon in 1814 and gone over to the Bourbons. The confidence that soldiers must have in their chain of command had not been fully restored. Again and again Napoleon was warned by soldiers to watch out for treason among the marshals and generals.

Of the many decisions made by Napoleon in the hectic days since his arrival was the reconstitution of the general staff. He sorely missed Berthier but had had him struck from the list of marshals. He was clearly of two minds and had said, 'That brute Berthier! [H]e will come back to us, we will forgive him everything provided he wear his uniform of the [Bourbon] garde-du-corps when he appears before me.' It sounded like a joke but for the undertone of petty humiliation, a facet of their relationship that kept Berthier in Bamberg.

In Berthier's absence, Napoleon was fortunate that he had at hand Berthier's former deputy, Gen. François Gédéon Bailly de Monthion, a 39-year-old, tall, distinguished officer from an old aristocratic family who had joined the armies of the Revolution in 1793. At Marengo as a captain in 1800 he had sufficiently impressed Berthier, who immediately transferred him to his staff. He had an excellent reputation as a gifted organizer. No one knew the general staff system better than he did.[15]

Within a year of Monthion's attachment to Berthier's staff, Napoleon had given him the Legion of Honour. In the 1806–7 campaigns, Berthier made him his chief subordinate, first assistant major general. In that position, he was:

> the chief of staff to Berthier, and directed all branches of the general staff. His department was the biggest, and was divided in its turn into three different bureau, each commanded by an *adjutant-commandant* who held the rank of colonel and who

served as *chef de bureau*. The first division dealt with troop movements, passwords, transmission of orders, etc. The second division . . . looked after the quarters of the general staff, police duties, the Gendamerie, supplies and hospitals. The third division . . . was responsible for prisoners of war and deserters, requisitioning, and conscripts, councils of war, laws and . . . orders or decisions . . . of government.[16]

For his service at Austerlitz in 1805 Monthion was promoted to colonel and received the Officer's Cross. Napoleon promoted him to general of brigade in 1808 for his service in Portugal and made him a count of the Empire for his service in the 1809 campaign, where he had had three horses shot out from under him. During the invasion of Russia he was described as 'the moving spirit of the staff' and as commanding a vast number of officers of all grades. He had stood in for his superior when illness took Berthier away from the army during the battles of Dresden and Leipzig in 1813 and was rewarded by the Emperor with the Grand Cross of the Legion of Honour. When even Berthier had abandoned Napoleon at Fontainebleau in the events that led to the abdication, Monthion remained with the Emperor. With the restoration of the Bourbons and the disbandment of the general staff, he was put on the inactive list but tossed the Bourbon order of a Chevalier of St Louis. Soldiering was all he knew, but the destruction of the organization with which he had served so brilliantly did nothing to predispose him to the Bourbons. Without hesitation, he rallied to Napoleon upon his return.[17] It was to Monthion that Napoleon had asked Captain Coignet to report.

Napoleon sorely missed Berthier upon his return. Apart from his genuine affection for the man with whom he had waged so much war, he had not hesitated to bully and subject him to his tantrums. Monthion was someone altogether different. He refused to be intimidated by Napoleon, who for his part remarked that he could feel no warmth for the man. Nevertheless, Napoleon had to admit that Monthion knew his job and had been steadfastly loyal.

Monthion was in a state of high expectation when he reported to the Tuileries on Napoleon's order. There could be only one reason the Emperor would have him report – the recreation of the general staff. With Berthier now struck from the marshalate and not stirring from his Bavarian castle, Monthion fully expected to be confirmed as major general and to be made a marshal of France. By any standard, he deserved it.

When he left his audience with the Emperor, he was reminded of the saying from antiquity that what the gods give with one hand, they take away with another. He had indeed been charged with reconstituting the general staff for duty with the Army of the North. But there was no mention of the position of major general (chief of the general staff) or a marshal's baton. He remained a general of division. He was not happy. Perhaps it was Napoleon's way – to dangle these rewards to be earned in the fighting to come.[18]

8 April – The Hofburg Palace, Vienna

Pavel Bulyagin, the recently departed Russian chargé in Paris, bowed low before His Imperial Majesty, Alexander I, and handed him a bomb in the form of a letter. It was a gift from Napoleon. As the Russian Emperor began to read, he flushed with high colour and went storming off to find Metternich. The bomb was a copy of the Anglo-Franco-Austrian treaty of alliance against Russia and Prussia. Napoleon's foreign minister, Caulincourt, had found it in the diplomatic archives. The Allies had been having serious arguments over the fate of Saxony and Poland, coveted by Prussia and Russia respectively. Britain and Austria had seen their own interests threatened, and Talleyrand, spotting the opportunity to assert France's role as a Great Power, had supported them. The Austrians in particular considered that their forces would be in the first wave against Napoleon with 400,000 Russians and 200,000 Prussians in their rear. Napoleon had recognized the opportunity for mischief and cast this golden apple of discord among delegates in Vienna.[19]

Alexander stormed off, treaty in hand, and confronted Metternich in an ugly scene. When the news reached Berlin, the King and his generals were outraged. They believed the British had gone back on their agreement over Saxony and were now willing to ally themselves with Prussia's historical French enemy and Austria, its rival for dominance of Germany. But the most serious damage was done in the mind of Alexander, a religious visionary. He appeared to have got over the matter and joined his troops in Germany,

> But he wrote to his brother Constantine that he had no intention of throwing away any more Russian lives on behalf of foreign machinations. He would accept the British subsidy and make haste slowly towards France. Let Austria first show that she meant to fight and suffer losses. He would not make great efforts to reinstate the Bourbons who had insulted him and had tried to rob him of Poland. In any case, if Napoleon were to prevail, the Tsar had no doubt he would offer Russia the whole of Poland to secure a peace treaty.

10 April – The Hofburg Palace, Vienna

For the third time in his career, Schulmeister was masquerading in Vienna as someone else. There was little chance of his being recognized. He was a deft master of disguise. He had arrived in the uniform of an Austrian hussar officer from a distant regiment on the Turkish border with effusive letters of recommendation to Archduke Ferdinand. The Austrians were still so gullible, he observed. The staff were working overnight to prepare for the invasion of France and were glad of the help. At some point, he was able to take leave to go to Bamberg. The Emperor had a letter for him to deliver there.

He had seen the priceless opportunity presented by the bitter fallout over the exposed treaty. He fanned the fears of Russia and Prussia among the Austrian staff and delegation. To the Russians and Prussians he sold himself to deliver for a tidy profit forged documents that showed the depth of Anglo-Franco-Austrian perfidy.[20]

10 April – Wellington's Headquarters, Brussels

Wellington was thoroughly dissatisfied with the lack of urgency in Vienna to put paid to Napoleon's ambition. He wrote, 'It will suffice to bring between the Sambre and the Meuse 60,000 Anglo-Dutch, 69,000 Prussians, and 140,000 Austrians and Bavarians, to find ourselves in France with forces far superior to those of the enemy, and free to manoeuvre in the direction of Paris.' He felt that the decision to wait for the Russian army to be in position to act as a reserve was less important than to strike when Napoleon's strength had not been consolidated and increased. The opinion in Vienna was on the side of overwhelming numbers which would not be achieved for at least two months.[21]

11 April – The War Ministry, Paris

Soult was getting anxious. He had heard nothing more from the Emperor although he had sent in his written oath of allegiance. He wrote several times to his friend Davout, who had promised to have the matter finalized. Soult had no reply and wrote again, saying, 'I hope that Your Excellency will be so kind as to answer the letter I had the honour of addressing to you two days ago, in order that I may be prepared for His Majesty's ultimate decision concerning me.' Two days later Soult was invited to personally renew his oath to the Emperor. He was now back in Napoleon's good graces. Yet, no command was offered him.[22]

Anxious to prove his loyalty, Soult sought to provide something of value to the Emperor. Balloons? Napoleon had responded when Soult suggested the reconstitution of the French Aerostatic Corps. The 1st Company of the corps had accompanied him to Egypt, but its equipment had been destroyed onboard ship in the Battle of the Nile. The Directory had abolished the corps in that same year, 1799. Soult mentioned them in his latest missive, adding,

I saw them in operation at the Battle of Fleurus in Belgium against the Austrians. Colonel Coutelle's observations from the balloon were critical in our victory. In

Spain I often thought what a great advantage a balloon would have been to see what that damned Wellington was doing beyond the crest he was always hiding behind. Remember, sire, how we had planned on using his concepts for the invasion of England.

It clearly piqued Napoleon's interest. He was quietly desperate for anything that could give him an edge. 'Yes, Coutelle,' the Emperor said. 'A remarkable chemist fully worthy of the Legion of Honour I awarded him in 1805 and making him a Chevalier of the Empire in 1809.' Soult was not surprised at Napoleon's uncanny memory. The next day the former colonel Jean Coutelle was summoned to the War Ministry.[23]

15 April – Grouchy's Headquarters, the Midi

Grouchy had quickly put paid to Angoulême's comic opera revolt and captured him. He was sure the Emperor would be pleased but had no idea how much. He opened an imperial dispatch. If he had not been such a self-possessed member of the old aristocracy, he would have shouted for joy. Napoleon had promoted him to marshal of France. In a postscript, he instructed Grouchy to let the duke go, no doubt realizing he was more trouble than he was worth. Angoulême promptly fled to England.

19 April – Prussian Headquarters, Liège

Blücher arrived at his headquarters in a bad mood. Marshal Count von Kalckreuth, who had been beaten so thoroughly by Davout at Auerstedt in 1806, warned him that he should be prepared to lose all the fame and reputation he had earned in the 1814 campaign in a rematch against Napoleon. Because Napoleon had on a number of occasions in that campaign beaten him badly, the admonition stung. The first thing he said to his staff was that the army was not to lose a single battle.

He would have been enraged if he had known how many senior officers were against his appointment. There was a general feeling that the 73-year-old field marshal was too old and senile. The latter aspect had been apparent for a long time. His brilliant chief of staff, Gneisenau, felt he himself should have been given command of the Prussian army in Belgium. He was advised by Field Marshal Hardenberg, Prussia's representative in Vienna, 'All the good you do will be boasted about by someone else . . . The King will not deviate from the seniority list, or you would be in command of the army. Now in actual fact you are in command, but old Blücher lends his name to it. Not many people will be misled by this.'

Gneisenau's sense of duty persuaded him to join his old commander at Liège. He quickly realized that there was almost no financial support for the four corps of the army in Belgium. Gneisenau wrote to Hardenberg, 'We are in such financial straits here that the Field Marshal almost had to pawn his whiskers.' That meant that, unlike Wellington, who had plenty of British gold to supply his forces, the Prussians were fed at the Netherlands' expense. That, in turn, reminded the francophone Belgians of the benefits of Napoleon's rule. Making war against Napoleon for Prussia had meant British subsidies; Prussia itself had been exhausted by a decade of war, and the British subsidies had not resumed as yet.[24]

Blücher was not commanding the Prussian first team. The veteran elite elements as well as the Guards were still in Prussia, a hedge against just the sort of perfidy revealed in the secret Anglo-French–Austrian treaty. A high proportion of his units were inexperienced Landwehr (militia). Of the forty-four Prussian regiments, fully twenty-four were Landwehr. Similarly, of the thirty-seven cavalry regiments, eighteen were Landwehr. A number of Landwehr infantry regiments were from regions recently annexed to Prussia. Many of these were concentrated in I Corps, in which each of its four brigades contained a Westphalian regiment, and a fifth was in II Corps. Others such as those from the 24th and 29th Infantry Regiments (formerly the 1st and 2nd Berg Regiments) had actually fought alongside the French as allies as late as 1813. The Prussians were poorly armed and uniformed as well. Many were using captured French muskets or British weapons and wearing British-made uniforms and equipment. Significantly, a large number of the Landwehr were boys under 17 and men over 45.

Blücher's army consisted of slightly more than 130,000 Prussians and 304 guns when the last units arrived. There were also 14,000 Saxon troops under Blücher's direct command. In addition he 'had nominal command of another formation: a North German "federal" corps. The Nord-deutsch Armeekorps – 15,000 troops commanded by General der Infanterie Friedrich-Heinrich, Graf Kleist von Nollendorf, was composed of units from Hesse-Cassel, Mecklenburg, Anhalt and several other small German states.'[25]

The Prussian cavalry had undergone a major reorganization in 1815 that amalgamated a number of varied units into single regiments. They had not fully shaken down into cohesive and well-trained units. The artillery was also weak, lacking many gunners. It was seriously undergunned in calibre compared to the superb French artillery.

There were also great strengths in the Prussian army. It had a superb general staff copied after the French model. Gneisenau was one of the finest chiefs of staff of any army. Leavening the inexperienced ranks of the Landwehr were a strong cadre of experienced officers and NCOs. Finally, the Prussian soldier, regular or Landwehr, was fired by a powerful sense of German nationalism awakened and kindled by the wars with the French. The other side of that coin was an equally powerful hatred of the French.

19 April – The Hofburg Palace, Vienna

Under the presidency of the Tsar and under the influence of Schwarzenberg, the Allies held a council of war that decided to postpone the invasion of France by all the armies until at least 1 June. The key issue was the need to allow all the armies to assemble in full, especially the Russian army, which would follow the others on the Upper Rhine as a reserve. Eventually that date was moved back to between 27 June and 1 July. Wellington's rage was only restrained by his famous self-possession. In contrast, Blücher's response was as volcanic as befitted a slashing hussar.[26]

1 May – Prussian Headquarters, Liège

Karl Schulmeister could smell the burning fuse. He had been drawn to Liège where a major rift was about to erupt among Napoleon's enemies. A corps of 14,000 Saxon troops was assigned to Blücher's army, and they were not happy. Their beloved old king, Frederick Augustus, was imprisoned by the Prussians for his French sympathies. It was Napoleon who had advanced him from Elector of Saxony to King of Saxony, and he had stayed loyal to the Emperor even when his generals took his army over to the Allied side in 1813. The Saxons had fought as French allies until then, and much sympathy for Napoleon simmered in their ranks.

The greedy Prussians wanted to devour Frederick's entire kingdom but the Congress of Vienna would only let them take 57 per cent of the territory and 42 per cent of the population. The sticking point was that old Frederick refused to accede and so remained in captivity. Impatient, the Prussian king ordered Blücher to incorporate into the Prussian army those Saxon regiments that originated in the parts of the kingdom to be annexed – about half of the Saxon force. That plan was blocked by Saxon honour. The troops felt they could not swear loyalty to the Prussian king as long as Frederick refused to release them from their oaths to him. And they detested the Prussians who had so ill-used their king and country. This was the burning fuse that brought Schulmeister to Liège.

With wonderfully forged letters he arrived in the Saxon camp and quickly ferreted out those officers most loyal to Frederick. He presented them with letters that instructed the officers to go along with the Prussian orders but to a greater end than the Prussians anticipated. They were to await their king's further orders. Swords flashed as they vowed to obey their rightful king. From there, in the uniform of a Saxon officer, Schulmeister sought audience with Prussian Maj. Gen. Karl Freiherr von Müffling on Blücher's staff to assure him the Saxon corps would cause no trouble with its integration into the Prussian service. At his instigation, a stream of other Saxon officers followed to reinforce that impression. Müffling was quick to assure Blücher and his chief of staff, Gneisenau, that the integration would pass off without incident.

Schulmeister would be back. As he rode off, he thought that now Napoleon would offer him what he had most coveted – the Legion of Honour. Napoleon had poured gold into Schulmeister's hands for all his past services, and he was a very wealthy man who could have stayed comfortably at home. Napoleon knew what men would do for a bauble of honour; nevertheless, he had denied it to his master spy. The Legion of Honour was for gentlemen, and as a spy Schulmeister simply did not qualify. But now his master spy would lay victory at the Emperor's feet. Napoleon would then deny him nothing.[27]

2 May – The Tuileries, Paris

Napoleon's espionage service in Vienna and Brussels, in addition to remarkably indiscreet newspapers, provided Napoleon with a good understanding of Allied intentions and strengths. He knew that six Allied armies were to cross the French border simultaneously, though the date was uncertain. Much would hang on that. In Belgium Wellington's Army of the Netherlands would cross between Mauberge and Beaumont, and Blücher's Prussians between Phillippeville and Givet. The Russian army under Barclay de Tolly would cross by Saarlouis and Sarbrücken. The Austrians, Bavarians, Württembergers, and Hessians of the Army of the Upper Rhine would strike across the border between Sarreguemines and Basle. All four armies would march on Paris. The Army of Upper Italy, composed of Austrians and Piedmontese, and the Army of Naples (Austrians) were to pass the Alps aiming for Lyons and Provence respectively.[28]

Napoleon now gathered two score of his senior officers in his cabinet room. Standing in front of a large map of France and its borders, he quickly outlined the enemy situation – he did not underestimate the enormous forces assembling to invade France. He struck the map over Brussels just across the border:

> Here is where I will begin to unravel the enemy alliance. The British and Prussians are poised to invade France. I fully expect Wellington to be in command here. It is only logical that he be in command of what British troops are on the continent. I will break him and Blücher, take Brussels, drive the English off the continent, and abolish this new Kingdom of the Netherland. Then with the shock of those disasters unsettling the Austrians and Prussians, I will rapidly move east through

the Rhineland to strike them one at a time before they can cross the border and devastate north-east France again. I will not allow them to concentrate overwhelming numbers again as they did at Leipzig.

He put his hands behind his back and looked at them with that gaze that never failed to provoke awe and power. Good, he had them, he knew. Then he quickly pounded one fist into the other:

Speed, speed, speed will be the guiding spirit of this campaign! It is speed that will allow me to concentrate, strike, move, and strike again before the enemy can respond or gather his forces. That is what I did last year, and time and time again we beat them, but the army by then was too weak to prevail and the enemy too strong to not be able to recover. This time the army will have the resources to triumph. A string of victories will set the enemy back on his heels and give us time for our strength to grow. Eventually, they will tire, and I will make peace.

There is also a good chance that when I destroy Wellington's army, the Liverpool government in London will collapse, and the Whigs will come back into power. They will make peace, and when the English purse closes, the Allies will have no alternative but to deal with me.[29]

He then listed the forces and their commanders that would be needed to guard the French frontiers until his victories in Belgium with the Army of the North upset the enemy's equilibrium. They were:

Army of the Rhine, V Corps (Gen. Jean Rapp), three divisions;
Army of the Jura, VII Corps (Gen. Claude Lecourbe), two divisions;
Army of the Alps (Marshal Louis Suchet), two divisions, one cavalry division;
Army of the Var (Marshal Guillaume Brune), two divisions, one cavalry division;
Army of Eastern Pyrenees (Gen. Charles Decaen), one division;
Army of Western Pyrenees (Gen. Berrand Clausel) one division;
Army of the West (Jean Lamarque), two divisions.

That same day he passed out the major command assignments in the Army of the North. This army would consist of the reconstituted I, II, III, IV, and VI Corps as well as the Guard and the cavalry reserve. The corps were to be spread across 200 miles of north-west France in Metz, Lille, Valenciennes, Laon, and Mezières, as well as Paris, to give no hint that it was anything but normal garrisoning.

The I Corps was given to Gen. Jean-Baptiste Drouet, Comte d'Erlon, a loyal Bonapartist, as he had shown at Lille. He had been ennobled in 1807 for his command of a division at Austerlitz and for acting as Lannes' chief of staff at Friedland. He was one of the most able subordinate division and corps commanders in the fighting in the Peninsula and with Soult in the 1814 campaign in southern France.

Gen. Honoré Count Reille received II Corps. Reille had earned a reputation for being a gifted, fearless, and zealous commander in brigade, division, and corps commands in the campaigns of 1806–7 in Prussia, Poland, and Russia, and in 1809 against Austria. Sent to Spain in 1810, he had commanded a corps and an army. He also served under Soult in southern France.

'Renowned as a general for his courage, loyalty, frankness and plundering', Gen. Dominique Count Vandamme received command of III Corps. For all his criticism of Napoleon, he was loyal to the core.[30]

Gen. Maurice-Etienne Count Gérard was a veteran of titanic battles like Austerlitz, Eylau, Wagram, and Leipzig and Peninsular battles such as Fuentes de Oñoro and rallied to Napoleon, although his loyalty was to France rather than any man. Napoleon gave him command of IV Corps.

Napoleon gave VI Corps to Gen. Georges Mouton, Count Lobau. The Emperor had said of him, '*Mon Mouton est un lion*' ('My sheep is a lion'). He earned this praise for his valiant action in the 1809 campaign leading heroic and effective charges for which he received the title Count Lobau for the island in the Danube. He served as Napoleon's aide in Russia and distinguished himself at Lützen in 1813. He commanded a corps at Dresden that year, where he was captured. He unhappily acknowledged the Bourbons in 1814 and quickly allied himself to Napoleon on his return.

Grouchy's efficient dispatch of Angoulême had earned him not only a marshal's baton but now it also earned him command of the four cavalry corps of the Army of the North.

The choice for command of the Guard which was concentrated at Paris was easy – Marshal Mortier. He seemed perfect for that vital command. He too had found a marshal's baton in his knapsack, commanded a corps at Austerlitz and the Guard itself in 1812–13, and in the 1814 campaign he had conducted a series of brilliant rearguard and covering operations. Within Napoleon's calculations was the fact that Mortier, d'Erlon, Reille, and Gérard had fought against the British in the Peninsula. Without doubt he considered Wellington by far a more formidable opponent than Blücher. He was stacking his deck with that in mind.[31]

9 May – The Tuileries, Paris

Monthion was enraged. In the preceding month, he had done wonders to reconstitute and train the general staff. Then came the stunning news that the Emperor had appointed Marshal Soult in his place. He would revert to the position he had held under Berthier – first assistant major general. The marshal's baton now seemed only a cruel mirage. He did not know that Davout was perhaps the author of the Emperor's change of mind. That same day, Davout had submitted the following letter to Gen. Bertrand, Napoleon's Grand Master of the Palace:

> It is my duty to the Emperor to make observations on the choice of M. General Monthyon as chief of staff, that I consider very poor. This general is despised in the army, he is inept; his campaigns of 1812, 1813, 1814 unfortunately gave proof of this; I consider him less than sure; this could be kept in the realm of imagination, but what is not kept there, is his conduct in the armies. I ask you, Monsieur le Comte, to put my observations under the eyes of His Majesty; I will add that if the choice of the staff officers has been made by General Monthyon, it is desired that you take information about them before sending letters of employment.[32]

The origin of this warning is unknown. It does appear to have been the excuse for Napoleon to appoint Soult, on the very day that Davout wrote this letter. Perhaps Napoleon's irritation with his inability to overawe Monthion may have needed just this poison letter to cause him to appoint Soult in his stead. He justified his decision by stating that the position required a marshal of France. For Monthion, the solution was clearly for himself to be made a marshal. Napoleon could not have believed that Monthion was incompetent. After all, he had worked closely with him for years. Not only had Monthion stood in as chief of the general staff on a number of occasions, but he had also frequently briefed the Emperor in person in Berthier's stead, not a task for the faint of heart. Napoleon also apparently did not take the clear accusation of disloyalty seriously. If he had, it is difficult to believe he would have let him continue to function as the deputy chief of staff, the officer who actually managed the staff.

The ensuing weeks only stoked his anger. Soult seemed to go out of his way to alienate not only him but the rest of the staff – cold, irascible, with almost no personal touch. It was not as if Soult had no administrative ability – his deft administration of Andalusia in Spain disproved that – but he had no idea of how the precision clock of the general staff operated. Napoleon may have been more impressed that Soult was the hardest working of all his marshals, something Davout, one of his few friends, acknowledged in his support of the Emperor's decision.

Davout had another warning for the Emperor, and this one was based on more substantial grounds. The Emperor had sent Davout an indication that he wanted to find employment in the Army of the North for Gen. Louis A.V. Bourmont as commander of the 14th Division, who was, in the words of Colonel Elting, 'always a man of intrigues and treacheries but a first-class fighting man and recklessly brave'. Davout refused to take action; Bourmont's royalist sympathies were well known in the army. He had been active in émigré military operations against the Republic and in royalist plots against Napoleon. His activities found him in Spain in 1807, where he took advantage of amnesty before his anti-Napoleon activities landed him in French custody. Vouched for by a marshal, he entered the French army. He proved to be a capable officer and rose in rank. In 1814 he enthusiastically welcomed the return of the Bourbons and since then had been close to the Duke of Artois. At Besançon he had been one of Ney's officers, but Ney suspected him of having been sent to spy upon him.[33]

Napoleon demanded to know why his wishes had not been carried out. Davout stated that it was not a question of the man's ability but of his loyalty. Napoleon brushed that aside. He said that Ney and Gen. Maurice-Etienne Comte Gérard, leader of the IV Corps which included the 14th Division, vouched for him. Gérard had even said he would answer with his head. That seemed enough for Napoleon. It certainly was not enough for Davout, who replied,

> Sire, if these were ordinary times, your Majesty would not force the hand of his Minister of War, who would respectfully offer his resignation rather than subscribe to that which he believes would compromise the best interest of the Emperor and his nation. I will obey, regretfully and I wish, though with little hope, that your Majesty will not have to repent it.[34]

10 May – The Estate of Marshal Berthier, Bamberg, Bavaria

The man was announced to Berthier as a messenger from the King. The visitor was facing the window when the marshal entered the room. He turned to face Berthier with a bow. The marshal stopped suddenly. This man was no royal messenger. He instantly recognized Karl Schulmeister, Napoleon's master spy. His heart sank. He knew exactly why he was here. The decision he had tried so hard to avoid was now square in front of him.

He was almost overwhelmed by the dilemma. He remembered why he had taken his leave of the Emperor in April 1814: 'he had endured too long the Emperor's cruel gibes, and he could no longer spend the rest of his life as the butt of Napoleon's tantrums.' He felt his sixty-two years too much. And yet . . .

Schulmeister handed him the letter from Napoleon. Almost gingerly Berthier opened it. With the first line he caught his breath. By the last line, he was planning on how to get back to France.

The Emperor's spy enquired of the route he would take. He replied by way of Stockach (the Grand Duchy of Baden) and through Switzerland to Basle on the French border. Schulmeister just shook his head. 'The Prince of Hohenzollern has his headquarters at Stockach, and I seriously doubt they would let you pass. *Monsieur le Maréchal*, let me arrange things. And do take your *garde-du-corps* uniform.'[35]

11 May – Bois de Bologne, Paris

To say that Colonel Coutelle was having the time of his life was an understatement. For the millionth time he thanked God that he had not abandoned his passion for balloons. When Soult called him to the Ministry of War to present him with the imperial commission to re-establish the Aerostatic Corps, he could report that there was a balloon available, his latest experiment. Had there not been, the scarcity of cloth would have put a stop to the project right there. Now the balloon that he had tactfully renamed from *Rétablisssment* (Restoration) to *Marengo* was slowly expanding as it filled with hot air in a large grassy meadow in the park. He had been fortunate to find half a dozen former *aérostiers* of the corps along with his deputy. Another thirty men had been found and trained. Now they were practising filling the balloon. Coutelle was thinking of how fickle fortune was. After numerous successes in the wars of the Republic, he had sailed with Napoleon to Egypt with a balloon, only to see it burn up with the rest of the French fleet at the Battle of the Nile. Upon his return, the corps had been disbanded. Napoleon's star apparently had not needed it. Now that star was not as bright as it had been, and the Emperor remembered him.

12 May – Army of the Netherlands Headquarters, Brussels

A burden was lifted from Wellington's shoulders with the arrival of Lt. Col. Colquhoun Grant, a Scottish officer who had served as the best of his exploring officers and chief of his intelligence operations in the Peninsula. Wellington had found the French border opaque, and it would be up to Grant to pierce it. Grant was a gifted and daring intelligence officer. Captured in 1812, he had been sent to Paris, but on the way he deceived a French general that he was an American officer and escaped. He audaciously went to Paris, where he stayed for some time and developed a source within the French Ministry of War.

Exploring officers could not penetrate the French border because the Allies were not at war with France, but with Napoleon. The local francophone Belgian population was sullen and uncooperative. He was able, however, to activate his contact in Paris from whom he learned a great deal about the assembling Army of the North. But what Wellington needed most to know – what Napoleon was planning to do – Grant could not answer.[36]

15 May – The Tuileries, Paris

It was a day for bad news. Napoleon had hoped to avoid the social unrest the renewal of conscription would cause, especially in the royalist Vendée. Nevertheless, his recall of the furloughed soldiers and the class of 1815 sparked another uprising. The news reached him that day. The Bourbon rebels were supplied with arms by ships of the Royal Navy. The only element missing was the support of the Catholic Church, which to some degree supported Napoleon for taking no measures against it after his return.

The last thing he needed now was to shed French blood. He immediately sent for Gen. Jean Lamarque, gave him three divisions, two brigades of the Young Guard, and assorted gendarme units, to be designated the Army of the Loire, with the instructions, 'Suppress this revolt, but give them good terms. I need peace.'[37]

20 May – The Police Ministry, Paris

Napoleon's order to provide Bourmont a command continued to rankle with Davout. He could not shake his distaste and distrust of the man. He had made discreet inquiries among the senior officers of Bourmont's division. Now Davout paid a call on Fouché to convey his fears to the one man who could confirm them. He said, 'I cannot sit idly and watch this officer wear the uniform of this country; his treasonous statements concerning the Emperor are well known to all; the brigade and regimental commanders of the 14th Infantry Division despise him. Who would trust such a man?'[38]

Fouché smiled softly. 'That's interesting. I am making my own inquiries.'

Davout was lost in thought as his carriage bore him back to the War Ministry. He did not notice the two horsemen who suddenly flanked the carriage. A passer-by later recounted how he saw one of them shoot the driver and the other fire into the carriage. The spooked horses panicked and crashed the carriage into a bridge abutment, sending Davout bleeding onto the pavement.[39]

That same day the news of the Allies' declaration of war against Napoleon arrived in Paris. Ever a realist, Napoleon had never expected anything else.

21 May – Davout's Residence, Paris

Napoleon had been stunned by the attempt on Davout's life. Fouché had his blood-hounds out sniffing immediately. As soon as Davout had awakened, Napoleon was at his side, trying to cheer him up. 'Eh, Davout, for an old soldier you are lucky. The doctors tell me the wound is not serious. Get better fast; I need you at your desk.'

Indeed he did but, propped up in bed, his shoulder bandaged, Davout knew that it would be weeks at least before he could resume his duties. 'In the meantime, sire, I recommend General Clausel to be my replacement. I know of no one better.' That day Napoleon sent for Clausel to become Minister of War.[40]

23 May – The Élysée Palace, Paris

The news had reached Napoleon that the Allies had formally declared war on him. He had been hoping against hope that his protestations of pacific intent and all the letters unleashed by him and his family would somehow change minds. Instead they showed an adamantine resolve for war. He should have known that when his wife and son were not returned to him from Austria – the Allies never would negotiate with him. He teetered on the edge of gloom and depression. He distracted himself by focusing on another problem he must resolve.

Napoleon did not normally reprove his marshals for their style of command, especially ones he trusted implicitly. He had ignored the cold and brusque manner Soult directed at his subordinates. Reports, however, had reached him that Soult and Monthion were on the point of a serious falling out. Soult's style might have been effective with a fighting organization, but it only disrupted what should have been the harmonious working of a staff. Berthier had been all business, of course, and could work his staff near to death – Napoleon's comment was, 'Could they die a more noble death?' For all that, Berthier was also good-natured.[41] Soult was not. Monthion's misgivings about him reached the Emperor, as they were intended to do. The issue did not yield to Solomon's neat solution of cutting the baby in two. They seldom did. If Napoleon removed Soult without a good reason that preserved his honour, the implied insult would alienate an irreplaceable subordinate. If he moved Monthion, it would disrupt the general staff that he had worked so hard to put back together. There was no one else with Monthion's experience. It was a pity he had never warmed to the man.

Part of Monthion's grievance was a reflection of his former chief's intense jealousy and dislike of Soult. Berthier had been outraged to hear from Schulmeister that Napoleon had appointed Soult to be chief of the general staff. 'What choice did he have with you absent, *Maréchal*?' That his creation was in the hands of Soult was the emotional jolt that capped the spy's entreaty to Berthier.[42]

There it lay until Napoleon's secretary announced that Marshal Berthier was outside and requested an interview. Napoleon smiled. Problem solved.

Napoleon had never hesitated to browbeat Berthier, but now he advanced to meet him, tears in his eyes. He was genuinely fond of the man. 'My friend, I have missed you.' At that moment, Berthier was completely his again.

They spoke as friends, and Napoleon dined with him alone. The Emperor did not normally spend long at table – he was far too restless – but that night he lingered. The palace was quickly abuzz that the Prince of Wagram was back in the Emperor's high favour. Berthier, ever the diligent staff officer, let Napoleon know that it had been Schulmeister who had delivered his letter and helped him slip back into France and was waiting outside. Napoleon immediately ordered him brought in.

Napoleon was not a man easily impressed, but when Schulmeister gave his report, his eyes grew wide. Finally, he leaped from his chair and embraced his spy. 'I award you the Legion of Honour!' Schulmeister had just detailed the enemy's war plan, and most importantly the start date of the multi-front invasion of France – between 27 June and 1 July. Napoleon had pieced together some of the enemy plan from other sources and strategic common sense. But Schulmeister's gift was priceless in its comprehensiveness. The date especially was vital. He had to strike before the enemy armies were in motion. He knew that once he did, the enemy would advance their movement. But he knew that he who struck first struck twice.[43]

Alone later, his mind raced with the possibilities. One of those was for Soult, for whom he had an operational mission in mind worthy of the marshal's ability. It was one that harked back to 1804–5 when Soult had organized the army for the invasion of England at Boulogne. 'Go to Lille,' he told him the next day. 'Organize the forces assembling in the region as the Army of the North. Train them as hard as you did at Boulogne. You do not have much time.' Napoleon knew that Soult's focused energy was enormous. As their meeting closed, he commented, 'You fought along with Jourdan when he beat the Austrians at Fleurus near Charleroi in 1794. You are still familiar with the area, no?' Soult should not have been surprised by Napoleon's encyclopedic memory, but it still amazed him.

Soult strode out of the palace, fired up at the opportunity. He had actually been relieved when Napoleon told him he was being replaced as major general. This new assignment was far more to his liking. The army he had forged at Boulogne had won the splendid victories of Ulm and Austerlitz. With luck, that was an omen.

CHAPTER 3

'Napoleon Has Humbugged Me, by God!'

30 May–16 June 1815

30 May – The Police Ministry, Paris

The captain was obviously terrified. He had good cause. Fouché was a master of terror. Blood, including the most royal blood, dripped from his resumé. The captain knew it all too well. He was a well-known royalist, a creature of the Duke of Artois, and far too indiscreet for his own good. He should have been dismissed from the service after Napoleon's return, but someone had found a position for him on the staff of General Durosnel, commander of the Paris National Guard, a most gullible man, it seemed. It was there that Fouché's bloodhounds had sniffed him out. 'Now, captain,' said the interrogator. 'You will tell us about the nest of traitors whom you serve.'

In his last gasp of courage, the captain said, 'I demand my right to answer any charges before a military court.'

The interrogator smiled, 'Dear captain, we are trying to have a serious conversation here.'[1]

30 May – Army of the Netherlands Headquarters, Brussels

Wellington was finding it difficult to restrain Blücher from plunging into France after Napoleon. The Prussian field marshal had no talent for patience. As far as the Duke was concerned, his own preparations were complete, but he wrote to Schwarzenberg that 'The Marshal Blücher is ready and very impatient to start, but I have made it known to him today that we shall have to wait for the day when you order us to begin.' Gneisenau opined:

> The month of May passed without any event taking place worthy of record. It was in the interest of the Confederates to gain time, and to permit Buonaparte to be the first aggressor. They were not to risk the danger of exciting the popular feeling of France herself against their honourable views. It was the man, and not the nation, they warred with.[2]

Both Wellington and Blücher's armies were essentially complete by this time. The Duke commanded 90,200 men, divided into 68,350 infantry, 14,550 cavalry, 5,700 gunners, and 1,100 sappers, medical, and staff personnel with 157 guns. He initially organized his order of battle as below:

Anglo-Allied Army[3]

I Corps	William, Prince of Orange	(31,000, 58 guns)
1st Brit Inf (Guards) Div	Maj. Gen. Cook	(4,266)
1st Brit Bde	Maj. Gen. Maitland	(1,628)
2nd Brit Bde	Maj. Gen. Byng	(2,198)
Div Arty	Lt. Col. Adye	(440)
3rd Brit Inf Div	Lt. Gen. Count Alten	(8,091)
5th Brit Bde	Maj. Gen. C. Halkett	(2,274)
2nd KGL Bde	Col. Baron Ompteda	(2,087)
1st Han Bde	Maj. Gen. Count Kielmansegge	(3,315)
Div Arty	Lt. Col. Williamson	(415)
2nd Neth Inf Div	Lt. Gen. Baron Perponcher- Sedlnitzky	(8,017)
1st Bde	Maj. Gen. Graf van Bijlandt	(2,931)
2nd Bde	Maj. Gen. Prince Bernard of Saxe-Weimar	(4,689)
Div Arty & Train		(397)
3rd Neth Inf Div	Lt. Gen. Chassé	(7,559)
1st Bde	Col. Detmers	(3,298)
2nd Bde	Maj. Gen. d'Aubreme	(3,848)
Div Arty & Train		(413)
Neth Cav Div	Lt. Gen. Collaert	(3,305)
II Corps	Lt. Gen. Lord Hill	(27,000, 18 guns)
2nd Brit Inf Div	Lt. Gen. Clinton	(7,992)
3rd Brit Bde	Maj. Gen. Adams	(2,937)
1st KGL Bde	Col. du Platt	(2,072)
3rd Han Bde	Col. H. Halkett	(2,541)
Div Arty	Lt. Col. Gold	(442)
4th Brit Inf Div	Lt. Gen. Colville	(8,152)*
4th Brit Bde	Lt. Col. Mitchell	(2,007)
6th Brit Bde	Maj. Gen. Johnstone	(2,609)*
6th Han Bde	Maj. Gen. Lyon	(3,029)*
Div Arty	Maj. Brome	(269)*
Div Arty	Lt. Col. Hawker	(238)

Netherlands Corps	Prince Frederick of the Netherlands	(10,421)*
1st Neth Inf Div	Lt. Gen. Stedman	(6,692)*
1st Bde	Maj. Gen. d'Hauw	(3,299)*
2nd Bde	Maj. Gen. de Ereens	(3,168)*
Div Arty	Capt. Wijnands	(225)*
Indian Bde	Lt. Gen. Anthing	(3,729)*
Reserve Corps under Wellington's direct control		(21,000, 46 guns)
5th Brit Inf Div	Lt. Gen. Picton	(6,724)
8th Brit Bde	Maj. Gen. Kempt	(1,923)
9th Brit Bde	Maj. Gen. Pack	(1,697)
5th Han Bde	Col. von Vincke	(2,604)
Div Arty	Maj. Heisse	(500)
6th Brit Inf Div	Lt. Gen. Cole	(5,158)
10th Brit Bde	Maj. Gen. Lambert	(2,289)
4th Han. Bde	Col. Best	(2,669)
Div Arty	Lt. Col. Bruckmann	(200)
Brunswick Contingent (Div)	Col. Olfermann	(6,009)
Light Bde	Lt. Col. von Buttlar	(2,565)
Line Bde	Lt. Col. von Specht	(1,753)
Avantgarde Bn	Maj. von Rauschenplat	(635)
2nd Brunswick Bn	Maj. von Cranum	(684)
Div Arty	Maj. Mahn	(372)
Nassau Contingent	Maj. Gen. von Kruse	(2,841)
1st Nassau Bde	Col. von Haven	(2,841)
Cavalry Corps	Lt. Gen. Earl of Uxbridge	(11,000, 35 guns)
1st Brit (Household) Cav Bde (Hvy)	Lord Somerset	(1,319)
2nd Brit (Union) Cav Bde (Hvy)	Maj. Gen. Ponsonby	(1,332)
3rd Brit Cav Bde (Light)	Maj. Gen. Dörnberg	(1,401)
4th Brit Cav Bde (Light)	Maj. Gen. Vandeleur	(1,315)
5th Brit Cav Bde (Light)	Maj. Gen. Grant	(1,267)
6th Brit Cav Bde (Light)	Maj. Gen. Vivian	(1,504)
7th Brit Cav Bde (Light)	Col. Arenschildt	(712)
Han Cav Bde	Baron Estorff	(516)*

Note: * indicates units detached in the Hal-Tubize area during the upcoming battle.

Complicating Wellington's ability to command was the fact that four languages were spoken in the Army of the Netherlands – English, German, Dutch, and French. At least 45 per cent of his army spoke German as a first language. Wellington also worried that he had only 45,000 men in his army upon whom he could depend – the British and KGL battalions. For that reason, he mixed British and KGL battalions with Netherlands and the other German contingents within the corps and divisions. The British and KGL battalions were to add stiffening to those units of uncertain reliability.

If anything had described Wellington's style of war at the strategic level it was the care he took to protect his communications. He was loath to allow the enemy any opportunity to get across those communications and separate him from his lifeline to Great Britain. That lifeline, fixed to a major port, accomplished two things. It allowed a point of evacuation in one direction and a funnel of supplies in the other. 'It is necessary to attend to all this detail and to trace a biscuit from Lisbon into a man's mouth to the frontier and to provide for its removal from place to place by land or water, or no military operations can be carried out.'[4]

Ostend was his primary and Antwerp his secondary point of communication with Britain. Each was garrisoned by a British battalion in addition to any Netherlands forces. To protect those communications with Ostend against a potential attempt by Napoleon to cut them, he stationed almost 18,000 men under Lord Hill at Hal, halfway between Brussels and Ostend. This force consisted of the 4th British Infantry Division (4th British and 6th Hanoverian Brigades), the Netherlands Corps of the 1st Netherlands Division and the Indian Brigade, and a KGL cavalry brigade. The Dutch-Belgian units made up 64 per cent of the force and the single British brigade only 16 per cent.[5]

Blücher's army numbered 130,000 Prussians plus another 14,000 Saxons. The Prussian army had 78,300 infantry, 13,000 cavalry, 5,750 gunners, and 3,250 other with 283 guns. The Saxons numbered 12,900 infantry, 1,300 cavalry, 490 gunners, and 400 others with thirty-two guns. Unlike other armies, the Prussians employed brigades rather than divisions as corps-subordinated manoeuvre units. However, Prussian brigades were equivalent in strength to divisions in other armies.[6]

Prussian Army of the Lower Rhine

I Corps	Lt. Gen. Count von Zieten	(30,800)
1st Inf Bde	Maj. Gen. von Steinmetz	(7,835)
2nd Inf Bde	Maj. Gen. von Pirch	(6,876)
3rd Inf Bde	Maj. Gen. von Jagow	(6,709)
4th Inf Bde	Maj. Gen. Graf Henckel von Donnersmarck	(4,106)

Reserve Cavalry	Gen. Lt. Friederich von Roeder	
1st Cav Bde	Maj. Gen. von Treschkow	(1,526)
2nd Cav Bde	Lt. Col. Lützow	(1,339)
Reserve Arty	Maj. von Rentzell	(1,074)
II Corps	Maj. Gen. von Pirch	(30,269)
5th Inf Bde	Maj. Gen. von Tippelskirch	(6,498)
6th Inf Bde	Maj. Gen. von Kraft	(6,334)
7th Inf Bde	Maj. Gen. von Brause	(6,353)
8th Inf Bde	Maj. Gen. von Bose	(6,072)
Reserve Cavalry	Gen. Maj. Alexander von Wahlen-Jürgass	
1st Cav Bde	Col. von Thümen	(1,452)
2nd Cav Bde	Lt. Col. von Sohr	(1,321)
3rd Cav Bde	Col. Graf von Schulenburg	(1,196)
Reserve Arty	Lt. Col. von Röhl	(1,043)
III Corps	Maj. Gen. Lt. Gen. Thielmann	(38,404)
9th Inf Bde	Maj. Gen. von Borcke	(6,557)
10th Inf Bde	Col. von Kemphen	(4,130)
11th Inf Bde	Col. von Luck	(4,201)
12th Inf Bde	Col. von Stülpnagel	(6,199)
Reserve Cavalry	Gen. Maj. Friedrich von Hobe	
1st Cav Bde	Col. von Marwitz's	(849)
2nd Cav Bde	Col. von Lottum	(1,189)
Reserve Arty	Maj. Lehmann	(1,279)
Saxon contingent attached to III Corps		(14,000)
IV Corps	Gen. Count Bülow von Dennewitz	(30,692)
13th Inf Bde	Lt. Gen. von Hake	(7,221)
14th Inf Bde	Maj. Gen. von Ryssel	(5,863)
15th Inf Bde	Maj. Gen. von Losthin	(6,500)
16th Inf Bde	Col. Hiller von Gartringen	(6,285)
Reserve Cavalry	Prinz Wilhelm	
1st Cav Bde	Col. Count von Schwerin	(1,360)
2nd Cav Bde	Lt. Col. von Watzdorff	(560)
3rd Cav Bde	Maj. Gen. von Sydow	(1,836)
Arty Reserve	Maj. Gen. von Braun	(1,067)

The Allied army and the Prussian Army of the Lower Rhine totalled 234,200 men and 482 guns. Only at the Battle of Leipzig in 1813 had Napoleon faced a larger Allied force.

Although pledged to fight together, the communications of the two armies ran in opposite directions. Wellington's was north through Brussels and then to the Belgian ports – west to Ostend and north to Antwerp – which connected him with England. Blücher's ran east to Liège and then to Prussia. This salient feature was not lost on Napoleon. If he were to strike north between Mons and Lille in the direction of Ghent and the ports on which the British depended, it would only serve to force two options on Wellington. The Duke would be forced to withdraw suddenly west and/or north to evacuate through these ports to avoid having his communications severed and his army stranded on the continent. On the other hand, if Napoleon tried to turn Wellington's right flank, the Duke would be forced east to link directly with the Prussians. If Napoleon struck the Prussian left flank, it would force Blücher west to link up with Wellington. Forcing the two enemy armies to concentrate was exactly what Napoleon did not want. However, if Napoleon feinted west to Wellington's right to draw the Duke's attention and concentration in that direction, he could then strike the Prussians, who would be fighting alone; he could defeat them, and then deal with Wellington.

This possibility caused Wellington to attempt to deploy his army to both cover a threat to his western or right flank and to be able to come to the aid of the Prussians. Cavalry screened the border from the coast to Mons, a distance of forty miles. His infantry was dispersed behind the cavalry from Oudenaarde to Nivelles, a distance of over fifty miles. His army simply could not cover his right flank and be in a position to join with the Prussians with any celerity. For Wellington, the first consideration, to protect his communications and line of retreat, far outweighed the second. Napoleon shrewdly appraised the two enemy commanders. He knew that Blücher would come to the aid of Wellington if he were down to his last battalion. Wellington would put the safety of his communications above rushing to the aid of the Prussians. Napoleon did not realize that his own reputation was influencing Wellington to be fixated on a strike to the west. Wellington was aware how brilliantly and how often Napoleon had used the encirclement to the enemy's rear. He had also studied Napoleon's campaigns well enough to realize that Napoleon was liable to do anything. He simply could not predict him.

The only route by which either army could easily come to the aid of the other was the good road between the crossroads village of Quatre Bras and Sombreffe. By crossing the Sambre River on the French–Belgian border at Charleroi, Napoleon would be able to strike north and sever that road. The Prussian dispersal also offered the opportunity of beating them in detail as they attempted to concentrate.

The Prussian corps were also dispersed over a wide area. Zieten's I Corps was deployed with one brigade forward at Charleroi and the remaining three stacked up to the north-east. Pirch's II Corps was garrisoned around Namur and Thielmann's III Corps to the south-east. Bülow's IV Corps was concentrated at Liège. Between Zieten and Bülow was fifty miles.[7]

1 June – Champ de Mars, Paris

A vast throng had gathered around the great green sward outside the École Militaire on this bright, sunny day. The event was the ratification of the Acte Additional, the quasi-constitutional limit on Napoleon's once-absolute power. It was enormously popular: he had learned something from defeat and exile. One of history's great showmen, he sought to seal the enthusiasm for liberal government with a spectacle worthy of the Caesars, dubbed Revolutionary Bonapartism.

'The sun flashing on sixty thousand bayonets seemed to make the vast space sparkle,' observed the historian Thiébault. Archbishop Barral of Tours conducted a mass on an immense altar erected in the middle of the great field, in his fine double-forte voice. A *Te Deum* was sung to the accompaniment of rolling artillery salvos.

The Red Lancers were a splash of bright colour echoed by the glittering clothes and uniforms of the court, the judiciary, the Council of State, the diplomatic corps, and a mass of senior officers in blue and gold or their regimental finery, not to mention the sartorial and jewelled glory of their ladies, who did full honour to their city. The delegates of the electoral colleges approached the Emperor, and one of them read the loyal address. In a ceremony roughly modelled on a tradition of Charlemagne and dressed in a purple robe, Napoleon addressed 15,000 seated guests as a crowd of a 100,000 pressed around the vast space on which the mass of troops stood.

Napoleon swore an oath to the Constitution on the Gospels in the hands of the Archbishop of Bourges. Then he spoke. 'As emperor, consul, soldier, I owe everything to the people. In prosperity, in adversity, on the battlefield, in counsel, enthroned, in exile, France has been the sole and constant object of my thoughts and actions.' He wanted only 'to preserve for France only natural integrity, honour and rights.' He had been brought back to France only by the humiliations heaped upon France. He had wanted peace, but it was the Allies who had prepared for war and declared it. His final words, 'My own glory, honour and happiness are indistin-guishable from those of France', were received with thunderous, rolling cheering.

The most dramatic moment was when all the bearers of their new regimental eagles and the gold-embroidered red, white, and blue national colours formed a semi-circle around Napoleon. He addressed them, 'I entrust these eagles with the national colours to you. Will you swear to die in their defence?' Then he turned to the Guard, 'And you, soldiers of the Imperial Guard, do you swear to surpass yourselves in the coming campaign, and die to a man rather than permit foreigners to dictate to the Fatherland?' They all thundered back, 'We swear!' and '*Vive l'Empereur!*' The crowds picked up the chants as all 60,000 troops passed in review of the Emperor in a river of glittering bayonets.

Napoleon had done this to secure domestic peace and support throughout most of France. His Revolutionary Bonapartism had been able to secure broad support across the spectrum of French opinion.

Among those invited to the ceremony were Ney and his wife. Ney had been disappointed that the invitation contained no offer of a command. He was mortified to find out he was not invited to the banquet that followed. Worse was to come. Two days later he appeared at the palace to draw his arrears in pay from the treasury. He was surprised when Napoleon suddenly walked out of his office. Seeing Ney, he barked, 'You here! Well, well, Ney, I thought you had emigrated.' Stricken, Ney could only say, 'I ought to have done so long ago.' He stormed out of the palace and out of history.[8]

4 June – Army of the Rhine Headquarters, Namur

The subtle policy of waiting for Napoleon to attack was entirely lost on the Prussian field marshal. He was chomping at the bit to get at the French, acting more like a 20-year-old hussar than a 73-year-old field marshal. He wrote to his friend Hardenburg, 'I beg you, my dear sir, will you see to it that we soon come to operations? Our lingering can have the greatest disadvantages. If orders to advance do not arrive and the unrest in France increases, I shall do as I did in Silesia and go to battle. Wellington will probably go with me.' Wellington was not about to do any such thing. Hardenburg knew that and that level-headed Gneisenau would calm the old man down.[9]

6 June – Army of the North Headquarters, Beaumont

Secret orders were sent the to corps of the Army of the North on that morning. The I Corps was to march from Valenciennes to Avesnes, II Corps from Avesnes to Maubeuge while III Corps left Rocroi for Chimay; IV from Thionville to Rocroi and V from Soissons to Avesnes. At the same time, the Imperial Guard, which had been concentrated at Paris, took the road via Soissons to Avesnes. Having the furthest to go, the cavalry reserve began the ride from Metz, Lille, Valenciennes, Laon, and Mezières in perfect synchronization with the infantry corps. The couriers with these orders prepared by Monthion arrived precisely when they were supposed to, so that the timing of the concentration would work smoothly. Across a frontage of eighteen miles all the elements of the Army of the North assembled without the enemy detecting a thing.

The movement was a staff planning and operational security masterpiece. The precision of the Berthier–Monthion team was everywhere in evidence, as was the firm direction of Soult. As soon as the corps were on the march, their places were seamlessly taken by large National Guard contingents. The movement itself was masked by large manoeuvres of the National Guard to give the impression that an attack from the region of Lille was in the offing, reinforced by a layered misinformation operation based on false rumours. The mail was stopped in the area of operations, and all communications with Belgium and the Rhine provinces were stopped. Napoleon had ordered, 'Not a stage or carriage must pass.' Every sailing vessel, including fishing boats, was kept in port.[10]

7 June – Army of the Rhine Headquarters, Namur

By this time, with no evidence of French preparations, the Allies had a complete change of opinion and were convinced that Napoleon would not attack. Blücher wrote to his wife, 'We shall soon enter France. We might remain here another year for Bonaparte will never attack us.'

That same day Napoleon instructed Bertrand to prepare his field equipment, uniforms, horses, and carriages 'so that I can leave two hours after having given the order. As I will be camping often, it is important that I have my iron beds and tents.'[11]

9 June – Army of the Rhine Headquarters, Namur

As the Army of the North was in the midst of its major forward concentration, Gneisenau wrote, 'The enemy will not attack us but will retire as far as the Aisne, Somme and Marne in order to concentrate his forces.'[12] The 30,000 men of the National Guard who had been manoeuvring east of Lille were ordered to deploy forward as well, between Tournai and Mons in Belgium.[13]

The French were careful to feed the British information on the presence of this large force. Just as expected, it drew Wellington's eyes west, especially when French cavalry patrols exchanged fire with British cavalry picquets in the area of Mons.

12 June – Army of the North Headquarters, Avesnes

Soult looked at the deciphered message that had come from the Emperor over the semaphore system from Paris. He said to himself, 'So it begins.' He could expect Napoleon by the next day and would be able to report the readiness of the Army of the North for the coming campaign.

Napoleon would have every reason to be pleased; the concentration of the army had been as flawless as the deployment of the army from the camps around Boulogne to the legendary victory at Austerlitz in 1805. He thought it was the most experienced army that Napoleon had ever fielded. He was relieved that Napoleon had soon after his return called up the young veterans of the class of 1815 that had already seen service in the 1814 campaign. Almost 28,000 replacements had been distributed to the understrength battalions. Detachments of 500 were sent to the understrength regiments. He was particularly pleased with the way replacements had been found to bring every infantry battalion to a minimum strength of 500 men. Artillery batteries and trains had been brought up to strength as well. It took too long to train a cavalryman properly for there to have been any augmentation of their regiments except for veterans who returned to the colours. Soult had ensured that the replacements had been carefully integrated to maximize cohesion, though he knew that more time would have been better. He had personally inspected many of the regiments and took pains to question these young men, their NCOs, and company officers. He came away satisfied that the new men had been enthusiastically welcomed as the veterans they were. These drafts brought the army up to a strength of 150,000 men and almost 400 guns.

He was also generally confident in the commanders, with the glaring exception of the Emperor's younger brother, Prince Jérôme, a man of much pretention and little talent. In this he was an uncanny double of Slender Billy. Soult recognized that it was a weakness of Napoleon's to advance his family far beyond their ability. It was a wonder that he had not learned that lesson in exile when only his sister Pauline stood by him. It was part of his Italian-Corsican origin that he could not escape. No one more recognized it than Soult, having had to deal with the Emperor's older brother, Joseph, in Spain. It was a most painful memory.

Jérôme was, if anything, worse than Joseph. Napoleon had made him King of Westphalia, where the expenses of his court exceeded those of the Emperor himself. Napoleon gave him a corps to command in the invasion of Russia, but he returned to the luxury of his court at the first opportunity. Napoleon had tried to teach him about the art of war. In instructing him on the principle of war, the objective, he had said, 'When you set out to take Vienna, take Vienna.' It was like throwing eggs against a millstone. But Napoleon did not give up on trying to transform his younger brother into a soldier.

Nevertheless, Soult realized that to keep the Prince from blundering he had to be kept on a tight leash. He made a point of discussing it with his corps commander, Count Reille, and giving him firm instructions on the matter.

With that problem addressed, Soult felt the army was fit and ready for whatever task the Emperor set it. Yet one more problem nagged at him. He may have been confident of the army's commanders, but among the junior officers and men there was a strong undercurrent of distrust for those who had served the Bourbons, especially those who had done so enthusiastically. More than one old soldier had told him that to his face. One had even denounced his regimental commander in the man's presence.[14]

Soult had to admit that he much preferred organizing and training an army to being its chief of staff. That did not stop him admiring excellent staff work; what he was getting from Monthion was superb. The deputy chief of staff had moved with a good part of his staff to support Soult's efforts and prepare for the upcoming campaign. Soult sat back and reviewed the latest order of battle for the Army of the North prepared by Monthion.

Army of the North[15]

The Imperial Guard	Marshal Mortier	(20,563, 126 guns)
Imperial Gd HQ		(2,004, 18 guns)
Gd Artillery Res	Gen. Baron Desvaux de St. Maurice	(700, 18 guns)
Engineers	Gen. Baron Haxo	(219)
Marines		(209)
Train Det		(676)
Med Det		(200)
Grenadiers à Pied Div	Gen. Count Friant	(4,489, 16 guns)
Chasseur à Pied Div	Gen. Count Morand	(4,789, 16 guns)
Young Gd	Gen. Count Duhesme	(4,774, 18 guns)
Gd Heavy Cav Div	Gen. Count Guyot	(2,068, 12 guns)
Gd Lt Cav Div	Gen. Count Lefebvre-Desnouettes	(2,439, 12 guns)
I Corps	Gen. Count d'Erlon	(22,301, 46 guns)
1st Inf Div	Gen. Baron Quiot du Passage	(4,449, 8 guns)
2nd Inf Div	Gen. Baron Donzelot	(5,427, 8 guns)
3rd Inf Div	Gen. Baron Marcognet	(4,459, 8 guns)
4th Inf Div	Gen. Count Durutte	(4,575, 8 guns)
1st Lt Cav Div	Gen. Baron Jacquinot	(1,806, 6 guns)
Corps Arty Res	Gen. Salles	(803, 8 guns)
11/6th Regt	Capt. Charlet	(206, guns)
2/1st Engr Regt	Brig. Mortaincourt	(376)
Train Det		(100)
Med Det		(100)
II Corps	Gen. Count Reille	(27,917, 54 guns)
5th Inf Div	Gen. Baron Bachelu	(4,915, 8 guns)

6th Inf Div	Gen. Prince Bonaparte	(7,977, 8 guns)
7th Inf Div	Gen. Baron Girard	(4,574, 8 guns)
9th Inf Div	Gen. Count Foy	(6,095, 8 guns)
2nd Lt Cav Div	Gen. Count Piré	(2,162, 6 guns)
Corps Arty Res	Gen. Baron Le Pelletier	(847, 8 guns)
7/2nd FA Regt	Capt. Valnet	(216, 8 guns)
1/1st Engr Reg	Brig. Repecaud	(431)
Train Det		(100)
Med Det		(100)
III Corps	Gen. Count Vandamme	(19,432, 46 guns)
8th Inf Div	Gen. Baron Lefol	(6,000, 8 guns)
10th Inf Div	Gen. Baron Habert	(6,480, 8 guns)
11th Inf Div	Gen. Baron Berthézène	(5,123, 8 guns)
3rd Lt Cav Div	Gen. Baron Domon	(1,322, 6 guns)
Corps Arty Res	Gen. Dougereau	(507, 8 guns)
1/2nd FA Regt	Capt. Vollee	(204, 8 guns)
5/2nd Engr Regt		(103)
Train Det		(100)
Med Det		(100)
IV Corps	Gen. Count Gérard	(17,861, 46 guns)
12th Inf Div	Gen. Baron Pécheux	(6,400, 8 guns)
13th Inf Div	Gen. Baron Vichery	(4,462, 8 guns)
14th Inf Div	Gen. Count Bourmont	(4,362, 8 guns)
7th Lt Cav Div	Gen. Baron Maurin	(1,837, 6 guns)
Corps Arty Res	Brig. Baron de Pouilly	(400, 8 guns)
5/5th FA Regt	Capt. Lenior	(200, 8 guns)
Train		(100)
Med Det		(100)
VI Corps	Gen. Count de Lobau	(15,528, 48guns)
19th Inf Div	Gen. Baron Simmer	(6,400, 8 guns)
20th Inf Div	Gen. Baron Jeanin	(4,462, 8 guns)
21st Inf Div	Gen. Baron Teste	(3,004, 8 guns)
Corps Arty Res	Gen. Le Noury	(695, 8 guns)
	de la Guignardiere	
4/8th FA Regt		(224, 8 guns)
Marine HA Co		(200, 8 guns)
1/3rd Engr Regt		(95)
Train Det		100

Med Det		100
Reserve Cavalry	Marshal Grouchy	(12,216, 48 guns)
I Heavy Cavalry Reserve Corps	Gen. Pajol	(2667, 12 guns)
4th Cav Div	Gen. Baron Soult	
5th Cav Div	Gen. Baron Subervie	
II Heavy Cavalry Reserve Corp	Gen. Exelmans	(2,849, 12 guns)
9th Cav Div	Gen. Baron Strolz	
10th Cav Div	Gen. Baron Chastel	
III Heavy Cavalry Reserve Corp	Gen. Kellerman	(3,600, 12 guns)
11th Cav Div	Gen. Baron L'Héritier	
12th Cav Div	Gen. Baron dHurbal	
IV Heavy Cavalry Reserve Corp	Gen. Count Mihaud	(3,100, 12 guns)
13th Cav Div	Gen. Watier	
14th Cav Div	Gen. Delort	

12 June –Army of the Rhine Headquarters, Namur

When Gneisenau wrote this afternoon that 'the danger of an attack has almost vanished', Napoleon had already left Paris at 4:00 that morning to join the Army of the North.[16]

12 June – The War Ministry, Paris

Davout could not be kept at home any longer and was visiting Gen. Clausel when the Minister of Police was suddenly announced. He rushed in, a look of supreme satisfaction on his face. He laid out for them his findings on the case of Gen. Bourmont. Clausel burst out, '*Cochon!*' Davout was clearly furious as well, but there was a grim look of vindication on his face. 'I will send a courier with the report at once,' Fouché said. 'I would go, but my attention is required to root out the nest of traitors here.'

'No,' said Davout. 'I will take it myself.' Clausel and Fouché both objected for the obvious reason that Davout's arm was still in a sling. 'To the devil with that,' he retorted. 'I will go mad if I have to nurse this arm a moment longer!' Then he threw off the sling. 'Clausel, your fastest horse!'[17]

13 June – Army of the Netherlands Headquarters, Brussels

Wellington's intelligence system by this point had completely failed him. Napoleon's operational security had obscured both the concentration of his army and his preparations in Paris. The Duke wrote to a friend in London that, 'There is nothing new here. We have reports of Buonoparte's joining the army and attacking us, but I have accounts from Paris of the 10th, on which day he was still there; and I judge from his speech to the Legislature that his departure was not likely to be immediate. I think we are too strong for him here.' In reality, Napoleon had left Paris the day before.[18]

13 June – Army of the North Headquarters, Avesnes

By that evening, Napoleon had joined his army at Avesnes, only thirty-one miles from Brussels where Wellington was deprecating the Emperor's chances. Napoleon complimented Soult on how well the concentration had been conducted. They dined alone together that night. The Emperor was in a good mood at the superb condition of the army. 'Soult, the army reminds me of the army you presented me at Boulogne.' Soult took that as a great accolade. The army he had trained and organized had marched to glory at Austerlitz, and the Emperor was now acknowledging it. Napoleon was especially pleased with the reports that the English and Prussians were not stirring. The element of surprise was the pearl of great price in the art of war.[19]

Napoleon's meals did not last long, and he quickly got to the point. 'Soult, I want you to command the I and II Corps when we engage the enemy. You will take the crossroads to Quatre Bras and defeat any of Wellington's army you find there. In doing so, you will protect my flank as I beat the Prussians and prevent Wellington from coming to their aid.' He paused for a moment, and then turned his full powers of emphasis on Soult. 'I want you to charge like a bull at anything you meet on the Gosselies–Brussels road. Take up a position astride this road beyond Quatre Bras and hold this position. Keep strong advance guards on the Brussels, Namur, and Nivelles roads!'[20]

Napoleon smiled at the look of surprise on Soult's face. 'You and Reille and d'Erlon have fought Wellington before and are most aware of his tricks. I will take him by surprise, but he will respond quickly.' As an afterthought, he said, 'If you are satisfied with the staff you have, they are yours for the coming campaign.' Just then Bertrand entered, bowed and said, 'Sire, the Minister of War has just arrived and insists on an immediate audience.'

'Clausel is here?'

'No, sire, Davout.' Just then an impatient Davout entered the room on his own, bowed and immediately briefed Napoleon on Fouché's report.

'Sire, the Minister of Police has uncovered a treasonous plot of great danger that extends from Paris to your camp.' Napoleon's legendary ability to focus was now apparent. 'He arrested a captain whose interrogation led to the uncovering of a ring of royalist officers on the staff of the commander of the Paris National Guard. They were working for Artois. As I left Paris, the entire ring was being arrested. I have come in person to carry the news that Artois' plotting reaches into your army. General Bourmont plans to defect just before the coming battle with his entire staff to betray your plans to the enemy. They will pretend to ride out on reconnaissance, then change to the Bourbon cockade and approach the enemy's outposts shouting, "*Vive le Roi!*"'[21]

Napoleon got up so suddenly that his chair went flying backwards. 'You were right, Davout, to warn me.' It was a rare apology, indeed, and Davout recognized it. Then Napoleon turned to Soult, 'We must prepare something special for this Bourmont.'

After Soult departed, Napoleon told Davout to stay. He had been going to give Grouchy control of the III and IV Corps. Davout's appearance presented a better option. 'Davout, are you fit for action?' The marshal's response was emphatic. 'Well, then I want you to take charge of Vandamme and Gérard's corps when we meet the Prussians. I know how much you terrify them. They scare their children to sleep with stories of you at Auerstedt.' Yes, Auerstedt in 1806 where Davout had beaten the main body of the Prussian army with only the heroes of his III Corps. It had put Napoleon's own simultaneous defeat of the lesser part of the Prussian army in the shade. He had been jealous of him ever since. But Elba had cured him of much of that.[22]

Later than night, Gen. Monthion called on Davout. 'His Majesty informed Marshal Berthier that you are to command the right wing in the coming battle. The marshal believes a staff would be a necessity and has designated these officers and clerks for your use.' He then presented them. No one could have been more surprised than Davout by Berthier's assistance. They had not been on good terms since the Danube campaign of 1809. Fully aware of Berthier's dislike of Davout, Monthion helpfully added, 'It was the express wish of His Majesty that you have a staff, and a good one.' Another miracle, Davout thought.

His corps commanders were Vandamme and Gérard; he knew them both. Vandamme was the most ill-disciplined and insubordinate general in the French army, though a valuable and able commander in battle. In Davout's opinion he had a mortal failing, however – he was habitually late. Napoleon forgave that for the sake of the man's ferocity, saying that 'he would give Vandamme command of the vanguard were he (Napoleon) to launch a campaign against Lucifer in Hell'. He had served under Davout in the siege of Hamburg. The Iron Marshal refused to put up with Vandamme's eccentricities and quickly brought him to heel. He would bear close watching. Davout also knew Gérard, who had ably commanded a division for him in Russia. After the first restoration, Artois, in a studied insult, had sent Gérard to relieve him, though his honourable conduct of the defence had earned him better treatment. He had been thankful for Gérard's tact and courtesy.[23]

Similarly, Soult had commanded both d'Erlon and Reille in Spain and southern France, and they had all worked well together. They had made a good team, and Soult was confident that they would again. Wellington had driven them across southern France in the 1814 campaign, but they had skilfully avoided serious defeat. Wellington, if anything, was frustrated that they always evaded his crippling blows.

13 June – Just South of Charleroi

Blücher's impatience to come to grips with Napoleon had caused him to push cavalry patrols more aggressively along the border than had Wellington. Napoleon had ordered that his divisions camp in hollows to hide their campfires, but they reflected on the clouds and made an orange glow. That night Prussian cavalry patrols observed the seemingly endless glow of countless French campfires around Beaumont. Lt. Gen. Zieten, commanding I Corps, with his headquarters and lead brigade at Charleroi, heard these reports but was not sure if it was not all a deception. There had already been two serious false alarms in the preceding weeks.

Early in the morning French deserters reported that Napoleon was preparing to attack the next day. Comparing the reports of his cavalry and the deserters, Zieten was convinced and immediately dispatched warnings to Blücher and Wellington both.

14 June – Army of the North Headquarters, Beaumont

Napoleon had transferred his headquarters that night to Beaumont, in the centre of his army and where the Guard was arrayed. The weather was bad that night as the army bivouacked around the headquarters in a rectangle eight by twenty-two miles just south of the Sambre River and on the main road to Charleroi and Brussels. Wellington's and Blücher's armies, on the other hand, were spread across 100 miles from the coast to Liège. Couriers dashed out through the rain to the corps commanders with the already written orders to begin their forward movement into Belgium. The order was a masterpiece of planning fully up to his past achievements. As was his practice, Berthier sent each set of orders by half a dozen couriers to ensure delivery. All were promptly delivered on time.

The Army of the North would advance in two echelons, take Charleroi, and cross the Sambre River. Each echelon would number 70,000 men and would advance in three columns. In the first echelon, Vandamme's III Corps would form the centre column with Gérard's IV Corps on the left and Reille's II Corps on the right. In the second echelon, d'Erlon's I Corps followed Reille's corps. Behind Gérard's corps rode the 14th Cavalry Division. In the centre, the Guard, Lobau's VI Corps and Grouchy's cavalry marched in support behind Vandamme's corps.[24]

The couriers that carried the movement orders also carried the order of the day:

Soldiers, today is the anniversary of Marengo and Friedland, which on two occasions decided the destiny of Europe . . . Soldiers! At Jena against these same Prussians, now so arrogant, you were one to two, and at Montmirail one to three . . . Soldiers! We shall have to make some forced marches, fight some battles, run some risks, but with constancy victory will be ours. The right, the honour and the happiness of the country will be reconquered. For every Frenchman who has courage, the moment has come to conquer or die![25]

The Prussians were beginning to stir, but Wellington continued to be focused on the threat from the direction of Mons. The continued activity of the National Guard in that area had successfully fixed his attention. Napoleon had thus achieved a moral ascendency over Wellington at this moment by denying him any accurate knowledge of his movements and by blowing a cloud of disinformation over the Allied armies through his efficient agents and sympathetic francophone Belgians.

That afternoon, Bourmont and five members of his staff rode off from the 14th Division headquarters to reconnoitre the route of march. They had not gone far when a squadron of the Guard Chasseurs à Cheval rode out from the woods and blocked their path. More of the light cavalry appeared behind them. The commander of the Guard Light Cavalry Division, Gen. Baron Lallemand, rode grim-faced up to Bourmont. 'Your sword, monsieur. By order of the Emperor, you are under arrest for treason.'[26]

While this treason was being nipped in the bud, the 14th Division's senior brigade commander, Gen. Baron Hulot de Mazarny, was called to the Emperor's presence along with Gérard. They were both stunned when informed of Bourmont's treason and arrest. 'Hulot, you will assume command of the division. Not a word from either of you about Bourmont's treason. This is the last thing the troops need to worry about now. You will put out that Bourmont and his staff were captured by a Prussian cavalry patrol.' Then he turned to Gérard and reminded him that he had vouched for Bourmont with his head. The general blanched. Then Napoleon patted him on the head and said that he could keep his head since he still had need of it.[27]

14 June – Army of the Rhine Headquarters, Namur

Blücher was sound asleep when Zieten's courier raced into the headquarters just before 11:00 p.m. It was clear to the chief of staff what the direction of the

French army was. On his own authority, Gneisenau gave the orders for the army to concentrate on a line of Sombreffe–Fleurus. The plans had already been made for such a contingency. It now remained only to carry them out. In the hours before dawn the next day, the three closest Prussian corps (I, II, and III) were hives of activity as they made ready and then began their forced marches. Bülow's IV Corps was fifty miles away at Liège. If it moved out smartly and forced marched, it could arrive just in time to join the fight. There was a problem, though. Gneisenau and Bülow had had a serious falling out, and the corps commander was senior to him. Gneisenau had therefore been hesitant to write as peremptory an order to him as to the other corps commanders. In writing that order the chief of staff was overly polite – to the point of masking the urgency of the march.

The army commander chose this moment to wake up and groggily wander about looking for schnapps. He ambled over to Gneisenau, who had just finished his letter to Bülow. He never busied himself with paperwork, but he was bored and snatched up the letter. He squinted to read, and then snorted. 'Are you inviting him to a ball? Give me the pen.' He scribbled below Gneisenau's signature, 'Move your arse *sofort*, or you will miss the fight.' With a flourish he signed his name, scratched, and wandered back to bed. Gneisenau's sense of propriety twinged, but then he smiled.[28]

As the Prussian couriers thundered away to alert IV Corps, Gneisenau did not see fit to notify Wellington of the Prussian decision to concentrate.

15 June – Charleroi

Napoleon sat on a chair outside the Belle-Vue inn watching his infantry columns march through the town. They burst into cheers of *'Vive l'Empereur!'* as they saw him. Some even broke ranks to kiss his horse. He liked the spring in their step and their enthusiasm. Yes, it was like the old days.

At 2:30 in the morning twelve cavalry regiments had trotted through the mist to screen the forward movement of the army. Thirty minutes later the first infantry columns were on the roads fifteen minutes ahead of daybreak. There was one corps commander who had not taken seriously the intricate movement orders prepared by Berthier's staff. Vandamme was jolted out of his cot by Davout himself. 'Up, up, *Monsieur!* Remember, the Emperor will not make marshals of men who are late!' His staff officers were already ensuring the III Corps divisions were being roused at the same time.[29]

Soult's staff similarly were ensuring that the I and II Corps were up and ready. D'Erlon had been given peremptory orders from Soult to be on the road on time. He got the hint.

The movement was detected by Prussian picquets, and the signal of three rapid cannon shots were fired. The first combat of the campaign opened shortly after sunrise; when there was sufficient light a battery of Reille's corps fired at the 2nd Battalion of the 1st Westphalian Landwehr Regiment. They had already stood to arms, and the regiment's other two battalions, alerted by the three shots, were on their way. It was the sound of the French guns that woke a fully clothed Zieten from his sleep, and he sprang to his feet. He immediately dictated two letters. The first in German he dispatched to Blücher at Namur and the second in French to Wellington in Brussels.

Prince Jérôme's division made first contact at Thuin with the Westphalians and forced them back. Zieten sent a report to Namur at 8:15 that the French were too strong to be engaged and he was pulling back to another defence line. Critically, he also added, 'Napoleon is present with his entire Guard. It is thus probable that he has serious intentions. The enemy also has a considerable amount of cavalry.'[30]

All through the morning Zieten was conducting a fighting retreat back to Fleurus to give the rest of the army time to concentrate. Impatient to be near the fighting, Blücher left Namur at 1:00 p.m. for Sombreffe, eleven miles north of Charleroi and only three miles north of Fleurus, where he would set up his headquarters, arriving at 6:00 p.m.

The army marched smoothly forward in accordance with Berthier's precise march tables. Vandamme's lead division reached the bridge over the Sambre to Charleroi and immediately stormed the Prussian barricade, sending the defenders flying through the town. As the French troops poured over the bridge and through the streets, the inhabitants, especially the women, cheered enthusiastically and shouted their support of the Emperor. Napoleon was soon riding into the celebrating town to the wild acclaim of the francophone population.

As Blücher galloped to Sombreffe, Napoleon was roaring with laughter as the citizens of Charleroi told him how the French had arrived so fast that several Prussian officers had fled without their trousers. He was still laughing as he sat down to eat the lunch prepared for Zieten. Fortunately, in their haste to retreat, the Prussians had not destroyed any of the bridges over the Sambre, which were now being crossed by the French corps. As the army crossed the bridges, it split into two elements. On the left Soult led the I and II Corps towards Quatre Bras. The Emperor had been emphatic in his order to Soult that he must take that crossroads to prevent Wellington from joining with Blücher. And he must take it quickly. Having done so, he was then to march east and fall upon the Prussian flank which was be engaged by Davout's III and IV Corps at Sombreffe. The Emperor would maintain the Guard and Lobau's VI Corps as his reserve. Napoleon had expected to beat the Prussian corps in detail as they came up but had miscalculated how efficient Gneisenau's staff work would be in bringing most of the Prussians to the field in time to fight as an army.

Soult was impatient as Reille's corps after a sharp fight pushed aside a Prussian brigade conducting a delaying action at Gilly three miles north of Charleroi.

While the road was still blocked, he ordered up the 2,000 cavalrymen of Reille's 2nd Cavalry Division and the Light Cavalry Division of the Guard. 'Ride around the infantry and get back on the road and take Quatre Bras. Do not let anything hold you up. Bypass any infantry you find. Remember it is the Emperor's express order that Quatre Bras be taken with dispatch – and held. It is a vital part of his plan. Reille will catch up.'[31]

Unbeknownst to Soult, there were no enemy troops in Quatre Bras. However, the 2,500 men of the 2nd Nassau-Usingen Infantry Regiment were within easy marching distance. One battalion was 1.8 miles to the west at Houtain-le-Val; another battalion was 2.4 miles to the east at Sart-Dame-Avelines. The third battalion was at Frasnes-lez-Gosselies, 4.8 miles directly to the south. Any alert would push the two closer battalions into the crossroads hamlet.[32]

To Soult's surprise, after the Prussians had been seen off the field, Reille began to bivouac his corps. His men had been up and marching since 2:30, and he thought they needed rest. If he had ever forgotten Soult's harsh nature, he was reminded of it with even more heat than he remembered from Spain: 'Tired! I don't give a damn. They can rest at Quatre Bras!' Orders soon had the troops back on the road just as gunfire sounded from Frasnes about two miles up the road. The cavalry had apparently found some opposition. Soult growled to Reille, 'Vite, vite, vite! Looks like the cavalry needs help', and then rode forward.[33]

The hamlet of Frasnes on the road to Quatre Bras was burning. Prussian stragglers had alerted the Nassauer commander, who had put his small force in order to defend the town. He placed a few small German detachments to hold it, but the cavalry had just ridden around north of the town. There they found that the Nassau battalion backed by an artillery battery had blocked the road north. The lancers of the 2nd Cavalry Division forced the battalion to form a square. Only the first rank of lancers were armed with the lance. Napoleon had thought only the first rank had the necessary shock potential of the lance. The rest were armed with sabres and carbines. Now these rear ranks dismounted and began skirmishing with the Nassauers from cover, dropping man after man in their tight ranks as the battalion was forced to retain its square as the remaining mounted lancers threatened. With this unit fixed, the rest of the 2nd and the Guard Light Cavalry Division again rode around and moved swiftly towards Quatre Bras.

Soult arrived ahead of Reille's infantry to watch the 2nd's horse artillery battery unlimber and pour canisters into the Nassauers, blowing bloody gaps in their ranks. They were badly shaken and appeared stunned, which was all the lancers needed. They swarmed in through the gaps, spearing man after man until the rest quickly surrendered. Reille's infantry arrived and swiftly cleared the rest of the Germans out of the hamlet.

15 June – Quatre Bras

General Desnouettes pushed his chasseurs and lancers fast up the road. He knew His Majesty would accept no excuse, even though the horses were tired. Tired or not, he would get them to Quatre Bras. In doing so, they rode down the Prussian stragglers who had alerted the Nassauers in Frasnes. One wounded uhlan tried to lash his horse forward, but the animal gave out, and he could only surrender. The courier sent out by the Nassauer commander in Frasnes was also overtaken and died from a lance thrust.

The Guard Light Cavalry rode into the hamlet of Quatre Bras without opposition with an hour of sunlight left in the day. He quickly threw one of his regiments and his two horse artillery batteries north of the town on the road to Brussels. Other detachments picketed the roads to Namur and Nivelles. They engaged Nassau sentries at Houtain-le-Val. Now he just had to wait for Reille and his infantry. As sun set, he was reinforced by the 2nd Cavalry Division.

By 11:00 p.m. Reille's lead 5th Division entered the hamlet. They were exhausted, and at least a third had fallen out on the forced march, but they were there.

Soult had come with them. He was being briefed by Desnouettes when a Guard staff officer interrupted to say that a Prussian general had been captured on the Namur road with a dispatch for Wellington. He introduced a clearly mortified Gen. Müffling, Blücher's quartermaster general and his liaison officer to Wellington. Soult may have been a bear to his subordinates, but in such circumstances, he was considerate and chivalrous. It was clear that the Prussian was not about to provide anything of value, but that was not necessary. His dispatch, which the Prussians had the courtesy to write in good French to the Duke, was everything he could have wished. The dispatch was from Gneisenau and informed the Duke that 'Blücher had concentrated on the east–west *chaussée* at Sombreffe.' Soult immediately sent off a courier under strong escort with the dispatch to Napoleon at Charleroi.[34]

15 June – Army of the Netherlands Headquarters, Brussels

It was the middle of the day and Wellington was writing at length to the Tsar that it was his determination to begin offensive operations at the end of the month. He was completely unaware that Napoleon was already in Belgium. He did not receive Zieten's warning until 3:00 p.m. when a Prussian officer covered with dirt and sweat galloped into Brussels with a much-delayed dispatch. The Duke thought it a feint, with the real main French axis of advance to still come by way of Mons. He had another reason for not prematurely making a decisive move. Brussels was full of French émigré aristocrats and British tourists whom he did not want to panic.

That same afternoon Prince William arrived from his headquarters at Braine-le-Comte to the west of Nivelles on the same road that ran to Sombreffe. He reported that the Prussians had been attacked at Binche just inside the Belgian border and that he himself had heard gunfire coming from Charleroi. That decided Wellington to alert the dispersed elements of his army to collect at their division headquarters, between Grammont and Nivelles, and be prepared to march with one hour's notice. The Reserve Corps would stay in Brussels under his command. He ordered Lord Uxbridge to collect his cavalry at Ninove. The concentration was still aimed at the French coming from Mons. The orders went out between 5:00 and 7:00 p.m.

He still thought Mons was the most likely French objective because the road to Brussels ran directly northwards from it. He said, 'For this reason, I must wait for my advice from Mons before I fix on my rendezvous.' The source of that advice was Lt. Col. Grant. He had no idea, however, that Grant had divined the real French approach via Charleroi. Unfortunately, his dispatch to Wellington was intercepted by a puffed-up Hanoverian cavalry officer, Lt. Col. von Hacke, who had the temerity to read it, declare it nonsense, and send it back to Grant.[35]

In the meantime, Wellington meant to keep his promises to the Duchess of Richmond to attend the lavish ball she had planned. He intended that his attendance would indicate that the situation was not critical. It was also meant to show such confidence that Brussels' large pro-Napoleon faction would have no excuse to act. It was also the place where most of his generals were likely to be found.

15 June – The Roads to Sombreffe

As Wellington's orders went out, over 60,000 Prussians and Saxons were rushing down the roads and over the fields to answer the call to concentrate at Sombreffe. Thousands of men, especially the reluctant Saxons, fell out in exhaustion, but the main columns pushed on.

15 June – Allied I Corps Headquarters, Braine-le-Comte, Belgium

If Slender Billy was more valour than ability, he was lucky to have a superb chief of staff in Gen. Baron Jean de Constant Rebecque. He had also heard the Prince's personal report of hearing gunfire from the direction of Charleroi and took it most seriously, especially when a few stray Prussian cavalrymen spoke of a major movement in that direction as well as statments from the Nassauers at Frasnes of approaching gunfire. He could read a map. If the French were coming by way of Mons, the road to Brussels ran through his own headquarters and Nivelles ten miles to the east. If, however, the French were coming from Charleroi, the road to Brussels ran through the crossroads hamlet of Quatre Bras. He made the decision to order the 2nd Netherlands Infantry Division at Nivelles, commanded by Lt. Gen. Baron Henri de Perponcher-Sedlnitzky, to march to Quatre Bras immediately. At the same time, he sent an order to the 8,000 men of the British 3rd Infantry Division at Soignes, four miles south-west of Braine-le-Comte, to also begin marching to Quatre Bras. Shortly after he had sent off the orders, Wellington's order to concentrate at Nivelles arrived. Rebecque disregarded that and continued to organize the corps for the defence of Quatre Bras. A courier sped through the moonlight to Brussels.

Just as Perponcher-Sedlnitzky opened his orders, a courier dashed up to him from the commander of the Nassau battalion at Houtain-le-Val with word that his sentries had been attacked by French cavalry on the road to Quatre Bras. The general's mind raced over the ramifications. Was this the result of a deep French scouting patrol? Or more likely was it the disaster it surely appeared to be? If so, the French had snapped the only good lateral road between Wellington and Blücher's armies. He knew his duty demanded an immediate attempt to drive the French out of Quatre Bras. He would literally be attacking in the dark against an enemy of unknown strength and disposition. His division numbered 7,620, but only his 1st Brigade (2,931) was at Nivelles. His 2nd Brigade was almost twice as strong, but it was centred at Genappe, north of Quatre Bras. He sent off couriers to order its commander, Prince Bernard of Saxe-Weimar, to secure Quatre Bras at all costs. He desperately hoped that the Prince had news of the French as well and that he would move immediately on Quatre Bras. He had instructed the Prince in May that the point of alarm for his brigade was Quatre Bras. At the same time, he roused the 1st Brigade and led it into the growing dark, towards Quatre Bras.

15–16 June – Duke of Richmond's Rented Palace, Brussels

Wellington arrived fashionably late to the ball. Rumours of the French at Charleroi had circulated through the city, and every eye was keen to see if the Duke showed any nervousness. He was serenely calm, though one observer noted a sense of anxiety beneath his bonhomie. It was noted that he would break off a conversation to give orders to young officers who dashed off. Officers whose regiments were at any distance were leaving in response to the Duke's assembly order.

Shortly before the traditional late supper, a courier arrived and presented his dispatch to the Prince of Orange, who just handed it to Wellington. He read it, no trace of anxiety on his face, but officers were called, orders given or quickly written. He suggested that the Duke of Brunswick and Slender Billy join their commands.

It was a report from Mons that nothing was happening there. So, he concluded, the reports about Charleroi were true.

Then he went in to supper about midnight. Hardly had he sat down when the Prince of Orange returned to the room and whispered into his ear. Wellington looked incredulous but said nothing except to repeat that the Prince should return to his headquarters. After a decent interval, he said to the Duke of Richmond, 'I think it is time for me to go to bed.' As he was bidding his host goodnight, he whispered to ask if he had a good map in the house. Richmond took him to his library and showed him the map.

He needed to confirm the implications of the message from Baron Rebecque of 10:30 p.m. that the French may have seized Quatre Bras by *coup de main* in unknown strength. He had dispatched the 2nd Netherlands Division to secure the crossroads, whether the French were there or not. Now looking at the map, he realized that the hinge connecting the two Allied armies had been broken. He exclaimed, 'Napoleon has humbugged me, by God! He has gained twenty-four hours on me!'[36]

Richmond never forgot what the Duke said next: 'By God, he does war honour.'

15 June – The Road to Fleurus

The Emperor rode with his staff behind the cavalry screen onto the plain of Fleurus, his only escort a squadron of grenadiers à cheval. His eye was drawn to a steep height to his left on the otherwise flat plain, and he was soon examining it with his glass. It was clear that a number of dismounted cavalry were on the height, obviously not French. He called for a staff officer to reconnoitre the hill. Captain Coignet rode up. Napoleon recognized the man who had conducted any number of such dangerous missions. 'Do not get caught,' he said as Coignet spurred off.

Halfway up the hill, three officers mounted and quickly came zigzagging down to confront him. They were clearly Prussians. Coignet saluted them and turned about. When he reached the bottom of the hill, he stopped to offer a bow to his pursuers. The taunt succeeded. As he closed half the distance to the Emperor, one of the pursuers galloped after him. The other two stopped to give the younger of them the honour of taking him. Napoleon was concerned enough to send two of his escort to rescue Coignet. But it was not Coignet's first engagement. He recalled:

> I patted my horse to put him in a good humor. I looked behind, and saw that I had time enough to make a left-wheel, and attack him. He shouted to me, 'Surrender.' And I to him also, 'Surrender.' Wheeling to the left, I fell upon him. Seeing me make this sudden wheel-about, he turned, but it was too late; the wine was poured out, and he had to drink it. He had scarcely completed his turn, when I was at

his side, and pierced him with the point of my sabre. He fell head foremost to the ground, stone dead. Leaving my sabre hanging at my wrist, I seized his horse, and rode proudly back to the Emperor. 'Well, old grouser, I thought you would be captured. Who showed you how to make such a turn?'

'One of your picked gendarmes, in the Russian campaign.'

Napoleon was evidently pleased and admired the fine English-bred gelding and commented that had it been a stallion he would have bought it. His staff vied to buy it. He turned to Monthion, 'Make a note of this old grouser. After the campaign, we will see him.'[37]

15 June – Gilly to Fleurus

Napoleon had to exercise no little self-control. He was used to directing his corps closely, but Davout had pushed Vandamme's corps and the Young Guard forward and drove the Prussians back with a rain of blows. Napoleon concluded that Davout was doing everything he himself would do. He rode among the moving columns and asked the first officer he saw what regiment it was. The man replied, 'Sire, the 37th.'

'Ah, Gauthier's regiment? Your soldiers have poor greatcoats.'

'The Prussians have new ones.'

'They are there, go and take them.'[38]

Once Vandamme got into battle, he was a veritable Mars. He was ably supported by Grouchy and two of his cavalry corps. They pushed Zieten's 2nd Brigade back to the defence of the ridge near Gilly, three miles north-east of Charleroi. The Prussians had three battalions with artillery on the ridge, with four stacked up to the rear as a reserve in woods to the rear. Their left flank was guarded only by two squadrons of West Prussian dragoons.

The French artillery concentrated its fire on the Prussian line at which the advancing columns of the 15th and 23rd of the Line of the 8th Division aimed. Although tired after a long march, the adrenalin rush of combat gave them new energy as the drums beat the *pas de charge* and the battalions cheered, '*Vive l'Empereur!*' The artillery ploughed the way for them, blowing bloody gaps through the Westphalian Landwehr on the Prussian right flank. The Landwehr collapsed and fled as the 15th crested the ridge to see the cavalry coming up parallel with them. Now surrounded, the two remaining Prussian battalions on the ridge surrendered. Those in reserve began a hasty withdrawal through the woods, pursued by the 15th.

As Napoleon rode up he heard the crash of gunfire as Davout threw the cavalry and Vandamme at the Prussians. The Emperor reflected that Davout was showing exactly the aggressive initiative for which he had chosen him. He found ample proof in the 1,200 Prussian prisoners being hustled to the rear. The survivors fell back rapidly towards Fleurus, where Zieten had determined to rally his corps. He had to hold the French there to allow the rest of the army to concentrate. Zieten's 3rd Brigade had been bruised about as badly by Reille at Gosselies and was moving quickly to Fleurus. Delaying Napoleon had cost Zieten 4,000 men that day. The word spread through his exhausted men that Davout the Terrible, the author of their national trauma at Auerstedt in 1806, commanded against them. Zieten was quick to inform Blücher that Davout was on the field. The Prussian commander burned to avenge that day when he had flung his cavalry in bloody ruin against Davout's infantry squares. The news did not arouse any trepidation in the field marshal. Rather, it stoked his desire for revenge to white hot.

But the falling darkness effectively shut down the fighting. The congestion at Charleroi caused Gérard's IV Corps to be redirected to the east where they found an undefended bridge to cross the Sambre. They marched up through the dusk and went into bivouac along with Vandamme's men.

Napoleon found Davout and Vandamme by a fire. It was there that the courier from Soult delivered the captured dispatch. Reading it, he exclaimed, 'Fortune smiles on us!' He had worried that she had abandoned him, but here was proof she had not. Blücher was concentrating his army at Sombreffe. Napoleon had believed he would face no more than 40,000 Prussians the next day. Now he said, 'I have them!'[39]

16 June – Quatre Bras

The Prince of Saxe-Weimar was thankful for the moonlit night. It was the only way his 28th Nassau-Orange Regiment had any chance at all to secure Quatre Bras. They marched down the Brussels road from Genappe with the Prince at the head of the column, skirmishers out front. A pair of cannons fired, sending solid shot straight through the ranks. The men were staggered by the bloody furrow that killed or wounded forty-two men. Then a bugle blew, the sound of hooves on cobbles, and the French cavalry were among them, hacking and stabbing, the moonlight glinting off their sabres. The lead battalion disintegrated as the men fled across the fields, pursued by the horsemen. The Prince's body would be found the next day on the road.

CHAPTER 4

'La Ball Commence!'

16 June 1815

3:30 a.m. – The Netherlands Army I Corps Headquarters, Braine-le-Comte

Slender Billy rode into his headquarters at 3:30 a.m. and was immediately briefed by Rebecque on the situation. Reports had been coming in that the attempts of the 2nd Netherlands Division to secure Quatre Bras had been repulsed in the night. The 1st Brigade had pulled back to Houtain-le-Val and the 2nd Brigade to Genappe after the Prince of Saxe-Weimar had been killed. The British 1st and 3rd Divisions were on the march to concentrate at Nivelles. The Prince was back in the saddle in a few minutes.

4:00 a.m. – Grande Armée Headquarters, Charleroi

Napoleon rose at 4:00 and immediately began to read and discuss with Berthier the reports that awaited him. He dictated letters to both Soult and Davout laying out his plans. Against the Prussians he would employ Grouchy's cavalry to hold their left flank in place while he battered away at their right, forcing Blücher to commit his reserves and then throw his own reserve at the Prussian left to crush it. He expected the defeated Prussians to retreat in the direction of their communications through Liège. To ensure that Wellington did not come to the aid of the Prussians, Soult was to defeat the allied forces at Quatre Bras in detail as they came up. He had almost 50,000 men, sufficient to accomplish that task. After finishing the Prussians, Napoleon would march to join Soult then seize Brussels. As a postscript, he ordered Berthier to send an order to d'Erlon's corps at Gosselies to remain there and be prepared to march to support either Soult or himself.

Napoleon reflected to himself, though he would never admit it to Berthier, how glad he was to have him. No one knew him like Berthier did or could translate his orders with that unmistakable precision that it made misunderstandings impossible. He thought of the story that went around that an illiterate grenadier was kept at headquarters to whom all orders meant for the marshals were read. If he could not understand them, Berthier concluded, neither could the marshals, and they were rewritten.

Berthier tied all the loose strings together. To that point, he reminded the Emperor that Lobau's VI Corps would not be of any use if it remained at Charleroi. 'Yes, of course. Order it moved to Fleurus immediately.'[1]

4:30 a.m. – Army of the Rhine Headquarters, Sombreffe

Blücher and Gneisenau were also up early and preparing to ride forward when news arrived that Perch's II Corps was now not expected to arrive before noon, with Thielmann's III Corps not far behind. Zieten's I Corps, which had withdrawn from Fleurus before dawn, was taking up positions in the strong stone villages along Ligny brook but would not be fully prepared until 11:00. Even so, the corps' left flank would be wide open until the reinforcements arrived. Then they would be placed in support behind Zieten's corps between Sombreffe and Le Mazy. Given that it was fifty miles to Liège, only divine intervention would get Bülow's corps to the battle. Of course, the Nord-deutsch Armeekorps was so far away that it would play no role in the battle. Blücher was not unduly perturbed. When all three corps were in place, he would still have over 100,000 men to fight the French – more than enough. His combative nature would have sent him forward with one battalion, as Napoleon predicted. It was something the Emperor would welcome because it put his head firmly in a noose.

Quickly bolting some bread and sausage, at 6:00 a.m. they mounted and rode forward three miles south-west to the mill located on a hill at Bussy, perfect for observation. Gneisenau especially was worried that there had been no communications from Wellington in response to the report that Müffling had been taken the night before. His suspicions of the British general's motives were only heightened by that.[2] To close the loop he had sent Maj. Friedrich von Brünneck with a squadron of hussars the eight miles to Quatre Bras at 6:00 to find out what the British were up too. The chief of staff knew that the absence of the IV Corps in the coming battle would make the support of Wellington's army vital. Blücher remained confident, repeating Wellington's words to the Prussian emissary on 13 June: 'My army will be concentrated at Nivelles or Quatre Bras, according to circumstances, twenty-two hours after the first cannon-shot.' Gneisenau opened his glass to look down the road, saw nothing, and slammed it shut.[3]

5:00 a.m. – Quatre Bras

The Prince of Orange had been busy in the early morning hours. He was determined to drive the French out of Quatre Bras with his 2nd Netherlands

Division. He advanced Maj. Gen. W.F. Graf von Bijlandt's 1st Brigade of five battalions (2,930) – two were Belgian and three Dutch militia – to Houtain-le-Val. There he found the 2nd Battalion (800) of the 2nd Nassau Regiment which had been repulsed in its approach to Quatre Bras. This gave him almost 7,000 men. It was then that he learned of the death of the young Prince of Saxe-Weimar and the similar repulse of his brigade of 3,000 men.

He sent off the division commander, Gen. Perponcher-Sedlnitzky, to prepare to attack from Genappe with the 2nd Brigade. Rebecque arrived and counselled the Prince to develop the situation and await the arrival of reinforcements before attacking. The 2nd Netherlands Cavalry Division would not arrive until at least 3:30 p.m. and the British 3rd Division at 5:00 p.m. Wellington's reserve, even if it had been put on the road early in the morning, would not arrive until early in the afternoon. The Prince would not contemplate waiting. 'The crossroads is vital. The Duke told me so in no uncertain terms just seven hours ago.'[4]

Soult agreed. He beat the Prince to the punch and ordered Reille to organize an attack with his two divisions that had arrived in the night after his cavalry patrols alerted him to the movement of the enemy. Gen. Gilbert Bachelu's 5th Division emerged from Quatre Bras on the road to Nivelles just as the Dutch-Belgian units were getting into position. Bachelu's 5,000 men were from experienced regiments with many battle honours. Quatre Bras was masked to the east by the Bois de Bossu. Bachelu's regiments marched along the wood's northern edge. Gen. Maximilien Comte Foy's 9th Division moved north on the Brussels road. To the south of the woods the 2,000 chasseurs and lancers of the 2nd Cavalry Division rode out. At the same time, Prince Eugene's 6th Division, with 6,500 in strong regiments, was marching up the Charleroi road less than a mile from Quatre Bras. The Guard Light Cavalry Division, deployed to the west of Quatre Bras on the Namur road, was hidden behind the Haute Cense farm.

Once beyond the woods, Bachelu's infantry deployed in column and attacked on either side of the road, supported by artillery and preceded by a cloud of skirmishers. The Prince's 27th Dutch Jäger Battalion and the 7th Belgian Line were in the lead with the three Dutch militia on the flanks and in reserve. It was a very one-sided encounter. The well-directed French artillery completely outclassed their opponents, shredding the lead Netherlands infantry. Outnumbered four to one against tough veterans, the two lead Netherlands battalions wilted and fell back upon the militia battalions. Bijlandt was wounded in the thigh by a French bayonet and captured.

These battalions were wavering when the French 2nd Cavalry Division came up behind them in a charge. The 1st Chasseurs à Cheval got behind the enemy artillery and charged, sabreing the crews. The 5th Dutch Militia Battalion was wavering when the Prince rode up, rallied them and gallantly led them into a counterattack. He shouted, *'Allons, mes camarades, sabrons ces Français, la victoire est à nous'* ('Come on, comrades, let's put our sabres to these Frenchmen, the victory is ours').[5] A steady volley from the French 72nd of the Line staggered them. Stopped and dazed, the militia was a perfect victim for the 5th Lancers, who crashed into them, spearing one after another. The other two militia battalions tried to form square but the French infantry came up firing into them. They threw down their arms. Slender Billy barely survived the cavalry charge; being mounted, he was a magnet for the lancers, but his aides died around him. He spurred his horse to the shrinking square of the 7th Belgian Line Battalion. The French guns were blowing holes through the Belgians as the French infantry came up and the cavalry hovered, ready to charge. Through all this, the Prince did not lose his nerve. He was young and brave and determined to die well. The Belgians had other ideas. Suddenly men upended their muskets, the sign of surrender, as others shouted *'Vive l'Empereur!'* The Prince would rather have died than surrender his sword to the colonel of the 61st of the Line. He could not bear the thought of having let Wellington down.[6]

As he handed over his sword, his only surviving unit, the battalion of the German 2nd Nassau, fought its way in square off the field, pursued by the French cavalry.

The rest of the 2nd Netherlands Division was badly beaten by General Foy on the Brussels road. His brigades fixed the Nassauers as the Guard cavalry fell on their rear. It was over in minutes. The entire 28th Nassau-Orange Regiment was surrounded and forced to surrender. In less than an hour, Reille had destroyed an entire division and taken over 3,000 prisoners, including the Prince-Hereditary of the Kingdom of the Netherlands.[7]

The presentation of the Prince of Orange to Marshal Soult was a perfect example of French chivalry. The marshal offered him every courtesy and praised his gallantry. He offered him breakfast, which reawakened the Prince's good nature. Then Soult sent him off with a suitable escort to Napoleon at 9:30. As they rode off down the Namur road, he ordered Reille to push north up the Brussels road. He would not wait for Napoleon. The opportunity to bounce straight into Brussels was just too good to pass up.

6:15 a.m. – Napoleon's Headquarters, Charleroi

Napoleon was intent on dictating orders when the noise of battle came through the open windows. He rushed outside to cup his ear for the direction. It came from the north-west, from the direction of Quatre Bras. Berthier had dashed out with him. Napoleon said to him with evident satisfaction, *'La ball commence!'*

6:15 a.m. – Prussian Command Group, Bussy

At the mill at Bussy, every Prussian head turned in the direction of the sound of gunfire directly to the west. Blücher shouted in glee. 'You see, Gneisenau, Wellington is as good as his word! Now we will catch Napoleon between us. We must hold him here while the English fall on his flank.' Gneiseau was chagrined that his dislike of Wellington might be misplaced. But the efficient staff officer in him was calculating what would happen if Napoleon attacked before Pirch and Thielmann arrived.[8]

8:00 a.m. – The Roads to Quatre Bras

Wellington left Brussels at 8:00 a.m. and was cheered by the columns of British infantry along the road as he rode south. He stopped briefly at the farm of Mont St Jean, but there the sounds of battle to the south were audible and he spurred forward to Quatre Bras.

At the same time Maj. Brünneck was fighting for his life two miles outside Quatre Bras. He and his escort had been attacked by French cavalry concealed in a wood. A sabre slash across the face sent him reeling half out of his saddle as his horse carried him away. A Prussian hussar grabbed the loose reins and led him away, back the way they had come.

10:30 a.m. – Fleurus

Napoleon arrived in Fleurus and rode down the outpost line with Davout and Grouchy until they reached a windmill at Naveau at the western edge of the town. He ordered his engineers to knock a hole in its rounded roof to build him a balcony from which to survey the enemy.

In half an hour it was ready, and the three of them climbed to the top. The ground on either side of the Ligny brook rose but the French side was higher and better ground for siting artillery that would outrange the Prussians' guns. The ground on the French side had numerous hollows and dips that would conceal the French infantry as it moved to attack. Along Ligny brook were a number of stoutly built stone villages, often surrounded by thick hedges or stone walls. Napoleon could see very few of Zieten's men fortifying the villages. As he watched, the head of Pirch's corps marched down the road from Namur, spreading out behind Zieten's corps massed on the slopes above the brook. Napoleon was surprised that they positioned themselves right in the open on the slope. As an artilleryman, he almost salivated at the target. He also noted with surprise that they had not destroyed the bridges over the brook. He did not know that Blücher had ordered them left intact so that he could switch to the attack if the opportunity presented itself. Not long after, Pirch's columns arrived, the head of Thielmann's corps began to appear and extend itself to the left of Pirch to cover the open flank all the way from Sombreffe to Mazy on the Namur road, a distance of almost six miles. Most of that distance was lightly covered by cavalry. Blücher was delighted at their arrival earlier than expected, fulfilling the old military adage that if you are early you are never late.

Napoleon had what the great Russian general Alexander Suvorov called the most important attribute of a general – quick grasp, what the French called *coup d'œil*, the ability to make a quick comprehensive appraisal of a situation at a glance. Now he expounded to Davout and Grouchy what he wanted them to do.

Speaking to Davout, he said, 'The old fox will not stir out.' Pointing to the Prussian right, he said, 'See how he deploys to fight a holding battle until Wellington comes to his aid. It will prove to be a false hope.'[9]

To Davout, '*Maréchal*, you will attack and take those villages. The Prussians will feed in their reserves, and you will grind them up. When the enemy has committed his last reserves, I will throw my reserves, Lobau's corps and the Guard, at their right flank and smash it.' Turning to Grouchy, 'You will take two cavalry corps and threaten the enemy's open flank. That will prevent that corps –' he pointed to Thielmann's – 'from reinforcing the fight for the villages. If an opportunity presents itself to turn or penetrate the flank, you will take it immediately.'[10]

Davout indicated the village of Ligny. 'Sire, the enemy will rush to defend the villages along the brook as soon as we attack. Right now, he is organizing his forces. The key is Ligny. From there we can slice across the enemy's rear as he fights for the villages. May I suggest that Lobau's corps be placed opposite the village in reserve for that purpose?' He was taking a chance. Napoleon had always been jealous of his control of the reserve. So Davout was surprised when the Emperor assented.

An aide raced up the stairs to the balcony and presented Soult's summary report of the fighting at Quatre Bras. Napoleon read it and said, 'Gentlemen, the day has begun well. Soult has defeated the Dutch at Quatre Bras and will march on Brussels.' He was concerned that Soult had made no mention of English troops there.

10:35 a.m. – The Brussels Road between Genappe and Plancenoit

Wellington and his staff left Mont St Jean immediately with a small escort on hearing the sound of the guns coming from Quatre Bras. An hour later the noise died away, but they kept up the pace. They were halfway to Genappe when they came across the first Nassauers fleeing from the destruction of their brigade at Quatre Bras. Hundreds more came up the road in the next few minutes. There was only one gun and team. The Duke knew badly beaten men when he saw them. He heard incoherent accounts of being overwhelmed by the French. Then the cry went up, '*Die Franzosen!*' The Nassauers panicked and rushed past the English group. An aide rode forward to look over a small rise. He turned back suddenly, shouting, 'The French!' Behind him a group of chasseurs appeared and stopped for a moment. Wellington was not given to empty courage. 'Gentlemen, we must ride hard now!' They galloped back down the road to Plancenoit with the chasseurs charging after them. The English had the advantage of the better horses and outdistanced the French.

Outside Plancenoit Wellington saw the black-and-green uniforms of the six companies of the 1/95th Rifles with enormous relief. He found their commander on horseback. 'Barnard, throw your men across the road immediately. The French are right behind us.' Not far behind the 95th the road was bright with scarlet uniforms. The British 5th Division was coming up. The commander, seeing Wellington with the 95th, rode up. He was just the man the Duke wanted to see. Lt. Gen. Sir Thomas Picton was one of his most trusted Peninsular War generals, a fire-eater in battle who commanded what had come to be called the 'Fighting Division'. The Duke quickly told him that it appeared Quatre Bras had been lost and the 2nd Netherland Division routed. Just then the chasseurs came into view and right into the well-aimed rifle fire of the 95th. A dozen saddles were emptied, and the chasseurs withdrew. 'Bring your division up and deploy across the road north of the town with one brigade on each side. I don't have cavalry to cover your open flank. Refuse that flank with your third brigade.' The Duke was thinking of the ridge to the rear as a good place to fight. Just then Picton and he turned suddenly south as the rifles of the 95th began firing again.

A mile to the south, the French II Corps was approaching with Foy's division in the lead followed by Bachelu's. They were screened by the 2nd Cavalry Division. Soult had ordered Reille to leave Prince Jérôme's 6th Division to hold Quatre Bras along with the Guard Light Cavalry Division. Soult expected d'Erlon's corps and Kellerman's Reserve Cavalry Corps to reinforce him by 3:00 p.m.

10:45 a.m. – Blücher's Headquarters, the Windmill at Bussy

Aides galloped away with orders that guided the oncoming brigades of the II and III Corps to their positions. The urgency was extreme. Blücher and Gneisenau realized that the French were positioned for an attack while their own corps were still assembling. The bulk of Zieten's I Corps had withdrawn in the night across the Ligny brook to the rising ground behind it. He was only just starting to assign units to hold the villages along the brook.

The French were massed directly south of the brook from Ligny to St Amand le Hameau. Gneisenau recommended and Blücher assented to stack their arriving reserves behind I Corps. The Prussian left would be at the village of Tongrenelle, also on the eastern extension of Ligny brook. The brook meandered to the east and the bridges over it at the villages of Boignée and Balâtre were to be held by the sullen Saxons. The threat seemed manageable there. The French cavalry massing there could not cross the marshy brook except over the bridges in the villages. Without infantry of their own, they would not be able to force the villages.

11:00 a.m. – Napoleon's Headquarters, the Windmill at Naveau

Napoleon was alone on the windmill balcony surveying the field of the coming battle. Davout and Grouchy had been sent off to do their part. An aide appeared and whispered that he had a guest waiting below. As he exited the mill, his eye caught an orange sash over the blue coat of a young blond man. The officer who had escorted the man from Quatre Bras introduced him: 'Sire, I have the honour to present the Prince of Orange.'

The Prince bowed gracefully, though his pride was bleeding. Napoleon could read people. He said, 'Marshal Soult praises your valour in the fighting. I have soft spot in my heart for gallant young men. No matter what happens, you have covered yourself with honour.' He did not tell him he was going to turn his father off his brand-new throne.[11]

Their pleasantries were interrupted by the sound of the French artillery beginning the battle. The attack caught the Prussians in the middle of their deployment, and the massed Prussian columns moving about the slopes above Ligny brook suffered appalling losses. A French observer recalled, 'By what we could judge, our artillery did considerable mischief among the great body of Prussian troops that were posted in mass on the heights and slopes.'[12]

Vandamme threw his divisions down the slope at the villages along Ligny brook without even direct artillery support. Lefol's 8th Division surged forward to the stirring tune of *La Victoire en Chantant* from the band of the 23rd of the Line. They attacked in three columns with swarms of skirmishers preceding them through the high fields of rye for the village of St Amand. Zieten's artillery was not fully deployed, but what guns could bear tore holes in the onrushing columns. Still, they came on, rushing to drive the few Prussian skirmishers from hedge and stone wall. They rushed through the village to find the bridge over the brook defended by a half-company of Landwehr that melted away from the massed French musketry. Sword drawn, the commander of the 15th Light Regiment led the charge across the bridge with the eagle-bearer following. After him the rest of the regiment raced across with the 23rd of the Line behind.

On the left Girard's 7th Division (detailed from II Corps) moved against St Amand le Hameau and St Amand la Haye. Girard threw off his blue cloak and rode at the head of his division in his full-dress uniform of a lieutenant general.

Undefended, St Amand le Hameau was quickly occupied, though some of Zieten's men at St Amand la Haye resisted desperately, but overwhelming French numbers forced them out. The 11th Light followed by the 82nd of the Line quickly emerged from the village.

Fifteen minutes after the attack on St Amand, Gérard sent Gen. Baron Pécheux's 12th Division forward in three columns directly for the village of Ligny. Batteries of the Guard's artillery raced up, sited their guns, and added their fire to those of IV Corps. The 30th of the Line penetrated through the weak fire of a few Prussian skirmishers, raced through the village, crossed the two bridges over the brook, and into the fields on the other side. The 96th of the Line was close behind. From his balcony at the mill, Napoleon was pleased at the result of catching Blücher on the back foot.

If anyone could recover from being caught off-guard, it was Gebhard Blücher. He was an instinctive fighter whose first and last response was to attack. Had Napoleon caught any Austrian or Russian general in such a circumstance, it would have spelled disaster. The old hussar galloped down to Zieten. 'Strike them, Zieten!' Then he rode off to Zieten's cavalry reserve and drew his sabre as he rode down the front of the regiments of the 2nd Brigade. 'My children, we attack. No mercy!' The cavalrymen to a man shouted back their eagerness.[13]

Zieten needed no urging to respond quickly and aggressively to the French assault. He ordered immediately counterattacks to drive the French out the villages and back across the brook. His subordinate brigade commanders were so like-minded that they moved forward before their orders arrived. They knew the danger and responded with the aggressive initiative that suffused the new Prussian national army. But they were just meat for the massed French guns that savaged them as they moved forward. It was here that the butcher's bill began to mount for the Prussians; the French gunners were experts at their craft. But the Prussians just kept coming, the Landwehr with the same determination as the regulars. Their gunners worked their pieces with frantic speed to support the cheering attackers. They roared the loudest for Blücher as he rode by with 1,800 dragoons and uhlans. He drew ahead of Zieten's infantry and led the charge straight at the 30th and 96th deploying outside Ligny.

Blücher had led the cavalry out of a hollow that had protected them from the French guns. Now the guns had their range and scored gashes through the mass of men and horses. But the hollow had been close to Ligny, and they closed fast on the French. The 30th barely had time to form square, but this was not the first time that regiment had faced cavalry, and the men knew steadiness would save them. And it did. Their volley fire brought down the first ranks of the Prussian dragoons and uhlans in a tangled mass of dead and wounded men and horses.

The old hussar general had miraculously come away unscathed, as he had on countless fields, and rallied the cavalry and led them back for another charge and another crushing volley. The 96th was coming up to the right of the 30th forming square. Blücher saw his chance and gathered his horsemen once again. His thunderous voice had an electric effect on men, even after being beaten twice. This time he led them against the 96th and caught them before the square was formed. The battalion flew apart as the uhlans were among them stabbing with their lances and as the dragoons hacked down at the infantry. Some of the French were able to escape into the square of the 30th. Others fled back into Ligny to be met by the follow-on brigade.

Now Prussian infantry joined the fight against the 30th as their guns threw canister that swept away whole sections of the square. The French closed up and withdrew back into the village leaving a trail of dead and wounded with the Prussians hooting in excitement after them.

Napoleon was surprised by the determination of the Prussian I Corps' resistance. He did not realize that in its commander, Hans Ernst Karl, Count Zieten, he had found one of the most formidable opponents of all his wars. He had commanded a brigade in the Battle of the Nations at Leipzig in 1813. Now he was fulfilling with skill and spirit the primary role of a commander in battle – the allocation of the reserve. Everywhere the French seemed to break through the line of the Ligny brook and its villages, Zieten threw in his reserves. Time and again the French were driven back into the villages to be followed by the Prussians where the fighting was most vicious and costly for both sides. Combat in built-up areas sucks up and bleeds formations to death at a terrifying rate. Added to the horror of close combat was the fire of the burning villages as they were set alight by the artillery of both sides.

The ferocity of the fighting in Ligny was unparalleled in the experience of the veterans of either side. One French officer would recall, 'The dead in many places were piled two or three deep. The blood flowed from under them in streams. Through the principal street the mud was red with blood, and the mud itself was composed of crushed bones and flesh.' Bullets swept the streets, but inside the houses Prussians and French fought with bayonets, rifle butts, swords, and fists. Corpses filled the shattered houses, most of which caught fire, roasting corpses and the screaming wounded.[14]

While Blücher was throwing his cavalry at the French, Gneissenau ordered II Corps to reinforce Zieten's counterattack. Thielmann's corps was ordered to move forward to be prepared to join the fight.

11:30 a.m. – Mont St Jean

Wellington rode with Picton on the ridge at Mont St Jean, personally positioning each of the battalions of the 5th Division when they heard the crackle of rifle fire as the 95th Rifles engaged the leading elements of the French cavalry. The Rifles could only delay back into the safety of Plancenoit or would have been ridden down by the French cavalry. Wellington damned his own shortage of cavalry. The infantry of the British 6th Division, the Brunswick Division, and the brigade-sized Nassau Contingent, could be expected to arrive from Brussels at any moment, but such a long column would take some time to assemble. Eventually that would give him 20,000 men at hand, but he would still lack cavalry and have no idea what faced him. He sent out couriers to hasten the arrival of every possible unit, especially Uxbridge's cavalry, which was twenty-nine miles away at Ninove. It was then that an exhausted Lt. Col. Grant found the Duke. Grant's horse was lathered and shivering with exhaustion from the killing pace from Mons.

Grant had been enraged when his warning of Napoleon's arrival at Charleroi had been returned to him. But that had been a godsend. In that time, he confirmed that the division-sized garrison of Lille had crossed the border heading for Ostend. A dozen miles to the south, 15,000 National Guards also crossed the border. For Wellington, it was his worst nightmare. He was unable to unite with the Prussians, his communications with Britain were about to be severed, the French had defeated his advance force at Quatre Bras, and now he was about to face a force of unknown size with only one division and no cavalry. He dared not call on the 17,500 men at Hal. They would have to fend off the now very real threat to British communications that Wellington had so feared.

Two thousand yards to the south on the Brussels road Soult and Reille rode up to the Belle Alliance Inn to watch the last of the redcoats disappearing over the ridge to the north at Mont St Jean. The 2nd Cavalry Division cantered by on the move. Reille struck the side of his saddle with his riding crop. '*Merde!* That damned *Anglais* has found another reverse slope.'

Soult pointed to the large walled farmhouses on either side of the Brussels road in front of the ridge, referring to the large manor of the Chateau de Hougoumont and La Haye Sainte farm. 'You see.' He indicated the blue and red columns marching quickly from the ridge directly to them. 'Wellington has recognized that he has two natural redoubts to his front to hang up our attack if we attack him directly.'

'Yes, but he has backed himself up to the woods beyond,' said Soult, pointing to the Forest of Soignes.

'It won't matter if I can't knock him off that ridge. And that is the last thing I want to do.'

'Well, all your men won't be up for another few hours. By then it will be too late for a fight.'

Reille just grunted in approval.

'But we can put him in a bind for tomorrow when d'Erlon's corps should be available. I think this situation calls for a manoeuvre solution. You see that village?' Soult pointed to Braine l'Alleud, the village about a mile to the west of the ridge.

'Send a cavalry brigade to ride around the village and cut the Brussels road, and an infantry brigade to hold that village. Then we can at the very least block his withdrawal.'

Reille laughed, 'Do you think the Emperor will be displeased if we beat Wellington before he gets here?'

Soult was not amused. 'Don't get your hopes up,' he said. 'Remember this is Wellington.'[15]

12:00 p.m. – Nivelles

General Rebecque was desperately trying to assemble what was left of I Corps. Survivors of the shattered division had fled back into the town spreading panic among the trains and few troops there with news of disaster and the death of Prince William. Rebecque knew that help was on the way – the remaining four divisions of the corps were converging on Nivelles and would be available to attack the French at Quatre Bras. These were the British 1st (Guards) and 3rd Divisions and the Netherlands 3rd Division and the Netherlands Cavalry Division – altogether almost 28,000 men. Awaiting them at Quatre Bras was the amateur Prince Bonaparte with only 7,800 men. The Guard Light Cavalry Division had been ordered by Napoleon to join him facing the Prussians. Jérôme was on his own.

12:40 p.m. – Boignée

Further to the east on the French right, Napoleon's only infantry, Gen. Hulot's 14th Division, formerly under the command of the traitor Bourmont, under Grouchy's command, was deployed opposite the village of Le Docq where a bridge crossed Ligny brook. Next to the 14th was the IV Corps' 6th Cavalry Division and to the east of them Grouchy had massed his I and II Reserve Cavalry Corps. Hulot had attempted to seize Le Docq with a quick attack over the bridge, but Thielmann threw in his 32nd Infantry Regiment (11th Bde) into the town. The fighting became as vicious as in the other villages.

At Boignée nothing was happening. Grouchy had that aristocratic presence that tended to calm those around him. But he was not happy. The noise of battle flared and rumbled to the left, but his cavalry had nothing to do. They could not cross the brook because the villages were guarded by enemy infantry. He was frustrated. Here he was, a new marshal, with nothing important to do until it was time to pursue the Prussians.

It was then that an aide called his attention to two officers leaving Boignée on horseback riding to them with a flag of truce. They were intercepted and escorted to Grouchy. He was surprised to see that they were Saxons. The senior officer rode up and to the shock of the marshal and his staff exclaimed, *'Vive l'Empereur!'*, introduced himself as Oberst von Dohna, commanding the brigade defending Boignée. In excellent French he explained that the Saxons despised – and here he lapsed into German – *'diese Sheiss Preuss'* for how they treated the Saxons' country and king. Many of them had fought for Napoleon for years. Saxony would be better off allied to Napoleon than swallowed bite by bite by Berlin. Grouchy was shrewd enough to see the opportunity the Saxon was edging up to. 'I speak for all the Saxons, *Herr Feld-Marshall.* We swear our allegiance to Napoleon for the sake of our imprisoned king. Your path across the brook is open to you at Boignée and Balâtre.'

Grouchy acted immediately. He sent the other Saxon officer to the Emperor with a summary of the Saxon volte-face. Then he ordered Exelmans' II Reserve Cavalry Corps to cross the brook at Boignée and Pajol's I Reserve Cavalry Corps to cross at Balâtre and converge on Tongrinne, one mile north of Tongrenelle. There most of the remaining Saxon regiments were concentrated.

Davout was conferring with Gérard when he saw Grouchy's aide with a Saxon officer galloping by. His interest piqued, he rode out and intercepted them.[16]

1:00 p.m. – Napoleon's Headquarters, the Windmill at Naveau

Napoleon's attention was focused on the furious Prussian counterattack. Zieten's right flank was strongly reinforced and pushing forward, offering its flank. The Guard and Lobau's VI Corps were on the opposite side of the battlefield and could not strike in time. But d'Erlon's I Corps should be just where it could turn to march east and fall on the open Prussian flank. He was dictating his order to Berthier when an aide ran up the stairs. 'Sire, sire! You must come down. You will not believe what has happened!'

He listened to the Saxon officer and Grouchy's aide and then rushed back to his balcony. His glass searched to the east to see Grouchy's cavalry enter Boignée and exit on the far side. Behind them Maurin's 6th Cavalry Division (IV Corps) followed. Berthier pointed out the movement of Milhaud's IV Reserve (Heavy) Cavalry Corps in the same direction, the sun glittering off the polished armour and helmets of the cuirassier regiments. The Saxon infantry brigade marched after them and turned west to attack the Prussians defending Le Docq. Napoleon immediately sent to the 3rd Cavalry Division guarding the left flank to delay the Prussian advance there as he dispatched the Old Guard to smash them at Ligny. 'Yes,' he said. 'Let them keep pushing on that door while we are coming in through the back.' He paused, smiled, and said, 'It seems Grouchy has validated my making him a marshal.'[17]

1:00 p.m. – The Road to Tongrenelle

Davout made his decision instantly. He turned to Gérard: 'Grouchy has found the key to this battle. We must help him turn it.' He directed Gérard to march immediately with his 13th Division to join the 14th at Tongrenelle. The 13th had been waiting in reserve and was fresh. So were Lobau's 15,000 men. On his own authority, Davout ordered them to follow Gérard. In minutes the orders were given, and almost 20,000 men began their march to join Grouchy's 6,000 cavalry.

1:15 p.m. – Wellington's Headquarters, Mont St Jean

Soult could see Wellington and his aides riding along the ridge opposite him. He was recognizable by the very plain dark blue cloak he was wont to wear whereas the officers about him glittered in scarlet and gold. Wellington, for his part, had no idea who the French general in front of him was. He was concentrating on the French infantry deploying south of the ridge. More alarming were the French cavalry marching around his flank to Braine l'Alleud on his right. The consequences of his lack of cavalry were now apparent. Even with the greatest luck, his own cavalry would not arrive for hours. In that time, the French could sever his communications to Brussels. To add to his worries, he had had no news of Blücher nor of his Prussian liaison officer, Müffling. Another courier sped north to Wavre and then south to find out what the Prussians were up to.

Time was everything now. The head of his British 6th Division was just outside the village of Mont St Jean on the Brussels road. Closer, however, was the 5th Division's Hanoverian 5th Brigade already on the British right. He dashed over to its commander, Col. Ernst von Vincke, and ordered him to seize and hold Braine l'Alleud. Wellington was taking a gamble that time was more important than quality. The four Hanoverian battalions were all German Landwehr, despite their regulation British scarlet coats, mere militia. If he had waited for the lead brigade of the 6th Division, he would have had dependable British battalions. Risk, risk. It would also be a race. The Hanoverians had only 1,200 yards to go to reach Braine l'Alleud, but the French cavalry was rapidly approaching the village. Wellington rode up to the lead battalion of the 6th Division, which had now emerged from Mont St Jean. The Duke was enormously relieved. They were men he knew – the 1st Battalion, 4th Regiment of Foot. They had fought with Moore at Coruña and had returned to fight for the Duke in Portugal, Spain, and southern France. Thereafter they had been dispatched to fight the Americans but had returned just in time to be sent to Wellington. They cheered when they saw him, but he had no time for that. 'King's Own! Follow me at the double!' Without a break, the 667 men of the King's Own Royal Regiment broke into a trot after him.

1:15 p.m. – Ghent

Maj. Sir Harry Smith had arrived in Ghent to join the 10th Infantry Brigade of Maj. Gen. Sir John Lambert as its brigade major. He brought his wife along, too, an indulgence of officers at that time. Most of the brigade had just arrived at Ostend from America where it had fortunately been held in reserve in the disastrous Battle of New Orleans in January. Sir John, as the surviving senior officer, had seen further attacks were futile and withdrawn his force. The 10th was a strong brigade numbering almost 2,300 men in the 1/4th, 1/27th, and 1/40th Foot, all of them veterans of the Peninsular War. The 1/4th and the 1/40th had just fought in North America; the 1/4th had taken part in the burning of Washington.

Sir Harry recorded that their stay in Ghent was pleasant but short:

> As we anticipated, our march from Ghent was very sudden. In an hour after the order arrived we moved en route for Brussels. We reached Asche on the afternoon of the 16th June. The rapid and continuous firing at Quatre Bras, as audible as if we were in the fight, put us in mind of old times, as well as on the qui vive. We expected an order every moment to move on. We believed the firing to be at Fleurus.[18]

The firing was not from Fleurus but much closer, at Quatre Bras.

1:20 p.m. – French 6th Division Headquarters, Quatre Bras

Jérôme chafed at his minor role in holding this crossroads. His was the largest division in Reille's corps and in the army, and here he was sitting when he could be doing something worthy of a Bonaparte. He was determined to show his big brother that he was not the only man in the family with military talent. Rebecque was just about to give him the opportunity.

Fortunately, the amateur prince had a capable second in command, Gen. Count Armand Guilleminot, a former topographical engineer with a good eye for ground as well as being a man who had served on the general staff and commanded a division and a corps. Napoleon had shrewdly assigned him as second in command to hold his little brother's hand. And now he was doing just that. The Prince was the type of amateur who thought the laurels of victory could be gathered without the tedium of taking pains. He was glad to give Guilleminot a free hand in such matters.

Guilleminot saw that the Bois de Bossu immediately to the west of the crossroads was a barrier to an enemy who most likely would attack down the road from Nivellles on the northern edge of the woods or in the open ground south of the woods. To guard the northern route, he deployed his 1st Brigade, placing the 1st Light Regiment along the Nivelles–Namur road to the west of the crossroads, with the 2nd Light to the east. To the south of the woods the 2nd Brigade straddled the Brussels–Charleroi road with the 1st of the Line to the west and the 2nd of the Line, whose men had fought as marines at Trafalgar, to the east. Among them was the man who had fired the shot from the rigging that had severed Nelson's spine.

He had not neglected reconnaissance either. Reille had detached the 6th Chasseurs à Cheval to the 6th Division, and Guilleminot sent them out to scout to the west. They had little time to become bored. They quickly tangled with the advance squadrons of the Netherlands Cavalry Division's light cavalry brigade that was intent on cutting off the French south of the crossroads. Now alerted, the French 2nd Brigade (1st and 2nd of the Line) deployed across the Brussels–Charleroi road just as the first regiments of the 3,300-man Netherlands cavalry filled the fields south of them.

The chasseurs also came thundering back down the Nivelles road to warn of the approach of strong infantry columns of the 3rd Netherlands Division commanded by Lt. Gen. Baron David Hendrik Chassé. This Dutch general had fought for Napoleon until his abdication, earning the title of 'General Bayonet' for his brutal methods as well as the title of Baron of the Empire. Nevertheless, with the establishment of the Kingdom of the Netherlands, his natural Dutch patriotism came to the fore.

1:50 p.m. – Tongrenelle

Blood streaming down his face, the young officer found Gen. Thielmann as he was directing the moving columns of his corps in response to Gneisenau's orders. He blurted out that the Saxons had betrayed them and attacked the 3rd Kurmark Landwehr Regiment at Tongrenelle.

French infantry poured over the bridge at Tongrenelle and cavalry at Boignée (Exelmans' II Reserve Cavalry Corps) and Balâtre (Pajol's I Reserve Cavalry Corps). On the northern bank of the brook at Tongrenelle, the French troops marched past the dead and wounded Prussians and Saxons and heard the firing not far off to the north. The Saxons had engaged Thielmann's 10th Brigade.

Davout's courier found Grouchy as he was preparing to engage Thielmann's Reserve Cavalry Corps deploying across his front of Exelmans' eight dragoon regiments. He quickly read the dispatch and said, '*Bon!*' He handed it to his chief of staff, pleased that Davout had transferred Gérard and Lobau's divisions to his control. 'It seems Davout still knows his business. Now to our business. Blow the charge.'

2:30 p.m. – Napoleon's Headquarters, the Windmill at Naveau

Napoleon had watched the march of the division of the Young Guard behind the burning villages along the Ligny brook to the west. He could see they were on a path to intercept the movement of the Prussian II Corps around his flank. The enemy were putting their heads into that trap. He tore himself away to watch the smoke rising from across the brook to the east where Davout and Grouchy were enveloping the Prussian left. So far there was no indication that the Prussian command realized what was happening.

He was wrong. Gneisenau had been informed, but an army cannot be turned on a pivot. Blücher was organizing another attack on La Haye on the French left with Pirch's brigades. Standing in his stirrups to shout, 'My sons! Carry yourselves bravely, don't let that nation be your masters again! Forward! Forward in God's name!' They bellowed back, *'Vorwärts!'* Once more they surged forward as the French guns sent furrows of bloody death into their ranks. They took the village. Blücher rode west to lead the attack against Wagnelée to turn the French flank. But the attack was stopped by the fire of two battalions of French skirmishers hiding in the tall rye. Behind them came the rest of Vandamme's last reserve, Habert's 10th Division.

Stopped on his right, Blücher knew his last chance was to break the French centre between St Amand and La Haye – as long as his men kept the French from moving out of Ligny. He sent one of Thielmann's brigades to reinforce the fighting there. He then gathered his last reserves and led them to St Amand. He rallied the mass of dislocated men, separated companies, and fragments of units by the power of his personality. With these seven or eight battalions he reinforced the battered remains of three more brigades. He ordered an attack.

One of the brigade commanders said, 'My men have fired off all their cartridges and also emptied the pouches of the dead. They cannot fire a single shot more!' Blücher ignored him, waved his sword and shouted, 'Fix bayonets and forward!' The men were energized and followed him once more. But they were animated only by the last of their courage. To the left of St Amand, they ran into the wall of three regiments of the Guard Chasseurs à Pied and melted away under their fire.[19]

It was here that Gneisenau found him. Even the old hussar could recognize the danger. Gneisenau wanted to break off the attack and retreat north while Thielmann held the left flank against the French and Saxons. Everything in Blücher's aggressive nature resisted. Over the last two years he had hammered the French everywhere he had fought them. The men followed him everywhere and had rarely failed to do what he wanted. He would break Napoleon here. To Gneisenau he said, 'You must make Thielmann hold the French while I beat them here. Go now!' His chief of staff knew when the old man's blood was up. There was no arguing with him.

2:45 p.m. – East of Tongrinne

Almost 3,000 French dragoons drew their sabres, and with shouts of *'Vive l'Empereur!'* stabbed them into the sky. The charge blew and Exelmans' corps leaped forward. An equal number of Prussians echoed with shouts of *'Urah! Urah!'* Uhlans, hussars, dragoons, and Landwehr cavalry then charged.

The horses were as excited as the men as they trampled down the high fields of rye. It was the largest collision of cavalry since the Battle of the Nations at Leipzig in 1813. The French knew they were on the brink of victory, the Prussians that they were all that stood in the way. The French cavalry, despite the deadly work of the uhlans' lances, were better trained and more experienced especially against the Prussian Landwehr cavalry. Slowly the Prussians were being pushed back when Pajol's I Reserve Cavalry Corps crashed into their rear. They had been waved across the Ligny brook at Balâtre by cheering Saxons to come up on the cavalry battle. Pajol took in the scene instantly, ordered his 4th Cavalry Division to deploy, and charged. The Prussians were completely taken by surprise. The first intimation of what was to strike them was the shout of *'Vive l'Empereur!'* in their rear before the impact of the French. Panic ran through them as every man turned to escape. Those that could were pursued by Pajol's fresh 5th Cavalry Division so hard that they were scattered in every direction.

Napoleon recognized that the climax of the battle was approaching. He left the mill and personally led the divisions of grenadiers and chasseurs à pied to the fighting at Ligny. The Guard artillery prepared the way with massed fire that savaged the Prussian reserves in the open outside the village. The Guard marched across the bridge and through the burning hamlet. Seeing the Emperor riding at the head of the Guard, the exhausted men of the 12th cheered wildly, *'Vive Napoleon!'* The Guard cleared the Prussians out of the edge of the village with the bayonet, formed up in the corpse-strewn fields outside and attacked. Their steady and rapid volleys mowed down the spent Prussians trying to bar their way, adding to the death sent by the Guard artillery. Now the 1,600 cuirassiers of the 14th Cavalry Division (IV Reserve Cavalry Corps) clattered over the bridge into Ligny. On the opposite flank the Young Guards attacked the Prussians trying to take Wagnelée again.

2:45 p.m. – Braine l'Alleud

Reille's cavalry charged when the Hanoverian battalions started rushing in columns down the slope from Mont St Jean to Braine l'Alleud. First in their path, the Landwehr Battalion Hameln was ordered to form square, but their minimal training meant they were too slow. They panicked as the French rode through them sabreing left and right at the fleeing Germans. The remaining battalions fled back up the slope as the cavalry followed them. Wellington personally led the 1/4th Foot up the reverse slope as the fleetest Hanoverian Landwehr raced over the crest. The regulars came on line and topped the crest as more of the Germans pushed through the ranks to escape to the rear. No steadier battalion existed in the British army – these men had fought at Coruña, Badajoz, Salamanca, and Vitoria. French cavalry did not faze them. Their volley was delivered within yards of the horsemen. The entire leading ranks fell in tangled heaps of men and horses. The volley of the second rank brought down the chasseurs milling around behind the dead and dying. The French recall was sounded, and the remaining horsemen regrouped at the bottom of the slope. Wellington had been saved by his veterans, but his relief was tempered by the sight of French infantry entering Braine l'Alleud.

Soult and Reille watched the action from just east of the chateau of Hougoumont with no little satisfaction. At small cost the art of manoeuvre had led to the savaging of one of Wellington's brigades and a threat to his flank and communications. Prince Bonaparte's division was expected soon and would make that threat a reality.

Neither knew that the Prince had been delayed by Rebecque's attack while the 1st and 3rd British Divisions concentrating at Nivelles had set out, on Wellington's summons, for Mont St Jean, a bare seven miles away. Now an aide pointed out to the French marshal the long red-coated columns marching up the Nivelles–Brussels road. Soult realized that his plan had been suddenly negated. Instead of cutting Wellington's communications, he himself was about to be caught in a British vice. He gave Reille the order to withdraw back towards Genappe.

2:50 p.m. – Quatre Bras

Prince Bonaparte impatiently rode back and forth behind the 1st of the Line as the 3rd Netherlands Division deployed north of the crossroads – almost 8,000 Dutch and Belgian troops. He could hear firing from south of the crossroads where his 2nd Brigade was holding back the Netherlands cavalry. He wanted to attack the enemy to his front. Guilleminot cautioned him to wait. 'Let them attack and wear themselves down. When they have tasted French powder and then recoil, that is the time to strike.'

Jérôme was plainly not happy. 'My brother has given me the 1st of the Line, the oldest regiment of France. They have fought at Caldiero, Wagram, Salamanca, Lützen, Bautzen, Dresden, Leipzig, Montmirail, and Vauchamps. Listen to their steady volleys to the south. Do you think these Dutchmen are any match?'

'Your Highness, it is a matter of timing. Trust me.' In a rare act of good judgement, the Prince did just that. Of the twelve battalions in the Netherlands

Division, six were Dutch militia. There were only four line battalions (three Dutch and one Belgian) and two Belgian jäger battalions.

The Prince did not have to wait for long. The enemy's 2nd Brigade attacked on either side of the road preceded by its jäger battalion as skirmishers. The 1st Brigade struck from the Haute Cense farm on the French right with its line battalions in the first wave, the militia battalions behind. They were staggered by a perfectly delivered volley. A second and third volley from the next two ranks of the French line drove the Dutch troops back. At the Haute Cense farm the 2nd Light's fire was just as deadly. It took the enemy commanders a while to rally their men for another attack. The result was the same. Chassé urged his shaken battalions, personally leading the 1st Brigade back into the attack. 'With the bayonet!' he shouted as he rode down the line. His fearsome figure set a jolt of enthusiasm among his battalions, and they surged forward.

Right into the concentrated fire of the French divisional artillery. Captain Meunier had trained his 200-man battery to a high level, and now it paid off. His six 6-pounder guns fired solid shot that cut crimson furrows through the Belgian-Dutch. They fired not straight on but at an angle so that the shot travelled almost length-wise through the battalions. The gun crews turned to canister as the enemy came within range. The increasingly ragged battalions closed on the French infantry. Chassé still was mounted, showing himself to his men. He was their slender hold on the attack. But it was too slender and snapped when the French 1st Light fired again with cool precision. Chassé and horse went down along with his front ranks.

'Now, Your Highness, now is the time to hit them,' said Guilleminot. Jérôme drew his sword and rode to the front of the 1st. 'Forward!' The first man to dart forward was the giant of a soldier, Sub-Lt. Legros, a former engineer, waving an axe overhead. It is just such a moment in combat when a single image curdles the courage of one side, just as the Trojans panicked when they saw Achilles, all violent death, racing towards them. The Dutch melted away as the line of French bayonets surged forward. The 2nd Light also attacked, stopping only to fire at the disintegrating militia battalions of Chassé's 1st Brigade. Its Belgian battalion reversed their muskets and surrendered outright.[20]

To the south of Quatre Bras the 2nd Brigade had been able to hold off the Netherlands cavalry by forming squares. A few charges had collapsed in front of these steady troops. To the south, Gen. Count François Kellerman's III Reserve Cavalry Corps was coming up the road from Gosselies when the sound of gunfire became audible. Kellerman was one of the best of Napoleon's cavalry commanders; the son of a famous general of the Revolution, he had saved Napoleon from defeat at Marengo. Later, when Napoleon was brought evidence of Kellerman's looting, he brushed it aside, saying 'General, whenever your name is brought before me, I think of nothing but Marengo.' Now Kellerman ordered the pace to increase to a trot.

Rebecque watched the Netherlands Division retreat in ruins:

At this moment a cannon-ball ricocheted under the belly of my horse, covering me with earth and stones and I was bruised on the flesh of my left leg. Immediately afterwards, while I still had my sword in my hand following the final cavalry charge, a canister shot struck the sheath of my sword against my left leg . . . A canister shot passed through my horse's head; a fountain of blood came from its nostrils, covering me entirely, and it fell dead on the spot.[21]

The look of horror on his aide's face snapped him out of his shock. He prepared to resume the attack with the 1st and 3rd British Divisions which he thought were about to join the battle. It was then that he received an urgent dispatch from Wellington to send all the I Corps to Mont St Jean immediately. His orders to withdraw from the field did not reach the Netherlands Cavalry Division in time. Kellerman's cuirassiers thundered down on the unsuspecting Dutch 4th Light Dragoons and 8th Hussars threatening the French infantry squares. Big men on big horses, the cuirassiers crashed into the enemy, driving them back on the bayonets of the French infantry.

The Prince could not wait to send a courier to his brother to boast of his victory, six colours, and almost 2,000 prisoners. No one was more surprised than Napoleon to receive it.[22]

3:00 p.m. – Outside Ligny

Blücher was drawn back to the crisis at Ligny like a moth to a flame. He saw an unfolding disaster as the cuirassiers hacked into the collapsing Prussian defence. The volleys of the Guard infantry were shredding the rest of the defenders. The old hussar did what he always did in such moments – attack. He gathered the last cavalry reserve, the thirty-two squadrons of Lt. Gen. Friedrich Erhard von Röder's I Corps Cavalry Reserve. He flung them forward with himself at their head, regiment after regiment in succession. The 6th Uhlans' lances flew against a French square that its commander thought was a National Guard battalion due to the poor and varied state of their uniforms. It was the 4th Grenadiers à Pied of the Old Guard. The guardsmen waited until the last moment then fired, bringing down eighty-three of the uhlans. Regiment after regiment charged – the 1st West Prussian Dragoons, the 2nd Kurmark Landwehr, the Brandenberg Uhlans, and the Queen's Dragoons. Each was beaten back. Then Blücher led them all in one last great effort.

It too failed before the disciplined and accurate fire of the French. Blücher's white charger, a gift from the Prince Regent, was struck in the side by a shell fragment. The beast went on a few paces then staggered in its death throes. Blücher cried out to his aide as the animal fell, 'Nostitz, I am done for!' The horse fell dead, pinning the field marshal underneath. The faithful Nostitz dismounted and stood over Blücher with his sword in one hand and the reins of his horse in another. The uhlans came streaming back past them, pursued by the cuirassiers. One of the armoured horsemen brushed past Nostitz. Moments later the uhlans returned, driving back the French. Nostitz grabbed the reins of a riderless horse and stopped a few of the uhlans and ordered them to lift the dead horse off the field marshal.

Then once more the cuirassiers charged through again. Seeing the group of uhlans, they attacked. Nostitz fell to a sabre that cut him from neck to breastbone. The rest of the uhlans fell or fled. In the brief action one of the big French horses kicked the head of the old man sprawled next to the dead horse. It shied away, its hoof smeared with brains. A French officer glanced down at the glitter of the medals on Blücher's coat. He leaned over his horse to get a closer look and exclaimed, '*Mon Dieu!*' He immediately ordered half a dozen men to guard the body and galloped back through the smoke to where he had last seen the Emperor.[23]

3:00 p.m. – On the Sombreffe–Gembloux Road

Grouchy's cavalry fell on the Prussian trains clustered along the road and in the nearby field. Wagon drivers and supply and service troops fled in every direction, were hunted among the vehicles and tents, or surrendered by the hundreds. A few pugnaciously resisted but were cut down. A crippled Prussian captain determined to take his final revenge on the hated French slashed open a powder pack and fired his pistol so the spark fell on the spilled grains. He got his wish. The ensuing chain explosion of fifteen wagons took fifty French horsemen with him.

The rippling explosions turned every head on the field in their direction. For the collapsing Prussian defence, it was the knell of doom. Almost instinctively, the Prussian units that were still holding together began to pull back. Thousands of individuals, many of them Landwehr from the regions recently annexed by Prussia, simply fled to the rear. Whole battalions disintegrated. Thielmann's last two brigades were holding back Gérard and Lobau's corps and the Saxons in a heroic last stand so that the rest of the army could escape to the north. Behind them came the infantry of Vandamme that had held them so long in the villages along the brook.

Gneisenau was swept along in the chaos of escape. Here and there individual battalions, now shrunken from losses, mostly regulars, held together. They would turn to form square to keep off the cuirassiers and dragoons following them, helpless to halt the armoured Frenchmen from sabreing their way through the panicked crowds of individuals and fragments of units. Some of the cavalry that was left tried to shelter the fugitives and tangled with the cuirassiers in a losing fight. Thielmann's tough-fighting brigades pulled back to form a rearguard. Part of the army, especially the mass of individuals, instinctively took the road to Gembloux on the army's line of communications and ran straight into Grouchy's cavalry and surrendered en masse.

The rest of the army staggered north on the road to Wavre as a great rainstorm blackened the last of the daylight and soaked everyone. Gneisenau called for the army to regroup three miles north of the battlefield at the village of Tilly.

3:30 p.m. – Mont St Jean

As the afternoon wore on, Wellington felt some well-deserved relief as the rest of the Reserve Corps – British 6th Division, the Brunswick Division, and a Nassau regiment – arrived down the Brussels road. Uxbridge's cavalry came in as well, and late at night the remnants of the 3rd Netherlands Division and the Netherlands Cavalry Division. The Netherlands 3rd Division was barely 4,000 strong now and badly shaken. Its surviving senior officer was Maj. Gen. A. d'Aubreme, whose 2nd Brigade had hung back at Quatre Bras during Chassé's last attack. Wellington ordered them to garrison Braine l'Alleud.

By way of Nivelles in the late afternoon the British 1st and 3rd Divisions tramped in. Without firing a shot, their appearance caused the French to withdraw. From a wounded chasseur, Wellington learned that it was Soult who had commanded in front of him. Soult, he thought – the most capable and dangerous of the French marshals he had fought. Any other Frenchman would have fought it out, but Soult had the talent of not getting caught. In fact, when Wellington had been British ambassador in Paris after the restoration, he had come upon Soult at a reception and grasped him from behind, exclaiming that at last he had him. The Duke realized all too well how close Soult had come to putting him in an untenable position. He further realized that he had not seen the last of him.

4:10 p.m. – Ligny

The body of the fallen Prussian field marshal was brought by torchlight into the ruins of Ligny, where a battalion of grenadiers of the Guard presented arms. Napoleon himself knelt next to the stretcher. He then rose and said to all assembled about, 'A man is honoured by such an enemy!'[24]

CHAPTER 5

Hougoumont

12:15 a.m.–12:00 Noon, 17 June 1815

12:15 a.m. – Mellery

The trail from the battlefield of Ligny was 'covered by confused, broken battalions, splintered cavalry squadrons, and artillery columns. Drummers scattered over the fields to beat their different rallying rolls, calling their respective regiments.' North of Sombreffe, Gneisenau stopped in the village of Tilly to try to pull the army together and organize its retreat. The chief of staff of I Corps pointed out that few of the maps issued to the army showed Tilly, but they all showed Wavre to the north, so that would be a better place to regroup. In any case the army was already drifting north of Tilly. He would have preferred to have gone by way of Gembloux along the army's line of communications eastwards. He had been in command ever since Blücher had disappeared in that last cavalry charge against the grenadiers of the Guard. The word was spreading in his beaten army as it trudged north or huddled in shock waiting for orders that Papa Blücher was a prisoner or dead.[1]

Gneisenau would have preferred to march east. He was seething that Wellington had failed to come to the aid of the Prussian army as he had promised. He felt that the army had sacrificed itself in expectation of that aid. His dislike and distrust of Wellington was now brought to a bitter boil with a sense of betrayal. Yes, he would have preferred to march east and leave Wellington in the lurch, but Grouchy's cavalry had cut that route off. Wavre, thirteen miles to the north, was now the only choice. From there, the decision to move east or somehow help Wellington could still be made.

Staff officers disappeared into the dark to convey the necessary orders. Maj. Karl von Weyrach went to find Bülow at Hanat, to tell him of the battle and order him to concentrate three miles south-east of Wavre at Dion-le-Mont. Another officer, Maj. Friedrich von Massow, was sent by way of Wavre to find Wellington, who was thought to be at Quatre Bras, inform him of the Prussian reverse, and ask his intentions. Maj. Gen. von Grolman had reached Wavre and selected a headquarters in the town square. Other staff officers spread out to begin collecting troops and directing them to Wavre.

The word had also spread from French prisoners that Davout had commanded along the Ligny brook. That was enough to make every Prussian shudder. No man was more feared. With the rumours about Blücher spreading despondency, those about Davout, Homer's 'brother to bloodstained rout', spread panic.

3:00 a.m. – Sombreffe

The sergeants had their hands full waking the men. They had fallen into a deep sleep after the battle that had lasted until darkness fell. At least they had had five hours of sleep before shouts of their sergeants and more than one boot in the arse roused them.

That night, before he took to his own bed in Fleurus, Napoleon had read with satisfaction Soult's dispatches from Genappe that Wellington was concentrating at Mont St Jean and that a good part of the Netherlands army had been mauled. The last thing he did was to direct Berthier to prepare the orders to put the army on the road to La Belle Alliance at 7:00 in the morning. 'Make sure they are roused early enough for their soup.' The French army was famous for subsisting on a soup of whatever was at hand.

He had also greeted the senior Saxon officers, many of whom he knew personally. He was tactful enough not to mention how they had defected to the Allies at Leipzig. He had also conferred with Davout. Napoleon was clearly elated about the crushing victory inflicted on the Prussians – the cavalry had herded almost 16,000 prisoners south, a large number of them Westphalian Landwehr. As a column passed the Emperor, many of them shouted, '*Vive Napoleon!*' and 'We fought with you!' Another 15,000 Prussians were dead or wounded on the field. His own losses were not more than 8,000. It was also clear to the marshal that the Emperor was exhausted and was about to retire without organizing the pursuit. Davout was not going to let the opportunity slip away. Grouchy was still too awed by his shiny new marshal's baton and would not have dared raise the subject, much less insist. Davout had known Napoleon too long to be that deferential. He had run the Prussians down after Jena. That was how you dealt with them.

'Sire, we must pursue as soon as possible.'

'Early in the morning will be soon enough. With Blücher dead their animating spirit is gone. That old devil was a relentless enemy. For them he is irreplaceable.'

'The Prussians must be ground into the dirt. Remember they are either at your feet or your throat. If we don't reduce them to licking our boots, their hands will be on our throats again.'

'All too true, but the army is exhausted.'

Like a dog with a bone, Davout shot back, 'They can sleep later.'

Napoleon smiled, 'As you wish. Do it yourself with Exelmans' and Pajol's cavalry, Lobau's corps, and the Saxons.' He turned to leave, then stopped and returned. 'If the Prussians retreat on their communications, let them go with a kick in the backside. But you must then turn west and join me in trapping Wellington. That is your primary mission after you have seen the Prussians off.'

Pajol's horsemen trotted off to lead the pursuit in the starlit dark.

3:00 a.m. – Soult's Headquarters, Genappe

The campfires flickered for 50,000 sleeping Frenchmen at Genappe, the surrounding fields, and the road back to Quatre Bras. Officers ensured that the sentries kept an alert watch. Cavalry videttes were even further out to give a longer warning of any surprise attack. Patrols returned to the area south of Mont St Jean. There were so many campfires visible from the Allied army concealed behind the ridge. Those that could be seen stretched westward to Braine l'Alleud. They found a wounded rifleman trying to get back to his regiment and brought him to Soult's headquarters, where his wounds were tended and he was fed on French army soup. He gratefully revealed what he knew of Picton's division.

Soult had sunk into his cot with the opening moves of the next day already in his mind. The Emperor's courier had brought him news of his victory at Ligny and orders. 'You are to prevent Wellington from withdrawing to Brussels. I will destroy him where he is.' Soult pondered that it would be far less costly to simply threaten his communications and force him to evacuate through Ostend and Antwerp. Then again, Wellington had an enormous reputation among the Allies as the only general not to have been defeated by the French, the only man equal to Napoleon. That was certainly the Emperor's calculation: defeat the invincible general and send a stunning shockwave through Europe. That would affect the Allies' will to fight far more profoundly than driving Wellington off the continent. After all, he could always return and resume the contest. Wellington's defeat, especially if most of his army was lost or prevented from evacuation, would likely collapse the Liverpool government. A Whig government would rush to make peace. That would not only starve the remaining Allies of gold but transfer the priceless moral ascendency to Napoleon. Without English gold, the Allies would be hard pressed to stay in the field. The Emperor could have peace if he were not too greedy and overplayed his hand. That had been his mistake in the 1813 campaign when he could have had peace but decided that fortune would continue to favour him. She had abandoned him, weary of his hubris. His exile had taught him much.

Before catching what sleep he could, Soult summoned Reille and d'Erlon to brief them on the summary of the Battle of Ligny from Berthier and on the Emperor's order and the part they would play early the next morning. 'Remember, *messieurs*, how adept Wellington was in Spain and Portugal at not fighting at disadvantage. The Emperor's victory at Ligny has created such disadvantage. Wellington will slip away rather than accept battle under such circumstances. We must prevent that at all costs.'

3:00 a.m. – Wellington's Headquarters, Mont St Jean

Wellington's aide woke him to tell him a Prussian officer had arrived with a dispatch. One look at Maj. Massow and Wellington prepared himself for bad news. It was worse than he expected. He ordered his senior staff awakened, and when they stumbled in, still shaking the sleep off, he stunned them with the news of the Prussian defeat, that Blücher was missing, and their army was retreating to Wavre. Worse, Gneisenau was not able at this time to guarantee that the Prussians would be able to come to their aid. He did not relate to his staff the bitter undercurrent of Gneisenau's dispatch complaining that he had heard nothing from the British commander and that the Prussians had had to face Napoleon alone.[2]

Wellington knew he needed a Prussian corps to be able to risk a battle with Napoleon, especially since the Netherlands divisions had been so badly cut up. Gneisenau had left hanging in the air whether that corps would be forthcoming. Upon that would hang the Duke's decision on what course to take. But prudence required he plan for either contingency. He must take care of this army; it was England's primary field force. His staff quickly dispersed to begin working on preparing plans for a retreat. The Duke knew full well that such a retreat would require the abandonment of Brussels. That did not bother him; after all, he had abandoned Madrid to save his army and would not hesitate to do it again. Without the Prussians, he simply would not have the force to fight and defeat Napoleon. That retreat must of necessity end with an evacuation of his army, leaving Britain's Dutch ally in the lurch. If it came to saving his army or defending the Kingdom of the Netherlands, it was no choice at all. No doubt, William would be on one of the ships to England or galloping east to join his Prussian cousins. That was the essence of what he told Massow. He told him he would stand at Mont St Jean: '[Here] I will wait for Napoleon and give him battle, if I may hope to be supported even by a single Prussian corps. But if this support is denied me, I shall be compelled to sacrifice Brussels and take up my position behind the Scheldt.'[3]

Fulfilling the adage that it does not rain but it pours, a courier galloped in with a dispatch from Gen. Hill, commanding most of II Corps at Hal. A large French force, the Lille garrison and the National Guard force, had crossed the border and was moving in the direction of Ostend or Ghent. Hill was moving directly to intercept it.

Wellington's dilemma was now acute. Now he had to depend on two contingencies. The first was whether Gneisenau would be able to send a corps to reinforce his army; the second was whether Hill would succeed in defeating the French and keeping communications with Ostend secure. For a man of Wellington's prudence, it was one risk too many. That prudence, the ability to weigh risk against gain, and the ever-present knowledge that Britain had only that one army, was what had led to his success in the Peninsula. He had never once had Napoleon's belief in his lucky star. The logic of the situation was as clear as it was stark. He must avoid battle and march to Ostend to evacuate his army. He would have to move quickly. Soult would surely be back and Napoleon not far behind.

3:30 a.m. – Wellington's Headquarters, Mont St Jean

Like Davout's men at Ligny half an hour before, the soldiers of the French I and II Corps were kicked awake by their sergeants and corporals; they pissed, and wolfed down some cold rations. At 4:00, Lefol's lead regiment was on the road to La Belle Alliance. At the same time, British and Dutch sergeant and corporals began rousing their men awake in the eternal way of non-commissioned officers. Rebecque burst into Wellington's headquarters to demand an explanation. He did not like what he heard. The army would withdraw north and abandon Brussels. Rebecque burst out, 'His Majesty made you commander of his forces to defend his kingdom, not give it back to the French!'

'General, the defeat of the Prussians and the rough handling of the two Netherlands divisions makes it impossible to offer battle here.'

'You have never failed to beat the French before.'

'That was when I could be assured of fighting at advantage. There is none to be found here. Now, sir, see that your corps is prepared to march.'

Rebecque stormed out into the early morning darkness. He paused to consider the implications of the Duke's decision. A withdrawal would be a gift to the pro-French element among the Netherlands troops. Yet, he could not fault the Duke's logic. He had served as the Prince of Orange's aide in the Peninsular War and knew that Wellington's success was due to only fighting when the odds were on his side and that he had never carelessly risked Britain's army. All the same, it did not bode well for the Kingdom of the Netherlands.[4]

4:30 a.m. – On the Road to Wavre

'*Die Franzosen! Davout kommt!*' The cry echoed through the ranks of the trudging Prussian columns as the French cavalry fell on them. Already disorganized from

1. Napoleon escapes from Elba.

2. Napoleon reviews the Old Guard at the great parade.

3. The Red Lancers of the Imperial Guard.

4. The army renews its oath to Napoleon after his return to the throne, painting by David.

5. Marshal Jean-de-Dieu Soult was Napoleon's first choice as chief of staff until Berthier's return made him available for a field command.

6. Marshal Adolphe Edouard Mortier, Duke of Treviso, commanded the Guard in the 1815 campaign.

7. Marshal Emmanuel Grouchy was entrusted with command of the French cavalry for the campaign.

8. Marshal Louis Davout was Napoleon's finest commander, yet he chose him to be Minister of War, until unexpected events brought him to the field.

(from top, left to right) 9. General Jean-Baptiste Drouet, Comte d'Erlon, commanded the French I Corps at Mont St Jean.
10. General Dominique Rene, Comte Vandamme, commanded the French III Corps.
11. Prince Jérôme Bonaparte, the Emperor's inept brother, was given the largest division in the army to command.
12. Marshal Louis Alexandre Berthier, Prince of Neuchâtel and Wagram, returned in time to operate the French general staff in the campaign of 1815.
13. General Étienne-Maurice Gérard commanded the French IV Corps at Ligny and Mont St Jean, portrait by David, 1808.

(from top, left to right) 14. The Duke of Wellington.
15. Lieutenant General Henry William Paget, first Marquess of Anglesey and second Earl of Uxbridge, commanded the British cavalry at Waterloo.
16. Lieutenant General Sir Thomas Picton.
17. Richard Hussey Vivian, first Baron Vivian.

18. John Cameron, commander of the 92nd Foot at Waterloo.

19. William, Prince of Orange, commander of the Anglo-Allied I Corps.

20. General David Hendrik Chassé, 'General Bayonet', portrait by Jan Willem Pieneman.

21. Field Marshal Prince Gebhardt von Blücher commanded the Prussian army in Belgium.

22. General Count Neidhardt von Gneisenau, Blücher's brilliant chief of staff.

23. Hans Ernst von Zieten commanded I Corps at Ligny.

24. The Prussian attack at Ligny.

25. Gneisenau covering the retreat at Ligny.

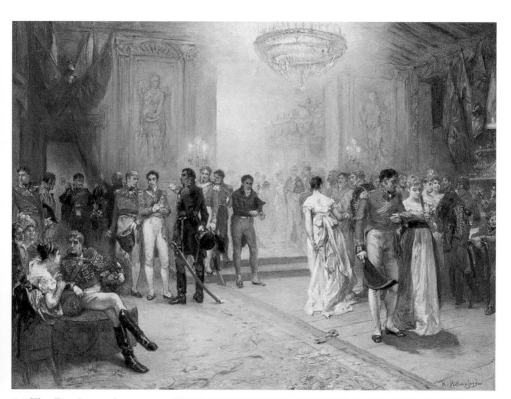

26. The Duchess of
Richmond's Ball, painted
by Robert Alexander
Hillingford.

27. A Prussian general
at Waterloo, painted
by R. Caton Woodville
(1856–1927).

28. A sub-lieutenant breaks through the courtyard gate at Hougoumont.

29. The French counterattack at Hougoumont.

30. The Scots Guards counterattack at Braine l'Alleud, painted by Lady Elizabeth Butler.

31. *Vive L'Empereur!* The attack of French hussars at Braine l'Alleud, by Edouard Detaille, 1891.

32. Sergeant Charles Ewart capturing the eagle of the French 100th Regiment of the Line at the Battle of Waterloo.

33. French soldiers presenting captured colours to Napoleon at his headquarters on Ronsomme Hill.

34. Early use of a French balloon in 1795. The French Aeronautic Corps was quickly re-established and employed at Mont St Jean.

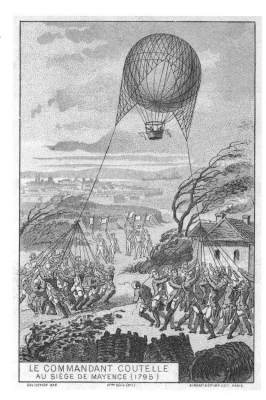

LE COMMANDANT COUTELLE
AU SIÈGE DE MAYENCE (1795)

35. 'To the last bullet' – the defence of La Haye Sainte.

36. The loss of a British colour in the collapse of Wellington's left flank, painting by Victor Huen.

37. Napoleon's forward headquarters at the inn at La Belle Alliance.

38. A general leading
the charge against
Wellington's right at
Waterloo.

39. Charge of the Red
Lancers of the Guard
through the gap in the
British line.

40. The final cavalry attack at Mont St Jean.

41. Napoleon
before the
storm of
Mont St Jean.

their retreat, their fears magnified by the dark, the force now shattered. Here and there a tough regular battalion stood firm, but around them the rest fled, were run down, or herded north by Pajol's cavalrymen. Davout was up close in the pursuit. He knew how to drive Prussians, and he would not let up.

6:00 a.m. – Fleurus

Napoleon was in a fine mood when he awoke. He could afford to be, with victories at Ligny and Quatre Bras, and Soult should be pinning Wellington to a position at Mont St Jean. Berthier had worked through the night making sure the army was assembling at Marbais, five miles from Quatre Bras. He had more good news for the Emperor. Davout had dispatched that thousands of prisoners had been taken as his two cavalry corps drove the disintegrating Prussians northwards. As the Emperor dressed, Berthier briefed him on the situation and showed him the most important of the dispatches.

'The situation could not be better. But my only worry is that Wellington will give Soult the slip. How many times did he do just that in the Peninsula? Eh? Soult has to keep him there long enough for me to arrive with the rest of the army and Davout to finish off the Prussians and put himself across the Duke's rear. Then, we shall crush England's field army, something my marshals never seemed to be able to do.'

'Sire, with luck all this will happen, but are we not making too many demands on fortune?'

Napoleon paused. His greatest fear, which he had never communicated to any-one, was that fortune, his star, had abandoned him. He had never felt so utterly ber-eft of the confidence in his fortune as when he had taken poison at Fontainebleau just before his abdication the year before. His triumphant return from Elba and now his stunning victory at Ligny has restored his faith in his star. He felt suffused with confidence now. That had a physical component. He was more fit than he had been in almost ten years. His uniforms had had to be taken in. His veterans noted that he seemed like the man of Austerlitz, slimmed-down and all nervous energy. That word has spread through the army, adding to its confidence in him.

Elba had been good for more than his physical fitness. He had had time for reflection on those around him. He said to Berthier. 'You know, my friend, I had thought my star had turned her back on me.' The marshal looked up startled at this admission. He had all too often felt the sharp edge of Napoleon's tongue and his tantrums. 'I do believe she is back. And how do I know that? She sent you back to me. What would I do without you, Berthier?'

The chief of staff was dumbstruck. He mumbled something about how it was due to Monthion that he had a proper staff, that it was largely due to Monthion's painstaking work that the army had been moved to Charleroi, and that he would have been just as well served by him. Napoleon knew that Berthier was about used up. He was running on sheer loyalty. This would be his last campaign. 'Have no fear, my friend, I will take care of Monthion. There are others that are also in need of reward.'5

By 7:00 he was at Marbais where his corps commanders, Vandamme and Gérard, as well as Mortier and Grouchy, were assembled. He rode up with Berthier at his side. Behind them was Monthion, who was confused why he had been summoned when he had so much work to do with the staff.

The assembled officers swept off their hats at his approach. 'Gentlemen, I congratulate you on our splendid victory of yesterday. You will be pleased to hear that Davout is running down the Prussians on the way to Wavre, a task of which he had had some practice.' The laughter was genuine. It was a byword in the army that the Prussians were more scared of Davout than the devil.

'Now, where, gentlemen, is the Count of Ligny?' He noted the looks of surprise. 'Gérard, why do you not respond when I call you by your title?' It dawned on everyone that Napoleon had advanced him from baron to count. 'What must I do to get you to respond, Marshal Gérard?' A marshal's baton, as well! Suddenly, Gérard was all profuse thanks. Napoleon laughed. 'Ah, I am glad I let you keep your head. How could you have thanked me if I had taken you up on your pledge?'

Then he turned to Vandamme, whose expression flickered between expectation and anger at not being rewarded as well. 'Vandamme, you scoundrel, if I had two of you, one would have to hang the other. But as I don't I must make you a marshal as well.'

All Vandamme could say was, 'About time!' The entire group, Napoleon not least of all, burst out laughing at Vandamme's rough tongue, another byword in the army. But there was method in his generosity. He knew men. The two new marshals would now compete to justify their batons.

Napoleon then asked loudly, 'Where is General Monthion?'

Now it was Monthion's turn to be surprised. He rode up. 'Sire? He said.

'There you are, general.' His eyes swept over the group. 'It has come to my attention that one of the Prussians who have copied our staff system has said that a good staff officer must be more than he seems.' He extended his hand in a sweep towards the general. 'Voilà, Monthion. Gentlemen, victory is a beautiful red flower, and you here gathered them for me yesterday. But the work of the staff is the stem without which the flower could never have bloomed. Also, remember, that without a staff, an army could not even peel a potato. Berthier has given me ample proof that it was the work of Monthion, the precise movement orders and faultless communications, that have ensured you were able to pick that bouquet. So, Monthion, I ennoble you Count of Charleroi for ensuring that they concentrated exactly as I wanted at that place, and I promote you marshal. Let us hope that d'Erlon and Reille earn their batons before this affair is over.'[6]

7:00 a.m. – La Belle Alliance

At that moment d'Erlon and Reille were trying to do just that. Reille's 2nd Cavalry Division chased the last of the enemy screening forces back behind the ridge just as the first of Wellington's divisions was about to march off to the west to cross the Scheldt and fall back on his evacuation port of Ostend. Most of the rest of the army was sorting itself out for the march. The guns had been withdrawn from the ridge and were concentrating with their teams, caissons, and limbers to begin the march. The garrisons had been withdrawn from Hougoumont and La Haye Sainte. Already, some of the cavalry had been sent ahead to screen the march. Wellington had planned a withdrawal, a retirement not in contact with the enemy. The sudden arrival of Soult's columns would make that a retreat, a retirement in contact with the enemy, one of the most arduous and difficult of all military manoeuvres.

Reille's corps was in the lead again with Soult riding in the front with the corps commander. Cavalry scouts reported to them that the enemy cavalry screen was falling back in stages. They had followed closely and seen the enemy leaving the two walled manors and that the guns were being pulled off the ridge. 'Our rabbit is about to bolt, Reille,' said Soult. 'At all costs we must keep him here until the Emperor arrives. The key is the same as yesterday. Take Braine l'Alleud so we can threaten his retreat on Brussels. Now hurry!'

Riding first in column just behind him was Jérôme's 6th Division. 'Come with me, Your Highness!' said Reille. The two and the division chief of staff with a cavalry escort galloped ahead until they came to La Belle Alliance, right under Wellington's nose. Pointing north-west to Braine l'Alleud, he said, 'You must take that town. That will make it a bone in the throat of Wellington's retreat. He will do everything he can to drive you out, but you must hold on until the Emperor arrives later today.' He noted the Prince's enthusiasm. He did not have to point out the opportunity for glory and his brother's praise. Just as they were turning their horses around, Reille said, 'Oh, yes, one more thing. See that walled manor?' He pointed at Hougoumont. Take that as well.'

7:00 a.m. – Wellington's Headquarters, Mont St Jean

Wellington had been tardily warned by his retiring cavalry of the French approach, confirming his opinion of the cavalry's all too careless attention to its duties. He rode up to the ridge to watch the French cavalry clatter up the road and veer towards his right. They obviously knew their business. A small party with escort stopped at La Belle Alliance. He muttered to himself, 'Soult, no doubt. Damn the man. He has caught me over a barrel.' Ruefully he considered that he had taught the Frenchman too well in Spain.

It was then that an aide put down his glass and pointed out the French infantry columns marching up the Brussels road. The Duke realized that Soult was again aiming to sever his communications as he had the day before. That would be bad enough if his army was in position. But his army had just quit their positions and was forming up for movement behind the ridge. If he took Braine l'Alleud, the direct road to Ostend would be blocked. At the same time, that position would allow Soult to threaten a retreat north up the Brussels road. The town was held by the remnants of the 3rd Netherlands Division. He spurred his way there immediately. An aide galloped back down the ridge to the nearest cavalry formation, the 3rd Hussars KGL Cavalry, commanded by Lt. Col. Meyer. 'Sir, the Duke orders you to drive off the French cavalry threatening our right.' Meyer immediately ordered his 700 hussars forward. The Duke himself rode up to the British 4th Brigade, commanded by Lt. Col. Hugh Mitchell, that had just returned to its position on the right of the ridge. 'Mitchell,' he said to its commander, 'you will support the Dutch and hold that town. Drive out the French if they beat you there.'

The French cavalry did get there first. The chasseurs charged through the streets, panicking the Dutch and Belgian troops already demoralized by their drubbing at Quatre Bras and now full of beer from the local brewery. Hundreds surrendered as the rest fled out of the back. The French lancer brigade followed, clearly intending to block any reinforcement. The Duke rode at the head of the 2,000 men of the 4th Brigade as it descended the ridge, but he returned to the ridge. The KGL hussars swept by to guard the brigade's flank and charge the lancers. The French lancers accepted the challenge; their commander, the much-wounded General Baron François-Isidore Wathiez, ordered the charge. The trumpets blew, and 800 lancers moved forward.

8:00 a.m. – The Ridge of Mont St Jean

Wellington's chosen line of defence was the Mont St Jean ridge, some 700 yards south of the eponymous farm. Rising gently 300 feet in places from the low ground to its front, it ran south-west to north-east, bisecting the paved Brussels–Charleroi road extending 1,500 yards on either side. Along the crest of the ridge ran the Braine l'Alleud–Ohain sunken road lined with hedges.

Wellington deftly redeployed his forces along the ridge. He placed a British division on either side of the Brussels–Genappe road. Picton's 5th British Infantry Division of 6,700 men in three brigades filled out to the east of the road – Kempt's

8th British Brigade, Pack's 9th British Brigade, and Vincke's 5th Hanoverian Brigade, still shaken from its rough handling of the day before. Best's 4th Hanoverian Brigade was posted between Pack and Vincke and was intended upon the arrival of Lambert's brigade to be part of the 6th British Infantry Division. The remnants of Perponcher's 2nd Netherland's Division, amounting to barely 2,600 men from various units, was a frail reserve for Picton. In any case, the Duke was more worried about his centre and right and the threat to the Brussels road than he was to his left.

After wolfing down breakfast, the army's gunners began hacking holes through the hedges to create embrasures for their guns. The Duke strictly ordered that the artillery was not to engage in counter-battery fire. The mission of the guns was to defend the ridge against French infantry attacks. Counter-battery fire would only attract the lethally accurate fire of the French artillery's heavier guns. That would incur unnecessary losses at the very time the Allied line needed the maximum defensive power of its guns. It would also diminish a British advantage in gunnery, shrapnel, or caseshot.

Of Picton's nine British battalions, four were Scots and of these three were Highlanders. The Highlanders were generally small, sturdy, and muscular men of remarkable endurance with a rock-like obstinacy in defence and a Celtic fury in the attack. Their regiments accepted English, Irish, and Welsh volunteers who soon adopted the Highlanders spirit. An exception was the 92nd Foot (Gordon Highlanders) in Pack's brigade, who 'were nearly entirely Scottish, predominately from Aberdeenshire and Invernesshire, and Gaelic was often spoken instead of English. By Waterloo these seasoned veterans were growing long in the tooth – the average age in Number 1 Company for example was 36.[7]

Of the Scots regiments, the 79th Foot (Cameron Highlanders) were assigned to Kempt's brigade. The 1st Foot (Royal Scots), the oldest regiment in the British army, the Highland 42nd Foot (Black Watch), and the 92nd Foot (Gordon Highlanders) made Pack's brigade almost entirely Scottish, save for the English 2/44th Foot.

To prevent the French from turning his left, the Duke had directed two of Best's four Hanoverian battalions to occupy the walled farms of Papelotte and La Haye and the hamlet of Frichermont, south-east of the ridge. Maj. Gen. Baron Charles de Ghigny's Netherlands brigade of light dragoons and hussars (Netherlands Cavalry Division) was transferred to support these battalions.

Alten's 3rd British Infantry Division of 8,000 men was posted on the right or west of the Brussels–Charleroi road. On Alten's right flank Cooke's 4,200 men of the Guards Division took position. On Cooke's right Clinton's division of almost 8,000 men filled in, hooking to the north. The Brunswick Contingent covered the flank across from Braine l'Alleud after Mitchell's brigade was sent to Braine l'Alleud. The remnants of Chassé's division had occupied Braine l'Alleud, which the Duke considered a quiet post for unreliable troops. Kruse's brigade of the Nassau Contingent reinforced Alten.

The Duke kept his cavalry in reserve. Behind Picton Wellington positioned three British cavalry brigades – the dragoons of Maj. Gen. Sir William Ponsonby's 2nd (Union), the light dragoons of Maj. Gen. Sir John Vandeleur's 4th Brigade, and the hussars of Maj. Gen. Sir Hussey Vivian's 6th Brigade. Somerset's Household Cavalry Brigade took position in support of Alten. Dörnberg's 3rd Cavalry Brigade and Arenschildt's small 7th British Cavalry Brigade supported Cooke and Clinton. Two brigades of the Netherlands Cavalry Division occupied the space between the village of Mont St Jean and the eponymous farm 400 yards to the south.

All three battalions of the 95th Rifles were on the field but numbered just under 1,300 men. The 1st and 2nd Battalions had only six companies rather than the normal establishment of ten. The 3/95th had only two companies. The 1/95th was attached to Kempt's brigade and the eight companies of the other two battalions were assigned to Adams' brigade (Clinton's division).

Seen from the south hardly a man of this host was visible save gunners along the sunken road, just as Wellington intended. Napoleon had never been confronted with an enemy he could not see.

8:30 a.m. – Quatre Bras

The courier from Soult found Napoleon just after he arrived at Quatre Bras at the head of the Guard. He could already hear the report of the guns rolling south from Braine l'Alleud. He opened the dispatch quickly. He smiled as he read it. He turned to Berthier. 'Soult has nailed Wellington to Mont St Jean. I would have thought he would be scurrying north by now. All the better. My brother's division is locked in battle for the key to Wellington's retreat, Braine l'Alleud. The rest of Reille's corps is in support of the Prince. D'Erlon's corps is threatening the enemy's other flank.' At that moment, another courier arrived along the Nivelles road. This time Napoleon positively beamed when he read it. 'Ah, perfect! The National Guard force and the garrison of Lille have interposed themselves across Wellington's communications with Ostend and are skirmishing with a British force at Hal.' He looked back at the glittering body of generals and aides and behind them the bayonets and bearskins of the Guard that filled the road into the distance. 'Gentlemen, let us make haste, or Soult will win the battle without us!'

Monthion had worked out the march organization to bring as much of the army to the battle as soon as possible. Since the Guard and cavalry filled the roads, Vandamme's and Gérard's corps were allowed several hours more sleep after their hard fighting of the day before. Between his map analysis and the aides he sent to explore the roads, he found a parallel route for Grouchy's cavalry corps to reach the battlefield quickly from Marbais. He had even found a place at the end of the main column for Coutelle and his balloon.

8:30 a.m. – Mont St Guibert

The Prussian rearguard tried to make a stand at this small town nine miles north of Sombreffe. Thielmann's III Corps was a shadow of its strength of the day before and was running out of ammunition. Its cavalry brigade had been shattered at Ligny, and the remnants had not rejoined the corps. Gneisenau had ordered Thielmann to hold the town and the road through it to Wavre until the rest of the army could sort itself out at the latter town. What cavalry he could find he left to support Thielmann. The Prussians had little time to prepare for defence. They had not eaten, and their ranks had been badly thinned by the fighting and the confusion of the retreat. Unlike I and II Corps, however, its Prussian Landwehr from the old Prussian province of Kurmark had largely stayed with their colours.

Unluckily for them, Davout knew how to press hard on the heels of a rout. His men were tired, but they were propelled forward by the intoxicant of victory while the Prussians were numbed by defeat. He was thankful that the Emperor had given him plenty of cavalry – the hussars, lancers, and dragoons of Pajol's and Exelmans' cavalry corps. To them was added the 7th Cavalry Division of Gérard's corps – over 6,000 horsemen in all. The last thing he intended to do was let himself be involved in the ruinous fighting for the town. Thielmann watched in dismay from a bell tower as the great mass of French cavalry bypassed the town and cut the road to his rear and kept on going. Around his other flank, dense columns of French troops also moved to bypass the town. He could do nothing to interfere with either column. The Saxons were attacking the town and his units on either flank. He turned to his chief of staff, Col. Carl von Clausewitz, and ordered him to prepare for a breakout to the east. He was fortunate to have such a capable staff officer, one of the group of brilliant reformers, including Gneisenau, who were transforming the Prussian army. The problem was that the Prussian army had to survive in order to be transformed.

9:00 a.m. – Braine l'Alleud

The crash of the French lancers and KGL cavalry had given Mitchell's brigade time to enter the town and drive out the French chasseurs with 23rd Foot and 1/51st Light Infantry. Mitchell left the 3/14th Foot (Buckinghamshire Regiment) in the field to support the KGL. The Bucks was one of the last battalions formed before the Peace of Amiens in 1803; it was scheduled to be disbanded and was only saved by Napoleon's return from Elba. The regiment had been recruited largely from militiamen, many of whom were underage. The battalion commander was about as experienced an officer to be found in the British army at that time. He was described by Ensign George Keppell: 'In my commanding officer, Major Francis Skelly Tidy, I found a good-looking man, above the middle height, of soldier-like appearance, of a spare but athletic figure, of elastic step, and of frank, cheerful, and agreeable manners.' Tidy was also inordinately proud of his battalion and ensured it avoided garrison duty after arriving in Belgium.

Tidy formed his battalion in square as the French lancers overcame the KGL hussars. The French lance was a deadly surprise to them. At the same time the French horse artillery, unable to influence the cavalry battle, turned its fire on the square. 'A bugler of the 51st, mistaking the square for his own, exclaimed, "Here I am again, safe enough!" The words were barely out of his mouth, when a round shot took off his head and spattered the whole battalion with his brains, the colours and the ensigns in charge of them coming in for an extra share.' More men were carried away by shot until Tidy ordered his men to lie down. Keppell himself was sitting on a drum, patting the nose of Tidy's horse, which was nuzzling his shoulder when,

> Suddenly my drum capsized and I was thrown prostrate, with the feeling of a blow on the right cheek. I put my hand to my head, thinking half my face was shot away, but the skin was not even abraded. A piece of shell had struck the horse on the nose exactly between my hand and my head, and killed him instantly. The blow I received was from the embossed crown on the horse's bit.[8]

Another shell blew up the battalion ammunition wagon, horribly maiming the horses. It was then that the beaten KGL hussars fled past and through the battalion, trampling many men underfoot. The French were among them, stabbing with their lances. Tidy shot one lancer out of his saddle as another one stabbed at his shoulder. The blow was mistimed and merely tore off his epaulette and scraped his shoulder. Keppell scrambled under one French horseman as another chased him. The only thing that saved the rest of the battalion was that the lancers chased after the KGL. As they galloped off, one of them was wounded and fell from his saddle. A comrade returned and offered an empty stirrup to the man. A light infantryman named Whitney took aim to shoot the lancer when Colour Sergeant Samuel Goddard said, 'No Whitney, don't fire, let him off, he is a noble fellow.' Tidy then hurried his survivors into the town, where Mitchell had skilfully positioned his other two battalions.[9]

The Bucks were just in time to see the French blue columns deploying for an attack on the town. Their skirmishers were driving the British in. Mitchell was a fine craftsman of war. He had fought in the Peninsula and southern France. As reliable were his other two battalions, 1/23rd (Royal Welch Fusiliers) Foot and

1/51st (2nd Yorkshire West Riding) Light Infantry, among Wellington's treasured veterans. If the 3/14th was almost the newest battalion in the British army, the 1/23rd was one of the oldest. Now they were about to be attacked by the oldest regiments in the French army – the 4,000 men of the 1st and 2nd of the Line in the 1st Brigade of Prince Jérôme's division.

9:00 a.m. – Hougoumont

The Prince would have thrown the whole of his division at Braine l'Alleud had not Count Guilleminot reminded him also to take the walled manor as Soult had directed. Jérôme offhandedly said, 'As you wish. Send the 1st Light.'

Both Wellington and Soult had recognized that the chateau and farm complex and its large walled English garden formed a perfect *point d'appui* (fulcrum) that would disrupt any attack on the Allied position. In French hands it would facilitate an attack on Wellington's right to cut off his line of communications along the Brussels road.

Hougoumont was an estate whose grounds measured 1,050 yards from north to south and 900 yards from west to east, almost all of which was enclosed by a substantial hedge. The walled chateau and farm buildings occupied the north-west corner and were separated by an interior gate into a northern and southern courtyard. The chateau building adjoined this interior gate and itself separated the two courtyards. There were also gates to the north and south of the chateau-farm. To the east of the southern gate was a walled garden. This complex measured 150 by 300 yards.

To the east of the chateau-farm buildings and walled garden was another much larger walled exquisite English garden open on the northern face. To the east of this was an apple orchard. Directly to the south of the chateau-farm and walled gardens was a wood 600 yards square. A hedge encircled the wood. To the east of the wood there was a field of grass and a field of tall rye also enclosed by hedges. To the east of the chateau-farm was a long hedge-enclosed vegetable garden. A road entered the grounds of the estate from its south-east corner diagonally through the rye field, woods, and between the chateau-farm enclosure and vegetable gardens to exit at the north-west corner of the estate.

The seizure of the walled fort-like chateau-farm, walled gardens, hedges, and woods would defy any quick military solution while soaking up large numbers of troops in the most vicious form of close fighting. It was just such a place the ancient Greek general Epaminondas would have called 'the dancing floor of war'.

So it was that both the French and British converged on Hougoumont at the same time for the dance of death. Sub-Lt. Legros, axe in hand, led his men through the southern gate of the chateau-farm followed by the rest of the regiment's 1st Battalion. Beside him rode the regimental commander, Col. Amédée Louis de Despans-Cubières.

Wellington had not forgotten the value of the complex and dispatched 2nd Guards Brigade's elite light companies, one each from the 2nd Battalion of the Coldstream Guards, 2nd Battalion of the 3rd Scots Guard, and the 1st Guards. They were led by Lt. Col. James Macdonell, second-in-command of the Coldstream battalion.

The men of the Coldstream's light company entered the north gate as the French entered the south. The two light companies of the 1st Guards came down the path between the chateau-farm and the vegetable garden. The two companies of the 3rd Guards followed the men of the Coldstream. At the same time the regulars of the Hanoverian Duke of York's Field Battalion in their green coats and grey trousers entered the English garden and the apple orchard just as the French 2nd Battalion of the 1st Light poured through the gate in the grass field south of the orchard. More French found a gap in the hedge in the south-west corner of the orchard.

Legros was the first through the open gate into the northern courtyard with his men crowding behind him. They came face to face with the redcoats of the Coldstream Guards coming pouring into the courtyard through the northern gate. With a shout Legros attacked. Like a Homeric hero seeking out another champion, he flew at Ensign Henry 'Vigorous' Gooch commanding the British and felled him with a vicious swing. Three guardsmen flew at Legros to avenge their comrade, but the Frenchman fought them off until his own men shouldered past to drive the English back. The courtyard was now a melee of stabbing bayonets, smashing butt strokes, and clubbed muskets as the best of French and British spilled each other's blood. Mcdonnell saw that after the first French companies through the gate, there would be only a moment before the rest streamed in. He rushed forward and put his shoulder to the gate and pushed the left half shut. Guardsman James Graham ran up to slam the second leaf when a Frenchman barged through and bayoneted him. It was too late. The next French company was pouring through. Mcdonnell fought his way back to the door of the chateau but was beaten down and killed.

Now heavily outnumbered with half their men down, the Guards retreated into the cow barn just east of the north corner of the courtyard, barred the door, and went to the windows to fire down at the French filling the courtyard. The French found a stout bench to use as battering ram on the barn's large double doors. One after another were shot down until Legros attacked it with his axe, sending chunks of wood flying. Other Frenchmen were concentrating their fire on the windows, killing the Guards or driving them back. At last the doors splintered open. The Guards were waiting. A volley brought down Legros and the first men through the doors. Col. Despans-Cubières was shot off his horse from a window at the same time. The French recoiled.

The struggle for the courtyard had reached that moment in battle when both sides hang back exhausted from their effort. It is a pause before that decisive single drop on the scales. Lt. Col. Charles Dashwood of the 3rd Scots Guards had followed Mcdonnell's men down the ridge and seen them disappear into the chateau-farm, heard the shriek of battle, then heard it taper off as a few wounded guardsmen staggered out, followed by a handful Frenchmen in pursuit. At a run, he led the light company of the Scots Guards through the northern gate to flood into the courtyard littered with bodies in blue and red. Now it was the turn of the French to be driven back through the gate. Many took refuge in the great barn on the western side of the courtyard and the chateau to fire down into the mass of guardsmen filling the courtyard. The only Frenchman left in the courtyard was a drummer boy standing over Legros. An Englishman grabbed him and threw him into a shed to save his life.

The Scots Guards tried to close the double interior gates, but they were jammed open by bodies. The French 3rd Battalion now attacked the gate. Instead of stout wooden doors it was the guardsmen shoulder to shoulder with lowered bayonets who now barred the opening.

The fight in the orchard was just as deadly. The three companies of Hanoverian regulars were tough and would not yield the orchard easily but French numbers overwhelmed them one at a time. The survivors retreated out of the apple trees and into the English garden from the unwalled northern portion to join the rest of the battalion. The Hanoverians inside the garden did not know they were trapped. The six-foot wall was too tall to fire over. Had they had the time, which they did not, they could have put loopholes in the walls. Now they were desperately trying to find anything to put up against the wall to act as a parapet, but aside from a few benches, there was precious little to accord more than a dozen men a firing position.

It was only a matter of time before the French 2nd Battalion found its way out of the orchard and into the garden. Now the Hanoverian men were trapped. A few tried to flee through the gate into the southern courtyard, but it was filled by French troops hammering at the Scots Guards. The walled garden proved a trap. Pressed by the French troops attacking from the north, up against the stone wall, and their commander wounded, the 500 survivors suddenly surrendered.

9:00 a.m. – La Haye Sainte

Soult's focus on Wellington's right made him overlook the importance of the walled farm of La Haye Sainte lying directly along the west side of the Brussels road just south of the centre of the ridge and the centre of Wellington's defence. It gave the Duke time to return the garrison that had occupied it the day before – the 400 men of the rifle-armed 2nd Light Battalion, KGL, commanded by Maj. George Baring. They were uniformed in dark green with black facings like the British 95th Rifles and equally experienced in the battles of the Peninsula.

The walled farm measured about 90 yards by 140 yards. Directly to the south was a large orchard bound by banked and ditched hedges. To the north of the farm there was a large kitchen garden, walled on the road side with the other three sides bounded by a hedge. Just below the kitchen garden on its eastern side and on the opposite side of the road was a large sandpit, ideal for the defence. Two companies of the 1/95th Rifles had been posted there. The KGL riflemen were spread thinly, with one man per two yards of the defended perimeter. No special extra ammunition was provided to resupply the men after their sixty-round basic load for the Baker rifle was expended. Baring immediately set his men to prepare loopholes through the walls and firing positions in the hedges.

9:00 a.m. – Quatre Bras

The corpses of Netherlands soldiers scattered north and south of the town was the first sign of war that Col. Coutelle and his *aérostiers* had come across. A few French ambulances were picking up the wounded of both sides. They came across a few stragglers moving north and couriers galloping south to Ligny.

Coutelle looked protectively at the wagon that held *Marengo* and the following one that held the bulky hot-air-generating equipment. He made sure the dozen soldiers assigned as an escort were alert. Their sergeant was a tough old veteran who kept them on their toes. No iron was allowed anywhere near that device nor in the making of the balloon and its wicker *basketùone* (basket), which would hold two men. One of them, of course, would be Coutelle. The other was an experienced engineer officer, too crippled for field service but capable of interpreting what was happening into the depth of the enemy's position. In good weather with a glass, Coutelle claimed rightly that he could see over ten miles.

The little convoy left the village on the Brussels road. The dead Dutch lay thick where they had been smashed. It was here that the courier from Monthion found them. Coutelle was able to scribble out a quick note that he was on schedule.

He wrote too soon.

He was handing the courier his note when the sound of thundering hooves drew his attention to the right. Lt. Van Doorn could not believe his good fortune when he spotted the little convoy leaving the village. His Dutch cavalry detachment had been concealed in a grove. They had been scouting the French border when Soult's corps had come storming up the Brussels road. They followed the direction of their cavalry division only to find evidence of the disaster that had overcome their side at Quatre Bras. Van Doorn realized the armies had moved north and hid his men while he decided what to do. Coutelle's little convoy answered that for him. He charged.

Coutelle saw the enemy attacking down the road. The courier drew his sword only to fly from his horse, shot by the officer leading the attack. Coutelle drew his own sword. The engineer major fumbled to draw his with his ruined arm, but a Dutch sabre came down on his neck. Van Doorn sought out Coutelle by his uniform as a French colonel and beat down his guard. His final blow shattered the guard on Coutelle's sword and severed two fingers. The French sergeant rallied his men. He shot Van Doorn in the back as his men fired from behind the wagon, emptying a few more saddles. With their officer down, the surviving Dutch turned tail.

10:30 a.m. – Braine l'Alleud

Soult and Reille from the inn at La Belle Alliance had been watching the fighting at Hougoumont intently. Soult had hoped that the Prince would have been fast enough off the mark to seize the chateau-farm before Wellington remembered its importance. Ah, well. Foy, whose 9th Division was moving into the rear of Hougoumont, might now have to be thrown into the fight. Bachelu's 5th Division was arriving as well to fill in to the east of Hougoumont. On the positive side of the ledger, the Prince's efforts were ensuring just what the Emperor ordered – keep Wellington committed to defending this place.

The real test, though, would be if the Prince succeeded in taking Braine l'Alleud, which would threaten Wellington's ability to retreat in safety. The marshal and the general now saw the Prince's attack going in as the noise of gunfire rose to a crescendo. He turned to Reille, 'I think the Prince may be in need of adult supervision.' Reille laughed and rode off.

Jérôme's cloud of skirmishers drove into Mitchell's light companies covering the approaches to the town. Mitchell had fewer than 2,000 men while the Prince was bringing 6,000 to the fight. The movement of such a force was apparent to Wellington from his vantage on the ridge. He sent to the Duke of Brunswick to send his Light Brigade of almost 3,000 men under Lt. Col. Buttlar and the Brunswick field artillery battery of six guns to reinforce Mitchell. Known as the Black Duke for the black uniforms of his men with the distinctive silver death's head on their shakos, Buttlar decided to accompany the brigade. They would need a firm hand and the reassurance of seeing their duke share their danger. The average age of the Brunswick soldiers was 18, with many junior officers and sergeants of the same age. It was a new national army built in 1813 with officers and NCOs who had served with Wellington in the Peninsula as thinly spread cadres.

Gen. Baron Jean-Louis Soye sought the cover of the low ground to shield his 2nd Brigade in its approach to the west of Braine l'Alleud from British artillery on the ridge. He was happy that the Prince had stayed on the high ground above so as to 'better observe' the action. It was a big brigade, over 4,000 men of the 1st and 2nd of the Line.

The Prince from his vantage watched the attack. So far, Reille, who was at his side, approved of the Prince's actions. A crash of musketry and then clouds of black powder smoke drifted up from the outlying garden walls where the 1/51st Foot was positioned. The French division artillery now had targets and opened up with plunging fire. In the hollow behind them, the 2nd Light Regiment waited as the division reserve – 2,300 veteran soldiers restless to get into the fight.

10:30 a.m. – Hougoumont

Wellington's batteries, by now repositioned on the ridge, concentrated their fire on the French swarming around the chateau-farm. Soult had also directed the batteries of II Corps' 5th and 9th Divisions to support the 1st Light. He could see another Hanoverian battalion coming down the slope to join the fight. The expertly handled French guns cut great bloody gaps in them. To his chagrin, the Duke watched the battalion break back for the safety of the reverse slope of the ridge. Then the French gunners turned their pieces on the chateau and the farm buildings around the north courtyard. Guardsman Private Leonard would relate later that the very air 'seemed to have been changed into an ocean of fire, all of the farm buildings were aflame. The soil underneath my feet began to shake and tremble, and large fissures opened before my very eyes.'[10]

The cobbled courtyards were carpeted with bodies in blue and red. The Scots Guards, now reinforced by the two light companies of the 1st Guards, still held the gateway between the courtyards, its doors smashed and splintered. The gateway was instead closed by bodies piled waist-high. The whole roof of the chateau was on fire. Holes gaped in its walls where the French balls had shattered them. Here and there fire darted from the holes. The fire from the English inside slackened as they had a more deadly enemy to combat – fire.

Only eight guardsmen at a time could fire from the gateway. The French in the south courtyard had a front of twenty-five, and their fire kept sweeping away the English. Yet their bodies also lay in heaps from the fire from the windows of the chateau.

At last one of Foy's guns was dragged into the courtyard and pointed at the English in the gateway. '*Feu!*' shouted the gun sergeant. The canister filled with little balls burst as it exited the gun muzzle in a fiery corona. The English in the gateway simply disappeared. A second spray of balls followed into the courtyard. A captain shouted, '*En avant!*' and the French ran forward, climbing over the bodies of the guardsmen. They jumped down to find a butcher's yard. Others cleared away the bodies. The rest of the 3rd Battalion and the remnants of the 1st rushed in to engage the stunned guardsmen. Others broke into the chateau to fight floor to floor with the English.

The Duke's glass was fixed on the burning chateau. When he saw French colours go up over the north gate, he slammed the glass shut and spurred his horse over to the 2nd Guards Brigade. Riding up to Maj. Gen. Sir John Byng, whose light companies had already been consumed in the fighting, he pointed and said, 'Byng, we must keep that place. It is the hinge of the battle. Take and hold it.'[11]

10:30 a.m. – Army of the Rhine Headquarters, Wavre

Gneissenau waited until the last possible minute to make his decision. At 6:00 that morning the Prussian staff officer had returned with Wellington's decision to abandon the field and retreat across the Scheldt onto his communications. That would take the British to the west and away from the Prussians. He did not know that events had overtaken Wellington and that Soult had fixed him to the field where he would have to fight. A second staff officer sent to confirm Wellington's decision had never arrived. The man had fallen off his horse and broken his leg. At this time, Gneissenau sorely missed Müffling, who had never returned from his mission to Wellington the day before. The staff officer who had returned earlier informed him that according to the Duke, Müffling had never arrived.[12]

Even more pressing than Wellington's betrayal – for that is what the Prussian called it – was Davout's relentless approach towards Wavre. Thielmann's corps was supposed to have delayed him, but nothing more had been heard from him. French cavalry prevented any couriers from getting through. It was all the remaining Prussian cavalry could do to slow down the French. Bülow's corps would not get to Wavre before Davout. If he stayed to fight Davout, it would be only with Zieten and Pirch's badly weakened corps, both of which were too short of ammunition for another battle. Ammunition resupply from depots along the line of communications to the east had been ordered but could not arrive in time. The army's trains had simply disappeared. The logic of the situation was as clear as it was desperate. He ordered retreat.

10:30 a.m. – Camps of the French III and IV Corps

The survivors of the savage fighting at Ligny were still half-numb from their ordeal as they woke slowly late that morning. There were many empty places in the ranks of the III and IV Corps as they assembled on the road. Each corps' 12-pounder battery had already departed with Napoleon's main body much earlier. Vandamme and Gérard were everywhere pushing their sluggish regiments onto the road to Brussels. The Emperor's couriers again and again urged speed. The battle had been joined at Mount St Jean. For tired men it was only an abstraction.

That imperial command had less effect than the sudden shift in the atmospheric conditions that had silenced the noise of battle until then. In a moment, the roar of the guns washed over the ranks. Every head turned. Not a man spoke. Then backs straightened. Men stepped more quickly into their ranks. Suddenly, the cry went up, '*Vive le Empereur!*'

11:10 a.m. – Soult's Headquarters, La Belle Alliance

D'Erlon rode up with his staff to report to Soult. His divisions were arriving and being guided by staff officers to their positions to the right of II Corps. A few minutes later Grouchy arrived with his staff. The shortcut Monthion had identified for his cavalry corps had saved a good deal of time. The first of his cavalry corps could be seen to the east by the dust plume generated by thousands of horses on the hot, dry dirt roads. The attention of this glittering array of marshals, generals, and staff officers was drawn to the scarlet columns coming over the ridge and heading for Hougoumont. 'Ah, Grouchy, you are a lucky man. You are with us the first to see Wellington come out from behind his damned reverse slope. We must not disappoint him.' He sent a staff officer with the order to Foy to send a regiment to reinforce the played-out 1st Light. 'Now, it is we who will bleed you, *Anglais*.'

Foy sent his closest regiment, the 93rd of the Line, which had also fought at Trafalgar as marines. Byng's 2nd Guards Brigade had the jump on them. Byng was about as good a British general as the army had and had the confidence of the Duke.

> In 1811 he joined the Peninsular army, recommended to Wellington by the Duke of York, the commander-in-chief, as 'an intelligent and excellent officer'. From then until 1814 he commanded a brigade in the second division under Lord Hill and was present at most of the major engagements of those years. For his intrepid conduct at Bayonne, 18 Dec. 1813, he was permitted to bear the colours of the 31st Foot, which he had planted in the enemy lines, as 'an honourable augmentation to his arms'.[13]

Now he led from the front as his two battalions double-timed down the ridge heading for Hougoumont. Waiting for them was the remnants of the French 1st Light in a natural defensive position. The chateau-farm buildings had no outfacing windows to fire from, nor was there time to loophole their stone walls. Instead the French filed out of the north gate to line the hedge that ran across the north of the grounds. Directly in front of the hedge was a sunken lane and just on the other side was a line of trees. It was here that French skirmishers placed themselves.

Halfway down the ridge, the British battalions shook out into line two men deep, the Coldstream on the right, and the Scots Guards on the left. The French artillery quickly ploughed round shot through them. The British just closed their ranks and pressed on until they approached the trees, where the fire of the French skirmishers began dropping men. They closed ranks again and did not slacken their pace. At fifty paces Byng ordered a charge. At the sight of the charging Guards, the French skrirmishers turned and fled back across the sunken road to scramble up the other side and through the hedge.

As the Guards surged through the trees, they were met by a devastating close-range volley that struck down scores, pitching many of the bodies into the sunken lane. No assault across the lane was possible. It became a firepower fight across the lane at a brutal ten yards distance. The advantage was with the French, who could drop down behind the banked-up hedge to reload, and it was only a matter of time before the Guards would wilt away.

The right two companies of the Coldstream had overlapped the sunken lane and come up directly against the north gate of the chateau-farm. In the open gateway was a French gun with the gunner lowering his glowing match. One guardsman could not resist the moment to repeat the prayer spoken at Fontenoy in 1745 by another guardsman: 'For what we are about to receive, may we be truly thankful!' Fifteen men were swept away when the canister burst at the gun muzzle spraying out a swarm of musket balls.

Three of the balls shredded the uniform of Col. Alexander Woodford, commanding, without cutting the skin at all. He was another Peninsular veteran and had commanded the 1st Battalion there. With an instinct for the main chance, he rallied the men and led them straight at the gate just as a gunner was swabbing the gun and a crewman was ready to load another canister. He shot that man with his pistol and ran the other through with his sword. Bayonets stabbed at him from the infantry guard of the gun, but his men were fighting past him to cut down the gunners and drive back the infantry into the abattoir of a courtyard. The French gave way and fled back to the interior gateway.

Watching the initial attack go in, Lt. Col. Augustus Frazer, of the horse artillery and attached to Wellington's staff, observed, 'I was delighted to hear that his Grace had determined not to lose a wood, 300 yards in front of the part of the line, which in reality was our weakest point.' Frazer now acted upon his own initiative to bring up a howitzer battery to the ridge to support the attack. Seeing that the attack had stalled, Wellington was relieved to see the howitzer troop hurry up. 'Colonel Frazer, you are going to do a delicate thing; can you depend upon the force of your howitzers? Part of the wood is held by our troops, part by the enemy.' He then explained what he intended.[14]

11:20 a.m. – Braine l'Alleud

The fighting for the town had become savage. The British turned each house and walled yard into a strongpoint that the French had to take by storm, littering the approaches with bodies. Fire licked at roofs here and there. The French brought their guns into the town to reduce the strongpoints. When the French broke into a house, it was with a swirl of bayonets, musket butts, and swords that the issue was decided, and often as not the survivors would stumble out, chased by the British. Then another assault would go in until the house was cleared or the defenders had fallen back to another building.

But the French were relentless. By this time Maj. Tidy had barely 200 men left, and the other two battalions were just as burned out. Pushed back to the centre of the town to the Church of St Etienne, which was filling up as a hospital, Mitchell's brigade was now reduced to the size of one of his battalions of that morning. The church itself was not defended but its surrounding buildings, the adjoining churchyard, rectory, and bell tower were. The high, wide windows on each side of the tower made it a perfect observation point.

Reille had found little to criticize and rightly concluded the attack was the work of the Prince's second in command. He did suggest that a division commander should be closer to the fighting. The opportunity now presented itself. Prince Jérôme was elated as courier after courier reported the approach of victory. He must be present at its culmination. He rode down into the town towards the town square and the British last stand around the church. He and his entourage stopped at a pair of guns firing down the main street to blow chunks out of the bell tower.

Ensign Keppel felt the shock of a ball smashing through the brick next to him, spraying him with brick dust and the brains of Private Wilson, the last enlisted man in the tower. All the others were dead or wounded, lying on the blood-soaked floorboards. He had been ordered to the tower to observe the movement of the French and had sent men repeatedly down the stairs to keep Mitchell informed. Now he was alone. Keppel peered out of the hole left by the French ball. The large window was too dangerous and attracted too much fire. A voice behind him said, 'Oi, it's an officer!' He turned around to see three men of the 1/51st come up the stairs. Behind them were half a dozen men in dark green with black shakos sporting silver death's heads and chattering away in German – Brunswickers. The Duke of Brunswick had sent forward a jäger company as his advance guard. Mitchell had also dispatched a squad to the tower with their hunting rifles.

Bullets were coming through the large window and wounded one of the light infantry. The tower shook with another ball that blew a hole on the other side of the window. A British sergeant crawled over to Keppel, who pointed out the guns through the hole in the wall. 'We must stop those guns, or they'll bring this tower down.' He turned to the Germans kneeling along the sides of the window. 'Do you speak English?' They looked blankly back at him until one of them understood and replied, '*Nein.*'

'Damn!' grunted Keppel.

The sergeant said, 'Not to worry, sir. I worked with the Krauts in Spain and picked up a little of their lingo.' He turned to the Brunswickers. '*Feldwebel, sie muss da cannonen shiessen.*'

The Germans smiled at hearing their language mangled, but they understood. They took off their black shakos and peered over the window ledge to judge the distance to the battery and watched the drift of smoke to gauge the wind. The British sergeant eased Keppel away from the hole and sited his Brown Bess through the wall.

'That's a 150-yard shot, sergeant. You'll never hit the gunners,' Keppel told him.

'Too true, sir, but I'm sure to hit something in that gaggle of fancy dans behind the guns.' He fired a moment after three of the Brunswickers. Two gunners fell, and another jumped back as a bullet pinged off the barrel he was about to swab. But the real excitement was among the horsemen as one man fell from his horse and the others seemed to take it much amiss.

11:40 a.m. – Hougoumont

Frazer was as good as his word. His howitzers quickly found the range of the French defending the embanked hedge. The bursting shells cut down scores of the defenders and blew away chunks of the hedge itself. Galloping down the ridge, Lt. Col. John Fremantle, Coldstream Guards, attached to Wellington's staff as an aide, watched the strike of the howitzers, the red burst of shells sending pieces of bodies and hedge flying. Wellington had sent him to get the stalled Guards moving again. He rode into the line of trees to find both Byng and Hepburn of the Scots Guards dead. As the senior man on the spot, he took command. Dismounting, he shouted, 'Forward, the Guards!' The men surged into the sunken lane and scrambled up through the holes in the hedge. He trusted Frazer to stop his guns when he saw the red uniforms swarm for the hedge. But the smoke from the musketry and now the shells hovered over the sunken lane and hid the Guards as they descended into the lane. It was only a sharp-eyed gunner who saw the colours of the 3rd waving above the smoke and moving forward – he alerted Frazer, who ordered an immediate cease fire.

Wellington's eye was equally sharp. He too followed the colours of the Scots Guards as they burst through the hedge. He saw the French defenders falling back across the English garden and into the apple orchard. The roof of the chateau was ablaze; he had seen the Guards break in through the north gate. He was too experienced to be satisfied – battles shifted suddenly all too often. He lifted his glass to scan the rest of the estate and spotted something that dampened his satisfaction – another large French regiment was quickly moving along the road that ran diagonally from the field of rye and through the woods south of the chateau-farm buildings.

At the same time, Guards drove the surviving 200 Frenchmen from the hedge and back across the garden, where they found themselves trapped just like the Hanoverians. A few found the open gate into the south courtyard and fled through, past the flaming chateau. More retreated inside the adjoining garden and lined the chest-high wall that separated it from the English garden. The rest found they were pinned against the six-foot English garden wall and pressed by the bayonets of the Guards. Only a few were able to scramble over with the help of their comrades when Fremantle demanded their surrender. The French were eminently realistic, recognized their situation was hopeless and threw down their weapons. On the ridge Wellington saw the French prisoners being hustled through the hedge and sunken lane and up the ridge. He ordered a Hanoverian battalion from Maj. Gen. Count Kielmansegge's brigade to reinforce the Guards.

Fremantle now found himself in a three-part fight. A few companies of the Coldstream Guards held the north courtyard. A few companies of the Scots Guards were fighting the French who had rallied in the orchard. Most of both battalions were in the English garden, attempting to break into the south courtyard through the gate in its eastern wall. They had picked up a log to use as a battering ram. Fire from the French behind the chest-high wall was hot and deadly as the Guards tried to assault the gate. They were firing diagonally at the assault parties of each attack on the gate. The concentrated fire was a scythe that swept away the head of every attack column. Only later would the French appreciate how they had turned British tactics on the Guards. In the Peninsula the French would attack in column against a British line two-men deep. The first volley of about 250 muskets from the British would strike the head of the fifty-man wide French column, bringing it down. Now the tactic was leaving a pile of dead and wounded British from concentrated French fire.

Fremantle saw that this was a losing game. 'Guards!' he shouted. 'A wall has two sides! Forward to the wall!' The firing line surged forward, trailing bodies until the redcoats came up to the wall, firing directly at the French and stabbing across the wall with their bayonet. At the same time, Fremantle threw one more attack at the gate. The men now safe from French fire picked up the log. A great heave made the double doors shudder. More men flowed into the adjoining garden, forcing the French back to where the outer walls were too tall to climb. Some scrambled through open first-floor windows. The rest, now exhausted and out of ammunition, threw down their muskets.

Wellington rode up to Frazer and pointed out the new French regiment (the 93rd) entering the woods in column from the road from Mont St Jean. His guns spat on their new target and fell accurately along the marching column with great effect.

It was then that an aide of Soult's said urgently, 'Sir, the Emperor arrives!' The staff parted as Napoleon rode up at the head of his staff and escort. He came up next to Soult, his attention focused on the struggle for Hougoumont, scanning it with his glass and then across the ridge. He slammed the telescope shut. 'Now Soult, what are you up to?'

CHAPTER 6

La Haye Sainte

12:00 Noon–3:00 p.m., 17 June 1815

12:00 Noon – La Belle Alliance

'See, sire, Wellington commits another brigade.' Soult was pointing to the Hanoverian dark-green-coated Grubenhagen Light Field Battalion from Kielmansegge's brigade moving rapidly down the ridge towards Hougoumont.

'Yes, I see. Aha, now we've got them – those English! We have ninety chances in our favour and not ten against.[1] We must encourage the Duke to weaken himself further. Send in another regiment.'

Soult nodded at Foy, who sped off to personally order the commander of the 92nd of the Line to reinforce the 93rd.

Then Napoleon pointed to La Haye Sainte. 'What about that walled farm? Why have you left it alone?'

'Sire, I was concentrating on his right to threaten his retreat and keep him in place.'

'Yes, you understand this battlefield in a way few of my marshals could. And we shall use that to do more than threaten his retreat. We shall leap upon it like a leopard hiding in a tree. But first we have to clear our front for when I attack, and I do not want to have to pass on either side of a defended position. Quiot is closest. Order him to take it. Even if it takes his whole division, he is to take it. Tell him it must fall for the main attack to succeed.'

Berthier quickly wrote out the order with such clarity that it could not be misunderstood.[2]

As he had ridden up to Mont St Jean, Napoleon had observed the accurate fire of Frazer's batteries. As an artilleryman, he was impressed with the handling of those howitzers. He thought that two could play at that game. Now that he was watching the fighting swirling around the burning Hougoumont, he ordered up the Old Guard's 'Beautiful Daughters', the three batteries totalling eighteen 12-pounder guns and six 6-inch howitzers. They were the best artillery in Europe. It would take at least half an hour for them to come up.

As Napoleon and Soult conversed, a trail of wounded from the fighting at Hougoumont began to trudge by to the nearby field hospital. The walking wounded stumbled along amid the ambulances and stretchers. Napoleon paused to look at what he had seen a thousand times before. He now did what he had done a thousand times before and nosed his horse over to the road. 'What regiment?' he asked.

'The 1st Light,' the closest replied.

Napoleon responded with, '*Mes braves gens!*'

Wounded men ceased their moaning to cry out, '*Vive l'Empereur!*'

He noticed one stretcher coming by on which lay a wounded man whose hand was clutched by a drummer boy. '*Mon enfant,*' he asked. 'Who is this?'

The boy did not let go of the wounded man's hand and saluted with his other. '*L'Enforcer, sire!*'

A wounded officer came up. 'Sire, this is Sub-Lieutenant Legros. He led the attack into the courtyard of the chateau, chopped open the gate with his old engineer's axe. Must have cut down a dozen *Anglais* before he was wounded.'

The column of wounded had come to a halt now. In a voice that could be heard down the road, Napoleon said. 'He is now Captain Legros. I award him for his ferocity the Legion of Honour.' The men cheered again. Napoleon lifted his hat in acknowledgement and returned to his vantage point overlooking Hougoumont.[3]

He had to admit to himself that Soult had done well in pinning Wellington to his position. It would take time for the Guard to arrive, and he used the time to ride the length of the field opposite the enemy's positions behind the ridge.

It was on this ride that Reille caught up with him. Napoleon had seen enough bad news in his life to know when it was approaching. Mortification was written all over Reille's face as he reported the death of Prince Bonaparte. Reille blurted out the particulars and then paused for the expected imperial fury.

Instead, Napoleon only asked, 'Did he die well?'

'Yes, sire. He was close to the fighting and shared the danger of his men.'

'Then he died like a Frenchman. He could not have a prouder epitaph.'

When Reille left, Napoleon rode under a tree, signalling his staff that he wanted to be alone. Only his escort, his chasseurs à cheval, formed their protective ring around him. Now alone, he wept for his little brother. How would he explain this to their mother?[4]

12:15 p.m. – 400 Yards South of La Haye Sainte

With the natural eye of a gunner, Napoleon immediately identified this spot as the ideal gun platform for his grand battery. It was a 1,300-yard-long ridge or spur of high open ground projecting gently north-east from the Brussels–Genappe road.

It ran roughly parallel opposite the ridge behind which the enemy sheltered some 600–800 yards away, putting most of their line within easy range of the guns. La Haye Sainte was barely 500 yards from the eastern edge of the Grand Battery. Between the guns and the enemy was a shallow depression which meant that an attacking force would for a time be sheltered from the guns firing overhead. Ominously, the spur was slightly lower in elevation than the enemy ridge. On the opposing ridge could be seen the thirty-four guns of the enemy's five and a half batteries. The enemy's 1,100 gunners would have been mightily impressed and no little apprehensive at the magnificent sight of the assembling Grand Battery.

The massing of guns into a grand battery was a tactic Napoleon had used with great success on many of battles. Although smaller than his greatest concentration at Borodino, this one would still be formidable. For the next hour battery after battery closed on the spur, each assuming a carefully designated position. The guns were aligned ten yards apart with another ten yards between batteries, eventually stretching over 1,000 yards.

To the east of the Brussels–Genappe road, the Beautiful Daughters of the Guard went into position along with more Guard batteries. They could fire at both the main British line and Hougoumont.

The artillery officers were thankful that the ground was hard. It had not rained for days. The downpour that had drenched the Prussians in their flight had not fallen here. Aside from losing his gun, a gunner's worst nightmare was getting his gun and team bogged down in thick mud. The locals warned them that when it rained hard here, the ground dissolved into a thick bog so sticky a man was likely to lose his shoes in it. Trying to move a gun through it would have been near impossible.

When the last of the guns arrived, there would be eighty-eight pieces. The most powerful were the twenty-four 12-pounders from the batteries of I through IV Corps. The three Guard batteries of 12-pounders, the Beautiful Daughters, were retained with the Guard. There were forty-two 6-pounders, including eighteen from the Guard. Of the twenty-two howitzers, there were fourteen 5.5-inch and eight 6-inch pieces, two attached to each of the 12-pounder batteries. The depression behind the spur offered protection for the 350 caissons and limber and over 1,000 horses. Over 2,000 men would serve these eighty-eight guns and howitzers. There was also a plentiful supply of ammunition – shot and shell. There was plenty of canister, too, but at that range there would hardly be any need for it unless the enemy was foolish enough to try and attack, but Wellington was no fool.

What ammunition the French guns did not have was the British innovation of shrapnel or spherical case or caseshot. Invented in 1784, it consisted of a hollow iron sphere filled with musket balls and gunpowder ignited by a fuse. Depending on the size of the gun, the sphere was filled with between 27 to 155 musket balls. In effect, it turned canister into a distance weapon. Napoleon had known of it but had never had it copied for the French artillery. The French howitzers relied on the older shell, a hollow projectile filled with explosive ignited by a fuse that caused it to burst, shooting the jagged shards of the ball at the enemy. Both sides also used solid shot and canister, cans of musketballs fired at close range like giant shotguns.

Four hundred yards behind the depression sheltering the caissons, limbers, and horses, the four divisions of d'Erlon's I Corps were assembling. For all of the power represented by the Grand Battery, Napoleon and his gunners had no idea what they were firing at other than the batteries lining the ridge. Napoleon's chief engineer of the Guard had personally conducted a reconnaissance and correctly reported that there were no enemy field fortifications. The only alteration to the site was the hacking away of parts of the hedges that lined the road that ran along the ridge for gun embrasures and firing positions for the infantry. What was behind the ridge was carefully hidden from anyone on the French side of the field. That was just what Wellington intended. It had served him well. This was the first battle in which Napoleon could not actually see the main body of his enemy, and it was to be unsettling, given all the warnings his commanders with experience in the Peninsula had given him.[5]

12:40 p.m. – Braine l'Alleud

The lucky shot that killed Jérôme and the last-minute arrival of the Brunswickers were all that prevented the French from overrunning the town. The Duke of Brunswick rode at the head of his Leib (Bodyguard) Battalion as the column double-timed down Rue de St Anne towards the Church of St Etienne, stopping only to question wounded British soldiers staggering out of the town.

Gen. Guilleminot had quickly taken command of the French division. Assault parties were driving the British out of the few remaining houses around the church. They burst into church itself, but one look at the scores of wounded men on the floors, and they backed out. Another party broke into the bell tower, cleared the first floor and stormed up to the stairs to find the snipers. The first Frenchman up the stairs shot one of the Brunswickers at the window. The man pitched over the edge. A cheer from the French outside greeted the thud of his body on the pavement. Keppel then shot the Frenchman. A Brunswicker rushed past him and bayonetted the next one. He then fell to a shot from another Frenchman coming up the stairs.

On the street outside, the scattered French were struck by the Brunswicker column rushing up the street. At the head of his men, the Black Duke was shot through the body. He cried out to his chief of staff, 'Oh, my dear Wachholtz, where is Olfermann?'[6] His second in command was with another battalion attacking through the southern part of the town and could not be readily found. The Leib

Battalion was enraged at the death of their duke and drove the French back down the street only to be stopped in a bloody shamble by the two French guns firing canister.

12:50 p.m. – Mont St Guibert

Officers in front, swords drawn, Thielmann's corps broke out of the Saxon cordon. They came with bayonet, they had so little ammunition left. The corps commander himself led the way. The Saxon guns shotted with double canister tore huge gaps in the black-clad mass as it surged forward, but they kept coming. Then the guns were overrun. The Saxon infantry in their way fired a volley and broke. A Saxon jäger turned to flee but saw Thielmann riding through the guns, urging his men on. The Saxon turned, aimed his rifle and shot Thielmann off his horse.

That was the last thing he saw as a Prussian cavalryman thundered past, bringing his sabre down in a bloody slice.

12:55 p.m. – The Ridge of Mont St Jean

The Duke's attention was drawn from the fighting at Braine l'Alleud and Hougoumont to the columns of the Imperial Guard as they arrived up the Brussels–Genappe road. He rode east along the ridge to ensure that his brigades were properly posted. He stopped to scan the opposite field when it became clear that it was Napoleon himself riding parallel to him on his white horse. It was then that an artillery officer 'came up to the Duke, and stated that he had a distinct view of Napoleon . . . that he had the guns of his battery well pointed in that direction, and was prepared to fire. His Grace instantly and emphatically exclaimed, "No! No! I'll not allow it. It is not the business of commanders to be firing upon one another."' Wellington watched his rival ride west to La Belle Alliance, and then he himself returned to his right flank.[7]

1:12 p.m. – The Inn at La Belle Alliance

Upon arriving at La Belle Alliance, Napoleon asked Soult and Reille their opinion of the British. Both had long and too-often painful experiences with them in the Peninsula. He also recognized that he had only fought the British once, at Toulon, twenty-five years before. Reille did not hesitate. 'I consider the English infantry to be inexpugnable [impregnable].' Soult emphatically added, '*Sire, l'infanterie anglaise en duel c'est le diable*' ('Sire, in a straight fight the English infantry are the very devil'). The Emperor did not appear pleased with the response. Soult and Reille fully expected one of his outbursts of temper. But to their surprise, he simply thanked them and walked away.[8]

His staff had learned to recognize when the Emperor wanted to be alone. He walked off to watch the Beautiful Daughters limber up on high ground overlooking Hougoumont, his hands clasped behind him. He walked slowly back and forth. Then a gun fired, and he opened his glass and put it up to his eye.

After a while he rejoined the group. 'Well, gentlemen, I have taken your advice into consideration. I will add to it something of Austerlitz as well.'

Then he said to Berthier, 'Where is that damned balloon that Soult wanted to try out?'

Monthion had the answer. 'He should be approaching any time now, sire.'

Napoleon merely said, 'Hmph.'

He walked up and down for a few minutes and then turned to Berthier. 'Order Soult to concentrate the rest of II Corps against Wellington's right. Take L'Alleud and threaten his escape to Brussels. Order Grouchy to also concentrate on our left to be able to either attack or cut off the retreat of the English. The Guard will remain in reserve just south of here along the road. The I Corps is to prepare to attack the enemy's left supported by the Grand Battery. Now, I'm going to take a nap.'

1:13 p.m. – Hougoumont

The expert gunners of the Guard needed only one ranging round to find their target. Now all three batteries spoke. A storm of iron fell on Frazer's battery, disabling two howitzers and killing or wounding thirty-two men and twenty-five horses. Frazer's men stood to their surviving pieces, but another French volley was too much. In the end only two howitzers would get away behind the ridge.

Now the gunners switched their fire to Hougoumont. Twelve-pounder balls smashed into the six-foot high garden wall. The six howitzers dropped their shells into the garden packed with the English Guards and Hanoverians. Most of the buildings of the chateau-farm were on fire, making the entire complex untenable. The French defenders of the southern courtyard were pulling out while the Coldstream Guard companies in the northern courtyard were also getting out through their gate.

The heavy guns kept up their firing until the garden wall was demolished, then they moved to the target of the massed troops in the garden. With large portions of the wall in ruins, a battalion of the 93rd came out of the woods to line its jagged edges and fire into the enemy reeling in the garden from the artillery's lashing. To their right another battalion was attacking the two companies of the Scots Guards in the orchard.

With the reinforcing 92nd of the Line came their 1st Brigade commander, General of Brigade Jean-Joseph Baron Gauthier. If ever there was a typical example of one of the fighting generals thrown up by the Revolution and the Empire, it was Gauthier. A volunteer in 1791, he rose through the ranks on ability and audacity. He fought in Germany, Italy, the Vendée, Germany, Austria, and Illyria. For his brilliant conduct at Essling in 1809 Napoleon created him baron and promoted him to command a brigade. After the Bourbon restoration, he was given command of the district of Lyons and promptly went over to Napoleon after he landed.

Gauthier had watched the fighting for Hougoumont closely. He saw that sending more men into the fighting would only feed the butcher's bill. His orders were simple: drive the English out of the chateau-farm and its grounds. How he did it was his business. So it was that he rode at the head of the regiment along with its commander, Col. Tissot, as it marched quickly through the wood. There he found the reserve battalion of the 93rd and gave the commander new orders. He caught up with the 92nd as it left the woods and marched along the western side of the burning chateau-farm. From the ridge the British saw the regiment enter the wood and expected it to join the fighting for the garden and orchard. The burning buildings and the smoke that covered the estate grounds hid them from view until they suddenly emerged by the north gate, to the complete surprise of the battered Coldstream Guards who had escaped the inferno.

The fire from the 93rd battalion at the broken wall added to the savaging of the enemy by the guns of the Beautiful Daughters. Men could stand no more. The Germans broke first for the holes in the hedges as the Guards backed up in small groups, all company cohesion lost as the guns and musketry harvested them. In the orchard the two Guards companies fought it out with the French battalion, giving ground one foot at a time, leaving red-coated bodies littering the ground among the trees.

There would be no escape. The 92nd drove the Coldstream companies into the sunken lane that was filling up with fleeing Hanoverians who were trying to scramble up the other side. Gauthier directed Tissot to move the rest of his regiment quickly to position itself in the trees above the lane. At the same time, the 93rd's reserve battalion turned the north-east corner of the estate and rushed to close the trap with the 92nd. Private Jean-Yves Bourhis of the 92nd edged through the smoke-shrouded carnage of the sunken lane when his foot caught on a cloth. He reached down to free himself and was amazed to find a gold and red flag. It was a king's colour. He pulled it up by the staff, but it was still held fast by hand. Bourhis knelt to see that it was the hand of the golden-haired ensign of the Coldstream Guards. He gently freed the hand and lay it across the boy's chest and saluted him.

Now it was the French who were firing down into the sunken lane. Hands went up quickly. Only the Scots Guards kept fighting along the hedge line front and back until only a few score were left in scattered knots, the largest around their colours. Six bearers of the king's colour and four of the regimental colour had fallen, but always a hand was ready to snatch up the fallen flags. Fremantle was the last field officer left standing. Three times he had been wounded but still stood next to the colours, sword in hand.

Then the French bugle call for cease fire rang out. Gauthier personally approached with an officer bearing a white flag. He saluted Fremantle, who returned the compliment. 'I ask you, colonel, to spare your men from certain death. This brave regiment has done everything and more that honour demands.' More than one guardsman wept as Fremantle surrendered the colours and handed his sword to Gauthier, who promptly returned it.[9]

On the ridge the shocked British officers on Wellington's staff groaned as it became clear what had happened. The Duke said nothing, but his jaw was set. 'Look!' one cried out and pointed down the ridge. A dozen men of the Coldstream Guards had survived the catastrophe of the 2nd Guards Brigade and were running up the ridge, one of them carrying their regimental colour. After them was a cloud of French skirmishers.

Wellington pulled his horse around and spurred him down the ridge a dozen yards to the 1st Guards Brigade and its nearest battalion, 2/1st Foot Guards. 'Light Company, follow me at the double!' He spurred back over the ridge and down the slope with the light company running after him. His stunned staff bolted after him. The company commander of the light company just followed the Duke and spread his men in a skirmish line. Gravity sped them fast down the slope towards the knot of Coldstream Guards around the single colour. The fresher French were gaining on them, eager for the glory and the Legion of Honour that would go to the man who brought Napoleon a colour of the famous Coldstream Guards. The surviving Coldstream Guards turned to defend themselves as Wellington rode up, his staff right behind him with drawn swords. Now the 1st Guards came running past them, towards the French. One look at the charging bayonets, and the French pivoted and raced back down the hill.

Maj. Gen. Maitland, commanding the 1st Guards Brigade, had sent the rest of the battalion after the others. They reached the crest just in time to watch the drama of the rescue. They cheered as the French ran and the Coldstream survivors trudged the rest of the way up the ridge. Wellington rode up stone-faced but thankful for snatching a small victory out of the disaster below.

The smoke billowing out of the burning chateau hid the carpet of bodies strewn about the two courtyards. After the battle a visitor walked the grounds and wrote:

I came first upon the orchard, and there discovered heaps of dead men, in various uniforms; those of the Guards in their usual red jackets, and the German Legion, and the French dressed in blue mingled together. The dead and the wounded positively covered the whole area of the orchard; no less than two thousand men had fallen there. The apple trees presented a singular appearance; shattered branches were seen hanging about their mother-trunks in such profusion that one might suppose the stiff growing and stunted tree had been converted into a willow. Every tree was riddle and smashed.[10]

Along the sunken lane between the blasted trees, the British could see the glint of a French eagle and its tricolour through the drifting smoke.

1:10 p.m. – La Haye Sainte

Major Baring watched the denouement at Hougoumont from the roof of the barn at La Haye Sainte. He could see French troops directly to the south moving into position and guns running up to high ground overlooking the farm. He saw Napoleon riding the trace of the French line and heard the cheers of '*Vive l'Empereur!*' All of this concentrated his mind on the desperate defence he must offer. He rushed to the courtyard, issued orders to the men to redouble their efforts to loophole the walls of the farm buildings and garden walls. Then he sent an officer to his commander begging for reinforcements and more ammunition. He roamed the grounds making sure his orders were being energetically carried out. Then all he could do was wait.

But he did not have to wait long. Napoleon's orders to take La Haye Sainte were immediately put into effect. The Great Battery unleashed its concentrated fire on the farm. The stone buildings and garden walls were quickly holed in scores of places. The orchard wall was blown to pieces. The farm buildings caught fire. Baring's casualties from the artillery were becoming serious. Braving the shot and shell falling onto the farm, he peered out of a window to see what looked to be 5,000 Frenchmen descending upon him.

The Grand Battery's fire also lashed Perponcher's amalgamated battalions only a few hundred yards north-east of the sandpit. To this day, no one can explain why that force that had been so badly handled just the day before was placed in such an exposed position unless it was to offer support to the defenders of La Haye Sainte. Survivors from twelve battalions had been pressed together. The men did not know one another or their officers. The casualties were horrendous as dozens of balls sliced through the packed ranks and shells exploded in their midst. Stunned and shocked, the inexperienced brigade started to unravel as men began to flee back over the ridge. First it was individuals, then sections, then companies, until unit after unit broke, stampeding to the rear. Finally, someone in command made the decision to withdraw the remaining men, leaving hundreds of dead and wounded behind.

By Napoleon's orders D'Erlon threw Gen. Baron Quiot de Passage's 1st Infantry Division against the farm with both brigades. They were reinforced by Captain

Emon and his company of sappers and a brigade of cuirassiers under Gen. Baron Dubois. There were to be no half measures in this attack.

The sappers demanded the honour of leading the attack. They trotted ahead armed with axes and pickaxes in two detachments towards the east and west sides of the farm, followed by the 54th and 55th of the Line (1st Brigade), experienced regiments that had fought at Austerlitz, Jena, Friedland, Ulm, and in the Peninsula. Col. Dubois' 1st Cuirassier Brigade guarded the flank of the 54th as it attacked the eastern face of the farm. The 55th attacked the western face as the 2nd Brigade advanced just to the west to ensure that the British were not reinforced from that direction.

A quarter of the defenders were already dead or wounded as the French attacking force approached. Yet the men had kept to their posts despite the shattered walls, dead companions, and burning farm buildings. Private Helmuth Keller would remember that the garden wall next to his loophole exploded as a ball struck it, killing Corporal Albert Brühl, with whom he had served for five years in the Peninsula. The wall was being pulverized, yet he stuck to his post. Through his loophole he could see what seemed a flood of Frenchmen approaching at quick march. He took careful aim and fired. He saw an officer drop as he was waving his sword at the head of his men. As Captain Dupont of the 55th stumbled dead into the dust, his men screamed in rage. He was a much-loved officer, brave to a fault, who took care of his men. He had come up through the ranks along with Sergeant Jean-Paul Aulard, to whom the men now looked for leadership. 'I was filled with rage when Dupont was shot. I only wanted revenge and to kill. My bayonet led the way.'[11]

The 55th of the Line struck the east side of the farm while the 54th hit the west. The sappers took the first lash of the British Baker rifles, and a dozen fell as the rest ran for the gates. The barn door on the east side of the farm had been foolishly burned for firewood earlier. Now it gaped open except for a hasty barricade. The sappers threw themselves on it with a fury. The defenders shot them down one after another, but the slow loading of the Baker rifles meant they could not kill fast enough. Behind the sappers crowded the bayonets of the infantry.

On the west side, sappers were hacking away at the main gate as the 54th swarmed through the shattered orchard walls. The KGL fell back through a gate into the farmyard. As at the barn door, the sappers left a clutch of dead at the main gate, but their axes had smashed it open. The 54th flooded inside. Baring would later heap praise on the courage of the French who attacked, 'showing the greatest contempt for our fire':

From two sides in two close columns, which, with the greatest rapidity nearly surrounded us, and despising danger, fought with a degree of courage which I had never before witnessed in Frenchmen . . . [They] threw themselves against the wall, and endeavouring to wrest the arms of my men through the loopholes; many lives were sacrificed to the defense of the doors and gates; the most obstinate contest was carried on where the gate was wanting [the barn] . . . On this spot seventeen dead Frenchmen already lay dead, and their bodies served as protection to those who pressed after them.[12]

Bursting through the barn barricade, Sergeant Aulard led his company of the 55th to fall on the defenders with the bayonet even as round shot striking the roof sent shards of slate among them. The KGL riflemen could only defend themselves with their short swords, an uneven contest against men trained in bayonet fighting. It was here at the barn entrance that Rifleman Frederick Lindau stood like a hero defending the opening. He heard the cry of '*En avant!*' as the French attacked. He laughed and said to a companion, 'The French were in such a hurry, it's as if they wanted to eat in Brussels today.' 'We opened such a murderous fire on the dense crowd that the ground was immediately covered with a mass of wounded and dead.' French fire was equally murderous, and Lt. Emanuel Biederman saw that 'our men fell by the dozens'.[13]

Baring remembered, 'Bleeding from two wounds in the head . . . I told him [Lindau] to go back, and the cloth about his head was not sufficient to stop the strong flow of blood; he . . . answered that "he would be a scoundrel that deserted you so long as his head is on his shoulders."'[14] Aulard went for him, and the two struck and parried with each other like two heroes on the plains of Troy. Finally, the blood dripping into Lindau's eyes made him miss Aulard's final thrust. The Frenchman twisted his bayonet and pushed Lindau's body aside and charged into the barn with a snarl.[15]

In advance of the 54th was a cloud of skirmishers who attracted the fire of the rifle companies in the sandpit. The skirmishers turned to swarm the sandpit, sending the Rifles scurrying back to the rest of their regiment in its position on the crest above the farm.

By this time, the KGL were fighting hand to hand in the farmyard and its buildings as more and more French infantry crowded in. The barn and stables were burning, flames shooting out of the holes in their roofs.

Alarmed at the fury of the French attack, Gen. Alten determined to relieve the pressure on La Haye Sainte with a counterstroke. He turned to the 50-year-old Hanoverian, Col. Christian Baron von Ompteda, commanding the 2nd Brigade KGL. Baring's battalion was Ompteda's and his brigade was closest to the besieged battalion. Alten pointed to the French regiment breaking into the eastern side of the farm. 'Strike them, Colonel, and drive them off. We cannot lose that position. Attack on line.' He specified Ompteda was to send in his 5th Line Battalion.

Ompteda was appalled. He could see French cavalry roaming the open ground south of the farm. He remonstrated that such an unsupported attack would be suicide. Alten firmly repeated the order. 'Then I will,' Ompteda replied. Alten then thought better of sending just one battalion and ordered Ompteda to take all his battalions, some 1,500 men.

Joining his command, Ompteda said to Lt. Col. von Linsingen, commanding the 5th Line Battalion, 'Try to save my two nephews,' who were no more than 15 years old and serving as junior officers in that battalion. Then he ordered his brigade forward. The three battalions (1st, 5th, and 8th Line) descended the slope in line and began to wheel to the east to attack the French 55th Line. The French could not miss the movement of so large a body of men and faced about to meet them. When they were within sixty yards of the French, Ompteda shouted, 'Charge', and his men surged forward with loud huzzahs.

Ompteda himself rode straight into the French. One of his captains remembered,

I saw that the French had their muskets pointed at the Colonel but they did not fire. The officers struck the men's barrels up with their swords. They seemed astonished at the extraordinary calm approach of the solitary horseman, whose white plume showed him to be an officer of high rank. He passed through them and reached the garden hedge. He jumped in and I clearly saw how his sword-strokes smoke the shakos off. The nearest French officer looked on with admiration, without attempting to check the attack . . . I saw Colonel Ompteda in the midmost throng of the enemy's infantry and cavalry, sink from his horse and vanish.

Even that extraordinary example of French chivalry had had its limits. Someone had finally lost patience and shot him in the throat.[16]

French Gen. Baron Dubois could not believe his eyes as he watched Ompteda's attack. Too good to be true, much too good. The best time for cuirassiers to ride down infantry was when they were in motion and not in square, and this was such a time. He instantly ordered his brigade of 700 cuirassiers forward at a trot and then within a hundred yards of the KGL they broke into a gallop over the hard, dry ground. They struck the open flank and unprotected rear of the 1st Line. Even the finest troops when so taken find it impossible to maintain themselves. They broke and fled but not fast enough. The cuirassiers just rode them down and then straight into the other two battalions, rolling them up. The two battalions dissolved as the survivors surrendered or tried to flee back up the slope only to be chased down. Barely 200 of over 1,500 men were all that made it back into their own lines.

The commander of the French 1st Cuirassiers, Col. Count Michel Ordener, was in the thick of the slaughter and said, 'I overthrew three officers with my own hand, their colour remained in our possession.' His cuirassiers chased the survivors up the slope, cutting them down as only a few could make the safety of the regiments there. They were met by a well-directed fire that emptied many saddles and brought down horses. Ordener was among those hit. 'They opened a murderous fire on us; my horse was killed. I was struck by a ball in the neck, but it was deflected by my cuirass.' He managed to get to his feet and stumble away, where his men picked him up.[17]

When Maj. Baring surrendered, his remaining men were hustled out of the ruined farm to join the 1,000 KGL prisoners being prodded to the rear by bayonet. Alten had watched the disaster unfold. He could taste the bitterness in his mouth as the column of prisoners stumbled into French lines. The loss of an entire brigade left a large whole in his line, made all the worse by the severe losses Kielmansegge's brigade had suffered in the fight for Hougoumont. Alten's division had been wrecked save for Halkett's 5th British Brigade. As if things could not get worse, the Duke rode up just then. The look on his face reminded Alten of Medusa, and he felt about ready to be turned to stone.

Wellington was livid at the loss of the brigade and even more at the loss of the farm. It had been the bone in Boney's throat, and now it had been plucked out by the French. After the loss of Hougoumont, his entire front was now suddenly vulnerable to a major and unimpeded French attack. Under other less dire circumstances, he would have relieved and arrested Alten for throwing away that brigade without orders, but now he could not afford to disrupt the command arrangement for this critical part of his line. A chastened Alten could be depended on to hold on. He ordered up Kruse's regiment of the Nassau Contingent from his Reserve Corps to fill the gap in Alten's line. It was a brigade-size formation commanded by the more than able Lt. Gen. August von Kruse. When Nassau was under the Empire he had fought well for the Emperor in Spain. After the disasters that fell upon Napoleon in 1813, he received secret orders from his duke to change sides and promptly marched his regiment into British lines. He then served Wellington as well as he had Napoleon. When his regiment joined the Allied army, Wellington said to him, 'I hope, General, that your actions today are as clever when you are fighting for me as they were in Spain when you were fighting against me.' Then he spurred away back to his right, where the fight for Braine l'Alleud was still in doubt.[18]

The Duke was all too correct in his appraisal of the loss of the farm. A British staff officer, Captain Shaw-Kennedy, observed:

> The possession of La Haye Sainte by the French was a very dangerous incident. It uncovered the very centre of the Anglo-Allied army, and established the enemy within 60 yards of the centre. The French lost no time in taking advantage of this, by pushing forward infantry supported by guns, which enabled them to maintain a most destructive fire upon Alten's left and Kempt's right, and to drive off Kempt's light troops that occupied the knoll in his front. By this fire they wasted most seriously the ranks of the left of Alten's and the right of Kempt's divisions; so much so that Ompteda's brigade having been . . . destroyed, and Kielmansegge's much weakened, they were now not sufficiently strong to occupy the front which was originally assigned to them.[19]

La Haye Sainte had gone from being the Allied advance position to disrupt the French advance to being the advance position, the *point d'appui*, from which the French could disrupt the Allied army's defence. A prisoner described the farm as 'completely destroyed, nothing but the rafters and props remaining. The floor . . . was strewed with the bodies of German Infantry and French Tirailleurs . . . The carnage had been very great in this place.'[20]

1:15 p.m. – The Inn at La Belle Alliance

Napoleon had just fallen asleep when Col. Coutelle arrived, with his little convoy following a mile behind. He reported to Berthier and recommended the best spot for his balloon to ascend. It was known as Rossomme Hill, just to the east of the road and by the eponymous farm. 'Good,' replied Berthier. 'Monthion has already recommended it as a place for the Emperor to set up his headquarters because it provides the best observation. The Emperor has agreed. Part of the staff is already there. Ask for any help you may need.'

Coutelle rode back and directed his convoy up the hill. The well-practised crew went about its work quickly. The hot-air-generating apparatus soon began filling *Marengo*, attracting a crowd of staff officers and soldiers at this wonder. Only some of the older men had seen Coutelle's earlier balloons in the wars of the young Republic. It was a wonder that seemed to fill them with confidence. Coutelle was more concerned that a careless spark would ignite his precious balloon. He addressed the crowd and threatened to run through any man with a lit cigar or pipe.[21]

1:20 p.m. – Wavre

The only Prussians left in Wavre were stragglers and deserters, all easily rounded up by Exelmans' cavalry, which clattered into town. Lobau's infantry were only an hour behind them, impelled forward by the sight of the detritus of the Prussian retreat – prisoners, weapons thrown away, lamed horses, broken down wagons and caissons. Ahead of them rode Davout and his staff. Pajol had reported that the mass of the Prussians had marched east along the road to Liège. Davout had directed him to harry them hard for ten miles. He would be sure to make the fear of God and Davout accelerate them east. He was then to double back to join the main body.

The Saxon courier rode past the columns of Lobau's corps as it entered Wavre. Gendarmes pointed him to the town hall where Davout had set up his temporary headquarters. The dispatch informed him that the Prussians had made a breakout at Mont St Gilbert. Perhaps 8,000 to 10,000 had got away, 5,000 prisoners had been taken with all of the Prussian guns. The dispatch continued that the Prussians had fled east in great disorder. The Saxons were marching to Wavre. The prisoners had been sent south. Among them was a Col. Clausewitz. Davout was pleased. The Saxons had done the job he had expected of them. Those Prussians had not hindered his seizure of Wavre and were out of the fight for good.

At the same time, another courier was on his way to Davout. This message was sent by Pajol to report that he had fallen on the rear of the Prussians as ordered and was driving them in panic eastwards. Thousands of prisoners were being taken. Pajol was delighted. It was a wonderful thing to drive the Prussians. It reminded him of the Six Days Campaign in 1814 when he commanded a corps under the eyes of Napoleon and helped inflict four sharp defeats one after another on the Prussians. They were Napoleon's last victories before his abdication. This time, the Prussians would stay beaten.

Bülow was about to have something to say about that. As Davout rode into Wavre, Gneisenau saw an enraged Bülow galloping so hard up the crowded road that men had to throw themselves to the side to keep from being ridden down.

If ever there was a man who hated Napoleon to his core and burned for revenge it was Gen. Friedrich Wilhelm Count Bülow. For him Napoleon represented intense pain. The deaths of his two children and wife were followed by the humiliation of Prussia in 1806. All that hurt, personal and patriotic, poured into an unforgiving hate. That hatred had been the forge of his professional excellence. He had become one of the great reformers of the Prussian army and a keen student of war. In independent command in the War of Liberation, he had defeated a French force at Grossbeeren and Ney himself at Dennewitz. For that he was ennobled as Count Bülow von Dennewitz.

He drew up so fast next to Gneisenau that his horse reared, flecking the chief of staff with its white lather. The general's first horse lay ridden to death miles behind. The men around them drew back out of range of his excited horse.

'Retreat? Gneisenau, I'll be damned if I retreat!' he shouted at the chief of staff. The men around withdrew further.

Gneisenau stood his ground. 'We have been badly beaten. Blücher is missing. Thielmann's corps is also missing. Zieten and Pirch's corps are almost out of ammunition. The army's trains cannot be found.'

Bülow snorted in derision. Before Gneisenau could attempt to respond, Bülow said, 'I assume command of this army. Now turn it around!'[22]

1:30 p.m. – Braine l'Alleud

The French II Corps was massing in and around the town, something that Wellington could not fail to see. The 2nd of the Line with 2,300 men was the largest regiment in the French army. It was the last regiment in reserve in the

6th Infantry Division and was now committed to the fighting in Braine l'Alleud. Soult reinforced the division with Foy's 2nd Brigade (2,700 men) supported by 1,100 cavalrymen of the 2nd and 7th Dragoons (1st Brigade, 11th Cavalry Division, III Cavalry Corps). Bachelu's 5th Infantry Division (5,000 men) was in reserve, ready to be committed if necessary as well as the cavalry division's 2nd Brigade of cuirassiers. Reille was pleased with the critical role his corps was playing. The prospect of what would come next was positively exciting. He could be nowhere else but with the advance. He could already feel a marshal's baton in his hand.

The 2nd of the Line entered the town from the west, and its numbers tipped the balance against the British and Brunswickers, forcing them back to the eastern edge of the town. At this point they found Foy's infantry brigade and the dragoons advancing through the fields on the eastern edge of the town. Watching from his vantage point on the ridge, Wellington knew then that Braine l'Alleud was finally lost. He had lost the remnants of the Netherlands Division and two brigades trying to hold it. He could not throw good money after bad.

Surrounded! The word leaped from man to man among the hard-pressed Brunswickers. Hundreds surrendered. A few joined Mitchell's shrunken battalions. Mitchell realized he had two choices. He could fight it out until his ammunition was exhausted. That would not be long. Or he could fight his way out across 1,000 yards of open ground to reach the British position on Mont St Jean ridge. The thought of handing over his sword to some damned Frenchman made the bile rise in his throat. He would not be blamed if he surrendered after his ammunition gave out. Honour would be satisfied, but, by God, Hugh Henry Mitchell would not be.

1:50 p.m. – The Road to Mesnil

The 2,000 lancers and chasseurs of Gen. Hippolyte Piré's 2nd Cavalry Division (II Corps) trotted around Braine l'Alleud, smoke from the burning town masking their movement. Piré was a talented and energetic, slightly built man who took good care of his men. Confident in their leader and from earlier brushes with the English and Dutch, they were in good spirits. Their initial objective was the little village of Mesnil, 1,000 yards north of Braine l'Alleud. From there another 1,500 yards led to the Brussels road. In between was a small wood through which the road passed. Piré thought his luck was running well; the wood would allow his cavalry to approach the enemy under cover. Then a quick dash, and his lancers and chasseurs would be upon them.

Soult's orders still rang in Piré's ears. 'Cut that damned road. Spread panic in their rear.' For Piré this was a cavalryman's dream – the opportunity for decisive glory and eternal fame. Yet patience was the prerequisite for glory. For French cavalry to show up in the enemy's rear when his attention was fixed on his front would be the priceless stroke. Soult had cautioned to wait until he heard the roar of the Grand Battery which would signal that the main attack was about to begin. To the north of Braine l'Alleud was string of hamlets in a hollow that led to Mesnil. There he would wait.

Other cavalry was being readied at the same time to occupy Mesnil. The Netherlands Cavalry Division had been concentrated just south of Mont St Jean. The Duke had put them there in reserve when he had observed them coming into his lines after their mauling at Quatre Bras. They had not filled him with confidence. They had lost their Crown Prince as well, and their morale showed it. Wellington's orders now set them in motion. Commanding the division, the Dutch Lt. Gen. Baron J.D. Collaert must have been having second thoughts about his allegiance. For nineteen years he had been in the service of a French ally or in French service itself. He had fought with Napoleon to the bitter end in 1814, then had offered his services to the new King of the Netherlands, who appointed him to command his cavalry. The day before, his old comrades had run him off the field. He had started the day with 3,200 men and was lucky now to muster 2,000. The Duke's orders were to protect the Brussels road north of Mont St Jean in case French cavalry tried to get behind him. He was told to deploy at Mesnil. The Duke had noted the year before in his reconnaissance of the site that the village was surrounded by depressions on either side and would be ideal for defence against any threat coming from Braine l'Alleud. Collaert was now taking longer than he would have wished to get his regiments going. They were too sluggish. The French cavalry he had served with would never have allowed themselves to show so little dash.

There were more British cavalry on the move. The Duke had ordered Ponsonby's and Vandeleur's brigades from his left to his right behind the village of Merbe Braine, which lay 1,000 yards east of Braine l'Alleud. Should that town fall, the threat to the Brussels road would come from cavalry, and he had to be able to meet it with his own cavalry.

2:00 p.m. – The Ridge of Mont St Jean

Napoleon was doing exactly what Wellington had feared he would do. It was clear to the Duke that the Emperor was manoeuvring his forces to threaten the army's line of retreat. He had hoped Napoleon would pound himself to pieces against the British reverse slope position as had so many of his marshals. Apparently, the ogre had taken some good advice. He supposed it was too much to expect otherwise. After all, how many times can you expect to use the same trick before even a dullard catches on?

Tricks would not do now, he realized. The essence of victory is to defeat the enemy's strategy, and right now Napoleon's strategy hinged upon taking Braine l'Alleud. By attacking the town he had already blocked the Duke's ability to retreat to the west and to Ostend. Now by taking the town, he would strike to cut the Brussels road. Wellington's army would be trapped against the woods to his rear. It occurred to the Duke that Napoleon was doing a good job of defeating Wellington's strategy. Napoleon must think he has nailed me to this position, he thought to himself. Or so Napoleon believes. Wellington concluded that Napoleon thought the Brussels road was the army's only line of retreat. If it had been, the Duke would be close to despair.

The town was burning in places as house-to-house fighting still raged. The masses of French infantry moving to the right would soon overwhelm it. But the Duke also had a line of retreat through the woods to his rear. He had explored it on his reconnaissance last year. It was an open wood, used efficiently by the local people. Undergrowth was kept clear and dead wood hauled away. The careful logging left sufficient space between trees for formations to move easily, even guns and wagons over the firm, dry ground. A good road to Brussels ran through the wood as well as a number of good logging roads crossing the woods going north. He had no doubt he could pull the army out, but it had to be under the cloak of night. All he had to do was hold off the greatest soldier of the age for the rest of this long, long summer day. That was all. There would be almost seven more hours of daylight. What could a man like Napoleon do with seven hours? He was a man who measured battle in minutes. The Duke watched the columns of the French II Corps and Grouchy's cuirassiers massing on his centre-right. He decided it was time to move a few of his knights across the chessboard.

2:10 p.m. – Braine l'Alleud

Mitchell thinned out his men holding off the French and massed the rest along with a few hundred Brunswickers in the north-east corner of the town. Wellington was watching the denouement in the town. Smoke from the fires and the black powder smoke from musket fire drifted over it. It seemed concentrated now in the eastern corner. He scanned that part of the town with his glass and was startled to see a British battalion emerge from the town. As it advanced, it became clear that it was Mitchell's brigade moving in battalion squares, two by two – the fourth being the Brunswickers who had refused to surrender. The squares formed a diamond pointing at Merbe Braine with the 1/51st in the lead, the 3/14th on the north, the 23rd on the south face, and the Brunswickers on the tail.

The Duke instantly recognized that, without help, Mitchell's shrunken brigade would not survive. An aide sped to take his order to Uxbridge to commit the Union and 4th Cavalry Brigades to drive the French cavalry away and escort Mitchell's brigade to safety. The brigades had already been ordered forward to replace the Netherlands Cavalry Division.

Wellington could only admire Mitchell's boldness in attempting to run the same gauntlet he had run earlier in getting to the town. Now his brigade was much reduced in numbers. And out of luck, too. Gen. Baron Piquet did not wait for Reille's order but ordered his dragoons to advance on the little battalion squares. They formed a good target for the British guns on the ridge. Shot ploughed through their ranks and shrapnel scattered lead balls to empty more saddles. Still the dragoons surged forward, forcing the squares to halt and prepare to receive cavalry.

As soon as the squares halted, the dragoons rode around rather than charge home. Their job was to force the enemy squares to stop and thus make themselves vulnerable to artillery and other infantry. A French horse artillery battery raced forward, unlimbered and fired canister into the face of the 23rd. Behind the guns Foy's brigade moved rapidly forward to engage the British. It was perfect demonstration of French combined-arms tactics.

When the guns swept away half the face of the shrunken 23rd, the dragoons charged before the ranks could close. They rode over the dead and wounded into the centre of the square, which promptly dissolved into knots of men, bayonets out and fugitives. A dozen men rallied to the battalion commander, Lt. Col. Sir Henry Ellis, and the colour-bearers in the centre of the square. The dragoons swarmed them. Ellis shot an officer at point-blank range. Bayonets bristled to lunge at the closing dragoons. But the band was too small, and the horses too close and it was over quickly. Two dragoons rode off waving the king's and regimental colours in triumph.

It would be too soon to celebrate. As the 23rd died, Vandeleur's 4th Cavalry Brigade of light dragoons poured down the slope at the charge, straight for the French dragoons. On their left came Ponsonby's Union Brigade aiming for the flank of the infantry of Foy's 2nd Brigade. Twenty-six hundred British cavalry were thundering onto the field to the complete surprise of the French. In the lead was Uxbridge himself.

Vandeleur's men swept aside two companies of French dragoons and fell upon the horse artillery battery which was just limbering up to move forward and blast the next square. The gunners fought back with ramrods and swords but were no match for the light dragoons on their nimble horses. It was a massacre; the only survivors hid underneath their guns.

Foy's 2nd Brigade was desperately trying to redeploy from column to square to face the oncoming Union Brigade. The French 100th of the Line got off a partial volley in the middle of its attempt to redeploy. Barely a dozen cavalrymen went down before the brigade struck the French. The regiment staggered back in confusion with the British horsemen hacking their way through the packed infantry. Named for their magnificent chargers, the Scots Greys were the first to cut through the heaving mass of infantry. The 100th was an experienced regiment but was overwhelmed and outnumbered by the mass of British dragoons. Most of them rushed back through the ranks of its sister regiment, the 4th Light, which had had the time to form to meet cavalry. Sergeant Charles Ewart of the Scots Greys saw the eagle of the 100th shining above the crowd. He ploughed through the milling infantry, sabred the colour-bearer, and seized the eagle. He rode forward brandishing the 'French cuckoo' above his head.

In chasing the fleeing infantry, the Scots Greys fell on the battery of 6-pounders that had been advancing between the two regimental columns. The gunners who did not flee to the ranks of the 4th Light died amid their guns. The Scots Greys then reformed and charged right into a disciplined volley from the 4th Light that brought down eighty-seven men. The rest of the brigade's dragoons were chasing down those of the 100th who had not found refuge in their sister regiment. The battle-crazed dragoons were simply uncontrollable at this point. One of the British officers recalled, 'In fact our men were out of hand. The General of the brigade, his staff, and every officer within hearing exerted themselves to the utmost to re-form the men, but the helplessness of the enemy offered too great a temptation to the dragoons, and our efforts were abortive.'[23]

Gen. Baron Guiton commanded a small brigade of French cuirassiers, barely 540 troopers, but they were large men on large horses. He was without orders at the time the British fell on the 100th, but he knew his duty. He attacked immediately. They came on in formation at a trot and within 100 yards of Ponsonby's dragoons broke into a gallop. The British cavalry were milling about having chased the surviving men of the 100th into the bayonet hedge of the 4th Light. Their horses were blown from their impetuous charge. They had no chance to form for a counter-charge or simply get away as the armoured French hit them. The impact of the cuirassiers shattered them.

Uxbridge was only too aware at that moment of his mistake in joining the charge like any ordinary *beau sabre*. Had he remained on the ridge he could have led a second line of cavalry to decisive effect. Instead he now found himself surrounded by cuirassiers who knew their business all too well. Recognizing his rank, they called on him to surrender. He declined by attacking the nearest Frenchman, beating down his guard and driving his sword through the man's throat. The others were on him in an instant and cut him out of the saddle, their horses trampling his body.

As the cuirassiers savaged Ponsonby's command, the survivors of Mitchell's brigade staggered over the crest of the British line to safety, Vandeleur's brigade covering their rear. The Union Brigade dragoons would continue to suffer as they tried to escape as well. Their tired horses left too many of them to the swords of the cuirassiers who only turned aside from their killing as they approached the slope. Determined to cover the retreat of his command, Ponsonby, though wounded in both arms, brought up the rear but his horse slowed to a walk, and he was overtaken by four cuirassiers.

I was carried on by my horse, till, receiving a blow on my head from a sabre, I was thrown senseless on my face to the ground. Recovering, I raised myself a little to look around, and when a lancer passing by exclaimed, *'Tu n'est pas mort, coquin'* ['You're not dead, you rascal'] and struck his lance through my back. My head dropped, the blood gushed into my mouth, a difficulty of breathing came on, and I thought all was over.[24]

Wellington had been a witness to the entire action. His iron self-control did not betray his distress when the gallant 1/23rd was destroyed. He remembered reviewing them in March and writing, 'I saw the 23rd the other day and I never saw a regiment in such order. They are not strong [in numbers], but it was the most complete and handsome military body I ever looked at.' He was not a sentimental man, but he truly regretted this loss, but in the end he would have agreed with Napoleon that soldiers 'are made to let themselves be killed'.[25]

2:20 p.m. – Rossomme Hill

Across the field, Napoleon woke from his nap refreshed and alert. Those short periods of sleep were a secret of his battlefield lethality that kept him at his best. He congratulated himself once again for the decision to lose weight and improve his vitality on Elba. As he rode back to the new headquarters at Rossomme Hill, he could not avoid seeing the great balloon almost completely swelled with gas. He rode over to find Coutelle, clearly impressed. 'Well, colonel, I can see I was right to have given you the Legion of Honour.'

He plied Coutelle with endless questions on how the balloon worked. He was clearly impressed with the distance that could be observed on a clear day, and today was a fine clear day. He asked how the observer communicated with the ground. Coutelle explained that messages were attached to little bags of sand and slid down a special cable. Then he noted the colonel's bandaged hand and enquired about it. When he learned of the loss of Coutelle's observer, he said, 'Well, I shall have a replacement for you.' He turned and saw his man. 'Ah, Bertrand, I shall make you famous.' Gen. Henri Gratian Bertrand stepped forward. This master military engineer was possibly the man who was the most loyal to Napoleon in all of France. They had met in Italy in 1797, and he had faithfully served his Emperor in a number of trusted positions. His bridges over the Danube in the 1809 Wagram campaign Napoleon had compared to the finest work of the Romans. He had been one of the few to volunteer to go into exile with Napoleon. 'I need you to ascend in this contraption and keep me abreast of what Wellington is doing. You are the only one I trust to do this, Bertrand.' The man positively swelled with pride at his master's public display of his confidence in him.

As Napoleon walked away, Berthier said to him that there was a surprise waiting for him. Napoleon looked puzzled as Berthier called out for a sergeant. The staff gaggle parted as a soldier of the 92nd of the Line appeared with a British regimental colour. The staff parted even more as eleven more men, six cuirassiers and five infantrymen of the 55th and 93rd of the Line, marched forward with king's and regimental colours of the KGL, spoils of the fall of La Haye Sainte, and two Hanoverian battalion colours taken at Hougoumont. It was a fine piece of battlefield theatre. Pvt. Bourhis, in a state of awe, approached the Emperor and dipped the colour so that its red folds fell out. Napoleon instantly recognized that it was the regimental colour of the Coldstream Guards. As with so many things military, he had an astonishing memory for detail.

'Ah, you see, gentleman, it is the king's colour because of the crown. And below it is the garter star that commemorates the march of General Monck in 1660 to restore order in London.' He then laughed as he pointed out the sphinx embroidered below the star. 'Egypt! Yes, yes, they were there, too, and helped gobble up all our gains. But who laughs now?' Of course, the staff laughed at his jest.[26]

2:30 p.m. – Wavre

Davout wasted no time after receiving Pajol's report on the continued flight of the Prussians. Ever since he had arrived in the town, the rumble of battle at Mont St Jean had been audible. Three couriers riding different routes arrived with the same dispatch from the conscientious Monthion. The Emperor reported he was engaged with Wellington in the area south of Mont St Jean. Davout was to join him as soon as possible. The Emperor assumed the Prussians had been seen on their way. Davout, therefore, was to cut off Wellington's retreat by way of the Brussels road and attack south. He ordered Exelmans' and Lobau's corps to march immediately in that direction. His chief of staff pointed out that they would arrive sooner on the field if they marched by way of the road through Fridmont, Chapelle St Lambert where it crossed the Lasne brook, and then to Lasne some eight miles away. That would place him just outside the Bois de Paris. The roads were dry. It would take three hours of hard marching to arrive to assist the Emperor. If they marched as the Emperor ordered, it would take them seven hours to reach the battlefield. By then night would have fallen. Davout did not have to agonize over the choice. Napoleon had made him a marshal to know when to disobey his orders.

2:45 p.m. – Rossomme Hill

Monthion read the dispatch from the courier and approached the staff clustered around Napoleon, who had been intent on the fighting west of Braine l'Aleud. He whispered into Berthier's ear and showed him the dispatch. The marshal thanked him with a curt nod and said, 'Sire, a dispatch from Vandamme. He and Gérard's corps are passing through Quatre Bras. He estimates he will arrive on the field in three hours at most. He is pushing his men hard.' Napoleon merely replied, 'Good.' For him, the news was another piece of the fluid work of art he was creating on this battlefield. One by one he had seized Wellington's advance posts – Hougoumont, La Haye Sainte, and now Braine l'Alleud – and inflicted significant casualties on his army.

At this time, the two dragoons who rode towards Napoleon's headquarters were cheered with shouts of *'Vive l'Empereur'* as they passed the battalions of the Old Guard in reserve. They were carrying the king's and regimental colours of the 23rd Foot, rewarded for their valour in seizing them by having the honour of presenting them to the Emperor himself.

Napoleon had been keeping close watch on the action with his glass and had just shut it when he heard the shouting of the Old Guard. Berthier pointed out the two approaching dragoons. They rode up to him, raised the captured standards and shouted *'Vive l'Empereur!'* and then lowered them in submission to the Emperor. He strode over and took the king's colour in his hands, saying, 'Brave dragoons, I award you the Legion of Honour!' He then waved the colour over his head to the applause and shouts of his staff, 'Brave dragoons!'

When he returned to observing the battle, the two colours were added to the bright row now stirring in a gentle breeze.[27]

On the road below, Maj. Lemmonier-Delafosse was waiting to lead some artillery forward as he paid close attention to the Emperor working on the hill. He wrote:

> Seated on a straw chair, in front of him a crude farm table, he was holding his map open on the table. His famous spyglass in hand was often trained on the various points of the battle. When resting his eye, he used to pick up straws of wheat, which he carried in his mouth as a toothpick. Stationed on his left, Maréchal [Berthier] alone waited for his orders and ten paces to the rear were grouped all his staff on horseback. Sappers of the engineers were opening up ramps around him so that people could reach the Emperor more easily . . . I left at last, with our artillery and I never saw him again. I have this ever-present memory.[28]

He just missed the arrival of Soult. He had come to confer with the Emperor on the conduct of the battle. Napoleon was in a good mood, pleased with Soult's battle management so far. In particular, he was glad to see that Soult had taken the intelligent initiative inherent in the siezure of Braine l'Alleud, following Napoleon's stated intent. Now Napoleon in quick strokes laid out his plan: 'I shall strike this Wellington two blows then impale him. First d'Erlon will attack his left and drive it in against the forest. Then we shall strike him on his right as he is reeling from the collapse of his left. With Reille in his rear, he will be trapped. *Voilà!* There it is.' He paused for a moment, then said, 'I am surprised that Wellington has not retreated. I studied his campaigns in Spain; he had the brilliant ability to slip out of every trap my marshals had set for him. Why is he still here? It will cost him dearly now.'[29]

2:50 p.m. – Mont St Guibert

Col. Wilhelm Count von Schwerin's face was set in deep anger as he rode through the town which had seen disaster fall on the Prussian III Corps. Prussian bodies littered the countryside to the east of the town where Thielmann's men had broken out. The streets of the town were filled with fallen Prussians as well. His fury was mirrored in the faces of the men of his 1st Brigade, the advance guard of Bülow's hard-marching corps. The corps commander's peremptory order to Gneisenau to stop the retreat and attack had worked miracles. The Prussian infantry that had shortly before been fleeing the French cavalry turned and stood their ground. A few steady volleys had convinced Pajol that the rout was over. He could only hope that they would just march away. Had he known how little ammunition they had, he would have pressed the issue, but Gneisenau's bold front was a successful bluff.

Leaving part of Zieten's corps to continue the bluff, Gneisenau joined Bülow and rode with him behind Schwerin's cavalry. Given the decision to fight, he had picked out a direct route for IV Corps, reinforced with a few brigades of Zieten's I and Pirch's II Corps that were still in tolerable shape. From Mont St Guibert it was only a nine-mile march to Lasne on the Rue d'Anogrune, three hours of hard marching. With luck, Schwerin would arrive on the edge of the battle in four hours. Hatred of the French would lengthen the stride of the following infantry. Two officers on the fleetest horses was sent separately to alert Wellington that the Prussians would soon join him.

Chapter 7

Pas de Charge!

3:00 p.m.–5:00 p.m., 17 June 1815

3:00 p.m. – The Ridge of Mont St Jean

With the fall of Hougoumont, La Haye Sainte, and Braine l'Alleud, a lull fell over the battlefield. It was then that Sergeant Ewart presented Wellington with the eagle of the 100th of the Line. The Duke was gracious to the sergeant, but to himself it meant little. He had a nice collection of them from the Peninsula. Of more importance, he would have to explain to the Prince Regent how the Coldstream battalion had been destroyed and its regimental colour lost. He tucked that worry away; far larger worries loomed. It was clear that a strong blow would come on his left. An equally strong force was on his right, and the French Guard was opposite his centre-right. The presence of the Guard especially focused his attention on the threat to his right and centre-right.

He could see great numbers of French infantry massing behind the ominous Grand Battery. It was impressive to see the French manoeuvre into position so expertly as their bands played. He remarked to no one in particular that the French truly were capital soldiers.

He also had to admit, though he kept this to himself, that Napoleon was everything he had feared him to be. In bold strokes he had crossed the Sambre to split the Allied army and Blücher's; then he had crushed the Prussians and he had manoeuvred to cut him off from his strategic reserve at Hal and the route of withdrawal upon his port of embarkation, Ostend, by the taking of Braine l'Alleud. That loss had also threatened his alternative route of withdrawal up the Brussels road and the route to his alternate port of embarkation, Antwerp. If he could not hold that open, he would be reduced to withdrawing through the Forest of Soignes, preferably at night. Even that was problematic. If he were Napoleon, he would grasp him by the belt buckle and make it impossible to withdraw. It is always useful to think that the enemy will do what he ought to do.

He weighed his alternatives and concluded that it would not be possible to pull the entire army out through the forest. He would have to use both routes, his right by the Brussels road and his left by the forest. To secure the former, he had ordered the Netherlands Cavalry Division to cover the road by occupying Mesnil. He was not aware of how slowly his orders were being carried out.

All eyes instead were on the balloon that had risen over the hill south of La Belle Alliance. Very few men in the Allied army had seen a balloon on a battlefield. Certainly, it was a novelty for Wellington. He had seen a demonstration in England and remembered distinctly how the aeronaut had been able to describe the countryside in detail for a dozen or more miles. He and his staff stopped as they rode east along the sunken road to peer at it. The realization struck him instantly that his dispositions behind the reverse slope would now become an open book for Napoleon.

Only the few men on the ridge – gunners, observers, officers – saw the balloon. But the word quickly spread to the ranks on the reverse slope. Something that exotic only added to the men's unease. On Wellington's left, the only men the French could see were Perponcher's Dutch-Belgians and Nassauers driven back to man the sunken road behind the hedges. Right behind them was the 1/42nd Highlanders (the Black Watch). Lt. Mackenzie MacDonald recalled, 'We knew the Prussians had been beaten . . . we felt no confidence in the Belgian troops with whom we were associated.' Another officer, Ensign George Gerard stated that 'people pretend to be attached to the House of Orange – the great majority of them really were not so'. 'Gerard had been told by an English resident in Brussels that the Belgian soldiers were not to be trusted as the greater part of them had served under Bonaparte, to whom they were much attached, and that he had little doubt the most of them would go over to him as good opportunities occurred.'[1]

The only element of the 2nd Netherland's Division that had retreated in good order at Quatre Bras was the Dutch horse artillery battery of six 6-pounders and two 5.5-inch howitzers commanded by Captain Adriaan van Bijleveld. His battery provided the rearguard behind which the remnants of the division had retreated. Now it took its place in the road only 300 yards from the crossroads.

3:00 p.m. – Rossomme Hill

As Wellington pondered, Napoleon looked up at the balloon swaying gently in the light breeze several hundred feet above his headquarters. He looked up, shading his eyes, and muttered, 'Well, Bertrand, what do you see?'

He walked a short distance to his right to observe the assembly of d'Erlon's corps with Soult. He was feeling voluble. 'I have made a great study of Wellington, Soult.' He did not say to him that he considered Wellington his only peer. As early as 1810 he had concluded that, 'In Europe there are only Wellington and myself.' Still, no need now to build up the man Soult was about to attack. Instead, he said,

'Wellington has used this same trick of hiding behind a hill against every one of my marshals. He is a one-trick general, a very good trick, I must admit, but you can only use it so many times before your enemy catches on.'[2]

Soult was pointing out how d'Erlon's left was secured now that La Haye Sainte was in the hands of Quiot's division. It was more than secured, it was now bristling with guns. 'We could not ask for a better jumping-off point for an attack. Quiot should be able to rupture Wellington's front just as d'Erlon's other divisions close on the ridge. Unfortunately, we do not know where Wellington has placed his reserves.'

Napoleon commented, 'If he hasn't thrown up over the side of the balloon, Bertrand should be able to tell us something about that.' Wellington's all-too-successful trick of the reverse slope might well be out-tricked by Coutelle's balloon.

As a hedge against the late arrival of Vandamme and Gérard, Napoleon had earlier ordered the Guard up to the open ground just to the west of La Belle Alliance. Should d'Erlon rupture the Duke's flank, the Guard would then smash into his right. He retained the 1st Grenadiers (the 'Oldest of the Old') as his personal reserve. The 3rd Regiment of the Grenadiers and the 1st and 3rd Regiments of the Chasseurs à Pied, 6,000 men, would make up this assault force. The Young Guard of almost 4,800 men remained in reserve. He could afford such a small reserve because even if III and IV Corps did not arrive in time for the assault, they would arrive in time to form a reserve if needed, he calculated.

3:00 p.m. – Epinay

Lambert's 10th Brigade had entered Brussels earlier in the afternoon, dropped off the 81st Foot as garrison and marched south with almost 2,300 men. One of its officers later wrote that Brussels was:

> The scene of confusion, the flying army baggage, etc., was an awful novelty to us. We were directed by subsequent order to halt at the village of Epinay, on the Brussels side of the forest of Soignies [sic], a report having reached his Grace that the enemy's cavalry were threatening our communications. The whole afternoon we were in a continued state of excitement. Once some rascals of the Cumberland Hussars, a new corps of Hanoverians (not of the style of our noble and gallant old comrades, the 1st Hussars), came galloping declaring they were pursued by Frenchmen. Our bugles were blowing in all directions, and our troops running to their alarm posts in front of the village. I went to report to Sir John Lambert . . . who says coolly, 'Let the troops —; this is all nonsense; there is not a French soldier in the rear of his Grace, depend on it, and sit down to dinner.'[3]

3:15 p.m. – Braine l'Alleud

Reille's II Corps now firmly held the ruined town. Smoke from dozens of burning buildings hung above it, drifting north on the soft breeze. Reille said to his staff that the Emperor's star had returned. The smoke was concealing the movement of his last fresh division, Bachelu's 5th. They followed the track of Piré's cavalry division. The smoke hid the dust cloud of 5,000 marching infantrymen and a dozen guns.

3:30 p.m. – Above Rossomme Hill

As the balloon ascended, Bertrand was amazed as the entire battlefield unfolded before him. He could see everything. No copse, no fold in the ground could hide troops or guns from him. The ridge behind which Wellington's army sheltered gave up its cloak of invisibility. When the balloon reached its maximum height, the strong rope cables that would give it stability were pulled taut by the ground crews and tied to stout stakes driven into the ground. Bertrand immediately unfolded his little field-draftsman's table and began to sketch everything he saw. In twenty minutes, he was finished. Coutelle took the map, folded it into a small tube and put it in a small sand-filled bag that he tied to a loop on the special message cable. He sent it sliding down while shouting to the waiting sergeant to alert him. His orders were to run with it straight to Berthier. The marshal took one look and exclaimed, '*Mon Dieu!*'

Napoleon looked up at his old friend's uncharacteristic excitement, as Berthier said, 'Sire, you must read this.' He laid it on the farm table.

Napoleon studied intently, marvelling at the treasure before him. Bertrand in an engineer's precise hand had drawn a map of the deployment of Wellington's forces. Now it was his turn to exclaim. 'Soult, come here!' The marshal bent over the table, and his eyes grew wide. 'Just as I expected. Wellington's left is the weakest. And he has precious few reserves. Look, on his left flank there are no infantry reserves, only one cavalry brigade.'

He turned around to look at his staff and saw Coignet. 'Old grousser! Get a fast horse and take this map immediately to General d'Erlon. Tell him he is to study this and make dispositions accordingly!' Coignet tucked the folded map in his coat and raced over to the nearest chasseur á pied of the Emperor's escort, jumped up, grabbed the man by the collar, pulled him off his horse, and in an instant was in the saddle whipping the poor beast down the hill.

'Berthier, remind me that man is to be promoted *chef de battalion* after this battle.' Then to Soult, 'Best follow him and make sure d'Erlon makes the most of this treasure from heaven. My throne rides on d'Erlon's success. I do not make it a practice to burden my generals with too much detailed instruction but to rely on their judgement. But in this case, I will make an exception. Meet me back at La Belle Alliance. This hill has a fine view, but it is just too far from the battle. I must be closer.'[4]

3:30 p.m. – The Great Elm

Maj. Helmuth von Beildorf had used up his fine horse in carrying Bülow's message to Wellington. By the time his mount limped into the Allied army's left flank, the poor creature was spent. Fortunately, he was found by Vivian's 6th Cavalry Brigade patrolling the army flank. He was escorted on a fresh horse to the Duke, who was at the great elm that grew at the intersection of the Brussels and Ohain–Braine l'Alleud roads.

He read the dispatch quickly. His staff was watching him intently. They all knew that Gneisenau would not be coming to their aid. The loss of Prussian assistance obviated the very reason why Wellington had decided to fight here. Now, though, a Prussian courier had arrived. The question of why hung in the air. The Duke's sudden and very rare expression of animation alerted his staff. 'Gentlemen, Bülow has assumed command of the Prussian army and is marching with 50,000 men to our support. He promises to reach us between 5:00 and 6:00.'

Suddenly, the thunder of the Great Battery struck every ear and turned every head.

3:30 p.m. – The Grand Battery

'*Feu!*' Almost 200 miles to the south-west, the windows of Paris rattled. Over 100 guns on either side of the Brussels–Genappe road erupted. Two French artillery officers later remembered:

> Gunners were standing in line inserting the charges, ramming them home and swinging the slow matches to make them burn more fiercely . . . Behind them stood the captain of the guns, nearly all of them elderly and they gave their orders as if on parade. Eighty guns fired together, drowning out every other sound. The whole valley was filled with smoke. A second or two later the clear calm voices of the captains could be heard again; 'Load! Ram! Arm! Fire!' This continued without break for half an hour. We could scarcely see our comrades while across the valley the English had also opened fire. We could hear the whistle of their cannon balls in the air, the dull thud when they struck the ground and that other sound as muskets were smashed to matchwood and men hurled twenty paces to the rear, every bone crushed.[5]

The effects of Napoleonic artillery fire on humans could be terrifying . . . artillery roundshot was virtually guaranteed to cause dramatic and gory casualties. The cannonballs themselves were subsonic, and lobbed slowly through the air, loudly whistling as they approached. Even at the end of its effective range, rolling shot would bowl men over and cause widespread injury. If flying shot hit a horse, it was not just a matter of the horse falling over; the ball might strike the saddlebags, scattering the contents in every direction as the horse went spinning, splattering pieces of the animal closely behind the chunks of leather and cloth. At close range, artillery fire would punch holes straight through entire sections of units.[6]

Lt. Col. James Stanhope, of the 3rd Battalion, 1st Guards, remembered how grim the effect of the guns was:

A number of Staff officers were soon killed & wounded who were the first alone exposed to the cannonade. General Cooke lost his arm, shells began to fall in our squares & though many men were blown up & horribly mangled I never saw such steadiness. As the poor wounded wretches remained in the square it was a horrid sight in cold blood.[7]

For half an hour the guns would pound that section of the Allied line that was the objective of d'Erlon's corps. The Grand Battery fired into a box roughly 1,200 feet wide and 375 yards deep that included the 14,000 men in twenty-two infantry battalions of Alten's and Picton's divisions but did not extend to where the one cavalry brigade lay in reserve. The Guards' Beautiful Daughters and other guns in the battery near Hougoumont targeted a smaller box on Cooke's division on the Allied right.

The only visible targets were the Allied guns. At first many of the French shots struck just below the edge of the ridge. But the ground was dry, hard clay, perfect for ricochets that spun into the gun crews. Soon the French gunners lifted their range to target the guns themselves. The strike of shot on an artillery piece is a terrible thing, smashing the carriage or the gun tube itself, sending splinters of wood and metal into the surrounding crew. Captain Friedrich Wiez later reported, 'Three guns of a recently arrived battery were smashed before firing a single shot, and one of this battery's caissons blew up just as it was passing near the front of the 1st Battalion.' With the caisson ablaze, its horses panicked and hauled it straight towards the large artillery park from where it had come. Some dragoons hurried over and attempted to sabre the animals but failed before the horses ran in among the closely parked caissons. Crashing into another caisson, the fire set off a chain explosion in the park that consumed hundreds of men and horses. The explosion shot up in a red-streaked black cloud over the Allied line. Napoleon clapped his hands in the delight of a gunner who sees what his profession has done.

The crews of the Grand Battery stopped long enough for a wild cheer, then bent to their guns again. Captain Alexander Cavalie Mercer of the Royal Artillery paid tribute to this terrible fire:

> The rapidity and precision of fire was quite appalling. Every shot almost took effect, and I certainly expected we would all be annihilated. Our horses and limbers, being a little retired down the slope had hitherto been somewhat under cover from the direct fire in front; but this plunged right amongst them, knocking them down by pairs, and creating horrible confusion. The drivers could hardly extricate themselves from one dead horse ere another fell, or perhaps themselves. The saddle bags, in many instances were torn from the horses' back, and their contents scattered over the field. One shell I saw explode under the two finest wheel-horses in our troop – down they dropped.[8]

The first French rounds struck the slope below the road, but the gunners quickly adjusted the elevation of their guns. The dry ground was an ally of the French guns. Had it rained recently, the shot and shell would have buried themselves in the soft ground. Instead those that hit the edge of the road embankment ricocheted among the guns and their crews. Those that fell over the road landed on the reverse ground amid the infantry lying prone on the ground. The ricochets flew along the ground, killing and maiming. Shells exploded in the air over the crouching troops spewing jagged iron among them. Other shells landed and bounced on the ground with sparking fuses until they exploded. Any man foolish enough to try to stop a skidding ball with his foot was sure to lose it, and it took a brave and lucky man to tear a burning fuse from a spinning shell.

The French gunners in the Grand Battery concentrated on the thirty-six Allied guns along the road to the left of the Brussels–Genappe road. Most of the French guns were just at the range where their accuracy was high. Allied gun after gun was silenced, filling the road with wrecked guns and dead and wounded gunners.

The batteries of the Guard joined the fire of the Grand Battery, aiming at the British centre and right. The eighteen 12-pounder howitzers of the Beautiful Daughters arced to fall into the British salient packed with infantry of five brigades of the British 1st Infantry (Household) and 2nd Infantry Divisions. In that space, approximately 1,000 yards square, were almost 12,000 British, KGL, and Hanoverian infantry as well as 2,000 British and KGL cavalry, numerous horse teams, and limbers of the guns lining the ridge. The large shells burst among the red-coated battalions with horrendous effect.

3:40 p.m. – French I Corps Headquarters

Coignet did not have far to go to find d'Erlon. His headquarters was on the long high ground behind the depression in which the Grand Battery's caissons and limbers waited. His 2nd, 3rd, and 4th Infantry Divisions were strung out on either side.

Coignet pulled his horse to such a quick stop that its hooves set a spray of gravel at d'Erlon and his division commanders. The captain got the tail of what was a heated argument. Gen. Pierre Durutte, commanding the 4th Infantry Division, stated flatly, 'I absolutely refuse to deploy my division in such an imbecilic formation!'

Then they all turned to see Coignet as he jumped off his horse, saluted, and said, 'Sir, by command of the Emperor, you are to study this map and plan your attack correspondingly.'

'What is this?' asked d'Erlon.

'I believe it was drawn by Gen. Bertrand from the balloon.' They all looked back to see the *Marengo* floating above Rossomme Hill.' D'Erlon unfolded it and said to his commanders, 'Observe, gentlemen.' The map elicited the same response that Berthier had made. 'Look, there is only one cavalry brigade on their left.'

The commander of the 3rd Infantry Division, Gen. Pierre Binet de Marcognet, added, 'And not one reserve infantry brigade. Everything is along their line.'

Durutte announced with no little vindication, 'Your formation is no longer necessary. All we have to do is break their line in one place, and it all will collapse.' D'Erlon was about to respond, when Soult arrived. The marshal asked what conclusions they had reached after reading the map. D'Erlon summarized their conclusions that the enemy line was vulnerable because of its lack of reserves.

Durutte spoke up. 'There is the issue of the formation of battle.' He was not a man to hold his tongue. He had been one of the first to receive the Legion of Honour but his Republican principles had made him refuse to sign his approval of Napoleon's assumption of the throne. At the same time, he would not let his subordinates follow his example lest it harm their careers. A period of exile as governor of Elba had followed, but he had redeemed himself commanding a division in the Wagram and Russian campaigns. He had achieved the distinction of bringing his division intact out of the debacle of the Russian winter.

D'Erlon shot him an evil look. But he had no choice but to explain that he wanted to attack with his division in *colone de division par battaillon*. It was an unusual formation, to say the least, and one that had never been used before. Clearly, his experience fighting the British in the Peninsula prompted this formation. The usual French attack formation was two companies wide with sixty men in the front rank and nine men deep (*colone de battaillon par division*). This gave the formation speed and manoeuvrability. These fast-moving columns would be preceded by clouds of skirmishers who would disorder the enemy who fought on line. Horse artillery and cavalry supported these columns. The guns would rake the enemy lines with canister while the cavalry threatened the enemy to switch from line to square, which was then even more vulnerable to artillery and the attack of the French infantry.

This worked well with all enemies except the British. It was Wellington who devised the combination of tactics that invariably defeated the French attacking columns. He employed superior skirmishers armed with the Baker rifle, the green-uniformed 95th Rifles and Portuguese *cadadores*. They drove off the French skirmishers and shot down the French artillery horses and gunners. The French column then found itself facing a British battalion in two lines, bringing 250 muskets to bear in the first volley on the head of a French column with only sixty muskets.

D'Erlon concluded that to match British firepower he had to march up his battalions in a three-rank formation to have a fighting chance to pound it out. The French had been known to employ the line in the attack, but d'Erlon's innovation was to stack up all eight battalions in each division in that manner, one behind the other. He argued that once the division approached the enemy ridge, the following battalions could slide out to the right or left and bring even more muskets to bear.

The look on Soult's face shouted scepticism. In general, he agreed with the Emperor that the corps commanders should not be overly controlled, but this situation was an exception. D'Erlon was clearly overreacting to his experience with the British in Spain. He saw no need to employ tact which, in any case, was not his nature. He looked d'Erlon in the eye. 'I speak in the Emperor's name now. Your formation is too complex, and it will slow you down as you cross the beaten zone, and it will cause the enemy artillery to rejoice at such packed targets. *Colone de battaillon par division* is the appropriate formation. Your battalions can easily go on line when they approach within musket range of the enemy.' He added that the Emperor had directed Gen. Milhaud's IV Reserve Cavalry Corps to support the attack.

D'Erlon summoned what dignity he could by saying to his commanders, 'Gentlemen, you have your orders.' The guns would be firing for one hour. The corps would have to attack then. Fortunately, the three divisions were already in formation of *colone de battaillon par division*.

Durutte strode away, doing his best to hide his smirk. His division would be on the far right. He had already scouted out the hamlets that ran parallel to his direction of attack. They were defended by Nassau troops. He would have to drop one of his brigades to protect his flank.

Quiot's 1st Infantry Division on the far left would not have to march that 700 yards to the enemy line. It already occupied La Haye Sainte, which it had seized earlier. It had now been reinforced with several artillery batteries. Only a few hundred yards separated the farm garden from the enemy line. The distance was even less from the knoll to the right of the sandpit, now filled with skirmishers peppering the enemy, picking off the gunners of Maj. Rogers' horse artillery battery. The French guns duelled with the battery, eventually knocking out most of its pieces. At 150 yards the French skirmishers and guns were also duelling with the 1/95th Rifles lining the road from the battery to the road intersection above the farm. Showers of canister at close range cut through the hedge to pepper the road with green-clad bodies. Their fire also kept down the Dutch-Belgian troops huddling nearby in the road. As the duelling went on, Quiot's 2nd Brigade moved to the dead ground below the knoll and into the sandpit. A British sergeant recounted the determination of the French light troops:

> The skirmishers in advance of their columns about La Haye Sainte, the knoll and sandpit and along the valley right and left, threw out a rattling fire for the purpose of harassing and weakening our line, to clear the way for the grand attack . . . this fire was repelled vigorously by our troops, who were partially covered from the enemy's fire by the hedgerow and banks on our part of the front . . . The fire increased, and it appeared as if all would be borne down by it. The banks on the road side, the garden wall, the knoll and sandpit swarmed with skirmishers determined to keep down our fire in front.[9]

Maj. Gen. Baron François Donzelot's 2nd Infantry Division would attack to the east of Quiot's. Marcognet's division was next in line, linking up with Durutte on the extreme right. These three divisions would attack in echelon so that the enemy line would suffer a series of rippling shocks as each division closed.

3:45 p.m. – The Inn at La Belle Alliance

Napoleon's concentration on the attack was wrenched away when Berthier presented him with Bertrand's latest report. Reille's cavalry was in Wellington's rear with infantry following. Far in the other direction long dark columns were marching from Mont St Guibert towards Lasne. He gave his attention to the greater threat first. 'Berthier, it can only be Prussians. How could Davout have let this happen? Send another courier to Davout to countermarch and intercept these Prussians. Send Coignet.'

Monthion showed Coignet a good map and helped him plot the fastest route to Davout. The old grouser wasted no time and spurred off.

4:00 p.m. – Outside Lasne

Coignet was fast, and Monthion's map accurate. He rode behind the army's right flank and skirted the Bois de Paris. He had no idea that a Prussian cavalry patrol just within the Bois de Paris watched him ride by. They had crossed the Lasne River over the bridge at the little village of Aywiers barely two miles south of Lasne.

It was only four miles on a decent road to Lasne, but to his surprise outside the town he came across a Prussian officer riding towards him.

> A hundred paces . . . he stopped and awaited me . . . I also halted, and, drawing my pistol, I sent a ball past his ears. He got angry, and started in pursuit of me. I wheeled about. He no longer followed me, but turned back. Then I wheeled round to the left, and charged him. Seeing me again, he came back at me. I sent him a second pistol-shot. He got angry, and came hard at me. I wheeled about and rode off. He pursued me . . . in a rage. I faced about, and fell upon him. He came close to me, and tried to stick his sabre into me. I struck his sabre up above his head, and, with the same stroke, brought my sabre down upon his face with such force that his nose went down to find his chin. He fell stone-dead.[10]

Coignet seized the Prussian's horse before it could trot off and noticed a dispatch case attached to the saddle. He reached over and took it. Opening it, he found a letter addressed to Wellington from Bülow. The Prussian had the courtesy to write in French, the mutual language of the Allies, and the lingua franca of Europe. Coignet's eyes grew wide as he read it, exclaiming 'O, la la!' He whipped his horse into Lasne.

The town, more a village, lay along the Lasne River which ran through a steep wooded ravine. At the southern end of the village, a bridge crossed the river to Mont St Guibert. His road continued north through Chapelle St Lambert to Wavre and, he hoped, Davout.

Just at the crossroads he saw a Prussian uhlan patrol crossing the bridge in his direction. They shouted and gave chase as he sped north the two miles to Chapelle St Lambert. Just outside the town, a pistol-shot hit his horse. The animal stumbled and fell to its knees. Coignet barely had time to jump off before it fell over, thrashing about in pain. As he leaped, the reins of the other horse slipped his hand. The uhlans had shouted in triumph as his horse fell. Now they couched their lances. Coignet drew his own sabre, not sure whether to fight it out or jump down into the ravine.

A yell in French and then a dragoon raced past him, followed by twenty more. The outnumbered uhlans tried to turn about, but the dragoons were on them. In a few moments the survivors were racing back to Lasne with half the dragoons in pursuit. The rest returned with five prisoners. Four bodies lay on the road. The young lieutenant, his sword dripping red, looked down at Coignet. 'Well, captain. You have the devil's own luck. May I offer you a horse?'

4:10 p.m. – The Brussels Road

Piré peered through the small wood at the Brussels road a few hundred yards away. The usual assembly of tents and supply wagons of an army's train, along with the far less tidy collection of camp-followers – not to mention English tourists – spread out into the fields. The road itself was busy with traffic. Some of the wounded of the day's fighting were being moved to Brussels by wagon. The walking wounded trudged along on their own or with a companion who thought he had a good excuse for absenting himself from the fight.

The head of Collaert's cavalry division were making slow headway through the traffic, which no one was controlling. Finally it reached the intersection with the road leading to Mesnil and turned in that direction. At that moment Piré's lancers and chasseurs charged out of the woods. The lead 6th Lancers charged with lances levelled into the head of the Netherlands's column, the 1st Dutch Carabiniers. The column came apart as the Dutch flinched in panic at the tide of stabbing steel. The following regiments peeled to the south, forming on line to strike for the road. The French poured through the wagon parks and tents, scattering the supply troops, laundry women, and tourists in their path. The Netherlands cavalry struggled to deploy but were too hemmed in by the buildings lining the road and the mass of wagons and tents, and the French were upon them too soon. They were packed so tight that many could not escape. Their two batteries clogged the road completely. The French were cutting down the crews, who either surrendered or fled as best they could.

Bringing up the rear of the Netherlands Division behind the guns was its 2nd Light Brigade with the 6th Dutch Hussars and the 5th Belgian Light Dragoons. They were just approaching the intersection of the Nivelles and Genappe roads in the middle of the village when the catastrophe rolled down the Brussels road straight to them. To his credit, their commander, Maj. Gen. J.D. van Merlen tried to attack, but he fell to the sabre of a French hussar. His command dissolved and fled down the Nivelles road. The panicked mob raced right into the rear of the salient on the far right of the British line that Soult was about to attack. Nothing will shatter morale faster than terrified soldiers screaming that the enemy is in the army's rear, especially when there are actual enemy chasseurs hacking at them as they flee. More panicked survivors of the Netherlands cavalry and mob of quartermasters, camp-followers, and British tourists came pouring out of Mont St Jean down the Genappe road. Hard on their rear were French lancers, Piré at their head. He was riding the lead tide of the French attack. Collaert had to surrender to a French junior officer amid the wreckage of his division. The French cavalry had not known a more glorious exploit. Nike seemed to be offering the laurel of victory to the French at that very moment.

Confusion shuddered through the Allied right. The old hands gritted their teeth. Many of them, no doubt, thought of the 57th Foot at the blood-soaked Battle of Albuera in 1811. The regiment had been on the point of being overwhelmed by the fury of the French attack. The commander, lying wounded in front of the firing line, had cried out, 'Die hard, the 57th! Die hard!' Out of 570 men in the ranks, 420 were lost as well as twenty of the thirty officers. It was going to be a day like that. Commanding the army that day, Lord Beresford wrote that the men lay where they had fallen, every wound in the front. There was a difference between Albuera and Mont St Jean: Wellington had not commanded at Albuera.

Wellington was sitting on his horse at the great elm. He kept his head, which is just what his veterans, British and the Germans of the KGL, expected. The effect on the inexperienced British regiments whom he had never commanded, and especially among the Netherlands and assorted Germans, was entirely different. They were like a glass on the point of shattering with the smallest additional pressure. Already deserters were bolting from the ranks and fleeing into the woods.

The 700 Hanoverian hussars of the 3rd KGL (7th British Cavalry Brigade) had turned in their saddles to see what all the noise was about. Veterans that they were, they were still shocked by the sight of the panicked mob of Netherlanders rushing towards them. They flew through the Hanoverians, disrupting their ranks and carrying many of them along. Wellington rode to the nearest infantry regiment, the 1st KGL, whom he knew and trusted, and ordered it to reverse front to block the mass of fleeing Netherlanders. They charged bayonets to warn them off.

Next Wellington galloped over to Maj. Gen. Wilhelm von Dörnberg, commanding the 3rd British Cavalry Brigade. 'Dörnberg, strike the French coming up the road. They must be broken.' Dörnberg, a Hessian in British service, drew his sabre and ordered his British and KGL light dragoons to wheel about and follow him. The mass of Netherlanders had come to a halt in front of the infantry. The following French hussars were mixed in with the 3rd KGL cavalry in dozens of individual combats when Dörnberg's regiments struck the mass of struggling men.

As the Netherlanders fled down the Nivelles road, the mass of terrified noncombatants had poured out of Mont St Jean onto the Genappe road, right into the rear of the 1st British (Household) Cavalry Brigade which was rapidly trying to wheel about. Riding through the crowd were Piré and his lancers. Piré led his 6th Lancers in a wedge, running down the fugitives straight into the Household Cavalry.

The wedge struck the four squadrons of the Royal Regiment of Life Guards. Wellington was the colonel of this regiment. The 5th Lancers came up to hit the neighbouring 1st (King's) Dragoon Guards. The shock of their attack hitting cavalry at its most awkward moment and the deadly lances broke both regiments apart, despite the fact they were heavies, big men on big horses. The diminutive Piré found himself trying to parry the anvil sword-blows of one guardsman who had kept his wits about him. The Frenchman's arm was numb. The next blow would probably have been the last, but a lancer rode up and drove his lance into the Briton's side. Piré saluted the man and shouted, 'Follow me, my children! *En avant!*'

In front of them were the terrified Nassau battalions of Kruse's regiment, which had taken the place of Ompteda's sturdy KGL slaughtered around La Haye Sainte. The men were green and inexperienced, and panic was running through them despite the desperate efforts of their veteran officers to keep them in line. They could get only a ragged volley off before the lancers hit them. The entire regiment dissolved, many fleeing down the slope in the direction of the French to escape the stabbing lances. In a rage, Kruse rode among his men, rallying them as best he could.

Kielmansegge was stunned to witness this disaster sweep away the Hanoverians on his left. His men watched, slack-jawed, shock and surprise draining away their courage. Kielmansegge snapped out of it. He bellowed out the command to form square. The order to do something that was almost an automatic response was seized upon by his officers to shake their men out of their fear.

Wellington had found himself almost in the path of the lancers. His staff drew their swords, attracting the attention of a squad of lancers, who rode into them. His young aides threw themselves in front of their Duke and died. Because of his dark cloak and clothes, Wellington did not attract as much attention as his brilliantly accoutered aides did. This was no time for personal courage. He spurred his horse Copenhagen towards the forming square of the Hanoverian Duke of York's 1st Field Battalion. Copenhagen leaped inside.

4:20 p.m. – Chapelle St Lambert

The dragoons that had saved Coignet were part of Exelmans' advance guard. Coignet found the cavalry general just entering the town and showed him the letter. He immediately dispatched his 1st Brigade of dragoons to seize and hold the bridge at Lasne. As the brigade clattered off, Davout rode up and was given the letter. 'Coignet, if the Emperor does not make you a baron of the Empire for this, he is a damned fool. Now, off with you. Give the Emperor this letter and tell him I will hold the Prussians here. They will not interfere with his conversation with Wellington.' As he was saying this, Exelmans' 2nd Brigade was trotting past. He went on to say, 'Lobau's corps is right behind them and my Saxons after that. We will give Fritz a bloody nose.'

4:30 p.m. – French I Corps Headquarters

On command, the three divisions moved forward in *colone de battaillon par division*. Each division had two brigades of two regiments. The brigades marched in parallel with their regiments in column. They descended into the depression filled with the caissons and limbers of the Grand Battery. The men there had been alerted and moved to create lanes through which the columns moved easily. They marched up the slope, and as they mounted the high ground, the Grand Battery's guns fell silent. The columns filtered through the guns and cheering gunners with admirable efficiency and descended into the low ground that led to the enemy ridge. As soon as the columns were out of the line of fire, the Grand Battery resumed its fire.

D'Erlon positioned himself in the centre of his corps, 'and with a strong, clear voice pronounced these few words: "Today it is necessary to vanquish or die!"' These were the vivid recollections of the young conscript, Louis Canler: 'The shout of "*Vive l'Empereur*" came from every mouth in reply to this brief speech and with the drummers beating the charge the columns moved off.'

Two officers in the 45th of the Line in Marcognet's division left fascinating accounts of the spirit of the French troops. Lt. Jacques Martin, a French-speaking Swiss in French service, remembered:

> the order arrived to climb the position and to seize 'à la baïonette' the English batteries and anything else that offered resistance. The ridge line bristled with their cannons and was covered with their troops; it appeared impregnable. No matter, the order arrived, the charge was beaten, the cry of '*Vive l'Empereur*' came from every mouth, and we marched ahead, closed ranks, aligned as on a parade.
>
> I can testify to the fact: in this critical moment, I did not see a single cowardly thought painted on the face of our soldiers. The same ardour, the same gaiety shone there as before. However, the shot had already killed many, and this prompted the thoughts that the carnage would be terrible when we arrived at their guns.[11]

Captain Kinkaid of the 95th Rifles was awestruck at the scene spread out before him:

> The scene at the moment was grand and imposing . . . each regiment . . . rent the air with shouts of '*Vive l'Empereur!*' nor did they cease after they had passed; but backed by the thunder of their artillery, and carrying with them the *rubidud* of drums, and the *tantara* of trumpets, in addition to their increasing shouts, it looked, at first, as if they had some hopes of scaring us off the ground.[12]

The drummers were beating the rolling *pas de charge*, the stirring music that always animated a French attack. A young British officer remembered the rhythm as 'the rum dum, the rum dum, the rummadum dummadum, dum, dum', followed by a pause in which the massed troops would shout *'Vive l'Empereur!'*

Captain Pierre-Charles Duthilt of the 45th wrote, 'Our turn came, and the order to attack was greeted with a fervent shout of *Vive l'Empereur!* The four columns moved down the slope . . . with ported arms. We were to climb the opposite slope where the English held the ridge and from where their batteries blasted us.' He estimated that a normal man could cross this beaten zone in no more than five minutes.

Canler recounted:

At this moment the enemy batteries which had only sent cannon balls and shells decimated our columns with canister [shrapnel – case shot]. We had scarcely gone one hundred paces when the commander of our second battalion, Marins, was mortally wounded. The Captain of my company, Duzer, was struck by two balls. Adjutant Hubaut and eagle-bearer Crosse were killed . . . at the second discharge of the English guns the grenadiers' drummer, Lecointre, lost his right arm.[13]

Drummer Lecointre marched on, striking his drum with only one hand, then collapsed from loss of blood. He was to survive. Instead of the slow solid mass that would have come at the gunners had d'Erlon had his way, rushing columns were quickly cutting through the high rye. The columns were harder to hit, but when they were the damage was horrific: 'if a round-shot ploughed into the thick mass, several files of men would fall back "as if pulled by a rope".' As the French were little over halfway to the ridge, 300 yards, the gunners switched to a load of double canister and shot. Amid this carnage, the men stepped over the fallen as their officers relentlessly shouted, *'Serrez les rangs! Serrez les rangs!'* ('Close ranks').

4:30 p.m. – 1,000 Yards East of Plancenoit

The Prussian lieutenant stood up in his stirrups to see better and muttered, *'Liebe Gott!'* He had just seen d'Erlon's corps move through the Grand Battery. It was the sight of a lifetime. And he had seen enough to know that his report of it must be delivered to Bülow as fast as his horse could gallop. His cavalry patrol waited in the trees nearby. He raced past them, shouting, 'After me!' It was only 2,500 yards to the bridge over the Lasne at the village of Aywiers where he had crossed.

4:30 p.m. – The Inn at La Belle Alliance

Few men had seen so much of war as Napoleon, but even he had not seen anything as remarkable as when Piré's lancers crested the ridge in front of him chasing the

Nassauers down the slope. Gasps and cries of surprise rippled from his staff. He put his glass down and shouted for Mortier, the commander of the Guard. 'Now, Mortier, now! Attack with the Guard. I cannot wait for Vandamme and Gérard. Hit them hard, and they will crack wide open like a melon.' He was fuming that Vandamme was late again.

4:35 p.m. – The Ridge of Mont St Jean

The lancers now paid the price for their impetuous attack. In their wake Sommerset rallied the Household Brigade and charged those scattered over the ridge, spearing gunners and Nassauers. With their horses now blown, they fell to the heavy swords of the Guards out for revenge at the insult they had just suffered. Piré himself was surrounded by three guardsmen, but there was no lancer to save him this time. A downwards slash from a powerful arm split him from neck to breastbone.

Dörnberg's brigade had driven Piré's hussars back up the road through the village of Mont St Jean. Ponsonby's and Vandeleur's brigades joined in wiping out the last of the lancers. Wellington rode out of the Hanoverian square and ordered his last reserve, Col. Hugh Halkett's 3rd Hanoverian Brigade, to fill the gap in the line left by the destruction of the Nassau Brigade. Halkett was a Scotsman who had distinguished himself in the Peninsula and commanded Germans of the KGL. He entered Hanoverian service after Napoleon's abdication. If ever there was an unlucky position in military history, it was the one now being occupied by the 3rd Hanoverian Brigade. Ompteda's brigade had held it and perished in front of La Haye Sainte. The Nassauers had replaced them, and they too fell to the fury of French cavalry. It had been a bad day for Germans, something not likely to encourage Halkett's men.

4:40 p.m. – Lasne

The 1st West Prussian Uhlans came trotting over the bridge at Lasne. Numbering over 600 men, they extended for some length down the road. Their advance patrol had not reported back, and Lt. Col. Beier, commanding, assumed they had continued on their mission. He was about to be disabused. A disguised horse artillery battery at the intersection on the far side of the bridge fired. Two 6-pounder balls ploughed through the uhlans packed on the narrow bridge. Then two more 6-pounders fired canister. Beier was among the dead and wounded men and horses clogging the bridge.

Bülow was quickly informed and hurried the 14th Infantry Brigade forward to seize the bridge, but its attack only added to the carnage on the bridge. At the same time Lobau's lead brigade entered Chapelle St Lambert and kept going with orders to take over the defence of Lasne from Exelmans' cavalry. A patrol soon informed Bülow that that route was also now blocked. More patrols had been sent south to find a way over the Lasne.

4:40 p.m. – *Pas de Charge!*

As soon as the attacking troops had descended into the depression, the Grand Battery resumed firing, not only to inflict damage but to add to the immense psychological effect of the mass of infantry with the thunder of hundreds of rounds coming the enemy's way. The Duke had given strict orders that there was to be no counter-battery fire. The full attention of the guns must be upon defeating the attacking infantry. The rash officers who forgot this injunction were given a brutally colourful piece of Picton's mind. Captain Mercer, commanding a Royal Horse Artillery battery, received his equally brutal lesson from the French gunners, who were far better at counter-battery fire.

Because d'Erlon's divisions were attacking in echelon, Quiot's division was the first to hit the ridge as they had the shortest distance to go from La Haye Sainte. His men were elated at having taken the farm and were eager for another go. The men of his 2nd Brigade rushed out from behind the knoll and from the sandpit with its 28th of the Line on the left and 105th on the right. With their skirmishers rushing out ahead, they swept up the 150 yards to the ridge and shouted triumphantly as they watched their skirmishers disappear through the hedge. The Rifles had lost most of their senior officers by this time and, not used to crossing cold steel, scrambled over the second hedge to reform as a second line behind Kempt's brigade. The French skirmishers leaped onto the road amid the wrecked guns and dead gunners and Rifles. They rushed to the second hedge and began firing down at Kempt's men, who still lay on the ground.

Picton witnessed the flight of the surviving gunners and the Rifles on the flank drawing back as the French skirmishers came over what was left of the hedge. Behind them was Quiot's rapidly advancing brigade. He ordered Kempt's brigade on the reverse slope onto its feet. They advanced to the second hedge, where Picton shouted, 'Charge! Charge! Hurrah!' Waving his black top-hat, he drew the attention of a French skirmisher, who promptly shot him, putting a bullet in the middle of his forehead.

Kempt's three battalions of Peninsular veterans jumped over the hedge. The skirmishers fled back over the slope in the face of this red-coated attack. The 79th, the Cameronian Highlanders, were in the centre, with the 28th Foot on the right and the 32nd on the left – 1,800 of some of the toughest soldiers in Europe. They moved up to the hedge and fired into the oncoming French at twenty paces. Almost the whole front rank fell. The rest were staggered by the blow and backed up, but *'Serrez les rangs!'* made these Frenchmen – who were also tough Peninsular veterans – stand and return a volley that sent many of the British pitching back into the road or onto the hedge. 'Close ranks!' and 'Advance!' propelled the British over the hedge straight into the volley of the second French rank. Now a hot fire blazed between the two lines so close that burning wadding set men's clothing on fire. Highlander Private Dixon Vallance recalled, 'My face, hands, and clothes and belts were bespattered with the blood of my killed and wounded companions.'

Next in echelon to strike the ridge was Donzelot's division, following Quiot's by 200 yards. He thanked God that Soult had been so right. The attack in *colone de battaillon par division* added speed to the attack and less of a target for the enemy's guns. Despite the high rye, the dry ground gave firm footing to the men's eagerness to get at *les Anglais*. They had crossed the beaten zone so fast that the death toll was far lower than he expected.

Within 100 yards of their objective, the leading French columns evolved quickly into line. Within fifty yards, the remaining guns of Dutch Captain Bijleveld's battery fired double canister, shredding the lead battalion of the 17th of the Line. The French officers shouted, *'Serrez les rangs!'* to close up the bloody gaps. A weak fire from the Dutch-Belgian troops was shaken off as the officers shouted again and again, *'Serrez les rangs!'* and *'En avant!'* For Corporal Canler it was not a demoralizing command. 'This cry, far from causing fear or despair in our hearts, produced a completely contrary effect. It inspired us with courage and not only with the determination to overcome, but also to avenge our unhappy brothers in arms who died before our eyes.'[14]

Captain Bijleveld held his men to their guns to ram home one more load of canister then told them to save themselves. Then he walked along the battery, firing each gun as he went. The smoke roiled back over the guns as he ran off to join his men. He barely got away as French skirmishers jumped over the hedge onto his guns. The 13th and 19th of the Line and the 51st Light were all on line with their first battalions and sent a crushing volley into the Dutch-Belgian battalions. Perponcher and the few senior officers were killed or wounded. Their ad hoc battalions wilted under the fire and began to come apart. The rest did not wait for the French to charge through the ruined hedge onto the road.

Gen. Pack saw some of them racing down the reverse slope, many trying to force their way through his own battalions. 'A collective groan with hisses and cat-calls rose up from the British lines to their rear.' Pack ordered his battalions forward. Captain Mercer was disgusted that each genuine casualty had 'ten or even more attendants' – men who had obviously lost all stomach for the fight. *'Monsieur!'* they cried, *'Tout est perdu!'* ('All is lost!').[15]

Despite the flight of so many men, the majority of Perponcher's force, mostly Belgians, remained in the road. They now raised their rifle butts up in surrender. The cry went up, *'Vive l'Empereur!'* and *'Vive Napoleon!'*

Next in the French line, Marcognet's lead battalions also now formed on line. The two officers of the 45th again left their vivid recollections. Captain Duthilt remembered, 'Our pace quickened and to repeated shouts of *"Vive l'Empereur!"* we rushed the batteries.' Lieutenant Martin of the 45th of the Line saw the hedge just ahead, 'Our soldiers did not await the order to cross it; they rushed over it, jumped over the hedges and broke ranks to run against the enemy.'[16]

They advanced through the hedge, crossed the road, and then the second hedge. Marcognet was shouting, *'Victoire!'* when the shrill sound of the pibroch, the piercing martial music of the Highlands, signalled the advance of Pack's brigade – the 1st Foot, the 42nd Foot (the Black Watch), the 92nd Foot (Gordon Highlanders), and the 44th Foot.

The 42nd Highlanders had originally been sheltering behind the hedge that bordered the Chemin d'Ohain. They rose and advanced to the hedge but would not go through it. One Highlander explained that they were hesitant to plunge into the thorny hedge because they were barelegged under their kilts. Marcognet's column was in the process of crossing the Ohain road when the Frenchmen realized they were only a few yards from the Highlanders. They began to deploy but were hit by a hail of lead from the Black Watch. The column staggered but recovered and unleashed a volley that momentarily disordered the 42nd. It was much the same for the nearby 92nd Highlanders. The Gordons levelled their muskets and fired when Marcognet's men were only about 30 feet away. The lead ranks were shredded, but the French recovered and replied with their own volleys.[17]

Covering the French flank, Durutte had a less straightforward mission. He had to mask the Nassau troops in Papellote and the other hamlets on the right. He committed his stronger 2nd Brigade to drive out the Nassauers, whom he thought would put up a stout resistance from the shelter of the farm buildings and hamlets. Milhaud's 1,700 cuirassiers of the 14th Cavalry Division waited in support. That left him with only the 1,700 men of his 1st Brigade to strike the enemy on the ridge. On his right rode the 1,600 lancers and hussars of Gen. Baron Claude Jacquinot's 1st Cavalry Division to cover his flank.

Durutte's objective was the flank of the Allied force on the ridge – the 4th and 5th Hanoverian Brigades – over 5,000 men. It would take longer for Durutte's battalions to attack since they had the furthest to go as the enemy line bent away slightly to the north-east. Despite moving quickly, the Hanoverian and Royal Horse Artillery batteries punished them more severely than those of the other divisions.

No one was no more surprised at the collapse of the Nassauer defence than General Brue, commanding the 2nd Brigade. His mission had been only to mask them. The Germans simply abandoned their position at the advance of the French skirmishers.

Seizing the opportunity, he notified Gen. Baron Jacques Delort, commanding the cuirassiers. He then rushed his regiments through the hamlets.

As soon as his battalions exited the hamlets in column, they found themselves threatened by the 1,000 light dragoons and hussars of Maj. Gen. Baron Charles de Ghigny's 1st Light Brigade. De Ghigny had been appalled when the Hanoverian battalions had fled the village. His mission had been to support them in keeping the French off the army's flank. Now it all devolved upon his brigade. If he felt any qualms about facing his former comrades in the French army, it did not show. A French-speaking Belgian, he had joined the French army of the Revolution and had soldiered his way brilliantly through one regime after another until he threw his loyalties to Napoleon, who rewarded this gifted Belgian cavalry commander with almost every honour the Empire could bestow. He had fought with Napoleon to the end, and then sought service in the new Kingdom of the Netherlands. As much as he may have admired Napoleon and valued his own life's experience, he could not now break his oath to the Dutch king.

Now he was looking at the French columns wondering, for more than one reason, if there were any cavalry with them. He feared he would be facing the 12th Chasseurs with whom he had served first as trooper than as commander from 1782 to 1814. Old and dear friends, his heart would break should he have to cross sabres with them. Thankfully he saw no chasseurs. His old friends were elsewhere on the field.

He advanced his small brigade, made smaller by action at Quatre Bras – 4th Dutch Light Dragoons and 8th Belgian Hussars – to threaten the French into forming square. This they did. For the moment they were stopped, which was all de Ghigny needed.

To further ensure that they did not move forward in square, he brought up the four-gun horse artillery battery he had been given. Now he was more than a threat to the French squares. He was an actual danger. Guns could blow holes in a square through which cavalry could charge, collapsing the formation. It was another example of the Napoleonic war game of stone, paper, scissors. His guns had only just started to begin a butcher's bill when behind them from the hamlets began to emerge an endless column of cuirassiers.

4:45 p.m. – The Inn at La Belle Alliance

The Old Guard battalions thundered '*Vive l'Empereur!*' as they marched past Napoleon to deploy for their attack on the English centre-right. Their bands played '*La Victoire est à Nous*' ('Victory is Ours'), stirring and fitting music for the grand display of martial strength. Nothing more embodied the romance and audacity of the age of Napoleon than these rolling drums and flaring trumpets.

Mortier saluted as he and staff rode by. Napoleon raised his hat in return. No men in his army were more devoted to him; they had fought and bled with him on countless fields, each one selected for his high conduct and valour in battle. They were the divisions of grenadiers à pied and the chasseurs à pied – 8,500 of the best soldiers in seven regiments. Trailing just behind in support were the 2,000 grenadiers à cheval and dragoons of the Imperial Guard Heavy Cavalry Division, without doubt the best heavy cavalry in Europe. Their officers were specially selected by Napoleon himself. With them were batteries of the Guard horse artillery. Napoleon kept back in personal reserve the 1,280 men of the 1st Regiment Grenadiers à Pied and as army reserve the Young Guard divisions of almost 4,800 men.

'There is no one I trust more at this moment with the fate of France than Mortier le Blanc,' Napoleon said to Berthier and Soult who watched with him as the spectacle marched past.

'Sire,' Soult said, 'Mortier is my dearest friend. We first met near here on the field of Fleurus long ago. I wish to ride partway with him now.'

Napoleon was moved by this sentiment. He felt it was a sign that his star was in the ascendant again. 'Go, *Maréchal de France*, your feelings do you honour!'

Soult was not thinking of honour but only of the joy of his friendship. Mortier grinned when he saw him. 'Ah, *mon ami*, thank you for coming along. To think we met near here so many years ago.'

Outside the inn, Napoleon continued to survey the march of the Guard when he heard the loud neigh of an exhausted horse. He turned to see an animal fall to its knees, dripping lather just as Coignet jumped off. Napoleon said, 'You are hard on horses, old grouser.' Coignet saluted and gave his report. The Emperor was clearly surprised. He thought he had seen the last of the Prussians, as Davout's report had earlier indicated. 'Ah, these Prussians,' Napoleon said. 'They take a lot of beating.' He then questioned Coignet closely about the details of what he had seen and when Davout said his forces would be in position to block crossings of the Lasne. He also asked about the terrain in that area, and then called for a map. The captain pulled out the one Monthion had given him and showed his route to Lasne. Napoleon studied it intently, tracing the river with his finger. 'You said Davout was on the point of defending St Lambert and Lasne.' His finger rested on Aywiers, south of Lasne. 'What about here?' Coignet replied he did not know. It had not been mentioned.

He turned to Berthier and Monthion. 'The last thing I need is a surprise from this direction. Send to the commander of the Young Guard that he is to be prepared to march to here –' he pointed to a crossroads 1,000 yards west of Aywiers – 'to block any force from getting out of the ravine. He is then to put a battalion and a battery to defend the bridge itself.'

4:45 p.m. – The Brussels Road North of Mont St Jean

Lambert rushed his brigade at the double to the sound of the guns. Maj. Arthur Rowley Heyland led the column with the 862 men of his 1/40th Foot, 140 of whom were very young, short-service men recruited for this emergency. He had been with the regiment ever since he had joined the army and fought with it through the entire war in the Peninsula, save for four months, where he rose to command. Upon his return to Britain in 1814, he had retired on half pay but was recalled to resume command of the 40th when it was being hurried to support Wellington.

Suddenly he heard firing in the hamlet up the road. An officer rode back to inform him that the road ahead was filled with French infantry. Heyland immediately ordered his battalion on line. Lambert rode up to be briefed and ordered him to advance and engage the enemy.

Heyland's light company had come up to the intersection of the Mesnil and Brussels roads and found both roads filled with French troops marching south towards the sound of fighting. Their officer took the initiative to place his men in nearby buildings and hedges and opened fire on an irresistible target. Gen. Bachelu was conferring with the commander of his 2nd Brigade, Gen. Baron Campi, at the intersection, surrounded by their staffs, a glittering array, as the brigade was beginning to march through. The sudden fire dropped both generals from their horses along with half the staff in a tangle of dead and dying men and frantic wounded horses. The old British military toast in the officers' mess, 'Confusion to the French', took on new meaning.

The confusion could last only so long among such experienced troops but long enough for the French to suffer another 100 casualties. Lt. Col. Duheux took it all in with a glance; he was a battalion commander with that calm and murderous presence of mind the French call *sang-froid*. Within ten minutes he organized a counterattack. *'Charge, mes enfants! A la baïonnette!'*

Men fell around him, but no bullet could touch him. He had the *baraca*, that amazing invulnerability and good fortune that is granted to a few great warriors. That is why his men followed heedless of the bullets, their bayonets seeking out the redcoats, driving them from the hedges and out of the houses. Behind them the second battalion of their regiment advanced.

Heyland heard the crash of gunfire ahead, then saw scattered members of the light company racing desperately for the protection of the advancing battalion. He rode in front of the 40th and called a halt to dress their lines. 'The battalion will advance in line of attack!'

5:00 p.m. – The Great Elm on the Ridge of Mont St Jean

Uxbridge and Picton were dead. The Duke's centre-right was a shambles. His left was teetering on the edge of collapse. The French were in his rear, and he had only the thinnest of reserves, and they were exhausted. And, oh yes, the Old Guard was clearly preparing to attack. At this supreme moment of crisis Sergeant Cotton watched the Duke, who betrayed not a trace of doubt. He was 'coolness personified'.

> Numerous applications reached the Duke for support and reinforcement, or to be relieved by the second line, as divisions, brigades and regiments had dwindled away to skeletons and handfuls of men. The only reply was 'They must hold their ground to the last man'... the Duke told Sir Colin Halkett, that there must not be the least symptom of falling back, as everything depended on the steadiness of the troops. Frequently, as the Duke passed the men, he heard murmurs, such as, 'Are we to be massacred here? Let us go at them, let us give them *Brummegum!*' i.e. the bayonet and he would calmly reply, 'Wait a little longer, my lads; you shall have them presently.'[18]

Wellington looked at his watch and said to himself that it would not go amiss if the Prussians were early.

CHAPTER 8

The Storm of Mont St Jean

5:00 p.m.–7:30 p.m., 17 June 1815

5:00 p.m. – The Allied Left

The space between Kempt's battalions and the French was less than twenty yards, filled with gun smoke and the flash of discharges from muskets. Sprawled bodies in blue and red marked each side's firing line. In one of the oddities of war, the 28th Foot found itself trading blows with the French 28th of the Line. So hot was the fire that both brigade commanders were shot down. Kempt's wound was too severe for him to still be able to ride, but he refused to be taken from the field while the issue remained in doubt. Baron Charles-François Bourgeois was also too good a target on his horse and fell into the arms of his aide as he slipped from his horse.

The commander of the Camerons, Lt. Col. Sir Neil Douglas, saw that the firefight was a stalemate, and with the loss of Kempt, something decisive had to be done. He called Piper Kenneth Mackay to him. He shouted above the din, 'The Cameron's Gathering!' It was the battle cry of the Clan Cameron, and its Gaelic name was also the slogan of the regiment – *'Chlanna nan con, thigibh a seo 's gheibh sibh feòil'* ('Sons of dogs, come here and get meat'). The staccato tune of 'The Cameron's Gathering' roused the battalion. Douglas bellowed, 'The Camerons will advance!' then, 'Charge!' Private Valance shouted as his friend next to him reeled back, shot in the head. Douglas raced ahead of his line waving his basket-hilted Scots sword with his men howling their Celtic fury. The 28th and 32nd caught the fire and moved only seconds after the Camerons.

The French flinched and recoiled at the advancing bayonets. The Celts struck them first, stabbing and clubbing those who could not get away. A few stood to fight in a rapid snarl of bayonets and musket butts. The French were rapidly falling back. The colonel of the 28th of the Line rode among his men shouting, 'The 28th to me!' Men rallied to him, but the brigade was on the point of breaking.

Quiot quickly led his 1st Brigade to reinforce the 2nd Cuirassiers and horse artillery came up on his right at the same time. The guns unlimbered quickly. '*Feu!*' shouted the battery commander. Then canister swept away the left flank companies of the 28th Foot. The British had already been disorganized by their charge, and now the 7th and 12th Cuirassiers came thundering into their flank and rear. The 1/95th had come into the road as a support for the brigade and now shot down the gunners and dozens of the armoured horsemen. But it was too late for Kempt's brigade. The advancing French, who now heavily outnumbered them, were overlapping the flanks, while the 2nd Brigade rallied to the shouts of their officers, 'En Avant!' The drummers again beat the *pas de charge*, and they advanced.

Now it was the turn of the British to retreat. A French officer raced ahead and ran his sword through the colour-bearer of the 32nd's king's colour. The men behind him cheered and ran up to defend him from the handful of Britons who tried desperately to retrieve their colour. The Camerons formed a rearguard grudgingly giving up each foot. The retreat turned into a run as the cuirassiers rode among them hacking and riding down men. In minutes the remnants of the 28th and 32nd, behind the Highlanders' stubborn rearguard, jumped over the hedge behind the protection of the Rifles. The French infantry and cuirassiers had the Camerons nearly surrounded. Douglas was shot dead. His colour-bearer had the shaft of the colours shattered in three places before he too was shot. A cuirassier officer rode into the centre of the defenders, reaching down to retrieve the colours. In a rage, Vallance lunged with his bayonet and caught the horseman under his arm. The man cried out as Vallance pulled him off his horse and smashed his face with the butt of his weapon. He had barely pulled up his bloody musket butt when the long, heavy sword of another cuirassier came down on head. Barely 100 Highlanders were able to gain the shelter of the sunken road.

The collapse of the Dutch-Belgian force left a 250-yard gap in the Allied position on the ridge. The 13th Light, a large regiment of almost 1,800 men in three battalions in Donzelot's division, advanced right through it. The 17th of the Line followed them, as did Gen. Baron Dubois' cuirassier brigade, together with another 1,500 men. On a new horse, with his neck wound wrapped in a scarf, Col. Ordener again led his 1st Cuirassiers. The sight of French infantry and cavalry pouring over the ridge had the effect of a bomb among the trains spread out behind the ridge. Already stunned by the earlier explosion of so many caissons and limbers, they panicked and fled towards the Forest of Soignes, cutting the traces of the artillery and quartermasters' horses to get away more quickly. Others simply ran. Amid the men were the wives, children, and other camp-followers of the regiments. They had the least to worry about, for the armies of both sides put them off limits to any harm.

Pack's brigade was struggling with the rest of Donzelot's division and part of Marcognet's when the 13th broke through the gap. Its second battalion wheeled to the right and attacked the Royal Scots from the flank and rear to widen the gap. Seeing the French break through on their left and Quiot's brigades advancing on them, the survivors of Kempt's brigade pulled out, running down the reverse slope. The French followed onto the road, where they burst into wild shouts of 'Vive l'Empereur!' as they waved their flags.

The Duke had returned to his elm tree command post just as Kempt's brigade retreated. He instantly rode down to rally them. The sight of him riding on his magnificent horse, Copenhagen, brought them to a halt. He faced them about, to create a new flank. The sight of him alone restored their confidence, but the new flank still hung in the air. He looked intently at the French flooding down the reverse slope and realized that Bülow was now too late.

Durutte's 1st Brigade had the furthest to go and was just approaching the road. The 4th and 5th Hanoverian Brigades, over 5,000 men, awaited them. Durutte was outnumbered by two to one. Yet it was the Germans who were filled with dread. The ranks rustled with apprehension as word spread of the French breakthrough to the right. The cry went up, 'The Big Boots are behind us!' It took everything their officers had to keep these green militia battalions together. Despite that, the rear ranks that could actually see the cuirassiers began to bolt to the rear and the safety of the woods.

Durutte's 2nd Brigade had driven the Nassau battalions out of Papellote and the other hamlets with surprising ease. Milhaud's 14th Cavalry Division quickly followed. The Germans had not retreated to the main line but along the road to Ohain to the north-east. They were now out of the battle.

Sir Hussey Vivian watched in horror as the ridgeline ruptured. The sight of the French waving their flags on the ridge as more regiments and cuirassiers flooded down the reserve slope screamed disaster. Pack's brigade was sorely pressed while the Hanoverians just stood on line. His brigade was the only force able to check the French breakthrough. He put his 1,500 cavalrymen on line and advanced.

Above Papellote, Delort's cuirassiers charged de Ghigny's Dutch and Belgians. Delort fully expected that the small force would flinch in the face of his armoured tide. Instead, they counter-charged. Delort would later recount how the 8th Belgian Hussars fought with insane bravery that matched if not exceeded anything he had seen before from Austrians, Prussians, or Russians. Behind the swaying, hacking mass of men and horses, Durutte's brigade could only stop and watch.

5:10 p.m. – Aywiers

The Prussian 1st Cavalry Brigade trotted over the bridge at the village of Aywiers. Half a mile behind them Bülow rode at the head of his hard-marching corps. He rode up and down the column saying, 'You must hurry, my children. You hear the guns. The English are waiting for us to save them from the French!' His Prussians got a good laugh from that and found new energy. He also urged them to avenge, 'Alte Vorwärts!' This time they did not laugh. Their faces only hardened and their stride lengthened.

Watching them from the woods up the road to Lasne was a French cavalry patrol. The officer scribbled a note and sent one of his men galloping up the road to find Davout.

5:15 p.m. – Above Rossomme Hill

'Look!' Coutelle said to Bertrand as he pointed to the east at the black-clad cavalry column crossing the bridge. Bertrand put his glass to his eye and could see the long columns of infantry not far behind. He hurriedly wrote a note, put it in a sand-filled bag and sent it sliding down the cable. At the same time, a French cavalry patrol saw the Prussian cavalry and turned around instantly to gallop back and report.

5:20 p.m. – Between Hougoumont and La Haye Sainte

It was now the turn of the Guard to take some long-range pounding from the enemy guns as they came within range. These veterans did not need to be ordered to close ranks as the balls sliced through them or case shot scythed down a dozen at a time. The chant, *'Vive Napoleon!'* was the only sound, besides the relentless rolling of the *pas de charge*, that came from the ranks of almost 10,000 guardsmen as they advanced through the trampled rye and the bodies of Ompteda's brigade. The troops they passed shouted enthusiastically, *'Vive l'Empereur!'* 'Even the wounded rose to cheer the columns as they passed by. A soldier with three stripes, a veteran of Marengo whose legs had been crushed by a shell, sitting near the embankment of the road repeated in a loud, firm voice: "This is nothing, comrades. Forward and long live the Emperor!"'[1]

These were the elite of the elite, called 'The Immortals' by the rest of the army, the subject of strict entry requirements dictated by Napoleon himself. No candidate for the Guard could be over 35 years old at the time of selection; he must have at least three campaigns and ten years' service under his belt; he had to have faced enemy fire in battle; and to be above average height. Their training was harsh and imbued with aggressiveness far beyond that of the rest of the army. Bayonet and close-combat skills were practised intensively . They were known for the single gold earing that many of them sported. On countless fields, the Guard had been the element that had clinched victory or held off the enemy. The rest of the army had an almost childlike faith in their invincibility.

The Prussians, Austrians, and Russians had had plenty of painful experiences at the hands of the Guard. Yet the British had none, save for the effect of the Guards' reputation. Now that reputation was coming to life. Most could not see them now as they were lying down behind the reverse slope. Only word of them came, spread by the few observers on the ridgeline itself. Their image in the imagination now loomed larger than life.

Behind them walked the Guard Heavy Cavalry Division, 2,000 troopers of the Grenadiers à Cheval and the Dragons de l'Impératrice (Dragoons of the Empress) Regiments, arguably the best cavalry in Europe. With each regiment rode a horse artillery battery of four 6-pounders and two 5.5-inch howitzers.

This force represented the classic Napoleonic combined-arms attack – horse, foot, and artillery – its combat power multiplied many times over that of any single arm.

In the other arm of the attack Marshal Grouchy led the massed cuirassier, dragoons, and carabiniers of Kellerman's III Reserve Cavalry Corps and the Chasseurs à Cheval and Red Lancers of the Guard Light Cavalry Division – over 5,000 first-class horsemen. They emerged from the depression between the Brussels–Nievelles road and the walled farm of Pospol 1,800 yards to the west. Simultaneously, Gen. Foy's 9th Infantry Division emerged from Braine l'Alleud and advanced on the British right.

5:20 p.m. – The Ridge Road on the British Left Flank

Engaged in front by Donzelot's infantry and struck in the rear by Ordener's cuirassiers, the Royal Scots' thin firing line came apart. All formation lost, the men fought on alone or in small groups. These sturdy Celts fought so hard, man-on-man, that the French would later say in praise that it was not enough to kill a Scot but you had to knock him down, too. Many a cuirassier died when a Scot simply leaped on the back of his horse and drove a dagger into his neck. Now French numbers told as one by one the Scots were brought down or driven to take shelter among the neighbouring Black Watch. Pack quickly ordered the 42nd to refuse its flank, just in time to send a volley into the charging cuirassiers, bringing down the front rank, causing the rest to stop or wheel away.

The two Highland regiments charged repeatedly to drive the French back and were only temporarily successful. The French just as often rallied and returned to the fight. The ground between their firing lines was littered with the dead and wounded. The French too charged, only to be beaten back. The ferocity of the Highlanders' defence cost them the lives of both commanders. The Black Watch's Lt. Col. Sir Robert Macara fell early in the fighting. He had been wounded in a charge, fallen to his knees, to be surrounded by Frenchmen who swarmed him, driving their bayonets into him. In a rage his Highlanders charged again, shouting, 'Where's Macara?' killing every Frenchman who tried to surrender.

Col. John Cameron of Fassiefern, of the Gordons, stood next to his colour-bearer in such fire that the man was shot though the heart and his flagstaff was shattered in six pieces by three musket balls. Cameron soon lay dead next to him in the rye. Still the Highlanders fought on.

The 92nd had started the battle with only 338 men, and the 92nd was slightly stronger at 412, barely 750 men in all. Now much winnowed, they were fighting more than twice their number of Frenchmen to a standstill. That could not last much longer. The flood of French infantry that had crested the ridge was to wrap around them along with the cuirassiers.

Into this unfolding disaster rode Vivian at the head of his 1,500 hussars. He intended to catch the French infantry as it wheeled to take Pack's brigade in the rear. The 13th's illustrious history was not about to get a black eye. At the approach of the cavalry its three battalions formed square, as did the two battalions of the 17th Light directly behind. Vivian had no choice but to throw his hussars directly at the squares. He knew – as did every other cavalryman – that steady infantry in a square were practically impervious to cavalry. The modern Greek word for horse is *alogo* – the illogical one – but they are not stupid enough to crash into a wall of bayonets. The only hope was that the infantry might flinch. He could not wait for his horse artillery battery to blow a hole. The charge was desperation itself.

The battalions of the 13th did not flinch. The 10th Hussars crumpled into a mass of dead and dying men and horses at a volley from the 1/13th. The volley of the two battalions of the 17th Light into the ranks of the oncoming 1st KGL Hussars was just as crushing. Out of 605 horsemen, 132 went down in a tangled mass. But one terribly wounded horse threw itself wildly into the French 2/17th, falling and lashing out with its hooves, knocking down a dozen men. Ensign Heinrich Stauber saw his chance and spurred right through the hole, followed by half a dozen troopers. He rode into the cente of the square to cut down the colour-bearer, as more KGL broke into the square. The sight of the German waving their colour caused the French to either surrender or flee to the other nearby squares. The KGL chased them, sabreing as many as they could. They were only stopped by the fire of the squares. Now all Vivian's hussars could do was ride around the squares unable to come to grips with them. At least they drew the cuirassiers off Pack's hard-pressed brigade.

By this time Durutte's brigade had crested the ridge to engage the Hanoverian brigades. The charge of the British hussars had restored their waning spirits, and now they stood firm to fight it out with the French. Vincke refused his flank to counter the simultaneous arrival of Jacquinot's cavalry. Pack's brigade under the press of numbers was forced back onto the flank of Best's remaining two battalions, forming a U of the combined formations. This was the first combat for most of the German soldiers in these battalions, but they drew confidence from their veteran officers and NCOs and from their hatred of the French.

Nevertheless, the left of the Allied army had been severed. D'Erlon's attack had done exactly what Napoleon had intended. Pack's men and the Hanoverians might have still been fighting, but it was merely for survival at this point, and it was just about to get worse.

De Ghigny's brigade by this time was spent and bled white. The survivors could only fight their way out of the melee. Half were dead or wounded – 65 per cent of the Belgians and 38 per cent of the Dutch. Delort pulled his exhausted brigade together, paused for a few moments to let his men recover from their ordeal, and led it forward against the British left flank. Behind his cuirassiers Durette's brigade also advanced in battalion columns.

5:30 p.m. – The Brussels Road North of Mont St Jean

The death of Reille, his staff, and his senior division commander and the attack of Lambert's brigade had disrupted the attack on Wellington's rear. The elements of II Corps gravitated to the fighting rather than continuing south. It was all to Lambert's advantage since the French joined the fight piecemeal with no single directing hand that would have quickly overwhelmed his battalions.

Lambert, by marching to the sound of the drums and pitching into Reille's corps, had given Wellington an opportunity – a narrow one, to be sure, but an opportunity – to save what he could of his army. Had Reille been able to slam into the Allied rear, nothing, save divine intervention, would have prevented Wellington facing unprecedented disaster. He had taken that opportunity. As the French cracked his left, he dispatched his assistant adjutant, Lt. Col. Basil Jackson, to see whether a route of retreat through the Forest of Soignes was open. It was then that the fruit of Lambert's diversion of Reille's corps was evident. The crossroads of the Brussels–Genappe and Brussels–Nievelles roads was still in British hands, and only just so. French skirmishers had occupied it briefly before being recalled as the fight with Lambert developed. Now it was held by some British cavalry and a few guns. From this crossroads one road went north-east through the forest. It was a good road that could carry heavy traffic. Another smaller road went north-east from just south of the hamlet of Mont St Jean. Jackson rushed back to tell the Duke what he had found.

Wellington now faced a painful dilemma. The Prussians were arriving in strength to take Napoleon in the flank. Pointedly, they had not linked up with his left where they would have been of immediate utility. At the same time, his own position was deteriorating. The Guard in large numbers – horse, foot, and artillery – was marching in great strength against his centre, as was a major cavalry force on his right. The centre could collapse before the Prussians could shift the course of the battle. He could order the withdrawal of his army through the forest now and ensure the survival of a major part of it. That would be his first defeat in open battle and on a scale that would shake Europe to its foundations. It would also entail leaving the Prussians in the lurch, an act which would both tarnish his reputation and poison British–Prussian relations. But if he held on long enough for the Prussians to throw Napoleon's plans awry, he could pull off, if not a victory of sorts, at least a draw. That would be a strategic defeat for Napoleon, the ultimate goal in war. He decided to wait.

5:30 p.m. – The Inn at La Belle Alliance

The scout came tearing into the headquarters just as the rider with Bertrand's message arrived. The scout was yelling, '*Les Prussiens! Les Prussiens!*' It was as if a shell burst among the staff, but the Emperor's immediate escort of chasseurs à cheval moved to surround him. Someone had the presence of mind to alert Captain Dyonnet, commanding the Gendarmes d'Elite of the Guard, who were posted nearby to protect the Imperial headquarters. Monthion ran out and stopped the scout and was able to calm the man down and get his report. He ran to Dyonnet and pointed to a road leading east. 'Large numbers of Prussian cavalry are only minutes away. You must hold them up to save the Emperor.' He then grabbed a courier and sent him to the 1st Grenadiers à Pied on the other side of the road. Their commander had already seen the chaos surrounding headquarters, the dashing off of the Gendarmes and the concentration of the Emperor's immediate escort. He alerted his regiment to move immediately, and personally led the first battalion forward.

Dyonnet led his 104 Gendarmes in the direction the scout pointed. Almost immediately the Prussian 6th Hussars, almost 600 men, appeared, went into line, and charged. Behind them the lance pennants of uhlans could be seen. Although outnumbered six to one, Dyonnet did not hesitate to draw sabre and charge the oncoming Prussians. His Gendarmes had no other reason to exist than to protect the headquarters and the Emperor. They were big men on impressive horses and crashed through the Prussian hussars only to be met by the lances of the following uhlans. Half his men were down, but he turned the remainder to cut their way out again, only to be swarmed by the hussars. The Gendarmes sold themselves dearly. The young Prussian officers vied to kill Dyonnet. He was above middle age, an old infantryman of the Royal Army who had become a gunner under the Revolution, yet retained the strength of a younger man combined with the experience of an old soldier. Two Prussian subalterns fell to his sabre before a lance jabbed through his back and out of his stomach.

The Gendarmes were dead or wounded to a man but had bought vital time. When the Prussians charged on the Imperial headquarters they were met by a battalion of the grenadiers à pied. Their volley slammed into the onrushing cavalry. The entire front rank went down. A second battalion marched up to fill in next to the first and added another volley. Against the urgings of Berthier and his aides, Napoleon rode behind his grenadiers only twenty yards from the Prussians. Monthion hurriedly rushed Bertrand's report to him. He summarized it to the Emperor, who immediately called Gen. Count Philibert Duhesme to him. Duhesme commanded the eight battalions of the Young Guard waiting anxiously in reserve on the other side of the Brussels road opposite Rossomme Hill. They were former soldiers or young men recently recruited from Paris and Lyons, whipped into shape by officers and NCOs who had served in the Old Guard. They thirsted for glory as an eventual entrance ticket to the Old Guard. Duhesme was just the right commander – a brutal fighting man brought home from Spain on accusations of torture. The Emperor said to him, 'Take one brigade and hold Plancenoit and keep the enemy off the Brussels road. It is our line of communications. Use the bayonet!'

The Young Guard had just entered the town when Col. Hiller von Gartringen's Prussian 16th Brigade marched quickly down the road from the north-east. 'Having [been] given orders [by Bülow] to seize Plancenoit, Hiller formed six battalions into three columns, and having nearly demolished the village by a fire of musketry and howitzers, sought to force it at the point of the bayonet.'[2]

Two battalions of the 15th Infantry Regiment rushed into the town just north of the woods on the outskirts of the town. South of the woods two battalions of the 1st Silesian Landwehr attacked. To the south along the Lasne the two battalions of the 2nd Silesian Landwehr also advanced. The Young Guard's artillery lined the high ground south of the town and pounded the columns. The 15th Regiment was severely punished as it reached the church on the northern edge of the town, there to be counterattacked by the Young Guard who drove them back in disorder. The other columns were similarly driven back. Bülow sent them right back in, this time reinforced with eight more battalions.

> The Prussians entered the village, which contained 520 inhabitants, and began to bash in the doors to evict the French. Each house was fought through with musket and bayonet and swung rifle butt. The Prussians battered their way through the outlying farm buildings and into the maze of village streets, until the Silesian Landwehr came up against the high walls of the church. 'The open square around the churchyard was surrounded by houses,' Hiller recalled, 'from which the enemy could not be dislodged in spite of our brave attempt . . . a firefight continued at 15 to 30 paces,' in the narrow streets, Hiller remembered, 'which ultimately decimated the Prussian battalions.'[3]

At La Belle Alliance the Prussian cavalry withdrew to be replaced by the 6,500 men of the 15th Infantry Brigade of Maj. Gen. Heinrich von Losthin. Behind them the roads darkened with Lt. Gen. Georg von Hake's 13th Infantry Brigade,

7,200 men strong. They were ordered to attack north through Frichermont and Papellote to link up with the British left flank. In reserve was Bülow's reserve, his 14th Infantry Brigade, almost 5,900 men under Maj. Gen. Gustav von Ryssel. The Prussian IV Corps commander had brilliantly put 30,000 fresh troops on Napoleon's rear. Crossing the bridge at Aywiers were some of the brigades of Zieten's and Pirch's corps in decent shape that Gneisenau had pulled together. Facing them were barely 6,000 men of the Old and Young Guard.

The sight of the black masses erupting onto the field gave an enormous boost to the morale of the hard-pressed British and Hanoverians on the left. Standing amid his smoking guns of E Troop, Royal Horse Artillery, Captain Thomas Dyneley remembered that the Prussians 'advanced with a very heavy body of cavalry in front, with which they charged the moment they came on the ground . . . This was a remarkably fine sight and our army gave them three cheers.'[4]

From his position by the great elm, Wellington had a good view of the heavy black-clad Prussian columns falling on the French. His staff was greatly cheered. He realized, however, that the Prussians were not going to stop the massed attack of the Guard that was drawing closer.

Beyond his vision, Exelmans' cavalry came charging down the Lasne road straight into one of Zieten's brigades at Aywiers just as it crossed the bridge. Exelmans had acted on his own as soon as his scout reported the Prussians crossing at Aywiers. Davout immediately ordered Lobau and the Saxons south, leaving only one regiment to guard the bridges at Lasne and St Lambert.

5:30 p.m. – The Guard Attacks

There is a saying that time spent in reconnaissance is never wasted. Soult's staff officers had carefully examined the British centre for the best approach for an attacking force. The marshal was meticulous in planning, and as soon as La Haye Sainte had fallen, they were looking over the ground. They concluded that an approach 'straight up to the plateau from the lowlands of La Haye Sainte by the Brussels–Charleroi road, over which the column had barely 400 yards to traverse and where the embankments sheltered it from the slanting fire of the artillery, was the best possible way'. It was a superb piece of staff work. And now the Guards marched down the Brussels road straight into the deep space.[5]

The Beautiful Daughters sent their fire straight at the British guns that lined the centre of the ridge as their attached howitzers dropped their shells on the reverse slope. The Allies had seven batteries on the centre of the ridge – five British, one KGL, and one Belgian – thirty 9-pounders, three 6-pouners, and five 5.5-inch howitzers. The dry ground aided the strike of the rounds as it had on the eastern flank. Napoleon had given specific instructions that the Guard's 12-pounders were to target the enemy guns. These guns could only fire perhaps one round a minute because of the need for the entire gun crew to pull it back to its firing position after the recoil drove it back. Despite the slow fire, these master gunners were particularly accurate at this close range. Those guns of the Grand Battery that could be brought to bear added their fire to the barrage. British gun after gun was silenced and gun crews decimated.

The butcher's bill that the attacking Guard would pay was much reduced by this effective fire and by the protected approach. Further to the Guard's advantage was that there was no damaging fire from Hougoumont or La Haye Sainte. It was only when the head of the Guard columns marched to within 400 yards that the surviving British guns could find a target. The gunners stood to their pieces, firing as fast they could, their faces grimed with powder. Balls cut through the Guard and here and there a bearskin was propelled into the air. Case shot riddled a dozen men at a time. It was within range for canister, and the surviving guns that could bear spewed clouds of musket balls into the Guard. Still, it was nothing like the defensive fire the Duke had hoped for due to the partially sheltered approach and to the Guard's effective counter-battery fire.

Still they came on in two columns, the grenadiers and chasseurs, closing up their ranks smoothly whenever a man fell. A hundred yards before they crested the ridge, the lead battalions formed on line. Directly over the crest on the reverse slope was Col. Hugh Halkett's Hanoverians. Wellington now took a serious risk and rushed over to Maitland's Guards Brigade from the right to reinforce the point of impact. The 1st Foot Guards was the senior infantry regiment in the British army, and its 2nd and 3rd Battalions were larger formations. Unfortunately, it was the absent 1st Battalion that was most experienced from the Peninsula. He calculated that there appeared to be no French threat coming from their front, which faced the burning, corpse-strewn Hougoumont.

The Duke dared not take the only other brigade on his right, Maj. Gen. Frederick Adams' strong 3rd British Brigade. The massing of French cavalry and infantry there was all too obvious. Adams had almost 3,000 men, in the 1/52nd and 71st Light with about 1,000 men each. The companies of the two 95th Rifles Battalions added another 600 men – all of Adams' men were tough Peninsular veterans. Backing the infantry up was the sole cavalry reserve – Maj. Gen. Sir Colquhoun Grant's 5th British Cavalry Brigade of almost 1,300 sabres. Already the mass of French cavalry was moving forward.

Wellington had more to worry about than the shifting of battalions. The morale of his army was becoming as fragile as a crystal glass. The word had spread of the fighting in their rear on the Brussels road and of the disaster on the left. Casualties had already been more than heavy, especially among his Allied battalions. The Netherlands forces had largely ceased to exist. He knew he could rely on the British and KGL battalions and to a lesser extent the Hanoverian Landwehr, but he also knew that trapped men have already given up the hope of victory and think only of flight.

D'Erlon now saw victory within his grasp. He had ruptured the Allied left and was pressing the surviving British and Hanoverian battalions hard. His numbers were proving decisive. Vivian's hussars had fallen back from their failed counterattack as the French battalions began to encircle the mass of the enemy infantry from the left as Jacquinot's cavalry closed in from the right. Vivian's hussars were caught in the middle. Again, the French lance, in the hands of the 3rd and 4th Lancers, proved lethal. Caught between the volleys of the French infantry and the lances of the French cavalry, the surviving British hussars could only seek refuge within the Hanoverians or through flight. The only hope for the trapped force was to fight its way to the north-east along a road that led towards Ohain and the Forest of Soignes.

Durutte's brigade and the cuirassier division was moving to close off that retreat. But it never happened. Prussians began emerging from the string of hamlets in their rear, the division-sized Prussian 13th Brigade. The French had to turn about to face them.

Amid the fighting a French officer waving a white flag approached the Highlanders. The firing subsided as the French pulled back as he was admitted to enemy lines. He bore a message from d'Erlon to Pack asking him to surrender as his position was hopeless. The Frenchman was asking the wrong man. Maj. Gen. Sir Dennis Pack had been taken prisoner in the ill-fated British occupation of Buenos Aires in 1806 and did not intend to go through that experience again. He had fought in almost every battle in the Peninsula, and it galled him no end to be on the receiving end of a French demand for surrender. It did convince him, though, that d'Erlon had a point – his position had indeed been hopeless, with French infantry and cuirassiers closing the trap on him. But now, just before the French officer had delivered the demand, an excited Hanoverian lieutenant had delivered a message from Col. Vincke that the age of miracles had not yet passed. The large French force closing the trap on them from the east had turned about and marched back the way it had come. To the outrage of the French officer, Pack detained him to prolong the pause. In that time, he gathered Best and Vincke: 'We are leaving this death trap.' His shrunken battalions would form a rearguard while the Hanoverians broke through Jacquinot's cavalry marching in squares. It was desperate, but they had no choice.

5:30 p.m. – La Belle Alliance and Plancenoit

The 1st Grenadiers à Pied were also in a desperate situation. There were only 1,280 of them assailed by 6,500 Prussians, among whom the news flew that the hated Napoleon himself was before them, doubling their ardour. The fire of the grenadiers piled up the bodies of the Silesian Landwehr who did not flinch, so eager were they.

Only the arrival of the 2nd Brigade of the Young Guard saved the grenadiers from being overwhelmed as the Prussian 18th Regiment tried to turn their flank. Napoleon rode up to the Young Guard as they were rushing up. 'With the bayonet!' he commanded. Brig. Baron Nicholas Guye saluted with his sword as his men surged by. Another son of the Revolution, he had been serving with distinction since 1792, and was now repaying Napoleon for all the honours he had showered upon him. His men cheered at the command of bayonets and charged. The Prussians were struck as they were manoeuvring to swing around the grenadiers. Eager for glory, these inexperienced new soldiers broke up the Prussian regiment with the impetuousness of their attack.

Their sister brigade was not doing as well. Bülow committed another brigade to the slaughter pen of Plancenoit. Outnumbered four to one, the Young Guard was being driven out of the village. Gen. Duhesme was everywhere keeping his young men fighting, but Prussian numbers forced them to abandon the village. Now the Prussians could see the Brussels road. And Napoleon had not a single man in reserve.

5:30 p.m. – Between Genappe and La Belle Alliance

Monthion's last courier had found Vandamme three miles north of Genappe. The sound of the guns had grown much louder and closer when the Prussians attacked. Vandamme realized that it did not bode well that the battle was approaching rather than receding. He had immediately increased the pace of his corps. He alerted Gérard to speed up his following corps as well. He ordered Gen. Habert, commanding the lead 10th Infantry Division, to hurry men on as fast as they could march: 'Increase the pace. Tell the men they are marching to the sound of the guns. We must save the Emperor!' Then he spurred forward with his only remaining cavalry, the 12th Chasseurs, de Ghigny's old regiment.

5:45 p.m. – Aywiers

Zieten had been sitting on his horse at the crossroads of the Lasne and Plancenoit roads watching his column march past from the bridge nearby. There was a shout, and suddenly he had to defend himself from two French dragoons. His staff was cut down trying to defend him. His sword was beaten down, and a stab to his shoulder disarmed him. He waited for the killing stroke, but the dragoon merely laughed and said, '*Tu es mon prisonnier, mon général!*' Within twenty minutes Davout arrived with the head of Lobau's 19th Infantry Division at the developing battle over the bridge at this little village. The dragoons had done their job of delivering a shock to the Prussians that the infantry could now exploit. French infantry cut the Prussian column in two; the bridge was now blocked.

6:00 p.m. – Centre of the Mont St Jean Ridge

The surviving gunners fired one last round of canister and fled back down the reverse slope to take refuge behind the British and German infantry. The Guard shook off the losses, closed ranks, and reached the crest of the ridge. The grenadiers and chasseurs then crossed over the side, their lead battalions on line. Just behind them came two horse artillery batteries. On the infantry left flank rode squadrons of the Guard Grenadiers à Cheval.

On the reverse slope Wellington had placed himself with the Guards brigade and had ordered them to lie down in the rye. He would never forget the sight of the bearskins of the Imperial Guard appearing on the crest and growing into the most magnificent military spectacle he had ever seen. He was disconcerted at what he saw as they began to descend the slope. He had thought, as they had done consistently in the Peninsula, that the French would attack in column, but here they were on line, the 1st Battalions of the 2nd Grenadiers à Pied and the 1st Chasseurs à Pied, each in three ranks on a front of almost 400 men. It was the first time since Fontenoy in 1745 that the Guards of France and England had met. It would be far less polite this time. When they were within twenty yards of the Foot Guards, Wellington shouted, 'Now Maitland! Now is your time!'

The Guards Brigade rose as one man in four ranks with a front of more than 250 men and fired. The French first rank was reaped as if by a scythe, but the second returned as deadly a fire into the English. The French fire was even more destructive since their line overlapped the English Guards on each flank. Halkett's Hanoverians now came up on the French left flank and fired into them. A Belgian artillery battery added its fire into the grenadiers, driving their flank back, just as the 3rd Grenadiers came up on the left in support. The fire between the French and English Guards was intense, neither side flinching as bodies piled up, marking each line.[6]

Two batteries of French horse artillery clambered over the sunken road, the riders on the lead horses whipping them up over the side. Positioning themselves to fire through the gaps between the French battalions, they sent canister into the Germans and British. Now the lead squadrons of the Grenadiers à Cheval came over the road and down the slope towards the Hanoverians, who were trying to close ranks after the canister had swept so many of them away.

On the British right Adams' brigade braced for the impact of the mass of heavy French cavalry trotting up the slope at them. It was a daunting sight – all of Kellerman's 3,600 troopers, the cuirassiers and carabiniers gleaming in polished steel or shining brass-plated breast and back armour, and the majestic helmeted dragoons. In the second wave were the 2,400 men of the Imperial Guard Light Cavalry Division, Chasseurs à Cheval, and the feared 2nd Chevaux-Légers Lanciers (Red Lancers). The mass came up the hill, each regiment in the first wave on line. Solid shot punched holes through them, sending men and horses flying in sprays of blood, leaving mangled men and screaming horses stumbling on the stumps of forelegs or disembowelled, legs kicking in the air. An artillery officer recalled in horror what his guns had done: 'The effect was terrible. Nearly the whole leading rank fell at once; and the round shot penetrating the column carried confusion throughout its extent . . . The discharge of every gun was followed by a fall of men and horses alike like that of grass before the scythe.'[7]

Adams' battalions lined the crest and fired at 100 yards. More men and horses fell, kicking in agony. The few guns fired canister, bringing down even more. Still they came on. Adams passed the order, 'Prepare for cavalry!' – the order to form squares, and it was a sight to behold as these tough veterans quickly and smoothly formed square. The French rode through the spaces between the battalions trying to find an opening to charge, only to be shot down at close range. Even if the cavalry could not charge these stout squares, the French were not powerless to kill and rode by, firing their pistols into the English ranks. One old soldier bit off his cartridge and muttered, 'We shall see who kills the longest', and shot a cuirassier officer off his horse just before he could discharge his pistol.[8]

It was then that Grant unleashed his hussars and light dragoons. They struck the French and drove them back. They in turn were hit by the next wave of cuirassiers and carabiniers whose big horses clearly outclassed the lighter British mounts in a melee. The French armour also put the hussars at a great disadvantage in such a fight. Grant's men had no choice but to retreat behind the squares.

Slower than the cavalry, Foy's infantry began to ascend the slope. Their march had been relatively unscathed by artillery, which had concentrated on the cavalry. He had put the 100th of the Line in the lead. He had told them that this was their opportunity to earn a new eagle.

Maj. Gen. Pierre Chabannais, commanding the Red Lancers in the second wave, saw his chance and swerved to the right to avoid the attack on the squares. His lancers rode straight through the gap left by the movement of Maitland's Guards.

6:00 p.m. – The Road to Ohain

The Hanoverian troops could not wait to get off the battlefield. Col. Vincke and Col. Best did their best to keep their battalions in some sort of march formation to speed their exit, but muskets and packs began to be thrown to the roadside and men slipped away from the column to find their own way out of the disaster that had overtaken the Allied left. Only Pack's diminished Highland battalions left the field with their honour intact. They fought as a rearguard supported by what was left of Vivian's hussars. Luckily for them they only had to fight off French cavalry by marching in square, stopping every once in a while to turn and fire a volley when it looked as if the lancers were becoming too aggressive.

Behind them, d'Erlon had turned his attention to organizing his corps to trap the British. He had sent Jacquinot's cavalry to see the enemy off. It had been good fighting, and he was proud that his men had covered themselves with glory. They could hear the tremendous combat just to the west. He rode among them, calling out, 'Hurry, my children, we must not let the Guard take all the glory!' They cheered him, shakos waving on their bayonets.

6:00 p.m. – The Brussels Road by Plancenoit

The Young Guard stumbled out of burning Plancenoit and onto the Brussels road. The Prussians followed like a black swarm of soldier ants. The Young Guard's first taste of glory had turned from sweet to bitter; the Prussians were master brewers of a toxic mix of hatred. Gen. Duhesme rode back and forth trying to rally his men. The paved road halted them; it was a natural barrier, and for a while they held until Duhesme was shot in the head and flew from his saddle and the Prussians surged forward with bayonets, shouting, '*Uhra! Uhra!*' The French broke and fled into the fields on the other side of the road with the Prussians after them, killing every man they could, showing no mercy to those who surrendered.

Vandamme took all this in with a glance as he rode up. Drawing his sword, he turned to the 12th Chasseurs and shouted, 'Charge!' Now it was the Prussians' turn. Their ranks had been disordered by their running pursuit of the Young Guard and now made a perfect killing ground for charging cavalry. The chasseurs cut right through the mass, Vandamme and his staff at the head. The general was as enthusiastic a killer as any man there. When he rode up to the hard-pressed Napoleon outside the burning inn at La Belle Alliance, his sword flicked blood as he saluted.

6:15 p.m. – Behind the Ridge of Mont St Jean

The struggle below the ridge raged on, neither side with a clear advantage. But the battle was like a glass full to the brim held by sheer tension. One more drop or a slight touch to the glass would be enough for the tension to break and water to spill over. Such an event could have been the decision by Maj. Gen. Sir Colin

Halkett, commanding the 5th British Brigade. The French Guard had attacked to the left, bypassing his brigade, whose battalions were staggered in squares. Another capable commander who had proved himself in the Peninsula, Halkett had made his reputation commanding the Germans of the KGL. Now he commanded four British battalions, only one of which, 2/30th Foot, had served in the Peninsula. The others had soldiered hard in India.

Halkett had been straining at the leash to strike but had no orders. 'Hang it,' he exclaimed and gave the orders that echoed through the battalions. They smoothly formed on line and advanced. The grenadier battalions behind those in contact with the Foot Guards were not insensible to this movement and faced left just in time to be staggered by a volley at 100 yards. Halkett realized that the situation would not go his way in a firefight, which eventually would only yield to French numbers. He ordered a bayonet charge. His battalions rushed forward with a shout. The French Guard had steadied and delivered one of their practised volleys straight into the charge, dropping hundreds.

What made the glass spill over was not Halkett's attack. Rather, it was the decision of Comte Pierre de Colbert-Chabanais to direct his Red Lancers through the gap left by Halkett and Maitland's brigades. They came over the ridge crest, easily crossed the shallow sunken road and plunged down the reverse slope. Ahead of them Halkett's battalions were engaged in their fight. The French lances with their colourful red and white pennants came down.

Their charge stopped by the steady fire of the French Guards, Halkett's battalions were trying to pull themselves together when the Red Lancers charged into their rear. The impact of almost 900 horses and their lance-wielding riders cut right through the British, who had had no inkling of what was heading their way until the last few moments. At the same time, more squadrons of the grenadiers à cheval came over the crest and also charged the stunned and disorganized infantry. Here and there clumps of redcoats formed to fight off the horsemen, but those that were now left alone were relentlessly hunted down and finished off with lance or sabre. Hundreds tried to make their way to the shelter of Hugh Halkett's Hanoverian brigade but were run down. Those who did not surrender never made it to safety, save in joining the 73rd Foot, which had time to form square and was backing away from the disaster to safety within their own lines.

On the right, Adams now realized his position was untenable. Seeing his brigade on the point of being cut off by the cavalry on his left and Foy's approaching infantry on his right, Adams ordered a retreat by square to link up with Halkett's Hanoverians. It was an exemplary movement as they marched and fought their way through the French cavalry that tried to break into them, ably supported by Grant's hussars. Foy's 100th had topped the crest and, witnessing Adams' retreat, saw their opportunity for redemption being snatched away from them. Col. Joseph Braun, their commander, rode along their front, standing in his stirrups and pointing with his sword to the last British battalion, the green-clad 2/95th Rifles. 'There, *mes enfants*, in the middle of that square is your eagle!' Seeing the enemy in green, the men of the 100th instantly knew who they were. They had spent most of six years fighting in Spain and had been tormented once too many times by the Rifles. They responded with a thunderous '*Vive l'Empereur!*' and advanced to win their new eagle.

A battalion marching in square, especially with enemy cavalry hovering about and the need to stop and fire a volley to keep them off, moved more slowly than one in column. Braun took full advantage of that as his regiment closed with the Rifles. Cuirassiers had masked their approach until they were within fifty yards. The cavalry rode away to give their infantry room to attack. The face of the square facing the 100th fired, and every shot took down a man and sometimes two – the muzzle velocity of a rifle was so much greater than a musket. But that was only about a hundred, for that was how many men in one face of a four-sided square could fire in the first rank of two in a 600-man battalion such as the 2/95th. It took twice as long to load a Baker rifle as it did a musket, cutting the rate of fire in half. The French fired volleys from all three ranks one at a time in quick succession and advanced over their casualties at the bayonet. The whole French regiment had fired at that single face of the square, knocking down three out of four men. The cuirassiers, seeing the face of the square swept away, charged. It was a race into the heart of the square, and it looked as if the horsemen would win.

The British hussars had been quick too, and a squadron charged to intercept the cuirassiers. Maj. Norcott, commanding the Rifles, had been one of those killed in the French volley, and his subordinates were moving to try to close up the square, but the French were on them too fast. It was then a melee with bayonet, sword, and musket or rifle butts. The French lunged and clawed towards the clump of men in the centre of what had been the square, where every soldier knew the colours were kept. Numbers were about even, and the Rifles fought with a desperate fury, until the 100th's sister regiment, the 4th Light, came crashing into the battle. With the hussars finally driven off, the cuirassiers prevented any rifleman from escaping. When it was over, barely 150 unwounded riflemen survived to surrender. The French frantically searched for the colours, turning over the bodies that carpeted the ground. Then they demanded of the prisoners where their colours were. The Rifles had the last laugh. A wounded officer told them, 'Our regiment has no colours.' He explained that the regiment was never issued colours to reflect its skirmishing role. The 100th did not take it well.

Wellington was a tight-lipped observer of this debacle following Halkett's disaster, and then realized that the Prussians would never make a difference. He had waited too long, far too long. He was now faced with the most difficult task any commander could face – to conduct a retreat while in contact with the enemy. To do so he must buy time. Only the cavalry could do that for him. Immediately at hand were the Cumberland Hussars, a Hanoverian regiment of wealthy young men who provided their own horses, commanded by Lt. Col. Hacke. To the Duke's surprise, he saw them retreating and sent a staff officer to bring them up.

> On delivering the order to the colonel, he told me that he had no confidence in his men, that they were volunteers, and the horses their own property. All this time the Regiment continued moving to the rear, in spite of my repeating the order to halt, and asking the second in command to save the character of the regiment by taking the command and fronting them. I was unsuccessful, and in the exigence of the moment I laid hold of the bridle of the colonel's horse, and remarked what I thought of his conduct; but all to no purpose.[9]

But there were more cavalrymen of far better mettle: the remnants of Household and Union Brigades and Vandeleur and Dörnberg's KGL and British Light Dragoons. As they appeared, the French cavalry was also rallied – Kellerman's cuirassiers and dragoons, the chasseurs à cheval and Red Lancers of the Imperial Guard Light Cavalry Division. With the arrival of the Empress's Dragoons to join the grenadiers à cheval, the Imperial Guard Heavy Division was now complete. Altogether, almost 14,000 cavalrymen of both sides flew at each other.

6:15 p.m. – The Inn at La Belle Alliance

If anything, Napoleon's immediate situation was more dangerous than Wellington's. He had greeted Vandamme with immense though temporary relief. His grenadiers were dying around him as the inn burned. Still they closed ranks to keep a living wall between the Emperor and Prussian vengeance. The Young Guard brigade that had reinforced the grenadiers was bent back at an angle across the Brussels road. The ground around them was black with Prussians. They knew the Emperor was there; they had seen him riding behind the grenadiers, encouraging them and telling them that III Corps was almost there, but try as they might no bullet seemed to able to touch him. There were three bullet holes through his hat and two through his coat, but aide after aide fell to the bullets meant for him.

For a while he stood behind the Young Guard, when suddenly a company broke and rushed to the rear. In their path was Napoleon, stock still, his hands clasped behind his back. They rushed up, saw him, and stopped abruptly. He just looked at him with the countenance that had commanded the hearts of men for more than twenty years. They turned around and rushed back to resume their place in the firing line.

A disaster was unfolding for the French. The Prussian cavalry now turned on the mass of limbers and caissons in the depression behind the Grand Battery. The

Prussian infantry was lapping around La Belle Alliance and cut the road in both places. The 2nd Chasseurs charged again and again to keep them from completely surrounding the Emperor.

The Prussians directly fighting the grenadiers were clearly preparing for a bayonet charge that would surely overwhelm them. The last of the Emperor's staff surrounded him, swords drawn. Then the Prussians came forward shouting, '*Uhra!*' The grenadiers met them in a blur of stabbing bayonets. These young Landwehr were eager but had not the skill with the bayonet of the grenadiers, who killed and killed. But their lines had so thinned that those in front of the Emperor were finally submerged in the black-clad tide. Coignet seized a musket from a fallen grenadier and threw himself in front of Napoleon. He had learned this killing business as a grenadier on countless fields, and he was fast and deadly. The first to be run through was an officer who was drunk with the thought of taking Napoleon himself. Coignet took him under his upraised sword arm, wrenched it out and stabbed the man just behind him. A man came at him from the left but his scream died as the sword went through his throat. Coignet glanced to see Napoleon himself fighting at his side.

Then shells began exploding among the Prussians and shot gouged their ranks. The guns of the Grand Battery had turned around and were firing into the massed Prussians. Napoleon shouted in relief, 'Bravo, my little beauties!' Then in the distance he heard the *pas de charge*.

The men of Habert's 10th Division had marched double-time to reach the battle after Vandamme had given him his orders. The men had not fully recovered from the bloodbath at Ligny. The march had drained them, but the sound of battle drew them forward. When the cry went down the ranks, '*L'Emperor en danger!*' it was like a shot of adrenalin, and their pace increased as new energy pulsed through them. Habert did not let them stop to fire at the Prussians but ordered them to go in '*à la baïonnette!*' They cleared the road with the same absence of mercy the Prussians had shown the Young Guard. Veterans that they were, to them the bayonet was an old friend and they killed with unthinking instinct. The 34th and 88th Regiments drove the Prussians off the road and linked up with Napoleon at La Belle Alliance.

Habert's 2nd Brigade came up next and attacked the Prussian flank. Lefol's 8th Infantry Division followed and attacked into Plancenoit, driving the Prussians back in another wave of brutal house-to-house fighting.

In the near distance, Lobau's 19th and 20th Infantry Divisions were marching on Plancenoit from the east. The 21st Division was holding the bridge at Aywiers. Davout's Saxon divisions were now beginning to pass through the village. Exelmans' II Reserve Cavalry Corps was moving across country towards the fire at La Belle Alliance. Bülow watched victory slip away. He had had Napoleon himself just about within his grasp. He would have put him up against a wall and shot him outright, just as Blücher had so earnestly demanded in 1814. Now his men were being pushed back by French reinforcements. He would quickly learn that he was now trapped.

6:15 p.m. – Behind the Ridge of Mont St Jean

Grouchy knew that this was his moment to justify the Emperor's award of the marshal's baton to him. The British cavalry had counterattacked to drive to buy time for their infantry and artillery to begin their retreat. The cavalry of both sides had fought and snarled at each in attack and counterattack. The infantry of the Old Guard aggressively followed the retreat of the British Guards Division so closely that they threatened to stop their retreat. Near-suicidal charges of Arenschildt's 3rd Hussars, KGL, were the only means to arrest the Old Guard's pursuit. Regiment by regiment, the rest of the British cavalry disengaged to cover the retreat.

Grouchy waited only long enough bring his heavy regiments on line to ensure a crushing attack. A bugle gave the signal for the entire host to advance at a trot. A British sergeant, Edward Cotton, in his old age vividly remembered the advance of the French cavalry:

> They are the far-famed cuirassiers of France, let on by a Kellerman: gallant spirits, that have hitherto overcome the finest troops that could be brought against them and have grown grey in glory. Trumpets sound the charge; in the next instant our ears catch the low thundering noises of their horses' hoofs, and your breathless excitement is wound to the highest pitch as the adverse lines dash together with a shock, which at the moment you expect must end in their mutual annihilation.[10]

Corporal John Dickson of the Scots Greys was similarly impressed. 'The grandest sight was a regiment of cuirassiers dashing at full gallop over the brow of the hill opposite me, with the sun shining on their steel breastplates. It was a splendid show. Every now and then with sun lit up the whole country. No one who saw it can ever forget it.' Ensign Rees Gronow of the 1st Foot Guards took a similar impression with him to the grave: 'Not a man present who survived could have forgotten in the after life the awful grandeur of the charge. You perceived at a distance what appeared to be an overwhelming, long moving line, which ever advancing, glittered like a storming wave of the sea when it catches the sunlight.'[11]

They were indeed impressive and just as deadly. They were mounted on large horses, Norman-bred on the finest stud farms in Europe – the greatest heavy cavalry in Europe. 'The cuirassiers are of greater value than any other type of cavalry,' Napoleon had commented in 1809. They were the elite of the cavalry. Their ability to intimidate an enemy and then smash through his ranks en masse was what Napoleon had in mind in his comment. They could simply ride down infantry and even other, lighter cavalry. The carabiniers à cheval were, in effect, cuirassiers but considered the best. The Imperial Guard added two more large heavy cavalry regiments. Except for the light cavalry of the Red Lancers and chasseurs à cheval of the Imperial Guard Light Cavalry Division, the French cavalry host was all heavy.

Against them only the survivors of the Household and Union Brigades could be considered heavy. All the rest were light cavalry – hussars or light dragoons. With the death of Uxbridge, command of the cavalry fell upon Maj. Gen. Somerset, commander of the Household Brigade. He had commanded only light cavalry in the Peninsula. The Household Brigade command was his first with heavy cavalry. It was ironic that the great majority of the men he now commanded were light cavalry.

The commander of the French Guard Heavy Cavalry Division, Maj. Gen. Comte Claude Guyot, brought his regiments on line with Grouchy's. Marshal Mortier prepared to renew the attack of the Guard infantry. Soult rode with him to ensure Grouchy and Mortier worked in concert.

Wellington placed himself with Somerset to give him his instructions. He was especially nervous since he had little faith in the British cavalry as a disciplined force. Its bravery was unquestionable, but what he needed now was discipline, for only that would protect his retreat. He had nothing but praise for the well-controlled charges of the KGL cavalry, but then they were Germans. His KGL cavalry in the Peninsula had been so effective that he had chosen them to be his own bodyguard. For that reason, he ordered Somerset to detach the two KGL light dragoon companies as the Duke's personal reserve.

The retreating infantry and guns were converging on the crossroads in Mont St Jean that led into the forest. The smaller road that ran south of the Mont St Jean farm was quickly under fire by the movement of d'Erlon's divisions, causing a panic among the wagon drivers, who abandoned their vehicles and fled on foot. The road was now blocked. The troops that were supposed to use it diverted to the crossroads and jammed it shut. Panic was lashing this mass along only to find itself dammed up. Many abandoned the road and fled across country to the woods. One soldier recorded his indelible impression of the chaos.

> Disorder and confusion continued in our rear, the roads were crowded with broken carriages, baggage, wounded officers, soldiers, dismounted dragoons, and trains of followers from the combined army; more particularly the foreigners, many of whom gave as a reason for abandoning the field, that Napoleon and his legions were invincible, and would certainly be victorious, and to contend against them would be quite absurd. In fact, what with the killed, wounded, and those in attendance, with others who had gone to the rear through fear, our fighting army

became reduced, towards the close of the day, to a handful of men, a mere wreck of its former self. It is on record that upwards of twelve thousand had sought refuge in the wood of Soignes, whose desertion imposed great hardships on those who so gallantly remained.[12]

Those who tried to escape by the Brussels road ran straight into the rear of II Corps engaged with Lambert. This shock just turned them around to flee directly into the woods or back to the intersection to spread even more panic.

Grouchy rode down the front of his armoured host, sword aloft, shouting, *'Victoire est à nous!'* to be answered with a thunderous, *'Vive l'Empereur!'* with thousands of swords and lances thrust into the air. The bugle sounded 'Boot to boot', the *charge à la sauvage* (the wild charge). The mass of horsemen trotted forward. The French cavalry had not attacked in such numbers across the same field since Murat's wild charge at Eylau in 1807. Then there had been plenty of room on that frozen day. Now the French were crowded together so tightly that it slowed their charge. Never before had so many cavalrymen been deployed on such a narrow field. Somerset counter-charged, and it was the largest attack of British cavalry in the wars of the Revolution and Napoleon. There was no question of receiving the French charge at a standstill, the worst position for cavalry to be in.

Napoleon in the midst of the intense fighting around La Belle Alliance clearly heard the great crash as the cavalry hosts met. The close ranks of the heavy French cavalry allowed no room for the two sides to 'thread' or for the lighter British horse to swerve to the side. Instead they were pushed brutally back onto each other or ridden down. It was only the Life Guards on their heavier horses that could meet such a charge on equal terms. Somerset himself remembered of the Life Guards that 'they hammered on the cuirasses like coppersmiths at work'.[13]

The struggle quickly turned into a melee of man against man. Once the weight of the attack had been spent, it was swordsmanship that mattered. Private Cotton of the 7th Hussars watched:

A hussar and a cuirassier had got entangled in the mêlée . . . the hussar was without cap and bleeding from a wound in the head, but that did not hinder him from attacking his steel-clad adversary. He soon proved that the strength of cavalry consists of good swordsmanship . . . and not in being clad in defensive armour . . . after a few wheels a tremendous fencer made the Frenchman reel in the saddle . . . a second blow stretched him out on the ground.[14]

It was in this clash, too, that the British hussars felt the full impact of the lance as man after man was speared off his horse, causing one French general to observe, 'Never did I realize before the great superiority of the lance over the sword.'[15]

The impact of the armoured French carried the 2nd and 3rd Cuirassiers through the lighter British cavalry. In view was the road clogged with infantry and guns. The French brigade commander urged his men forward to fall on them. The remnants of the Guards Brigade brought up the rear of the retreat. They turned and fired into the cuirassiers, who had no time to swerve, and brought down the entire first rank.

Wellington then waved on his KGL reserve with his hat. The dragoons came racing past him to take the French in the flank as they were trying to reform and drove them back. With any luck, he thought, I can get this army away now.

Spoken too soon. The British cavalry was being driven steadily back by the heavier French until their line fell apart on the right under the attack of the Guard's heavy cavalry regiments and the Red Lancers. After them poured the Guard infantry battalions.

On Wellington's left d'Erlon directed his divisions to the north past the burning farm of Mont St Jean. There was nothing to stop them as they swept over the Brussels road by the farm, packed with men, wagons, and guns held up by the traffic jam at the crossroads. More pressed up past the road to the east to cut off the branch of the road that led through the forest. The retreat turned into flight but no fight. Those who were cut off either tried to disappear into the woods or simply surrendered by the hundreds. Abandoned guns, caissons, limbers, and wagons of all kinds blocked the road. The escape of any organized force was now becoming impossible.

By this time Col. Hacke and his Cumberland Hussars were riding through Brussels shouting that all was lost and the French were on their heels. The royalist element in the city and especially the horde of English residents panicked. Others looked into their chests and closets to bring out their tricolours.

6:30 p.m. – Behind Plancenoit

Bülow was finding himself in the same situation. Rarely has victory turned so quickly to disaster. Two French divisions had come up the Brussels–Genappe road and were pushing his men out of Plancenoit, with a third in the distance. The 15th Brigade had been on the verge of ridding the world of Napoleon until the Grand Battery had turned their eighty-eight guns on it, inflicting huge casualties and driving it south. A large French force was also pressing on his rear, having cut him off from the follow-on forces of Zieten and Pirch.

His 16th Brigade was being driven out of Plancenoit. The 15th Brigade had been driven south. The 13th Brigade was fighting over Frichermont against Durutte's brigade. His only reserve, the 14th Brigade, was already fighting with the French that had come from Aywiers. The situation had the makings of a first-class catastrophe. It would take a genius to find a way out.

So he turned to Gneisenau, who was ready with an escape route. To the south lay the impassable Lasne with its heavily wooded steep banks. The east was blocked by Davout. The French were attacking from the west. It would have to be north up the road to Ohain bypassing the Bois de Paris and avoiding the fighting around Frichermont. Gneisenau thought bitterly to himself that this was becoming a pattern.

Napoleon was exhibiting his ability to juggle multiple crises. Couriers from Soult kept him informed of the growing success on the other side of the ridge. He knew he could trust his marshal to finish off that matter while he concentrated on the problem at hand – *les Preussiens*. They had been the most obdurate and hate-filled of his enemies. Now he would grind them into the dirt. They would not rise again. This would receive his personal attention. Bertrand had informed him that a large French force – Davout, of course – had cut the Prussians in two at Aywiers and was pressing on their rear towards Plancenoit. He could also read a map in a glance. Armed with this, he directed Vandamme's 10th Infantry Division to attack due east to cut the roads to Ohain. They collided with the 15th Brigade, which was badly cut up from its struggle with the grenadiers and the brutal attention of the Grand Battery. The Prussians were pushed off the high ground north of Plancenoit to join the retreat out of the village.

Habert had earned the epithet of the 'Ajax of Catalonia' for his heroic tenacity in the defence of Barcelona. He had been equally tenacious only a day before at Ligny. And today he was tenacious in the fulfilment of the Emperor's orders. He planted his flag at the nexus of three roads over which the Prussians would have to march were they to try to escape, and dared them to try.

Bülow reacted violently. The French had stepped on his throat. If Habert was not driven off that road nexus, his army was doomed. He drew his last reserves and threw them in turn at Habert's 3,000 Frenchmen. First came the 2nd Pomeranian Landwehr Brigade, inexperienced but ardent young men who were no match for the steady, disciplined fire of Habert's veterans. They were living on sheer adrenalin now, but it lasted long enough to force the Pomerians to fall back behind piles of their dead and wounded. They made way for the attack of the 1,800 sabres of Maj. Gen. von Sydow's 3rd Cavalry Brigade. The French quickly formed battalion squares, and again their steady, disciplined fire drove off the enemy. But now they were spent, their ammunition near empty, as once more the Prussians were preparing to attack.

It was then that Napoleon rode among them, encouraging them that relief was coming. 'We are out of ammunition,' some called out to him. 'Eh, you still have your bayonets! And I have my sword!' He waved it, and the men nearby could see the blood on it. The men caught the fire of the moment and cheered wildly, chanting, '*Vive Napoleon! Vive Napoleon!*' The Prussians stood stock still.

7:00 p.m. – On the Field of Mont St Jean

Soult now ordered a halt in the attack and sent for Foy. 'You know him, Foy. Tell him he has done everything that the honour of his country demands.' He turned to Mortier, 'Courtesy requires the rank of a marshal and courtesy requires someone who speaks English. Go along, too.' An air of expectation hung over the two armies. The French horse and Guard stood ready to go in for the kill. The Allies, or at least the British and KGL, were equally ready, but to sell themselves dearly. Every eye watched the two horsemen ride from the French side, one carrying a white flag as a trumpet played truce.

It was not difficult to find Wellington. 'Ah, Foy, I am pleased to see you in one piece this time,' the Duke said. He knew perfectly well what Foy would say and had steeled himself for this moment. But there was not a trace of that in his face. Foy would write later of Wellington's imperturbable dignity at this time, the supreme display of British self-possession. He agreed to meet Soult in the field between the armies and rode out with only an aide and one man to carry the white flag. Fifty thousand men watched in dead silence as the two parties met. They spoke for twenty minutes. Just before they rode back, Soult said, 'I will present your position to the Emperor.'

Two miles away, Napoleon was accepting the surrender of Bülow near Plancenoit. He was determined the Prussians knew that they had been crushed. He demanded that they march past to surrender their colours to him personally. He did not return Bülow's sword. As the colours were being hurled at his feet by their weeping Prussian bearers, Foy rode up to present Soult's message. His staff burst out cheering.

7:30 p.m. – On the Field of Mont St Jean

The meeting of Napoleon and Wellington was immortalized in a vast painting by Jacques-Louis David that now hangs prominently in the Louvre – Napoleon on his white charger and Wellington on Copenhagen, both lifting their hats to each other. The Emperor had been specific in his instructions to David that the Duke was to be honourably depicted.

Captain Mercer was one of the tens of thousands of men who watched the historic meeting of the two greatest captains of the age. He observed that the heavens too were redolent of the moment.

> The sky had become overcast since the morning, and at this moment presented a most extraordinary appearance. Large isolated masses of a thunder cloud, of the deepest most inky black, their lower edges hard and strongly defined, lagging

down, as if momentarily about to burst, involving our position and everything on it in deep and gloomy obscurity.

Somewhere a gun was fired, seemingly to punctuate the event, and must have 'burst the clouds overhead for its report was instantly followed by an awful clap of thunder, and lightning that almost blinded us, while the rain came down as if a waterspout had broken over us. The sublimity of the scene was inconceivable. Flash succeeded flash, and the peals of thunder were long and tremendous.'[16]

CHAPTER 9

Fin

The Convention of Waterloo stunned Europe. In an act of chivalry and reconciliation, as Napoleon grandly publicized it, Wellington was allowed to evacuate his army through Ostend and Antwerp in exchange for the parole that no man would be allowed to wage war against the French Empire until exchanged.[1] That most definitely included the Duke of Wellington. Napoleon also allowed the British and KGL regiments that had retained their colours to keep them. He had more than enough of those taken in battle. He heard of the disappointment of the 100th of the Line that they had found no colours with the Rifles. The British were politely asked to return the eagle, which Napoleon personally presented to the regiment.[2]

When he rode into Brussels to the acclaim of the francophone population, Napoleon was gratified to see how many tricolours were displayed. He calmed the English expatriate community by calling on the Duke and Duchess of Richmond and hosting them and Wellington at a small dinner. Everyone was looking to see how the defeated Duke behaved but aside from an occasional moment when he stared out of the windows, he was gallant if somewhat withdrawn.

Things were not as genteel in London when the news reached it. England had not received such a shock since de Ruyter's Medway raid in 1667. The Liverpool government fell in weeks, to be replaced by the Whigs who promptly sought peace terms with Napoleon and even more promptly cut off the flow of English gold to their erstwhile allies. This was all as Napoleon had foretold.

The Prussians, Austrians, and Russians immediately fell out. The Prussians were positively catatonic from the shock. Blücher, their national hero, had been killed and his army destroyed with the same catastrophic effect of the disasters of 1806. The Austrians retreated into their traditional cautiousness. Only the Russian Tsar was still breathing fire until his advisers had to bring him down from his cloud and remind him that of the three things necessary for war – money, money, and more money – he had none.

Here Napoleon showed a restraint that was all cleverness. His terms were arresting in their modesty. He said, 'There are only five things that France desires

– Belgium, the borders of the Rhine, the recognition of the French Empire and his dynasty, and peace.' Then he added, 'There is only one thing that Napoleon desires for himself – my wife and son.'

The Austrian Emperor was only too eager to send his daughter back to Paris as a goodwill gesture. The very inconvenient child she had had by her lover was quietly turned over to a childless couple in the extended Imperial family. Her lover was detained and conveniently disappeared, such were the subtleties of French diplomacy even without Talleyrand. Of that old and faithless former bishop and Napoleon's several times former foreign minister, the Emperor announced that all was forgiven and he could return home. Talleyrand moved straight away to Russia, where the first winter chill carried him off.

The Allies hemmed and hawed for the sake of tradition, but in the end, gave Napoleon what he wanted. They told themselves that Napoleon appeared to have tamed himself, so moderate were his demands. He was happy to let them believe that. Of course, what accelerated the negotiations was the increase in Napoleon's demands as they dithered, and the concentration of his army for an invasion of Austria. That brought Vienna around. To make the Prussians choke on the bitter pill, he added that they disgorge that part of Saxony they had awarded themselves. It was the least he could do to reward the Saxons who had come over to him at Ligny. It was an astute move to bind Saxony to France and provide a position from which to influence German affairs. The Austrians and Russians were only too glad to stunt Prussia's growth. Austria would have a much freer hand in Germany. An unappreciated consequence of the 1815 campaign was the discrediting of the Prussian military reformers whose effect on subsequent Prussian military development was far less than expected. The French general staff system remained the model for the next century.

Russia was bought off when Napoleon agreed to the Tsar's assumption of the Polish throne. As much as King William of the Netherlands screamed in Vienna and London about losing half his kingdom, he was bluntly told in both places to be thankful he got to keep the other half at all.[3]

Napoleon's victory parade in Paris was the grandest the French capital had ever seen and marked the Emperor's last great military campaign. It was a spectacle that lived forever in French national memory. Representatives of every regiment in the Army of the North marched. At their head were the bearers of a forest of captured colours. The applause of the crowds became thunderous when they saw the British colours. D'Erlon, Vandamme, Gérard, and Monthion all formally received their marshal's batons. The army was feted as never before. Promotions, titles, and medals were showered on it. Reille's widow was presented with her gallant husband's marshal's baton in a tearful ceremony.

To claim that he had been at Mont St Jean was a statement of pride that a soldier would take to the grave and his family cherish for generations. Those who had missed the battle held 'their manhoods cheap', as an English playwright once put it. For all this *gloire*, the army was tired of war and wanted years of peaceful garrison and home life. Mont St Jean swept away all the shame and bitterness of 1814 as well as the bad taste of the Bourbons.

Berthier retired – for good this time. Monthion succeeded him and refined the general staff system upon which all others in the modern world are modelled. The General Staff Academy was named after him.

Napoleon did not forget Jean-Roche Coignet. For his gallant valour in the campaign and for saving his life, the Emperor made him a baron of the Empire, promoted him colonel and gave him command of a special detachment of the Guard responsible for the safety of the Imperial family.

For his fallen brother, Napoleon built a splendid monument at the renamed Place Jérôme in central Paris.

While in Brussels after the battle he sent a cavalry detachment to round up old Louis and his entourage. He gave him a fine chateau on the Loire and a generous allowance. Napoleon shrewdly calculated that in a foreign refuge, he would just be the focus of more émigré plotting. It was safer to have this enemy closer, where he could be watched. Ironically, he would outlive Napoleon by three years. His sons and grandsons were told never to set foot in France again. He made it clear that, should they be so foolish, the generous consideration that had allowed Angoulême to be released would not be repeated. Napoleon made it clear he would not make a gift of that man's life a second time.

He did indeed settle down with Marie Louisa, kept her pregnant and closely watched. He devoted himself to building up the French economy and putting people back to work. A favourable commercial treaty with Great Britain was an important step in that direction. He also discovered that the National Assembly under the liberal constitution he had established upon his return from Elba had developed a mind of his own.

Having learned the cost of Albion's enmity, Napoleon now cultivated a new and friendly relationship with Britain. He sent Soult to London as his ambassador, where he was a great success in negotiating a treaty in which France promised to support Britain in preventing Prussia from seizing Hanover. He invited the Prince Regent to come to Paris as an honoured guest. The British nobility had already descended upon France and especially Paris in great numbers. For some, the hardest part of the more than twenty years of war was to be denied Paris. Napoleon broke new ground in promoting a joint expedition to crush the Barbary pirates to which even the United States was invited to contribute some of their wonderful frigates. Of course, there was more than goodwill in offering to provide the ground forces commanded by Gen. Foy for the expedition. Once Algiers fell to British–American naval bombardment and French ground assault, the French remained in possession.

Napoleon also busied himself with writing his memoirs, which were published after his death. His comment on Wellington's conduct at Mont St Jean caused no little stir across the channel. 'Wellington's troops were admirable, but his plans were despicable; or should I rather say, that he formed none at all. He had placed himself in a situation in which it was impossible he could form any.'[4]

Wellington, who lived to an old and honoured age, commented privately that he bore Napoleon too great a debt for his gallantry to comment. His reputation had recovered remarkably, and he was remembered as the man who had driven the French out of the Peninsula and bore an outsize responsibility for unravelling Napoleon's iron domination of Europe. The British comforted themselves that Napoleon had so respected Wellington and the British army that he could only honour him with terms of the Convention of Waterloo. Such was the emphasis on that aspect of the campaign that the British referred to the battle as Waterloo rather than Mont St Jean as the French and the rest of the world did.

A family man to the core, Napoleon sought reconciliation with his brothers and sisters who essentially had betrayed him after his abdication – all save the loyal Pauline whom he showered with good fortune. He took care of his family, but never trusted them again. His mother, Madame Mère de l'Empereur, was another matter. She had shared his exile in Elba, and he doted upon her. She would outlive him by fifteen years. After the peace he realized that he had more family than siblings. He had two other sons. He acknowledged Charles Léon (1806–81), by Louise Catherine Eléonore Denuelle de la Plaigne. He also acknowledged Alexandre Florian Joseph Colonna Walewksi, who was born in Walewice, near Warsaw, on 4 May 1810 to Napoleon's Polish mistress, Countess Marie Walewska. Charles turned out to be a ne'er-do-well and wastrel, but Alexandre proved to be a distinguished soldier and Napoleon II's invaluable foreign minister and minister of state. The younger Napoleon and Alexandre were devoted to each other. The success of Napoleon II's reign owed much to the loyal and sagacious support of Alexandre.

As much as Napoleon desired the affection of his wife, he realized what her limitations were. Instead he doted on his son, the Little Eagle, the Prince Imperial, who grew into a beautiful blond, blue-eyed boy with a fascination for everything military. Napoleon took him everywhere with him to apprentice him to rule. In this he became the darling of France, the promise of an able, vigorous dynasty. Napoleon with the future in mind insisted that his son learn Enlish well. With the birth of George III's granddaughter, Victoria, in 1819, Napoleon put out feelers to explore her betrothal to the Prince Imperial. It was a new strand in his plan to placate Britain. The British had raised the problem of religion. Only her father and brother William stood between her and the throne. British sovereigns by their law could only marry Protestants. Napoleon was not put off and remarked that Henry IV had famously said, 'Paris was worth a mass.' The death of Victoria's

Fin 201

father and George III the next year put that in abeyance when Victoria became the only heir of William IV. Napoleon's death the following year removed the greatest proponent of the union.[5]

Victoria fell in love the moment she saw the blindingly handsome young French emperor when he arrived for her coronation in 1838. He was equally smitten. They were constantly in each other's company. She informed the government of her intention of marrying the French emperor in defiance of the law forbidding marriage to a Catholic. The resulting constitutional crisis in Britain shook the nation. There were speeches in the House that decried the prospect of Boney's eventual grandson sitting on the British throne. At one point the young Victoria was reputed to have said she would give up her throne for the man she loved. In the end she bowed to constitution, bid adieu to the French Adonis, and announced that she would marry another suitor, the German Prince Albert of Saxe-Coburg. He was young, handsome, and Protestant. She insisted on an immediate wedding. Seven and half months later their first son was born.[6]

Endnotes

Introduction

1 Winston Churchill, 19 December 1940, cited in Richard Langwroth, ed., *Churchill by Himself: The Definitive Collection of Quotations* (New York: Public Affairs, 2008), p. 365.

1 'What a Canary!'

1 Philip Henry Stanhope, *Notes of Conversations with the Duke of Wellington, 1831–1851* (London, 1888), p. 32.

2 John R. Elting, *Swords Around the Throne: Napoleon's Grande Armée* (New York: The Free Press, 1988), p. 629.

3 Georges Blond, *La Grande Armée* (London: Arms & Armour, 1998), p. 453.

4 R.F. Delderfield, *Napoleon's Marshals* (New York: Stein and Day, 1980), p. 191.

5 Andrew W. Field, *Waterloo: The French Perspective* (London: Pen & Sword, 2015), p. 10, citing Pierre-Charles Duthilt, *Mémoires du Captaine Duthilt* (Lille: J. Tallandier, 1909), p. 292.

6 Elizabeth Longford, *Wellington: The Years of the Sword* (Harper & Row, 1975), p. 78.

7 S.J. Watson, *By Command of the Emperor: A Life of Marshal Berthier* (London: Bodley Head, 1957), p. 63.

8 Henry Houssaye, *Napoleon and the Campaign of 1815: Waterloo* (Uckfield: Naval & Military Press, 2004), p. 32.

9 Elting, p. 83.

10 Michael Glover, *The Peninsular War 1807–1814* (London: Penguin, 2001), p. 39.

11 Randal Gray, 'The Big Mortier', in David Chandler, ed., *Napoleon's Marshals* (New York: Macmillan, 1987), pp. 312–23.

12 Peter Young, 'The Bravest of the Brave: Ney', in Chandler, *Napoleon's Marshals*, p. 363.

13 Elting, p. 638.

14 Longford, *Wellington*, pp. 378–9. Mark Adkin, *The Waterloo Companion* (Mechanicsburg, PA: Stackpole Books, 2001), p. 87.

15 Xenophon, *Memorabilia, Oeconomicus, Symposium, Apology* (Cambridge, MA: Harvard University Press, 1923), p. 253. *George H. Wilkens, *Napoleon and Wellington* (London: Collier Publishers, 1955), pp. 99–103. Wilkens made an

extensive study of the health and vigour of the two men, noting that both were 45 years of age, but both men exhibited at Waterloo the energy of 25-year-olds.

16 Raymond Horricks, *Marshal Ney: The Romance and the Real* (London: Ardway Publishing, 1988), p. 191.

17 Blond, p. 463.

18 Andrew Roberts, *Napoleon: A Life* (New York: Viking, 2014), p. 716.

19 Bob Carruthers, ed., *Soldier of the Empire: The Note-Books of Captain Coignet* (Barnsley: Pen & Sword, 2012), p. 253.

20 Roger Parkinson, *The Hussar General: The Life of Blücher, Man of Waterloo* (Ware: Wordsworth, 2001), p. 208.

21 Blond, p. 465.

22 Field, *Waterloo: The French Perspective*, p. 10, citing Lieutenant Chevalier, *Souvenirs des guerres napoléouiennes* (Paris: Hachette, 1970), p. 313.

23 Carruthers, pp. 253–4.

24 Blond, p. 467.

25 Carruthers, pp. 254–5.

26 John Foster, *Napoleon's Marshal: The Life of Michel Ney* (New York: William Morrow, 1968), pp. 152–3.

27 Blond, p. 467.

28 Longford, pp. 394–5.

29 Blond, p. 468.

30 Henry Houssaye, *The Return of Napoleon* (London: Longmans, Green and Co., 1934), pp. 141–2.

31 John G. Gallaher, *The Iron Marshal: A Biography of Louis N. Davout* (London: Greenhill Books, 2000), p. 300.

32 Andrew Roberts, *Napoleon and Wellington: The Battle of Waterloo and the Great Commanders who Fought it* (New York: Simon & Schuster, 2001), p. 742.

33 John M. Trudeau, *The Emperor's Spy: The Life of Karl Schulmeister* (New York: Gotham Books, 1988), p. 21.

34 'Karl Schulmeister: The Forgotten Spy who Aided Napoleon's Triumphs', Look and Learn History Picture Library, http://www.lookandlearn.com/blog/18265/karl-schulmeister-the-forgotten-spy-who-aided-napoleons-triumphs.

35 'Karl Schulmeister: The Forgotten Spy'.

36 Peter Hayman, *Soult: Napoleon's Maligned Marshal* (London: Arms & Armour Press, 1990), p. 221.

37 Paul Britten Austin, 'Oudinot, Father of the Grenadiers', in Chandler, *Napoleon's Marshals*, p. 394.

38 *Michael Paddington, *The Campaign of 1815* (London: Ross & Sons. 1925), p. 45.

39 *Nicholas Davout, *La Battaile de Mont St Jean* (Paris: Rachette, 1825), p. 32.

40 'Pierre David de Colbert-Chabanais', Wikipedia, https://en.wikipedia.org/wiki/Pierre_David_de_Colbert-Chabanais.

41 Adam Zamoyski, *Rites of Peace: The Fall of Napoleon and the Congress of Vienna* (New York: Harper Perennial, 2007), p. 470.

42 Longford, p. 389.

2   Forging the Sword

1   When Georg Ludwig, ruler of the Duchy and Electorate of Brunswick-Lüneburg (Hanover) in the Holy Roman Empire from 1698, became King George I of Great Britain and Ireland in 1714, Hanover became a possession of the British Crown.

2   The Congress of Vienna in 1814 had established the Kingdom of Hanover from the former Electorate of Hanover. By this, George III, as the Elector, acquired the throne of Hanover which remained in his family until Victoria became queen in 1837. Under the Semi-Salic Law, a woman could not inherit the throne thus ending the 123-year personal union of Hanover and the United Kingdom.

3   Philip Guedalla, *Wellington* (New York: Harper & Brothers, 1931), pp. 264–6.

4   Elizabeth Longford, *Wellington: The Years of the Sword* (New York: Harper & Row, 1975), p. 397.

5   Philip J. Haythornthwaite, *Who Was Who in the Napoleonic Wars* (London: Arms & Armour, 1998), p. 224. Mark Adkin, *The Waterloo Companion* (Mechanicsburg, PA: Stackpole Books, 2001), p. 9.

6   Charles Oman, *Wellington's Army, 1809–1814* (London: Greenhill, 1993), p. 118.

7   Michael Glover, *The Peninsular War 1807–1814* (London: Penguin Books, 2011), p. 349.

8   Christopher Summerville, *Who Was Who at Waterloo: A Biography of the Battle* (London: Pearson Education Ltd, 2007), p. 316.

9   Richard Holmes. *Wellington: The Iron Duke* (New York: HarperCollins, 2003), p. 206.

10   Lord Broughton, *Recollections of a Long Life*, vol. 1 (New York: Charles Scribners, 1911), p. 94.

11   Holmes, p. 32.

12   *Edward G. Swinton, *Sowing the Dragon's Teeth: Napoleon and Conscription* (London: Charing Cross Publishers, 1929), p. 287.

13   John R. Elting, *Swords Around the Throne: Napoleon's Grande Armée* (New York: The Free Press, 1988), p. 645. David Hamilton-Williams, *Waterloo New Perspectives: The Great Battle Reappraised* (London: Arms & Armour Press, 1993), p. 70. David Chandler, *The Campaigns of Napoleon* (New York: Macmillian, 1966), p. 1014.

14   *George H. Wilkens, *Napoleon and Wellington* (London: Collier Publishers, 1955), p. 211.

15   Henry Houssaye, *Napoleon and the Campaign of 1815: Waterloo* (Uckfield: Naval & Military Press, 2004), pp. 32–3.

16   Ronald Pawly, *Napoleon's Imperial Headquarters* (Botely: Osprey, 2004), p. 23.

17   'The History of a Regiment During the Russian Campaign – 1812', *Blackwood's Magazine*, vol. 67, May–June 1850, p. 574.

18   *François Gédéon Bailly de Monthion, *Mémoires du Maréchal Monthion* (Paris: A. Bossnage, 1835), p. 284.

19   Adam Zamoyski, *Rites of Peace: The Fall of Napoleon and the Congress of Vienna* (New York: Harper Perrenial, 2007), pp. 464–5.

20   David Hamilton-Williams, *Waterloo New Perspectives: The Great Battle Reappraised* (London: Arms & Armour, 1993), p. 69.

21   Houssaye, *Napoleon and the Campaign of 1815*, p. 53.

22 Houssaye, *Napoleon and the Campaign of 1815*, p. 33.

23 *Jean-Marie-Joseph Coutelle, *The History of the French Aerostatic Corps* (London: Greenhill Books, 1990), p. 132. Lionel Leventhal, the owner/editor of Greenhill Books and the grand old man of British military publishing, discovered this forgotten gem of French Napoleonic history published by Coutelle in 1829, had it translated and published as an important addition to military history.

24 Roger Parkinson, *The Hussar General: The Life of Blücher, Man of Waterloo* (Ware: Wordsworth, 2001), pp. 209–10.

25 'Prussian Order of Battle', http://www.napolun.com/mirror/napoleonistyka. atspace.com/Prussian_Order_of_Battle_Waterloo.html#prussians1815ziethen.

26 Houssaye, *Napoleon and the Campaign of 1815*, p. 53.

27 *Karl Schulmeister, *Mémoires* (Paris: Ernest Kolb, 1893), p. 299. Schulmeister's memoirs are considered one of the great accounts of espionage.

28 Houssaye, *Napoleon and the Campaign of 1815*, pp. 53–4.

29 *René Thiebault, *Napoléon et la Campagne de 1815* (Paris: Cosse, Marécheal, 1869), p. 98.

30 Philip J. Haythornthwaite, *Who Was Who in the Napoleonic Wars* (London: Arms & Armour, 1998), p. 327.

31 *Napoleon I, *La Campagne de Mont St. Jean* (Paris: Éditeur Imperial, 1818), p. 65. Napoleon's book is considered a definitive reference to the campaign of 1815, despite his downplaying or ignoring of mistakes, but then again he was Napoleon.

32 Stephen Beckett, *Waterloo Betrayed: The Secret Treachery that Defeated Napoleon* (Canton, GA: Mapleflower House, 2015), p. 37.

33 Elting, p. 650.

34 John G. Gallaher, *The Iron Marshal: A Biography of Louis N. Davout* (London: Greenhill Books, 2000), p. 307.

35 Houssaye, *Napoleon and the Campaign of 1815*, pp. 32–3. *Jerome Roberts, *Napoleon's Master Spy: The Life of Karl Schulmeister* (London: Greenhill Books, 1987), p. 232.

36 Bernard Cornwell, *Waterloo: The History of Four Days, Three Armies, and the Three Battles* (New York: HarperCollins, 2015), p. 43.

37 *Napoleon I, p. 45. Napoleon was particularly anxious to avoid harsh measures against opponents that could turn public opinion against him. He was firm, but generous with clemency.

38 David Hamilton-Williams, *Waterloo New Perspectives: The Great Battle Reappraised* (London: Arms and Armour Press, 1993), p. 155.

39 *Richard R. Simpson, *Betraying the Emperor: Conspiracies Against Napoleon in the Campaign of 1815* (New York: Samuels & Sons, 1938), p. 77.

40 *Nigel R. Witliff, *Napoleon and his Marshals in the Campaign of Mont St. Jean* (London: Spencer & Coe Publishers, 1938), p. 47.

41 *Peter G. Tsouras, ed., *The Quotations of Napoleon and Wellington* (London: Greenhill Books, 1996), p. 127.

42 *Monthion, p. 288.

43 *Roberts, *Napoleon's Master Spy*, p. 244.

3 'Napoleon Has Humbugged me, by God'

1   *Richard R. Simpson, *Betraying the Emperor: Conspiracies Against Napoleon in the Campaign of 1815* (New York: Samuels & Sons, 1938), p. 123.

2   General Count Gneisenau, *The Life and Campaigns of Field-Marshal Prince Blücher* (London: Constable and Co., 1996), pp. 402–3.

3   Mark Adkin, *The Waterloo Companion* (Mechanicsburg, PA: Stackpole Books, 2001), pp. 37–50. Maj. Gen. Sir John Lambert's British brigade was at sea at this time and would not land at Ostend until the middle of June.

4   Duke of Wellington, *The Dispatches of Field Marshal the Duke of Wellington During his Various Campaigns in India, Denmark, Portugal, Spain, the Low Countries, and France, 1811*, VII (London: John Murray, 1834–8), p. 406.

5   Adkin, pp. 49–50. Geert van Uythoven, 'The Dutch Indian Brigade', The Napoleon Series: Military Subjects: Organization, Strategy, and Tactics, https://www.napoleon-series.org/military/organization/c_dutch1815.html. The Dutch Indian Brigade was created to garrison the Dutch colonies returned to the Netherlands in 1814 and had not departed by the time of the 1815 campaign.

6   *Robert De Lancy, *The Saxon Corps in the War of 1815* (London: Richard Bentley, 1893), p. 89. *Albert von Boehn, *Geschichte des Feldzuges von 1815 in den Niederlanden* (Berlin: Posen Und Brombert, 1838), p. 48.

7   Adkin, pp. 39, 66. *Ulrich von Dohna, *The Saxons at Waterloo* (London: Greenhill Books, 1999), p. 32.

8   Andrew Roberts, *Napoleon: A Life* (New York: Viking, 2014), p. 749. 'Field of May (1815)', Wikipedia, https://fr.wikipedia.org/wiki/Champ_de_mai_(1815). Raymond Horricks, *Marshal Ney: The Romance and the Real* (London: Archway Publishing, 1982), pp. 205–6.

9   Roger Parkinson, *The Hussar General: The Life of Blücher, Man of Waterloo* (Ware: Wordsworth, 2001), p. 215.

10 'The French Advance into Belgium', The Napoleon Series, http://www.napoleon-series.org/military/battles/1815/hundred/c_chapter2.htm. Henry Houssaye, *Napoleon and the Campaign of 1815: Waterloo* (Uckfield: Naval & Military Press, 2004), p. 57.

11 Houssaye, *Napoleon and the Campaign of 1815*, p. 59. Roberts, *Napoleon: A Life*, p. 750.

12 Parkinson, p. 215.

13 *Lewis F. Wilson, 'The French Deception Operation in the Mont St. Jean Campaign', *Journal of Operational Art*, vol. 25, June–July 1986, p. 87.

14 *Henry G. Chappé, *La Vie Militaire du Maréchal Soult* (Paris: Capelot, 1908), p. 363.

15 *Louis R. Parquin, *La Grande Armée et la Campagne de 1815* (Paris: Flamarion, 1948, p. 126.

16 Parkinson, p. 215.

17 *Simpson, p. 285.

18 Bernard Cornwell, *Waterloo: The History of Four Armies, Three Armies, and Three Battles* (New York: HarperCollins, 2015), pp. 41–2.

19 *Napoleon I, *La Campagne de Mont St. Jean* (Paris: Éditeur Imperial, 1818), p. 79.

20 Andrew W. Field, *Prelude to Waterloo: Quatre Bras, the French Perspective* (London: Pen & Sword, 2014), pp. 58–9.

21 *Simpson, p. 288.

22 *Napoleon I, p. 92.

23 John G. Gallaher, *The Iron Marshall: A Biography of Louis N. Davout* (London: Greenhill Books, 2000), p. 215.

24 Peter Hofschröer, *1815: The Waterloo Campaign, Wellington, his German Allies and the Battles of Ligny and Quatre Bras* (London: Greenhill Books, 1998), pp. 168–9.

25 'French Orders and Reports from the Waterloo Campaign: Napoleon's Proclamation to the Army 15 June 1815', The Napoleon Series, https://www. napoleon-series.org/military/battles/1815/waterloo/Orders/c_waterlooorders1. html.

26 *John P. Corelli, 'The Bourmont Affair,' *The Age of Napoleon*, vol. 31, July 2001, p. 129.

27 *Simpson, p. 295.

28 *Otto Schwartz, *Der Krieg Gegen Frankriech in Jahre 1815* (Berlin: Heft, 1869), p. 38.

29 René Augoyat, *Le Maréchal Infernal* (Paris: Dumaine, 1860), p. 222. This is a classic military biography reintroduced to a modern public when it was translated and reprinted by Greenhill Books in 1990.

30 Hofschröer, p. 172.

31 *Sebastien Berthaud, *Mémories d'un Aide-Major de le Maréchal Soult* (Paris: Rothschild, 1870), p. 366. Berthaud was the staff major assigned to Soult and left this highly colourful and insightful portrait of Soult.

32 Mike Robinson, *The Battle of Quatre Bras 1815* (Stroud: Spellmount, 2010), p. 43.

33 *Berthaud, p. 367.

34 Elizabeth Longford, *Wellington: The Years of the Sword* (New York: Harper & Row, 1975), p. 415.

35 Longford, pp. 414–15.

36 *Michael R. Shaw, *The Great Ruse: Napoleon and the Art of Deception in the Campaign of 1815* (London: Greenhill Books, 2017), p. 148. Longford, pp. 416–21.

37 Bob Carruthers, ed., *Soldier of the Empire: The Note-Books of Captain Coignet* (Barnsley: Pen & Sword, 2012), pp. 250–60.

38 Andrew W. Field, *Grouchy's Waterloo: The Battles of Ligny and Wavre* (Barnsley: Pen & Sword, 2017), p. 51.

39 Field, *Prelude to Waterloo: Quatre Bras*, pp. 56–7.

4 'La Bal Commence!'

1 *Louis Thiry, *La Manoeuvre de Ligny* (Paris: Hachette, 1898), p. 88.

2 *Karl Schwartz, *Die Gegensätze zwischen England und Preussen* (Berlin: Heinzen, 1895), p. 67.

3 Henry Houssaye, *Napoleon and the Campaign of 1815: Waterloo* (Uckfield: Naval & Military Press, 2004), p. 80.

4 *William H. Shelton, *The Netherlands Army in the Campaign of 1815* (London: Horseguards Books, 1948), p. 97.

5 'Albert Dominicus Trip van Zoudtlandt', Wikipedia, https://en.wikipedia.org/ wiki/Albert_Dominicus_Trip_van_Zoudtlandt.

6 *Sidney Caldwell, *William II of the Netherlands: A Life* (London: Spencer & Sons, 1930), p. 85. Although his military reputation was ruined by his capture, his relation of his subsequent conversation with Napoleon was an important contribution to the history of the campaign.

7 *Jan Van Zandt, *The Netherlands Army in 1815* (London: Windsor House, 1937), p. 49.

8 *Schwartz, p. 95.

9 Houssaye, *Napoleon and the Campaign of 1815*, p. 89.

10 *Napoleon I, *La Campagne de Mont St. Jean* (Paris: Éditeur Imperial, 1818), p. 102.

11 *Napoleon I, p. 105.

12 Andrew Uffindell, *The Eagle's Last Triumph: Napoleon's Victory at Ligny, June 1815* (London: Greenhill Books, 1994), p. 93.

13 *Helmut Felker, *Das Heldenleben des Feldmarshalls Prinz Blücher* (Berlin: Hindrichs, 1835), p. 333.

14 Roger Parkinson, *The Hussar General: The Life of Blücher, Man of Waterloo* (Ware: Wordsworth, 1975), pp. 222–3.

15 Henri Fucart, *Soult: Maréchal d'Empire* (Paris: Combet, 1911), p. 336.

16 *Dieter Hindrichs, *Die Sachsen und Napoleon* (Dresden: Hauser, 1860), p. 278.

17 *Napoleon I, p. 147.

18 Lt. Gen. Sir Harry George Wakelyn Smith 1st Baronet of Aliwal G.C.B., *The Autobiography of Sir Harry Smith* (London: J. Murray, 1903), chapter 14, no page number, available at http://digital.library.upenn.edu/women/hsmith/autobiography/harry.html.

19 Houssaye, *Napoleon and the Campaign of 1815*, p. 102.

20 *Walter Crane, *The Playboy Prince at War: The Life of Prince Jerome Bonaparte* (New York: Grover Publishers, 1925), p. 235.

21 Christopher Summerville, *Who Was Who at Waterloo: A Biography of the Battle* (Harlow: Pearson Education, 2007), p. 93.

22 *William Ellis, *The Destruction of the Netherlands Army at Quatre Bras* (London: Borroughs, 1898), pp. 137–42.

23 *Felker, p. 340.

24 *Napoleon I, p. 130. *August von Gneisenau, *Der Schalcht bei Ligny* (Berlin: Heft, 1845), p. 289. Gneisenau's account of the battle was only published fourteen years after his death from cholera in Poland.

5 Hougoumont

1 Roger Parkinson, *The Hussar General: The Life of Blücher, man of Waterloo* (Ware: Wordsworth, 1975), p. 225.

2 *Karl Schwartz, *Die Gegensätze zwischen England und Preussen* (Berlin: Heinzen, 1895), p. 89.

3 Henry Houssaye, *Napoleon and the Campaign of 1815: Waterloo* (Uckfield: Naval & Military Press, 2004), p. 145.

4 Jean-Victor Constant de Rebecque, *The Betrayal: Wellington and the Battle of Mont St. Jean* (Geneva: Éditeur Suisse, 1845), p. 120.

5 *Napoleon I, *La Campagne de Mont St. Jean* (Paris: Éditeur Imperial, 1818), p. 122.

6 *Pierre Lachouque, *Les Maréchaux de Napoléon* (Paris: 1840), p. 328.

7 'The British Army at Waterloo', blog, http://britisharmywaterloo.blogspot.com/2015/09/92nd-foot-gordon-highlanders.html.

8 'A Very Pretty Little Battalion': The 3/14th Regiment of Foot in the Waterloo Campaign', The Napoleon Series, http://www.napoleon-series.org/military/organization/Britain/Infantry/c_3-14Waterloo.html.

9 'Waterloo Lives: Descendants Speak Out', Waterloo 200, http://waterloo200.org/themes/soldiers/waterloo-lives-descendants-speak-out.

10 Bernard Cornwell, *Waterloo: The History of Four Days, Three Armies, and Three Battles* (New York: HarperCollins, 2014), p. 209.

11 Walter Coleville, *Sir John Byng: A Soldier's Life* (London: Barrow & Woford, 1878), p. 202.

12 *Schwartz, p. 199.

13 'Byng, Sir John (1772–1860)', History of Parliament, http://www.historyofparliamentonline.org/volume/1820-1832/member/byng-sir-john-1772-1860.

14 David Hamilton-Williams, *Waterloo: New Perspectives, the Great Battle Reappraised* (London: Arms and Armour, 1993), p. 279.

6 La Haye Sainte

1 Elizabeth Longford, *Wellington: The Years of the Sword* (New York: Harper & Row Publishers, 1969), p. 453.

2 *Napoleon I, *La Campagne de Mont St. Jean* (Paris: Éditeur Imperial, 1818).

3 *John Forsythe, *The Struggle for Hougoumont 1815* (New York: Greenwood Publishers, 1966), p. 143.

4 *Walter Crane, *The Playboy Prince at War: The Life of Prince Jerome Bonaparte* (New York: Grover Publishers, 1925), p. 250.

5 Mark Adkin, *The Waterloo Companion* (Mechanicsburg, PA: Stackpole Books, 2001), pp. 296–9.

6 Peter Hofschröer, *1815: The Waterloo Campaign, Wellington, German Allies and the Battles of Ligny and Quatre Bras* (London: Greenhill Books, 1998), p. 300.

7 Andrew Roberts, *Napoleon and Wellington: The Battle of Waterloo and the Great Commanders who Fought it* (New York: Simon & Schuster, 2001), p 177.

8 Roberts, *Napoleon and Wellington*, p. 163.

9 *This event was the beginning of bad blood between the Scots Guards and the Coldstream Guards. The former insisted that, had their battalion been commanded by one of their own officers, they would never have suffered such a mortifying indignity.

10 Adkin, p. 343.

11 *Richard T. Foley, *The Men of Waterloo in their Own Words* (Washington, DC: Infantry Press, 1937), p. 76.

12 Robert Kershaw, *24 Hours at Waterloo 18 June 1815* (Haverton, PA: Casemate Publishers, 2014), pp. 156–7. Adkin, pp. 369–70.

13 Kershaw, p. 157.

14 Mike Chapell, *The King's German Legion (2) 1812–1816* (Oxford: Osprey, 2000), p. 33.

15 *Jean L. Renault, *The Life of a Sergeant of Napoleon* (London Burns & Church, 1969), p. 153.

16 Christopher Summerville, *Who Was Who at Waterloo: A Biography of the Battle* (Harlow: Pearson Educational, 2007), p. 299.

17 Kershaw, pp. 160–1. The 1st Cuirassier Regiment was the oldest armoured regiment in the French army.

18 *Verein für Nassauische Altertumskunde und Geschichte.* vol. 13–14, p. 38.

19 Andrew W. Field, *Waterloo: The French Perspective* (Barnsley: Pen & Sword Military, 2015), p. 172.

20 Chappell, p. 35.

21 *Michael Fleming, *History of the French Balloon Corps* (New York: Lighthouse Publishers, 1980), p. 83.

22 *Friedrich Steiner, *Die Schlacten bei Ligny und Mont St. Jean* (Dresden: Halter und Sohn, 1853), pp. 112–13. There was no little anti-Prussian gloating by this Saxon soldier who had as a young man fought in this campaign. The result of the campaign was to curb Prussian attempts to devour Saxony and other parts of Germany. It was written after the Revolutions of 1848 had succeeded in establishing a Second German Reich as a constitutional monarchy. The Prussian king was offered the throne and reluctantly agreed to accept.

23 Summerville, p. 328.

24 Adkin, p. 227.

25 'The 23rd Foot, the Royal Welch Fusiliers, Waterloo 1815, Fact Sheet: 1-A05-03', http://royalwelsh.org.uk/downloads/A05-03-23rd-Waterloo1815.pdf. J. Christopher Herold, ed., *The Mind of Napoleon: A Selection from his Written and Spoken Words* (New York: Columbia University Press, 1955), p. 210.

26 François Gédéon Bailly de Monthion, *Mémoires du Maréchal Monthion* (Paris: A. Bossnage, 1835), p. 438.

27 For generations after the war, British tourists at Les Invalides in Paris would wince and groan at the sight of these colours on display around Napoleon's sarcophagus.

28 Adkin, p. 146.

29 *Napoleon I, p. 235.

7 Pas de Charge!

1 Robert Kershaw, *24 Hours at Waterloo 18 June 1815* (Haverton, PA: Casemate Publishers, 2014), pp. 162–4.

2 Andrew Field, *Napoleon and Wellington: The Battle of Waterloo and the Great Commanders who Fought it* (New York: Simon & Schuster, 2001), pp. 77–8.

3 Lt. Gen. Sir Harry George Wakelyn Smith 1st Baronet of Aliwal G.C.B., *The Autobiography of Sir Harry Smith* (London: J. Murray, 1903), Chapter 14, no page number, http://digital.library.upenn.edu/women/hsmith/autobiography/harry.html.

4 *Soult, *Memoir du Napoleon* (Paris, 1832), p. 397.

5 Bernard Cornwell, *Waterloo: The History of Four Days, Three Armies, and Three Battles* (New York: Harper, 2014), p. 170.

6 James Burbeck, 'Napoleonic Artillery: Firepower Comes of Age', *War Times Journal*, available at http://www.wtj.com/articles/napart.

7 James Stanhope, *Eyewitness to the Peninsular War and the Battle of Waterloo* (Barnsley: Pen & Sword, 2010), p. 176.

8 Mark Adkin, *The Waterloo Companion: The Complete Guide to History's Most Famous Battle* (Mechanicsburg, PA: Stackpole Books, 2001), p. 280.

9 Edward Cotton, *A Voice from Waterloo: A History of the Battle Fought on the 18th June 1815*, Eighth Edition, Revised and Enlarged (Braine l'Alleud: Hotel Du Musee, 1895), p. 106.

10 Bob Carruthers, ed., *Soldier of the Empire: The Note-Books of Captain Coignet* (Barnsley: Pen & Sword), p. 268.

11 Andrew W. Field, *Waterloo: The French Perspective* (London: Pen & Sword, 2015), pp. 98–9.

12 Field, *Waterloo*, p. 100.

13 Cornwell, pp. 185–6.

14 Field, *Waterloo*, p. 100.

15 Kershaw, p. 166. Eric Niderost, 'Scottish Highlanders at Waterloo', Warfare History Network, http://warfarehistorynetwork.com/daily/military-history/scottish-high landers-at-waterloo.

16 Kershaw, p. 167.

17 Niderost.

18 Cotton, p. 285.

8   The Storm of Mont St Jean

1 Henry Houssaye, *Napoleon and the Campaign of 1815: Waterloo* (Uckfield: Naval & Military Press, 2004), p. 224.

2 Louis Adolphe Thiers, *History of the Consulate and the Empire of France under Napoleon*, vol. 12, trans. D. Forbes Campbell and John Stubbing (London: Chatto and Windus, 1894). p. 130.

3 Robert Kershaw, *24 Hours at Waterloo, 18 June 1815* (Haverton, PA: Casemate Publishers, 2014), pp. 270–1.

4 Kershaw, p. 269.

5 Houssaye, *Napoleon and the Campaign of 1815*, p. 225.

6 The last time the British and French Guards had fought each other was sixty years earlier at the Battle of Fontenoy in 1745. According to Voltaire, 'They were at a distance of fifty paces . . . The English officers saluted the French by raising their hats. The Count de Chabones [sic], the Duke de Biron who were in the front and all the officers of the French Guards returned the salute. Lord Charles Hay, Captain of the English Guards, cried "Gentlemen of the French Guards, fire." Count d'Auteroche, then lieutenant and later captain of the Grenadiers, replied "Gentlemen, we never fire first, open fire yourselves." The English commenced a rolling fire, that is, they fired by divisions, so that one battalion in four ranks having fired, another battalion made its discharge, and then a third, while the first recharged their weapons. The line of French infantry had not fired; it was alone in four ranks, the line rather elongated and not sustained by any other force of

infantry. Nineteen officers of the guards fell stricken at that single discharge . . . The first rank having been thrown into confusion, the three others looking to their rear and seeing only cavalry at three hundred toises [about 150 yards], they fled.' Voltaire, *Précis du Siècle de Louis XV* (Paris, 1768), p. 240.

7   Kershaw, p. 230.

8   Houssaye, *Napoleon and the Campaign of 1815*, p. 227.

9   'The Retreat of the Regiment of Cumberland Hussars at the Battle of Waterloo', http://www.waterloo-campaign.nl/bestanden/files/notes/june18/note.14.pdf.   In fairness to the regiment, a number of officers and men were so ashamed that they deserted to return to the battle and join other formations.

10 Edward Cotton, *A Voice from Waterloo* (London: B.L. Green, 1849), p. 64.

11 Kershaw, pp. 109, 228.

12 Cotton, p. 108.

13 Houssaye, *Napoleon and the Campaign of 1815*, p. 197.

14 Mark Adkin, *The Waterloo Companion* (Mechanicsburg, PA: Stackpole Books, 2001), p. 236.

15 Houssaye, *Napoleon and the Campaign of 1815*, p. 198.

16 Alexander Cavalie Mercer, *Journal of the Waterloo Campaign*, ed. Andrew Uffindell (Barnsley: Pen & Sword, 2012), pp. 152–3. The storm of Mont St Jean would come to rival and even outshine the legend of the sun of Austerlitz.

9   *Fin*

1   Armies would enter into a convention to exchange prisoners, usually rank for rank. So these parolled British troops could not fight the French again until they had been exchanged for an equal number of French prisoners.

2   The colours of the Netherlands army were most definitely not returned. Napoleon wanted King William to realize his place. The Belgian battalions of the army were immediately incorporated into the French army.

3   *Alexander Douglas, *The Peace of Vienna 1815* (Edinburgh: John Knox University, 1932), p. 252. Although Prussia continued to attempt to dominate Europe, French and Austrian support of Saxony and Bavaria and Britain's determined retention of Hanover fenced in the ambitions of the Hohenzollerns. The 1848 Assembly of Frankfurt drafted a liberal constitution for a unified German empire (the Second Reich).

4   *Emmanuel-Auguste-Dieudonné Las Cases, *Memoirs of the Life and Conversations of the Emperor Napoleon*, vol. 4 (New York, 1855), p. 160.

5   *Edward Stapleton, *The Grand Passion: Napoleon II and Victoria* (London: Blackstone Publishers, 1888), pp. 76–83.

6   *Edward Peale-Mason, *The Life of Napoleon II, Emperor of the French* (London: Spencer & Jerome, 1897), p. 239. It was remarked by those surviving Frenchmen who had known Napoleon as a young general, that the Prince of Wales bore a striking resemblance to him. *'Palace Suppresses Royals DNA Test Results', *Daily Mail*, 12 October 2019.